THE UNIVERSITY OF VIRGINIA EDITION OF
THE WORKS OF STEPHEN CRANE

VOLUME I

BOWERY TALES

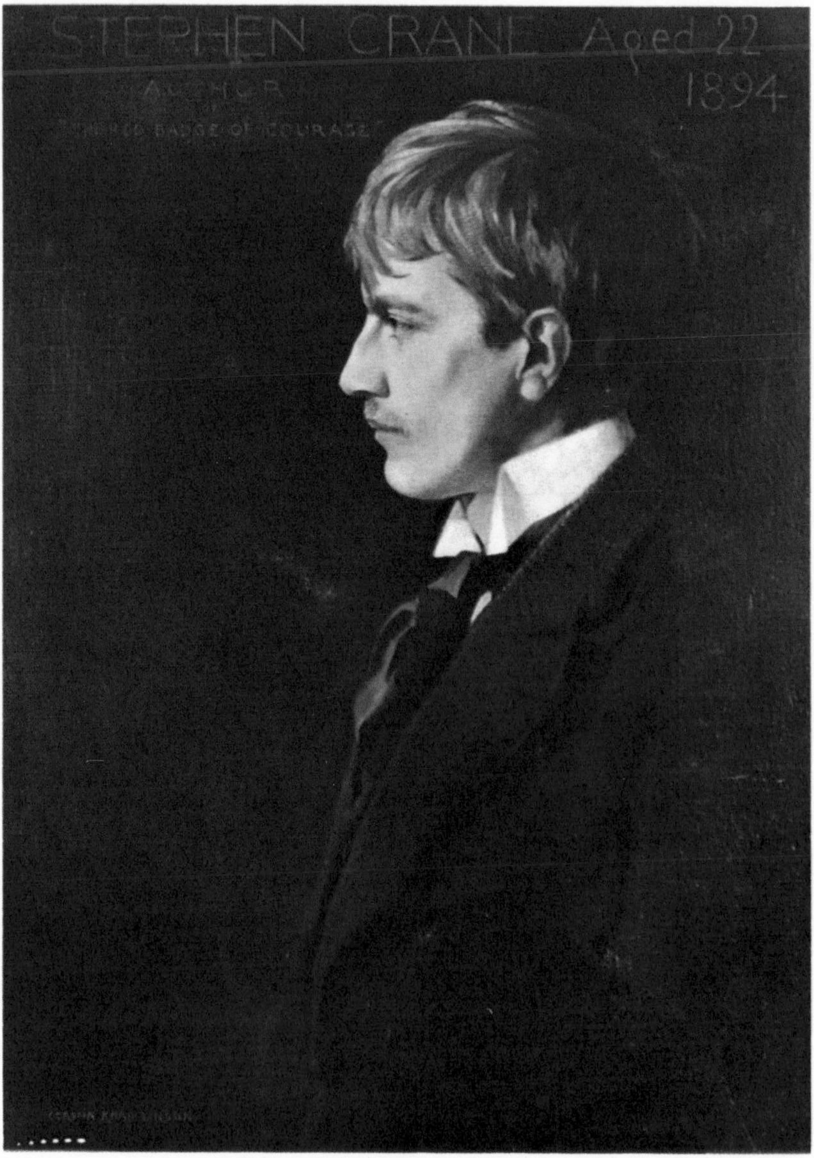
STEPHEN CRANE Aged 22
1894

STEPHEN CRANE

BOWERY TALES

MAGGIE
GEORGE'S MOTHER

EDITED BY
FREDSON BOWERS
LINDEN KENT PROFESSOR OF ENGLISH AT
THE UNIVERSITY OF VIRGINIA

WITH INTRODUCTIONS BY
JAMES B. COLVERT
PROFESSOR OF ENGLISH AT THE
UNIVERSITY OF GEORGIA

THE UNIVERSITY PRESS OF VIRGINIA

CHARLOTTESVILLE

The Bibliographer for This Edition Is
Matthew J. Bruccoli.

CENTER FOR EDITIONS OF
AMERICAN AUTHORS

AN APPROVED TEXT

MODERN LANGUAGE
ASSOCIATION OF AMERICA

®

Standard Book Number: 8139–0258–4
Library of Congress Catalog Card Number: 68–8536
Printed in the United States of America

To
Clifton Waller Barrett

FOREWORD

THE present volume inaugurates the University of Virginia Edition of THE WORKS OF STEPHEN CRANE, intended to contain every known piece of his creative writing and journalism but excluding his letters and memoranda. The principles on which the editing has been based are stated in the prefatory "Text of the Virginia Edition," which will appear only in the first volume. The Introductions in this edition are intended to offer what facts are known about the circumstances of the composition and publication of the works under discussion and to place these works in the literary and historical contexts of their time and of Crane's development as a writer. The Textual Introductions detail the physical forms of the text, their authority and transmission, and examine any specific problems involved in the establishment of the text in its present critical form.

The original research was forehandedly started in 1965 by a grant to the editor from research funds of the University of Virginia made available by President Edgar F. Shannon, Jr. Since 1966–67 the expenses of the preparation of the text with its introductions and apparatus have been generously subsidized by grants from the National Endowment for the Humanities administered through the Modern Language Association of America and its Center for Editions of American Authors.

The editor is much in debt for assistance and various courtesies to Professor Robert Stallman of the University of Connecticut, Professor Joseph Katz of Kent State University, Professor William Gibson of New York University, Commander Melvin H. Schoberlin, USN (Ret.), and to his colleagues Professors Matthew J. Bruccoli of Ohio State University, James B. Colvert of the University of Georgia, and J. C. Levenson of the University of Virginia. Mr. Kenneth A. Lohf, Librarian for Rare Books and Manuscripts of the Columbia University Libraries, has been of unfailing and particular assistance, and the editor is grateful to the late John D. Gordan, Curator of the Berg Collection at the New York Public Library, to Mr. William Cagle, Curator of Manuscripts in the Lilly Library of Indiana University, to Miss Alice Beer, Mr. Donald Gallup, and Mr. C. E. Frazer Clark, Jr., and to the librarians of Harvard, Yale, Princeton, Ohio State, Syracuse, Dartmouth, the British Museum, and the London Library for their courtesies. Mr. William Runge, Curator of Rare Books, and Miss Anne Freudenberg, Curator of Manuscripts, at the University of Virginia have been constantly helpful, and the services of Mrs. David Yalden-Thomson as research assistant have been much appreciated.

The editor's debt to Mr. Clifton Waller Barrett and his magnificent collection at the University of Virginia can be expressed only by the dedication of this edition to him. Both the portrait of Crane by Corwin Knapp Linson and the manuscript pages of an early draft of *George's Mother* are reproduced by courtesy of the Clifton Waller Barrett Library of the University of Virginia Library.

It is proposed to publish the novels in the early volumes, followed by the short stories, sketches, poems, and journalism; however, these volumes will not necessarily appear in order but as the convenience of preparation and the financing of the research dictate. Most of the volumes, being miscellaneous in their contents, will be given general titles. The present volume takes its title *Bowery Tales* from the collection of *Maggie* and *George's Mother* published by Heinemann in London, 1900, although no evidence is preserved to indicate whether or not Crane approved.

It is a pleasure to have the first volume of this new edition appear early in the year devoted to the sesquicentennial celebration of the granting of the University of Virginia's charter.

F. B.

Charlottesville, Virginia
September 1, 1968

CONTENTS

THE TEXT OF THE VIRGINIA EDITION

T HE University of Virginia Edition of Stephen Crane provides for the first time texts established according to the
standards and by the techniques of modern textual scholar-
ship. The general procedures governing this establishment are
outlined here, whereas the specific problems for each text are
treated in the separate Textual Introductions.

The text itself is a critical unmodernized reconstruction. It is
critical in that it is not necessarily an exact reprint of any
individual document: the print or manuscript chosen as copy-
text (i.e., as the major authority for this edition) may be
emended by reference to other authorities or by editorial decision. The Crane text, in short, has been established by the application of bibliographical and analytical criticism to the evidence
of the various early documentary forms in which the text has
appeared.[1] It is unmodernized in that every effort has been made
to present the text in as close a form to Crane's own inscription
as the surviving documents for each work permit of such reconstruction, subject to normal editorial procedure.

The first step in the establishment of a critical text is the
determination of the exact forms in the early documents and of
the facts about their relationship one to another. When manuscripts are extant, the establishment of the texts of these documents involves the checking of the written form of all words and
the determination of the texture of their spelling, capitalization,
word-division, and punctuation, i.e., the 'accidentals' of a text as
distinguished from its 'substantives,' or the forms of the words as
distinguished from the words themselves. Any manuscript alteration of the initial inscription is noticed, and whenever possible

[1] Various terms used here are discussed at length in Fredson Bowers, "Established Texts and Definitive Editions," *Philological Quarterly*, XLI (1962), 1–17.

the author's rejected forms are reconstructed from the available evidence and recorded for the information of critics.

Since the printed versions that derive from Crane's preserved manuscripts have a supplementary authority, the editor has attempted to identify and analyze any variation in the readings of the printed texts that in themselves have primary or supplementary authority. To this end a number of copies of the first—and of any other book edition possessing authority—have been mechanically compared for variation on the Hinman Collating Machine. Although it is too much to hope that every minor variant in the impression of these books has been discovered by the multiple collation, one can state that the readings of the text in such authoritative documents, even in relatively minor respects of form, have been substantially established from the evidence of the machine comparison by superimposition of a number of examples, letter for letter and word for word. In addition, other copies not possible to compare on the Hinman Collator have been sight-collated by hand in an especially scrupulous manner.

Printed texts that are ascertained to be simple reprints of earlier substantive printed forms and to possess no established authoritative revisions have not necessarily been collated in multiple copies for variation since the only purpose of such collation is to establish the exact form of authoritative textual documents. Thus the 1902 reprinting from the same plates of the Harper 1900 first edition in collected book form of the *Whilomville Stories* has been collated back against the first printing to see if any plate variants exist, but no need has been felt to collate different copies of the 1902 printing against each other. Indeed, no actual need existed to machine-collate the three Barrett copies of the 1900 edition since all of the stories except for the latter part of "A Little Pilgrim" reprint the *Harper's Magazine* version without authorial change. On the other hand, since this was the first collected edition, even though the text was without authority, there seemed enough intrinsic interest in its form to warrant the machining of the three duplicate copies available in the Barrett Collection at the University of Virginia Library.

Particularly when as in the *Whilomville Stories* or in "The Monster" the magazine form of a work is a substantive document in whole or in part, no useful purpose would be served by multiple machine collation of magazine copies in search of textual variation, and hence this form of search has not normally been made.

On the other hand, when a printed edition has any substantive authority, the textual history of impressions [2] subsequent to the original have a distinct interest through such time as the author or an authoritative agent could have ordered alterations in the plates. The history of the usual edition, therefore, is the history of the textual variation in its set of plates throughout the various printings. Plates may be altered between impressions, at times to correct errors in the edition typesetting, at times to incorporate editorial normalizations and fancied improvements, and at times to repair plate damage caused by handling accidents as well as normal wear on the press. Therefore, in order to establish the exact forms of the editions (in respect to the history of their plates), the first impression from the plates of any substantive edition typesetting has been compared on the Hinman Machine against the last ascertained impression within a few years of Crane's death, and those variants affecting readings have been recorded as between the early and late states of the plates, with the impression then identified in which any such variant had its origin. A specific statement is always made, even if it be no more than, as with the three identifiable impressions of the 1896 *Maggie,* to record no observed variation.

Following the establishment of the variant documentary forms of all substantive editions chosen as significant in the history of Crane's text, these different edition typesettings have been individually hand-collated against the first edition; all substantive, or word, variants recovered from this collation have been recorded, as well as such occasional variants among the accidentals as might bear on the question of the authority of any of the documents by which the texts were transmitted. From this evidence, printed in the Historical Collation appended to each edited work, the line of textual transmission can be traced from document to document and the general authority of each edition can thus be determined. This evidence also determines, in large

[2] In the Virginia Edition the use of the bibliographical terms follows not the popular but the technical definitions of *edition, impression* (or *printing*), *issue,* and *state* recommended in Fredson Bowers, *Principles of Bibliographical Description* (Princeton, N.J., 1949), pp. 379–426.

part, the specific authority of any document, since bibliographical and critical analysis of the textual variants will demonstrate
which are mere reprint editions—that is, editions in which the
cumulative transmitted error was never corrected systematically
but, instead, largely by chance. Evidence of this nature indicates
that no comparison of the printer's copy had been made against
any authoritative document, and thus that the various alterations observed (when not mechanical corrections) were in their
turn corruptions and could not represent, in some manner, an
editorial return to a purer version of the text.

On internal evidence like this, combined sometimes with external evidence, one can determine, usually with precision, the
printed texts that have Crane's immediate authority as against
the number that are simply derived reprints without authority.
In this connection, authority is defined as resident in any document printed directly from a Crane manuscript or from some
other document such as a typescript made from manuscript, or,
as with the 1896 *Maggie,* another edition that had been corrected
and revised by Crane. Such authoritative texts are called substantive, as contrasted with derived. Only substantive texts have
been used as documentary sources of revisory editorial emendation, although occasional correction may, for convenience, be
drawn from derived editions.

After the derived editions have been isolated, the next step in
the editorial process is the selection of the copy-text from among
the established substantive texts. In practice, the selection may
differ from literary work to literary work according to the distinc-
tive conditions; but the theory is firm: whenever practicable the
copy-text selected is that form of the text, no matter how it may
subsequently have been revised, that is nearest to the primary
authority of Crane's manuscript.

Obviously, when the manuscript or a derived typescript is no
longer in existence, the copy-text must be the first printed version that was set from copy deriving from the manuscript, since
only this printed form can preserve with any authority such
characteristics of the manuscript as have escaped the normalization of printing-house or editorial style imposed on the copy. If
Crane never intervened to revise or correct this text in any
subsequent edition, the first printed version remains the sole

authority. However, if—as happened between the first book and the first magazine versions of "A Little Pilgrim" in the *Whilom-ville Stories*—Crane did introduce revisions after the printing of an earlier form, the claims of more than the single, or copy-text, authority must be considered.

The editorial procedure in such cases follows the principles laid down by Sir Walter Greg.[3] That is, a double authority is recognized. The copy-text remains the supreme authority for the accidentals, since it alone was set directly from Crane's manuscript or an intermediate typescript. On the other hand, the substantive variants in other texts not thought to be printer's errors must be taken to represent Crane's revisions, and to these must be added such alterations in the accidentals as appear to derive from the author, although this last is a much more difficult matter to determine. For instance, when later editions show as a whole that they have not been set from copy of an earlier edition revised by the author but are simple reprints, chance alterations in such characteristics as punctuation that coincide with Crane's usual practice must be ignored even if an editor may be certain that they would have agreed better with the lost manuscript than did the substantive edition's styling. Changes in the accidentals may also occur by equal chance in a revised edition; hence the simple fact of established substantive alteration does not automatically demonstrate the equal authority of accidentals that in the revision tend toward the author's usual characteristics. As in the revised 1896 *Maggie*, where every seeming change in the punctuation toward Crane's usual preferences may be matched by an alteration that departs from the Crane practices transmitted from the manuscript to the 1893 print, an editor may be justified in believing that Crane seldom revised such accidentals, at least after they were in print. The question of authorial revision of the accidentals between manuscript and final typescript printer's-copy form is less certainly to be dismissed, and in such texts as the *Whilomville Stories* some variant accidentals in the print as against the preserved manuscript have been taken as reflecting authoritative typescript

---

[3] "The Rationale of Copy-Text," *Studies in Bibliography*, III (1950–51), 19–36. See also Fredson Bowers, "Current Theories of Copy-Text," *Modern Philology*, LXVIII (1950), 12–20.

changes. As a matter of principle an editor may be bolder in experimental mixing of the accidentals in two substantive texts when they radiate from a lost archetype than when, as in a revised edition, one derives from another.[4]

Hence the critical Virginia Crane text will incorporate in the copy-text such variants from later demonstrably authoritative editions as pass the editorial tests for authorial alterations or for authentic manuscript readings preserved in other texts that, like the copy-text, radiate from the lost original. In effect this procedure attempts to reproduce the lost marked-up printer's copy that Crane furnished for a revised text, or the lost archetype for radiating texts, and in this reconstruction to filter out the unauthorized printing-house variants that creep into any reprint and are thus found in the printed form even of a revised edition. Despite the fact the he 'accepted' them (provided he read the proof for a revised form of the text), Crane did not authorize these printing-house variants; hence they have no place in the pure text that the Virginia Edition endeavors to establish.

Correspondingly, when Crane's manuscript or typescript or

---

[4] Some few cases may grow very complicated indeed. All the evidence suggests that the first American appearance in *McClure's* for November, 1898, of "His New Mittens" was set from a typescript made from the manuscript that Crane had sent to Paul Reynolds, his New York agent. The story appeared, also in November, in England in the *Cornhill Magazine,* set from copy that could not have been proofs of the *McClure's* typesetting. The variants in the wording indicate also that the copy could not have been a carbon of the typescript sent to *McClure's* unless we are to posit more correction and editorial revision than seem customary. (In this case authorial proofreading of the *McClure's* typesetting seems improbable if not impossible.) The odds, then, favor the setting of the *Cornhill* version from an independent typescript made either from the manuscript or from the carbon of the typescript used by *McClure's.* The verbal variants in *Cornhill* appear to be downright errors and misreadings (whether of compositor or typist) or else English editorial intervention. In the present edition they have been rejected. On the other hand, certain of the accidentals characteristics in the *Cornhill* version favor Crane's practices more strongly than the *McClure's* text. Given the probable line of transmission of the text, it is at least as possible that the *Cornhill* compositor in these respects rendered his copy more faithfully than did the *McClure's* compositor, as that the *Cornhill* coincidences with Crane's characteristics are by chance. An editor may be justified, then, in contriving an eclectic text from the two authorities since they radiate from the archetype and are not in a direct line of derivation. Radiation is also found in various newspaper articles and sketches that would have been set by various compositors from proof copy furnished by Crane's syndicate employer. It is at least theoretically possible to reconstruct the hypothetical proof that served as copy from the various newspaper versions when sufficient have been preserved.

proof has been preserved, the earliest prepublication form becomes the copy-text. In each case this form has been collated against the first printed version and all details of substantive variance have been recorded. However, the printing-house style imposed on the authoritative manuscript or its typescript has been rejected except for necessary corrections, and only those variants from the manuscript in substantives or in accidentals that appear to have been inserted by Crane in the typescript or the proof have been accepted and incorporated in the critical text.[5] Thereafter, the determination of the history of the text and of the authority of all variants in editions after the first follows the regular procedures outlined above.

Crane's shorter works published in a variety of magazines and newspapers present a special problem. In general, the Greg theory of copy-text holds, and an attempt has been made to separate the authority of the substantives from that of the accidentals in the different versions of the text and thus to establish the most authoritative form of each in a critical text that may fairly be said to synthesize the most authoritative versions.

To repeat, the purpose of this edition of Crane is to establish the text in as close a form, in all details, to Crane's final intentions as the preserved documents of each separate work permit. This aim compels the editor to treat each work as a unit, with its own separate textual problems. That is, no attempt is made between texts (except as stated below) to secure a uniformity of style that is not authorized from those documents for the texts in question that establish their most authoritative preserved forms. It follows that the texture of accidentals in a work like *George's Mother,* published by Arnold, will differ from those in a work like *Maggie* that was privately printed. These, in turn, will differ in their accidentals forms from the critical text of *The Red Badge of Courage,* which uses the holograph manuscript as its copy-text.

When only printed versions of a text are preserved, the edito-

---

[5] In "The Angel-Child" from the *Whilomville Stories* at least 200 variants appear in the accidentals between the preserved manuscript and the *Harper's Magazine* form set from a lost typescript. In a text of about 3500 words the cumulative effect on Crane's own modes of expression is distinctly noticeable. Only the manuscript contains the full record of what must have been intentional Crane punctuation and the like according to the rhythms and expression that he heard in his style.

rial or printing-house style imposed on the text removes it in various respects from conformity with Crane's known practices in spelling, punctuation, capitalization, and word-division as seen in his manuscripts. One might be able to alter some of these forms in *George's Mother,* say, to bring the critical text, in theory, into a closer relationship with what one may reasonably suppose to have been certain of the details of the lost manuscript. But interesting as such an experiment might be, the result could never be wholly consistent, and since it would be impossible to be thoroughgoing in the process, no demonstrably established form of the text could result. Hence, with certain exceptions, each work in the present edition rests as a separate unit on the evidence of its own preserved documents and represents a faithfulness to Crane's full intentions in varying degrees of exactitude according to the authority of this evidence. It follows, then, that novels like *Maggie* and *George's Mother* (though appearing in the same volume of this edition) will exhibit different characteristics in their accidentals: each will have been edited independently from the evidence of the most authoritative printed documents, and these documents (the only authorities we have) differ in various respects in the treatment the different printers gave to the accidentals of the Crane printer's copy. The newspaper sketches, especially, will differ widely for the same reasons, but each has necessarily been treated as an independent unit and edited according to its earliest authority, whether manuscript, proof, or printed version as it appears in one or more newspapers.

An exception to this procedure is made under two specific and carefully limited circumstances.

First, as in *The Red Badge of Courage* or the *Whilomville Stories,* when substantive differences appear in the printed version that differ in their form of accidentals from the established and authoritative forms of the manuscript copy-text, the accidentals are altered editorially to agree with the higher authority of the manuscript texture. This would appear to be an unexceptionable editorial procedure. Its principle can be carried one step further, however. When similar departures from the 1893 copy-text appear in the revised 1896 *Maggie,* they too are altered to present a uniform texture with the copy-text. In short, they have been treated like variant forms of accidentals such as word-division or spelling within the copy-text itself, which have been made uniform as part of the critical editorial process.[6]

Second, the rule that separate works must be treated as independent units is broken when these works were written substantially as a unit, and when manuscripts are preserved but by bad luck a minority is missing. The *Whilomville Stories* are the example. Here the two stories for which no manuscripts have as yet been found are perforce edited from the *Harper's Magazine* text—set from a typescript, presumably—as copy-text. However, when in very prominent details such as almost invariable word-division practices found in the manuscripts their copy-texts differ from the usage represented by the manuscripts, some few judicious normalizations have been ventured but by no means any thoroughgoing recasting of the accidentals. This would be the logical editorial process to follow if the manuscript for certain chapters of a novel were missing; these stories were written so much in sequence that such an analogy may hold.

In general, then, editorial treatment of the text is primarily concerned with synthesizing the evidence of all manuscripts and authoritative printed editions in order to arrive in as logical a manner as may be at Crane's final intentions as nearly as can be determined from the preserved documents, with particular reference to the manuscripts. The characteristics of these manuscripts are sufficiently uniform to encourage the belief that Crane did indeed have final intentions in respect to many features of the accidentals, as well as of his words, with particular reference to his light punctuation system that must have reflected the way in which he heard his sentences in his inward

---

[6] When a copy-text varies in its accidentals, the editor has ordinarily normalized them according to the form that appears to be closest to Crane's usual practice as observed in manuscripts of the same date. The movement, then, will usually be in the direction of greater authority and this same movement will hold for the normalization of revised readings. Thus if the accidentals form of the revision appears in a known Crane preference, and the copy-text itself has been variant in its forms for the reading, the normalization of the copy-text would already have made the Crane form regular throughout the text and no clash would appear with the revised reading. On the other hand, it is possible for the copy-text to be completely uniform in respect to a spelling, say, like *curb* that is not characteristic of Crane. Perforce this spelling is maintained in the present edition since it occurs in this uniform manner in the only authoritative document for accidentals.

ear, with rhythms and intonations rather firmly established. Given the intent of the editorial treatment, any alteration believed to be Crane's must be adopted, regardless of critical estimate of its literary worth, although, of course, an editor's literary judgment is one of the various criteria that operate to establish any alteration as a Crane variant instead of one produced by the typist or printer. On the other hand, not all Crane revisions are literary in their origin. When Crane removed the profanity from the 1896 *Maggie* in order to have the work published by Appleton, the unrevised readings have been retained in the established text as more faithfully representing Crane's true intentions than the results of censorship, even though self-imposed. Sometimes, however, the line between imposed censorship and a softening of satire or of shocking detail may be difficult to draw since literary motives may well dictate on occasion a less extreme version, as seems to be the case in some of the alterations in the 1896 *Maggie* or, for instance, in the moderation of the overdrawn religious satire in "A Little Pilgrim," which concludes the *Whilomville Stories.*

Revision of the copy-text, therefore, can be admitted only from the evidence of authoritative documents. On the other hand, correction may be drawn from any source, whether a substantive or reprint edition, or from independent editorial judgment. Indeed, no correction from an unauthoritative document can have any more validity than editorial correction; hence reprint editions are noted as sources for emendation only as a convenience and not because there is any secondary value in the fact that the chosen emendation first originated in them.

Editorial correction is of five kinds. First, Crane did not always see proofs for his magazine or newspaper writings, and even when he read proof he was not always accurate in catching all of the printers' errors that manifestly need setting right; hence some substantive emendation has proved necessary.

Second, inconsistencies may be present in the manuscripts in respect to spelling, capitalization, and division of words that were regularized in the prints. Such regularization of a manuscript has generally been accepted when the printer's version appears to coincide with Crane's usual practice; however, if the print regularizes anomalies in opposition to Crane's more habitual practice, or else fails to normalize an irregularity, independent emendation has been admitted.

Third, if Crane's own usual practice (especially as of a given date) cannot be determined, the variant forms are retained in the established text whenever they cannot be regularized, with apparent justice, according to their majority form.

Fourth, whereas all characteristic spellings are followed in the present unmodernized text when they are acceptable variants of more common forms, and are regular in the text in question, misspellings like Crane's characteristic *missle* for *missile* are always corrected, as are such grammatical errors as his frequent *it's* for the possessive pronoun *its*.

Fifth, word-division is regularized according to the practice in the most authoritative documents for each text, ordinarily the copy-text. If the matter is in doubt within a given text, the form has been adopted that agrees with parallels within the text or that is most characteristic of manuscripts closest in date. When in the original documents a possible compound is hyphenated at the break between two lines, the editorial decision whether to establish the word as a hyphenated compound or as a single word conforms to the same principle.

No attempt has been made in this edition to reproduce the typographical details of the original documents such as the lineation, the number of lines of indentation for display capitals and the number of capitalized text letters following them, or the capitals or lower-case letters in running titles and chapter headings and the periods that usually follow them. Thus although the text itself has been scrupulously treated, its appurtenances have been silently modernized.

A few distinctions have been made between silent alterations of minutiae in manuscripts and their record in printed texts, chiefly because the notice of errors in the prints furnishes some evidence about the care in proofreading and thus about the general care with which the manuscript was transferred to type metal. In the manuscripts certain forms that Crane habitually favored, like *aint* for *ain't*, or *dont* or *cant*, are so constant that to record each occurrence of forms that would automatically be corrected by any compositor has seemed otiose. Similarly, the small change of manuscript carelessness like the occasional omission of a period after an abbreviation, as in *Mr* or *Mrs,* or the occasional omission of an apostrophe before the contraction *em,* has been silently corrected. Moreover, Crane was not consistent in the placement of punctuation in respect to quotation marks, and this has silently been set right. These matters, on the other hand, are recorded when they appear in printed copy-texts. Both for manuscripts and for printed texts, however, conventional abbreviations like *Dr.* have been silently expanded to *Doctor* and Arabic numbers have generally been spelled out. Otherwise, no variation of any kind from the copy-text (other than those enumerated) has gone unreported; hence, the interested reader at any point can reconstruct the copy-text from the Virginia print in tandem with its records of emendation. These records are contained in appendixes to each literary work, where specialists may consult the details at leisure. The basis for the record is the page and line number of the Virginia text, *viz.,* 42.15 means page 42, line 15.

The textual appendixes usually consist of the following:

Textual Notes: Whenever an emendation of the copy-text, or a refusal to emend, seems to require special notice, a brief comment upon the reading is offered.

Editorial Emendations: All alterations of the copy-text not specified as silently made are recorded, together with the immediate source of the approved reading, which is always the first appearance of the emendation in the documents consulted in the preparation of the particular text. Since the purpose of this emendations list is to present at a view only the departures from the copy-text, and the origin of each reading of the correction or revision, the history of the altered reading up to the point of emendation is provided, but not its subsequent history. For substantives the full history of all readings variant from the copy-text within the editions consulted can be found in the Historical Collation.

The basic note provides, first, the precise form of the emended reading in the Virginia text. Following the square bracket appears the identification of the earliest source of the emendation in the editions collated. A semicolon succeeds this notation, and following this appears the rejected copy-text reading with the sigla of the editions that provide its history up to the point of emendation. In these notations certain arbitrary symbols appear. When the variant to be noted is one of punctuation and nothing else, a wavy dash ⁓ takes the place of the repeated word associated with the pointing and thus the more readily calls attention to the exact feature of the emendation. An inferior caret ∧ indicates that punctuation is absent and that this lack of pointing is the variant being noted. Three dots indicate one or more omitted words in a series. The sigla for denoting the editions recorded are explained in the Textual Introduction for each work. American book editions are prefixed by the letter A, and English by the letter E. Unless specifically excepted, the reading listed as originating in a plated edition comes from the original state of the plates and is constant in all noted impressions made from these plates. An emendation assigned to V is made for the first time in the present edition if by 'the first time' is understood 'the first time in respect to the listed editions chosen for collation.' An asterisk preceding a reference indicates that a Textual Note discusses this reading. Discussion of a retained copy-text reading that has not been emended will also be indicated by the asterisk and the formula '*stet* A1' or whatever is the appropriate siglum for the copy-text.

Word-Division: Hyphenation of a possible compound at the end of a line in the Virginia text poses a problem for the reader as to the exact form of the copy-text. Moreover, end-of-the-line hyphenation in the copy-text itself requires editorial decision whether the reading should be reproduced in the Virginia text as one word or as a hyphenated compound. This double problem is faced in the appendix on Word-Division, which is designed to record all the essential facts about the forms of possible compounds both in the Virginia text and in the copy-text.

Hence it must be understood that no hyphen at the end of a line in the present edition is actually part of a hyphenated compound unless it is specifically listed in this section of the apparatus, as in the form: *class-|mates.* This notation indicates that *class-*, ending the line in the Virginia text, is printed as part of a hyphenated compound within the line of the copy-text. If this notation were absent, it must be assumed that the copy-text form was *classmates*.

Since many hyphens ending lines in the copy-text may actually break an original hyphenated compound, not just an unhyphenated single word, the second part of this appendix section lists all occurrences of established hyphenated compounding broken at the end of a line in the copy-text itself, except when the hyphen joins capitalized units where there can be no ambiguity. In this notation the reading is that in the established Virginia text; whether the compound is hyphenated or unhyphenated in the listing is in accord with the determined practice of the copy-text or (failing this evidence) of the manuscripts closest in date. Obviously, not every broken word in the copy-text is so listed, since most of these will be mere syllabicated single words; thus only words that have some possibility of being compounds are noted. It is to be understood, moreover, that each reading was broken in the copy-text at the point of the hyphen (*class-mate*), or where the hyphen would normally have occurred if the compound had been one that Crane could theoretically have hyphenated.

The third section lists those rarer examples when, by chance, the same compound reading is broken at the hyphenation in both the Virginia text and the copy-text. Within parentheses, the established correct form is thereupon provided for the information of the reader.

These precautions being observed, anyone may transcribe a passage from the Virginia Edition with no ambiguity about word-division in the copy-text.

Historical Collation: A list is provided of all substantive variants from the Virginia text in the editions chosen for collation. Variant readings in the accidentals are ignored because of their copiousness and their basic lack of significance save when they affect the sense in a substantive manner and thus qualify for listing, or when they have some special importance in connection with the tracing of the family tree of textual derivation. Moreover, the various accidentals forms in different editions of a recorded substantive reading are ignored.

The first reading, to the left of the bracket, is that of the Virginia Edition, which will not necessarily be that of the copy-text if emendation has taken place. To the right of the bracket is placed the variant and the sigla for the specific collated editions in which it appears. Whenever one or more of the collated editions are not listed in a collation note, their readings must be understood to be the same as that of the Virginia Edition.

> micks] mugs A2, E1–2
> uprose] upreared its form A1

In the first of these two illustrations from *Maggie*, the Virginia text reads *micks* with A1, the copy-text, as against *mugs*, the rejected variant found in A2 (the 1896 revised American edition), which is also followed by the two collated English editions, E1 and E2 of 1896 and 1900 respectively. In the second note, the reading *uprose* from A2, followed by E1–2, is chosen for the present text; hence only the rejected variant *upreared its form* from A1 is listed, the other collated editions agreeing with the Virginia reading to the left of the bracket. In short, the first reading is invariably that of the Virginia text; the reading to the right of the bracket is invariably a rejected variant reading found in one or more of the collated editions.

Special Lists: Whenever the textual situation warrants the addition of further information than that supplied in the standard textual appendixes, special lists record the necessary data. Whenever a manuscript or typescript is preserved, for example, every piece of recoverable evidence about altered readings in it from the initial inscription is recorded so that the complete textual history of the work from the earliest preserved form may be made available for critical study.

On the other hand, a full list of all accidentals variants between a manuscript copy-text and the first printed edition deriving ultimately from it would run to so many items as to be of doubtful evidential value compared to the mass of information of minimal import thus recorded at considerable cost. Hence the full evidence of the accidentals bearing on the choice of copy-text is not presented in this edition. The loss is of little or no consequence, however, since the theory of copy-text followed by

the editor automatically selects the document for basic reproduction that is closest in its authority to the initial authorial inscription and thus to the author's accidentals. However, all substantive variation for such works will be found in the Historical
Collation, with the Editorial Emendations list indicating those
readings in which the manuscript copy-text has been altered by
reference to a variant in some later authority.

In order to secure a common ground for collation of the
different Crane works, the following procedures have been
adopted.

When a printed book edition is substantive because it is the
earliest preserved document for the text or else because it contains authoritative revision of an earlier appearance of the text
either in preserved manuscript or typescript, or else in magazine
or newspaper, form, multiple copies have been mechanically
collated on the Hinman Collating Machine, usually in the Clifton
Waller Barrett Collection of the University of Virginia Library
but with the occasional assistance of copies in the Ohio State
University Libraries or in other libraries. When the dispersal of
copies makes machine collation impossible, scrupulous sight collation has been substituted. Magazine and newspaper appearances have not been machine-collated against duplicates, but
care has been taken to sight-collate all different typesettings, as
in the appearance of a work in more than one newspaper or
magazine. Moreover, within Crane's lifetime, and for a few years
after his death, all printings after the first of a substantive book
text have also been machine-collated.

Multiple copies of a substantive book text are collated not
primarily to search for alterations in type or in plates during the
course of the initial impression, for such alteration (though
possible in type) is not likely to occur in plates. Instead, the
main purpose is to attempt to discover whether previously unnoticed printings, or impressions, have appeared, the evidence
being wear and batter in type or plates, and thus whether variants from the first printing may have entered the textual tradition in a concealed manner. Similarly, known impressions later
than the first are machine- or sight-collated back against the
original printing in order to record any possible variation in the

text and its authority, although only one copy of these identifiable later impressions is commonly collated.

On the other hand, first book editions that are not substantive, in the sense that they are mere reprints without authorial intervention in earlier appearances of the work in magazines or newspapers, have not always been collated in multiple copies. The odds are strong against the possibility that concealed impressions (not discovered in our investigations) would contain authoritative revision in plates, given the circumstances of initial publication and Crane's general indifference to revision of works already in print. Yet within the crucial years, known impressions and editions of such books have been collated for the sake of the record and as insurance against the unexpected.

The establishment of the text has then proceeded by the determination of the family tree for the text of each work and of the authority or nonauthority of all textual documents that have been preserved, whether manuscripts, typescripts, or printed versions, the area covered being roughly that of Crane's lifetime and the few years immediately succeeding. After that point, reprints of Crane almost ceased for most of his books until modern times, whether in the United States or in England.

The modern tradition for Crane's text may be said to start with *The Work of Stephen Crane,* edited by Wilson Follett in twelve volumes for Alfred A. Knopf between 1925 and 1927, with introductions by various hands. This was not designed as a scholarly edition and hence care was not taken always to utilize the earliest and most authoritative editions as printer's copy. The text of this edition has been collated for the private information of the editor, and Follett's readings have occasionally been remarked in the discussion of cruxes in the Textual Notes. But there seemed little reason other than historical curiosity to record its variants in the Historical Collation, and thus they have not been noted. Most modern editions of Crane have been simple reprints for textbook purposes, and these have also not been noticed in the Historical Collation. However, when scholars like Schoberlin, Stallman, Gullason, and Fryckstedt have edited previously unpublished or unreprinted works by Crane, substantive variants from the Virginia text in their editions of such writings have been recorded, and similar treatment has been given to such scholarly annotated texts of Crane as those represented by the *Poems* edited by Joseph Katz.

In short, all the documents that could possibly be substantive, and all the documents preserving the text that appeared in Crane's lifetime or posthumously, whether substantive or not, have been utilized by the present editor for the establishment of the text, and their variant wording has been recorded in the Historical Collation, as is proper for an attempt at a definitive edition. A critic, therefore, has at hand in this edition a complete substantive textual record of the only documents that can be authoritative for Crane's text. In addition, the editor has taken care to consult the results of previous editorial ministrations when such editions have been intended as independent scholarly productions and, as seems appropriate, has recorded their substantive variants or discussed editorial choices of words in connection with specific emendations.

To ensure maximum accuracy, all hand collation of the different typesettings of later editions against the copy-text has been duplicated by different workers, the results have been conflated, differences checked, and every variant wherever noted has been rechecked through the whole list of collated editions. This process should have produced exactness of fact unless the collators simultaneously passed over a variant unique to that edition, in which case no system of double checking could catch the error. All proofs have been read at least five times, and by three persons; one or more of these readings have been against the original copy-text, whether manuscript, typescript, or print, in all cases when a transcript or an annotated print had to be used as printer's copy.

In the Textual Introductions the accounts of substantive editions are not intended to be complete on the scale of a descriptive bibliography, and ordinarily nontextual details like the bindings are not noticed when no variation is known. Fuller descriptions are readily available in Ames W. Williams and Vincent Starrett's *Stephen Crane: A Bibliography* (1948), and the Pittsburgh Series in Bibliography has announced the preparation of a new large-scale bibliography. On the other hand, all observed variation of any kind in documents that have textual authority is noticed and analyzed. However, when the Introductions deal with derived and unauthoritative editions, although some account may be given of minor nontextual variation no special effort has been made to discover unknown states and hence any mention of variation cannot be supposed to be complete.

F. B.

Maggie: A Girl of the Streets

INTRODUCTION

CRANE'S first major literary effort, *Maggie: A Girl of the Streets*, is widely regarded as a minor classic. First published in a private edition in 1893 and then in a reworked version by Appleton's in 1896, it is often cited as one of the earliest examples of American naturalistic fiction and, because of certain radical innovations in its style and method, an important precursor of the experimental fiction of the nineteen twenties. The studied concentration of its impressionistic style sets it conspicuously apart from the relatively flat, enumerative styles of other realistic fiction of the period. Hamlin Garland and William Dean Howells, leading critics and spokesmen for the new realism, recognized its significance at once when it first appeared; and it continues in our own times to command attention and respect, both for its historical interest and for its importance as a work of art in its own right.

Unfortunately, the history of *Maggie* is somewhat confused and incomplete. It is usually said that Crane started the novel in the spring of 1891 at Syracuse University, where as a notably unsuccessful transfer student from Lafayette College he was making his first serious attempts at fiction writing. Dividing his time between the baseball diamond, the city streets, and the police court—studying "humanity" as he later explained—he neglected the "cut and dried" lessons of the classroom and established a reputation with the faculty for rebellious unconventionality and undisciplined brilliance. He spent his afternoons in the cupola of the Delta Upsilon fraternity house reading and writing, but nothing in the record of his experience at this time or in the writing he was doing suggests that he was capable of anything resembling *Maggie*, at least as we know it.

These early sketches and stories show that he began as a humorist with imitations of Mark Twain's tall tales and Poe's satirical hoaxes. These include a spoof on international politics,[1] a yarn about a swarm of gigantic bugs overwhelming a locomotive,[2] and an improbable tale about a New York tenor on a concert tour among savages in Africa.[3] Another tall tale is about smuggling whiskey into Maine in the stomach of a camel and the awkward consequences of the drunken beast's disruption of a pious ceremony in dedication of a new church.[4] And still another piece probably dating back to this time, the unfinished "Dan Emmonds," which Crane later referred to as "an old thing, strong in satire," was apparently intended as a parody of Poe's *Narrative of Arthur Gordon Pym*. It tells of a wondrous sea voyage that ends in a shipwreck off the coast of Australia and the hero's rescue by a band of copper-colored savages.[5]

The influence of Poe and Mark Twain on the later Sullivan County sketches, published in the New York *Tribune* in 1892, has often been noted, but the Syracuse pieces show even more clearly how dependent on them Crane was at this time for his literary ideas. More directly imitative of their masters, often with strong overtones of parody, they show little or no promise of the style of *Maggie*. They seem to bear out Crane's remark to a friend in 1894 that when he first began to write he hardly knew what to write about.[6]

The external evidence for a Syracuse version of the novel seems weak and inconclusive. Crane's fraternity brothers Frank Noxon and Clarence Peaslee claimed that Crane drafted *Maggie*

[1] "A Foreign Policy, in Three Glimpses," *Bulletin of the New York Public Library*, LXI (January, 1957), 43–46; reprinted in *The Complete Short Stories and Sketches of Stephen Crane*, ed. Thomas A. Gullason (New York, 1965), pp. 56–59.

[2] "Great Bugs in Onandoga," New York *Tribune*, June 1, 1891, p. 1; reprinted in *Stephen Crane: Uncollected Writings*, ed. Olov W. Fryckstedt (Uppsala, Sweden, 1963), pp. 7–8.

[3] "The King's Favor," *University Herald* (Syracuse, N.Y.), XIX (May, 1891), 128–131; reprinted in Gullason, *Short Stories*, pp. 52–56.

[4] "The Camel," in Gullason, *Short Stories*, pp. 60–61.

[5] Gullason, *Short Stories*, pp. 61–62. R. W. Stallman in "New Short Fiction: Dan Emmonds," *Studies in Short Fiction*, I (1963), 1–8, suggests that the story imitates Defoe's *Robinson Crusoe*. The 1891 dating is uncertain. Lillian Gilkes in "No Hoax: A Reply to Mr. Stallman," *SSF*, II (1964), 66–71, argues that it was written in England in the late nineties, but the style is very similar to that of other pieces of 1891. Crane's 1896 reference to it will be found in *Stephen Crane: Letters*, ed. R. W. Stallman and Lillian Gilkes (New York, 1960), p. 121.

[6] Corwin K. Linson, *My Stephen Crane*, ed. Edwin H. Cady (Syracuse, N.Y., 1958), p. 59.

"at least in its early form" in the cupola of the Delta Upsilon house,[7] and it is generally assumed that their testimony is supported by that of Willis F. Johnson, day editor of the *Tribune,* who wrote that he saw a draft of the novel a few months later at Asbury Park, where Crane (having ended his formal education when he left Syracuse at the end of the term) was reporting resort news for his brother Townley's news agency. "One day in the summer of 1891," Johnson recalled, "he brought me a big bundle of manuscript and asked me to read it and tell him what to do with it. I found it to be not a Sullivan County sketch, but a tale of the slums of New York, the first draft of *Maggie: A Girl of the Streets.*"[8]

But all this may be a matter of mistaken recollections. No one else who knew Crane at Syracuse ever mentioned for the record the existence of such a manuscript. Indeed, Frederick Lawrence, who claimed especially close friendship with Crane in those days and who lived with him at the Delta Upsilon house and later at the Pendennis Club in New York, seems to assume in his account that Crane first began the novel in the fall of 1892.[9] Doubt is cast on Johnson's date by the fact that most of the Sullivan County sketches were written in April or May, 1892; thus Johnson, whose statement implies knowledge of several, must have seen them and the draft of *Maggie* (written in December, 1891) a year later, shortly before he published them in the *Tribune* in July and August, 1892.

Furthermore, Hamlin Garland, whom Crane met in August, 1891, when the critic was at Avon, New Jersey, conducting a seminar in American literature and art, had no knowledge of a *Maggie,* though it is hard to believe that Crane would have shown the manuscript, if it existed, to Johnson and not to Garland. Garland was already an established writer and advocate of realism and took a friendly interest in Crane after he discovered

---

[7] Noxon to Max J. Herzberg, Washington, D.C., Dec. 7, 1926, *Letters,* p. 334; Peaslee, "The College Days of Stephen Crane," *Monthly Illustrator,* XIII (1895–97), 27.

[8] "The Launching of Stephen Crane," *Literary Digest International Book Review,* IV (April, 1926), 289. The novel would have had no title at this time.

[9] "Crane and I were inseparable in Syracuse," he wrote Thomas Beer in 1923. "We lived together in our so-called Pendennis Club on Avenue A while I was more or less intermittently studying medicine and he was writing *Maggie*" (Philadelphia, Nov. 8, *Letters,* p. 331).

on inquiry that the youth was the author of a particularly accurate report in the *Tribune* of a lecture on Howells. But Garland remembered Stephen at this time only as a clever reporter and a skillful baseball player. "I considered him at this time," as the critic recalled in 1900, "a very good reporter and a capital catcher of curved balls—no more, and I said goodby to him two weeks later with no expectation of ever seeing him again." [10]

This meeting with Garland was a crucial event in Crane's literary career and very probably marks the real beginning of the history of *Maggie*. Crane at that time had no program, no viable conception of the art of fiction, and apparently no plan of action. Garland was in a position to supply everything the youth lacked. He had developed from Howells' criticism, his reading of Véron, and his study of the new impressionistic painting a theory of art (called "veritism") which emphasized the revelation of social truth through the discipline of artistic craftsmanship. His lectures entitled "The City in Fiction" and "Sharpening Social Contrasts" (and perhaps his talks with Crane personally) stressed the importance of a fiction dealing with important social problems of the times, including the problem of life in the big city slums.[11] Of this he had already furnished an example in his play "Under the Wheel" (1890), a story about the Boston slums which even then, or shortly thereafter, he was recasting as the novel *Jason Edwards*, published in 1892. It was very likely Garland's influence that sent Crane into the city in pursuit of a subject for a novel.

In any case, shortly after the critic's departure in August, Crane began his study of the Bowery. From his brother's house in Lakeview he roamed the city studying the saloons, the flop-

---

[10] Hamlin Garland, "Stephen Crane: A Soldier of Fortune," *Saturday Evening Post*, CLXXIII (July 28, 1900), 16; reprinted in *Letters*, pp. 299–305. R. W. Stallman reports in his *Stephen Crane: A Biography* (New York, 1968) his discovery of six new Sullivan County sketches, all of which appeared in the *Tribune* between February and May, 1892 (p. 568). But this important discovery throws little light on the doubtful question of a Syracuse version of *Maggie*. Johnson's claim that he saw Sullivan sketches and a draft of *Maggie* several months before the earliest known Sullivan piece was printed is still open to doubt. And the fact that neither Lawrence nor Garland knew anything of this early version of the novel leaves the whole question unresolved.

[11] The printed program of lecture topics is reproduced in Jean Holloway, *Hamlin Garland* (Austin, Tex., 1960), pp. 55–56.

houses, and human derelicts and describing his adventures to his friend Helen Trent, who was shocked when he appeared on one occasion with a black eye he got in a Bowery saloon. He quarreled with her when she objected to the slums as "not nice," saying that they were the most interesting place in New York and that he was going to write a "sincere" book about them. Sometime between September and late December he had completed the first draft.

He told a friend, Wallis McHarg, that he wrote it "in two days before Christmas" and gave it to McHarg to read after conducting him on a tour of the Bowery. McHarg's advice was to give the characters names—he found it hard to keep the people, identified only as "the father," "the brother," "the woman of brilliance and audacity," straight in his mind—and he also cautioned Crane that no one would dare publish a novel about a prostitute.[12] Crane may have added names at this time, for he wrote McHarg a few weeks later that his brother William had supplied a title, though the letter, known only through Thomas Beer's paraphrase, may not have actually stated Maggie's name. It is usually assumed that the novel was rewritten this winter, but the evidence is merely the doubtful note to McHarg.[13]

By March, 1892, it was ready for the inspection of editors, and armed with a note from Townley, Stephen called on Richard Watson Gilder, editor of the prestigious *Century*. Gilder, who had once known the Crane family slightly, recalled the visit: "He was thin, and his blue eyes seemed enormous. He sat wrapped in a grey ulster much too big for him, talking slowly about his family with whom I had lost touch. I saw that his manuscript was not long and gave him an appointment for the next day." [14] He found *Maggie,* or rather this version of it, whatever it was like, shocking. It seemed cruel and callous, offensive in its lack of sentiment, and he went over the manuscript with the author criticizing errors and excesses in style until Crane cut him short: "You

---

[12] Thomas Beer, *Stephen Crane: A Study in American Letters* (New York, 1927), p. 81.

[13] Beer, summarizing the note, says: "Brother William had named the book. It was now *Maggie: A Girl of the Streets*" (p. 82). He implies that all the characters were given names except the "woman of experience and audacity" (p. 81).

[14] Beer, *Crane*, p. 83.

mean that the story's too honest?" It made the rounds of several other editors, but no one wanted it.

Since none of the manuscripts of *Maggie* have survived, it is not possible to say what this version was like, but it was probably cruder than the *Maggie* we know. For when Crane established himself in New York more or less permanently the next fall, he revised it—apparently radically—once again. Frederick Lawrence thought he began it initially at the Pendennis Club, where they lived together that winter, and later Crane himself referred to a book he "wrote" at this time in "three months . . . of very hard work to S. Crane." [15] It was finished by January, and on William's advice, he applied to the Librarian of Congress for a copyright about January 18, 1893: "Enclosed find a printed copy of the title page of a book written by me, and one dollar, for which please send a copy of the record of the copyright which is applied for." The enclosed typewritten title page omitted the name Maggie, reading simply: "A Girl of the Streets, | A Story of New York—by—Stephen Crane." [16]

With this new version he wasted no time on editors. Borrowing money from William, he had *Maggie* printed in an edition of eleven hundred copies by a firm of religious and medical book publishers. The printers refused the use of the firm name on the title-page, and the author himself adopted the disguise of a pseudonym, perhaps for the reason he gave:

I hunted a long time for some perfectly commonplace name. . . . I think I asked Wheeler [a newspaper reporter] what he thought was the stupidest name in the world. He suggested Johnson or Smith and Johnston Smith went on the ugly yellow cover of the book by mistake. You see, I was going to wait until all the world was pyrotechnic about Johnston Smith's 'Maggie' and then I was going to flop down like a trapeze performer from the wire and, coming forward with all the modest grace of a consumptive nun, say, I am he friends! [17]

But he was disappointed, for when the ugly little yellow book appeared in February or March, no respectable book dealer ex-

---

[15] Crane to Lily Brandon Munroe, New York, [winter of 1893–94?], *Letters*, p. 20.

[16] Crane to the Librarian of Congress, New York, [about Jan. 18, 1893], *Letters*, p. 13.

[17] Quoted in Beer, *Crane*, p. 90.

cept Brentano, who took twelve copies and returned ten, would stock it. Crane presented elaborately inscribed copies to friends and acquaintances and, despite the unflattering characterization of the clergy, to a number of ministers, described to a friend later as "maniacs of reform." Professor Brander Matthews received a copy with a note requesting his opinion and an unidentified Miss Wortzmann was presented with a volume inscribed: "This story will not edify or improve you and may not even interest you but I owe your papa $1.30 for tobacco." "My first great disappointment," he wrote in 1895, "was in the reception of 'Maggie, A Girl of the Streets.' I remember how I looked forward to its publication, and pictured the sensation I thought it would make. It fell flat. Nobody seemed to notice it or care for it." [18]

II

This was not literally true, however. One of the first copies went to Hamlin Garland, and the critic responded immediately and enthusiastically: "the first paragraph described the battle of some street urchins with so much insight and with such unusual and vivid use of English that I became very much excited about it. Next day I mailed the book to Mr. Howells, in order that he might share the discovery with me. The author had the genius which makes an old world new." [19] Assuming the role of patron, he recommended Crane to various editors; and B. O. Flower's Arena Company, at Garland's urging, at one time planned to republish the book, though nothing ever came of the idea. "Hamlin Garland," Crane wrote, "was the first to overwhelm me with all manner of extraordinary language," [20] and when Garland reviewed the book in the *Arena* in June, he did indeed give it high praise. "It is a work of astonishingly good style," he wrote. "It is pictorial, graphic, terrible in its directness. It has no conventional phrases." As a stylist, he went on to say, the author "impresses the reader with a sense of almost unlimited resource."

[18] Crane to an editor of *Leslie's Weekly*, [about November, 1895], *Letters*, p. 79.
[19] Garland, *Sat. Eve. Post*, CLXXIII (July 28, 1900), 16. Crane, not Garland, mailed the copy.
[20] Crane to Munroe, New York, [April, 1893], *Letters*, p. 21.

But he also noted weaknesses, that it "fails of rounded complete-ness. It is only a fragment. It is typical only of the worst ele-ments of the alley." And he advised the author to "delineate the families living on the next street, who live lives of heroic purity and hopeless hardship," [21] a suggestion which he may have talked over with Crane personally before incorporating it in his review, since *George's Mother,* begun in the spring, fits the pre-scription.

Howells, though Garland urged notice of Crane on him, was slower to respond. Several weeks after sending the critic a copy (at Garland's suggestion), Crane wrote him, "having received no reply I must decide then that you think it a wretched thing?" Howells apparently did not find it as striking as Garland did, for although he admitted that he had "glanced through" it and was sure Crane was "working in the right way," he confessed that he had not really read it.[22] But Crane's note turned his attention again to *Maggie,* and Howells found, as he recalled years later, that he did "care for it immensely" and he invited Crane to visit him:

he came to tea and stayed far into the evening, talking about his work, and the stress there was on him to put in the profanities which I thought would shock the public from him, and about the semi-savage poor. . . . He spoke wisely and kindly about them, and especially about the Tough, who was tough because, as he said, he felt that "Everything was on him." [23]

But Howells, though generous with encouragement and with efforts to bring Crane to the attention of editors, did not review *Maggie* until June, 1895, and then only as a kind of afterthought in an article on E. W. Townsend's Chimmie Fadden stories, also about New York slum life.[24] The critic's attitude, apparently, was somewhat ambivalent. "You know how well I think you handled that subject," he wrote Crane in response to a request for a letter of recommendation to the editor E. L. Bodkin, "and if I could not agree with you in all points of theory, I thoroughly respected

[21] Hamlin Garland, "An Ambitious French Novel and a Modest American Story," *Arena,* VIII (June, 1893), xi–xii.
[22] Howells to Crane, New York, March [28 or 29], 1893, *Letters,* p. 17.
[23] Howells to Cora Crane, Annisquam, Mass., July 29, 1900, *Letters,* p. 306.
[24] "Life and Letters," *Harper's Weekly,* XXXIX (June 8, 1895), 533.

your literary conscience, and admired your literary skill." [25] In his belated review, he acknowledged the importance of *Maggie's* efforts at "grim, not to say grimy truth," but his emphasis was on the impropriety of its language, "the impossibility to cultured ears of a parlance whose texture is so largely profanity. All its conscience and all its art could not save it, and it will probably remain unknown, but it embodied perhaps the best tough dialect which has yet found its way into print." [26] *Maggie* shows little kinship with Howells' genteel realism, but the slanting of the critic's opinion may go far beyond the issue of profanity and "grimy truth." Unlike Garland, he was not much in sympathy with the radical experiments in art of the time, and one suspects that he found Crane's style too antiliteral for a properly functional social realism.[27] In his introduction to the 1896 English edition he praises *Maggie* for "that quality of fatal necessity which dominates Greek tragedy," but his emphasis is upon its values as a study of personality types and their psychological motivation, almost as if he is projecting upon the book the idea of characterization which was central to his own aims as a novelist.

III

Crane continued his studies of the Bowery in such pieces as the famous "Experiment in Misery" and "The Men in the Storm," but even before he fully realized that *Maggie* had arrived stillborn he had set out in new directions. He began *The Red Badge of Courage* and *The Black Riders* in the spring of 1893 as well as *George's Mother,* and by the end of 1894 all three were finished and awaiting publication. On the strength of a favorable public

[25] Howells to Crane, New York, April 8, 1893, *Letters,* p. 18.

[26] *Harper's Wkly.,* XXXIX, 533.

[27] Although generous and appreciative, Howells seemed to value Crane's promise more than his actual achievement. He did not especially like *The Red Badge of Courage.* "For me," he remarked in a letter congratulating Crane on the English success of the war novel, "I remain true to my first love, 'Maggie.' That is better than all the Black Riders and Red Badges." His thought apparently turning to Crane's future at this point, he added: "You have a lot of good work in you, and the whole of a long life to get it out" (New York, Jan. 26, 1896, *Letters,* p. 102).

response to a severely shortened version of *The Red Badge*, which appeared in the New York *Press* and in the Philadelphia *Press* in December, 1894, he was engaged by the Bacheller Syndicate as a roving correspondent and early in January set out on a trip through the Far West and Mexico. Appleton's accepted the war novel in February, and when he returned to New York in April, Crane found his *The Black Riders* already under scornful attack from newspaper paragraphers. But *The Red Badge* appeared as a book in September, and its growing fame through the winter of 1894–95 threw upon the obscure *Maggie* the light of new interest.

Ripley Hitchcock of Appleton's proposed its reissue early in 1896, and Crane set about preparing it for the printer early in February. His initial plan may have been simply to edit out some of the profanity to which Howells had objected, for he wrote Hitchcock shortly after he began work that he had "dispensed with a goodly number of damns" and promised to send it, presumably ready for the printer, "in a few days." [28] But a few days later, when he was well into the work, he wrote that he had "carefully plugged at the words which hurt," and that "the book wears quite a new aspect from very slight omissions." He now, as he said, planned to "send you *Maggie* by detail." [29] By February 15 he had worked through the first six chapters and on March 23, after his progress had been interrupted by a journey to Washington to gather material for a book on politics, he wrote the editor that he would "begin to drive Maggie forward." [30] By the end of the month, therefore, the rewriting was finished and the new version was in proof. "I am engaged on the preface," Crane wrote on April 2, but he declined to finish checking proofs. "Let somebody go over them—if you think best—and watch for bad grammatical form & bad spelling. I am too jaded with Maggie to be able to see it." [31] It was, after all, the third (possibly the fourth if an early 1893 revision is assumed) rewriting of this troublesome book, and when it finally appeared in June, 1896, relieved of some of the exuberant overwriting and graceless

[28] [Hartwood, N.Y., Feb. 4–6?, 1896], *Letters*, p. 112.
[29] Hartwood, Feb. 10, 1896, *Letters*, p. 113.
[30] Washington, D.C., March 23, [1896], *Letters*, p. 120.
[31] New York [April 2, 1896], *Letters*, p. 122. The preface, if actually written, was not printed.

phrasing that marred the earlier edition, Crane must have felt that he had at last made the final effort for *Maggie*.

IV

Looking back at *Maggie* across the brilliant fiction of the twenties, the book does seem to be, as historians often say, a conspicuous link between Crane's time and our own. It showed the way to the future, Spiller notes, "by its unprecedented candor of theme, its sense of fate, and its directness in dealing with sordid material," [32] and Berryman, to cite another representative opinion, says that the "phrase-by-phrase concentration, the steady brilliance, and the large design of the little novel" reflect the conception of art that "initiated modern American writing." [33] But *Maggie* seems easier to link with the work that came after it than to that before it. None of its predecessors are like it in style, method, and expressed attitude, and the sources of the novel have not yet been satisfactorily determined. Even to his contemporaries, Howells and Garland, Crane appeared to have sprung from nowhere at all, and a recent literary history dismisses the whole problem of accounting for him by saying merely that he was an artist of "amazing, almost miraculous prescience," and thus "that despair of the academic critic, a highly 'original' writer." [34]

Even so, historians have not been idle, and one of the main lines of inquiry has been into the question of the indebtedness of *Maggie* to European naturalistic writers. It is often said that the novel is derived from Émile Zola's fictional study of Parisian slum life, *L'Assommoir*. The idea, one of the oldest in Crane criticism, was first advanced by Frank Norris in 1896 when he wrote in his review of the novel that it "is a story on the plan of the episode of Nana in *L'Assommoir*, the dialect and local color

---

[32] Robert E. Spiller in *The Literary History of the United States*, ed. Robert E. Spiller and Others (New York, 1948), II, 1022.

[33] John Berryman, *Stephen Crane* (New York, 1950), p. 52.

[34] Edward Wagenknecht, *The Cavalcade of the American Novel* (New York, 1952), p. 212.

being that of the Bowery." [35] It was a common belief in the nineties, as Crane's complaint about the bad manners of people who accused him of "stealing" his books from European realists testifies: "For it has been proven to me fully and carefully by authority that all my books are stolen from the French. They stand me against walls with a teacup in my hand and tell me how I have stolen all my things from De Maupassant, Zola, Loti and the bloke who wrote—I forget the book." [36] The question has been examined in detail by Ahnebrink, who found in certain parallels in characterization, theme, episodes, particulars, and technique evidence that *Maggie* was indeed directly and significantly influenced by *L'Assommoir*.

But this does not seem very likely. It cannot be proved that Crane read *L'Assommoir* before he wrote *Maggie*; it does not seem necessary to assume, as Ahnebrink does, that the descriptive details of the tenements and the brutality and degradation of the life there could not have been derived from actual observation. The specific language of the descriptive passages in the novels bears little or no resemblance, and many of the themes, such as the destructive power of alcohol, were commonplace in American journalism of the time. But even if it could be shown that *Maggie* derived from *L'Assommoir*, it would explain very little about Crane's book as a work of art. Zola and Crane saw their subject in fundamentally different ways, as a comparison of their descriptive styles shows. The following passage is from a translation Crane had available:

As a matter of fact, the grey, dirty B. staircase, with its greasy hand-rail and stairs, and scratched walls showing the rough mortar, was still full of a powerful odour of cooking. On each landing passages branched off sonorous with noise, and yellow painted doors, blackened near the locks by dirty hands, stood open; while, on a level with the staircase window, a musty stench came from the drain-sink mingling with the pungency of the cooked onions. From the

---

[35] *Wave* (San Francisco), XV (July 4, 1896), 13.

[36] Crane to James Gibbons Huneker, [Ravensbrook, Eng., December ?, 1897], *Letters*, p. 160. In the most recent study of Crane, R. W. Stallman cites Flaubert's *Madame Bovary* as the source of *Maggie* (*Stephen Crane*, pp. 77–78), arguing the point chiefly on the inconclusive evidence of similarities in the characterizations of Emma and Maggie. Stallman also reaffirms the influence of Zola's determinism in *L'Assommoir* (p. 74).

ground floor in the sixth storey one could hear the clatter of crockery, the noise of saucepans being scoured, of pans being scraped with spoons to clean them.[37]

A description of a similar scene from *Maggie* follows:

Eventually [Jim and his father] entered into a dark region where, from a careening building, a dozen gruesome doorways gave up loads of babies to the street and the gutter. A wind of early autumn raised yellow dust from cobbles and swirled it against an hundred windows. Long streamers of garments fluttered from fire-escapes. In all unhandy places there were buckets, brooms, rags and bottles. In the street infants played or fought with other infants or sat stupidly in the way of vehicles. Formidable women, with uncombed hair, and disordered dress, gossiped while leaning on railings, or screamed in frantic quarrels. Withered persons, in curious postures of submission to something, sat smoking pipes in obscure corners. A thousand odors of cooking food came forth to the street. The building quivered and creaked from the weight of humanity stamping about in its bowels.[38]

Zola is literal, objective, and inclusive, as his theory of analytical style required. Details occur in ordinary "realistic" spatial and temporal order, and since the point of view is fixed in time and space, the narrator sees in familiar perspective what any other keen and literal observer would from the given point or moment. Crane, on the other hand, is figurative and exclusive. Details are few and carefully selected, and they never quite come into spatial or temporal focus: "buckets, brooms, rags and bottles" are merely "in all unhandy places"; infants "played or fought with other infants or sat stupidly in the way of vehicles" in an order of time and space not specified. The picture is almost without perspective, for we see nearly simultaneously "a dozen gruesome doorways" and "yellow dust . . . swirled against an hundred windows," a deliberate distortion carried further in the quasi-figurative "careening buildings" and the grotesque "loads of babies."

This is not the language of generalized summary, but rather the style which reflects Crane's characteristic vision. Zola's vi-

[37] Quoted in Lars Ahnebrink, *The Beginnings of Naturalism in American Fiction, 1891–1903* (University of Uppsala Essays and Studies on American Language and Literature, IX; Uppsala, Sweden, 1950), p. 252.
[38] P. 11.1–15.

sion encompasses a literal order; Crane's cuts under the surface of appearance to essences, and his figurative and rhetorical distortions refer to qualities and values apprehended not objectively but subjectively. The stylistic differences spring from radically different visions, purposes, and attitudes and suggest strongly that Crane could not have been influenced in any very significant way by *L'Assommoir*.

In one sense the view that Crane's art derived simply from a "miraculous prescience" is correct, for it was of course finally the power of his imagination, working on various conceptions and tendencies, that fashioned the instrument of his style. The imaginative power cannot be explained, but certain literary conceptions and tendencies can be cited in the record, unluckily too scant, of his literary experience in the years 1891 to 1893. His Sullivan County sketches, written between the first and last versions of *Maggie*, show like the earliest pieces he wrote at college the influence of Mark Twain and Poe. In the Sullivan tales he experimented with some of the devices of the local colorists and frontier humorists, and it was probably Mark Twain who suggested the literary possibilities of colloquial language. Like this master Crane had a strong feeling for the effect of the contrast between the colloquial and the elevated "literary" style, a device commonly used in *Maggie*. The Sullivan sketches also reflect Mark Twain in the frequent occurrence of incongruous contrasts and such rhetorical devices as anticlimax and understatement. The satires on resort life at Asbury Park, printed in the *Tribune* also in 1892, sometimes echo Mark Twain strongly: "The average summer guest here is a rather portly man, with a good watch-chain, and a business suit of clothes, a wife, and about three children." [39] The Sullivan tales also, as Berryman notes, reflect Poe's sense of the "clouded, the obsessive, the grotesque," [40] which may have come directly from Poe or indirectly through Poe's imitator Ambrose Bierce, whose story "The Suitable Surroundings" (in *Soldiers and Civilians*, 1891) apparently influenced Crane's Sullivan tale, "The Black Dog." But the fantastic, grotesque, and hallucinatory effects, though permanent

[39] "On the Boardwalk," New York *Tribune,* Aug. 14, 1892, part 2, p. 17; reprinted in Fryckstedt, *Uncoll. Writ.,* pp. 23–27.
[40] P. 41.

features in Crane's style, become in his mature work something
different—in *The Red Badge* a brooding sense of a vaguely hostile, animistic nature, or perhaps the muted sense of the sinister
and uncanny in "'The Monster."

Two writers who probably influenced Crane more significantly
were Hamlin Garland, whose influence in another connection
has already been mentioned, and Rudyard Kipling. Kipling provided a creed of art and showed Crane the possibilities of an
impressionistic method, and Garland provided a theory for both
the creed and the method. Kipling, Crane implied in his single
admission of a literary influence, was the model for his early
sketches, and though he claimed to have abandoned his "clever
Rudyard-Kipling style" sometime in 1892,[41] the Englishman's
influence was nevertheless apparently deep and permanent. It
has been shown that Crane took his famous wafer image in *The
Red Badge* from *The Light That Failed* (1891), which he probably read as a serial in *Lippincott's Magazine* in the spring of that
year at Syracuse University.[42] He apparently took over, point by
point, the artistic credo of the hero of the novel, Dick Heldar.
Heldar is an artist and war correspondent who specializes in
realistic paintings of battles. He is in rebellion against the false
romanticism of the day and, in accordance with his belief that
art is properly based on actual experience, goes to the battlefield
for his subject matter. He also lives for a while the life of an
outcast in the slums of London. Art, he says, deals with truth,
ugly, brutal, or beautiful, as the case may be. He also believes
that art should preach no moral, that it requires of the artist an
uncompromising integrity, selfless devotion, and willingness to
suffer.

This is also Crane's creed. "It seems a pity," he wrote, ". . .
that art should be a child of suffering; and yet such seems to be
the case." [43] In 1891 he was saying, "I cannot see why people hate
ugliness in art. Ugliness is just a matter of treatment." [44] In the
same letter in which he repudiated Kipling's style, he wrote that
"we are the most successful in art when we approach the nearest

[41] Crane to Munroe, New York, [March, 1894?], *Letters*, p. 32.
[42] See James B. Colvert, "The Origins of Stephen Crane's Literary Creed,"
University of Texas Studies in English, XXXIV (1955), 179–188.
[43] Crane to John Northern Hilliard, [Ravensbrook, 1897?], *Letters*, p. 159.
[44] Berryman, *Crane*, p. 21.

to nature and truth," and in 1897 he explained that he had "been very careful not to let any theories or pet ideas of my own creep into my work. Preaching is fatal to art in literature." [45] These ideas were common enough in the theories of the literary realists and impressionist painters of the day and were held, in part or whole, by writers as different as Garland, Howells, Norris, and Zola. But they probably came to Crane first through Kipling and prepared him for the later influence of Garland, whose theoretical ideas were similar.

Stylistically, Crane seems closer to Kipling than to any other writer he might have read before 1892. There are general qualities, difficult to illustrate, which show a similarity in attitude: a certain offhand, knowing air, a fondness for epigrammatic nicety and pithy utterance. And though Kipling is more conventional in imagery and sentence organization, his descriptions often have a strong impressionistic sense, as his account of a battle in *The Light That Failed* shows:

Gradually the scattered white cloudlets drew out into long lines of banked white that hung heavily in the stillness of the dawn before they turned over wave-like and glided into the valley. The soldiers in the square were coughing and swearing as their own smoke obstructed their view, and they edged forward to get beyond it. A wounded camel leaped to its feet and roared aloud, the cry ending in a bubbling grunt. Some one had cut its throat to prevent confusion. Then came the thick sob of a man receiving his death-wound from a bullet; then a yell of agony and redoubled firing.[46]

The fictional Heldar, describing his method in painting, might have been describing both Crane's and Kipling's styles: "All done in a shifting light for shifting effect. . . . I remember I went out of my way to foreshorten for the sheer delight of doing it, and I foreshortened damnably, but for all that it's the best thing I've ever done." [47]

Finally, Kipling's novel may have helped to develop Crane's special sense of the use of color, though Crane's interest in painting seems to date back to his school days at Hudson River

---

[45] Crane to Hilliard, [n.p., n.d.], *Letters*, p. 158. The date of the letter is uncertain.
[46] (New York, 1897), p. 179.
[47] *Ibid.*, p. 54.

Institute in the late eighties.[48] Crane himself said he was influenced in the use of colors for compositional effects by a passage in Goethe on color and psychology.[49] Kipling demonstrated a literary use, however, and perhaps more importantly an attitude toward it. "I met a fellow the other day," the hero Heldar says, "who told me that it was impossible that shadows on white sand should be blue—ultramarine—as they are. . . . He knew all about Art, confound him." Beer reports that Crane, walking with his brother, once asked, "Will, isn't that cloud green? But they wouldn't believe it if I put it in a book." [50] *The Light That Failed*, like the Sullivan sketches and *Maggie*, is brilliant with color imagery: "What color that was," Heldar exclaims describing the Sudan. "Opal and amber and claret and brick-red and sulphur—cocatoo-crest sulphur—against brown, with a nigger black rock sticking up in the middle of it all, and a decorative frieze of camels festooning in front of a pure pale turquoise sky." [51]

But if Kipling planted attitudes and gave some hints for a method, Garland confirmed and buttressed them with theory, lending, one might imagine, the authority of a real rather than a fictitious spokesman. His lectures at Avon, advertised as "Studies in American Literature and Expressive Art," discussed the novels and poems of Bryant, Cooper, and Whitman as "landscape" literature, and his discussion, judging from the printed program, included the painter Thomas Cole. Some of his ideas about the art of fiction had been advanced in the *Arena* in 1890, the central premise of his statement being that art is properly a matter of personal vision, not a rendering of objective reality.[52] His lecture on Howells, as Crane's summary in the *Tribune* shows, warned against the error of literalism. "The photograph is false in perspective, in light and shade, in focus. When a photograph can depict atmosphere and sound, the comparison will have some meaning." [53] As the critic put it in his *Arena* article,

[48] Joseph Kwiat, "Stephen Crane and Painting," *American Quarterly*, IV (1952), 331.

[49] See Frank W. Noxon, "The Real Stephen Crane," *Step Ladder*, XIV (January, 1928), 5.

[50] *Crane*, p. 138.

[51] P. 53.

[52] Hamlin Garland, "Ibsen as a Dramatist," *Arena*, II (June, 1890), 72–82.

[53] "Howells Discussed at Avon-by-the-Sea," New York *Tribune*, Aug. 18, 1891, p. 5; reprinted in Fryckstedt, *Uncoll. Writ.*, pp. 8–9.

italicizing the essential point, "Realism has only one law, to be true, not to the objective reality, but to the objective reality *as the author sees it.*" [54]

This sentiment Crane seemed to be echoing when he advised a friend in the summer of 1891 on the art of writing. Tossing a handful of sand in the air, he counseled, "Treat your notions like that. Forget what you think about it and tell how you feel about it." [55] And again some years later in a statement often quoted and cited as central in his artistic credo: "I understand that a man is born into the world with his own pair of eyes, and he is not at all responsible for his vision—he is merely responsible for his quality of personal honesty. To keep close to this personal honesty is my supreme ambition." [56]

In view of what he appears to have acquired from Kipling and Garland it is not surprising to find him at the end of his first year in New York living in the semi-Bohemian world of impoverished painters and actors. It was a world of refined artistic feeling, colored by the spirit of Aubrey Beardsley and the outrageous Baudelaire, whose decadent poem "The Buffoon and the Venus" Crane imitated in his "A naked woman and a dead dwarf." [57] The watchword of the studios was "style," as Corwin Knapp Linson, a painter in whose studio Crane lived in the winter of 1892–93, observed. "In that period, 'style' came near to being worshiped as the end of art, as the only thing worth while." [58] *Maggie* was already finished before Linson knew Crane, but the painter observed the early stages of the writing of *The Red Badge* and gave testimony to the exquisitely studied method of composition: "He had a way of noting random sentences on paper scraps long before he would find their fitting places. On such I find: 'A ghastly, ineffaceable smile sculptured by fingers of scorn.' 'A fierce little stove.' 'Littered with straw, tin cans, and children.' " [59]

In his review of *Maggie* Frank Norris noted that it was the style which accounted for its power and interest, Crane's "habit and aptitude for making phrases—short, terse epigrams struck

[54] *Arena*, II (June, 1890), 74.

[55] Arthur Oliver, "Jersey Memories—Stephen Crane," *New Jersey Historical Society Proceedings*, n.s., XIV (1931), 648.

[56] Crane to Hilliard, [n.p., January, 1896?], *Letters*, p. 110.

[57] Richard E. Peck, "Stephen Crane and Baudelaire: A Direct Link," *American Literature*, XXXVIII (1965), 202–204.

[58] *My Crane*, p. 31.

[59] *Ibid.*, pp. 32–33.

off in the heat of composition, sparks merely, that cast a momentary gleam of light upon whole phases of life." Except for this, he
continued, "*Maggie* strikes no new note. . . . Most of [Crane's]
characters are old acquaintances in the world of fiction and we
know all about—or, at least, certain novelists have pretended to
tell us all about the life of a great city. In ordinary hands the tale
of Maggie would be 'twice told.' " [60] Norris no doubt had in mind
the slum novels of Arthur Morrison, H. W. Nevinson, J. W.
Sullivan, and E. W. Townsend, which had appeared since
Crane's book was first published; but in a very real sense the tale
of Maggie Johnson was "twice told" even in 1893. A literature of
the slums written by reformers and philanthropists such as T. D.
Talmage, J. W. Buel, and Jacob Riis had already established the
main features of the slum story by 1890. These writers and
others had defined the character of the slum girl and analyzed, in
the chivalrous terms of the era, her typical response to her
plight. According to the common view her natural purity and
virtue were all too often overwhelmed by the corrupting power of
her environment. "There is not one person out of a thousand,"
Talmage wrote, inveighing against the cruel scorn of the respectable, "that will . . . come so near to the heart of the Lord Jesus
Christ as to dare help one of these fallen souls." [61] Her life of
shame, according to the myth, typically ended in suicide.

Crane probably knew nothing of these books at first hand, but
their point of view and typical constructions were more or less
commonplace in the popular thought of the nineties. The *Arena*,
a magazine of progressive social thought with a circulation of
more than one hundred thousand, published in the early months
of 1891 a series of articles on the slums which reflect faithfully
the common themes and ideas. The editor, B. O. Flower, was
himself a close observer of the social underworld and described
in a series of editorials such conditions as "the plight of poor
factory and sewing girls, whose fate is often so grim and tragic
that it is only their splendid moral strength which keeps them
from the abyss of vice." [62] Shortly before Crane arrived in the
Bowery the *Arena* published an essay which analyzed the deter-

[60] Norris, *Wave*, XV (July 4, 1896), 13.

[61] D. T. Talmage, *The Masque Torn Off* (Chicago, 1882), p. 65. See Stallman,
Crane, p. 73, for a discussion of the influence of moral tracts on *Maggie*.

[62] B. O. Flower, "Deplorable Social Conditions," *Arena*, XV (February, 1891),
375.

ministic effect of environment on the morals of slum dwellers, citing the saloon as the chief instrument of destruction.[63] Another writer denounced the sham of respectability, expressing the hope that the new realism in social thought would expose the hypocrisy which paralyzed constructive reformist action. "We are in the midst of an end of sham," he wrote. "We do not care so much that vice exists as that it can be well dressed." [64]

Crane invented the plot of *Maggie* in its details, but the large patterns were given. The characters (the pure, betrayed Maggie, the drunken parents, and the vicious brother), the point of view (the author's scorn of "respectable" people, his veneration of Maggie's innate, though vulnerable, purity), the action (the fights, the seduction, and the suicide), and the interpretation of causes (alcohol, social determinism, the scorn of Christian respectability) were all conspicuously accessible, waiting so to speak for a style and treatment capable of investing them with interest and viable meaning. Edgar Fawcett exploited the master plot two years before Crane began his study for *Maggie* in his novel of the slums, *The Evil That Men Do* (1889). Cora Stang, the heroine, is "a delicate blushing-rose in the midst of . . . smirk and soilure." And "though she had tried very hard to be good" and aspired to be "a flower of sinless and beautiful love," she is at last seduced and abandoned, victimized by "the savage forces of birth, heredity, and poverty." She is scorned by respectable people of "egoistic indifference" who "murder philanthropy," and her brief career as a prostitute ends tragically in her murder.

But Fawcett has no art of sufficient power to rescue this "twice-told tale" from its inherent banal sentimentality. It is Crane's art—the almost perfect detachment, the brilliant impressionism, the critical power of its irony—that saves what would otherwise be a lost literary cause. And if something of the banality of his untreated materials lingers in the little novel, it goes in the reading almost unnoticed—sufficient proof of Crane's power to "initiate modern American writing."

J. B. C.

[63] Arthur Dudley Vinton, "Morality and Environment," *Arena*, XVII (April, 1891), 574.
[64] Albert Ross, "What Is Immoral in Literature," *Arena*, XV (March, 1891), 439.

TEXTUAL INTRODUCTION

THE first edition (A1) of *Maggie*, 1893, collates: [unsigned] $1-10^8$ 11^2, pp. $1-3$ $4-163$ 164. The printing was from type metal and there could have been only one impression. The title (p. 1) reads: 'MAGGIE | A | GIRL OF THE STREETS | (A STORY OF NEW YORK) | BY | JOHNSTON SMITH | COPYRIGHTED'. The verso of the title (p. 2) is blank; the text with the head title 'A GIRL OF THE STREETS: | A STORY OF NEW YORK.' begins on p. 3 and ends on p. 163, with p. 164 blank. The book was bound in mustard paper wrappers with blank spine and back wrapper. The front wrapper is printed in black and red: 'Price, 50 Cents | [triple heavy rule in red] | MAGGIE | A Girl of the Streets | (A STORY OF NEW YORK) | By | JOHNSTON SMITH | Copyrighted | [triple heavy rule in red]'.

The printer is unknown except that it was a New York City firm specializing in religious and medical texts. Eleven hundred copies were printed at a cost of $869.[1]

After Crane had made his name with *The Red Badge of Courage*, Appleton & Co. encouraged him to revise the 1893 text [2] and in early June of 1896 published a revised edition (A2), clothbound, collating 1^8 $2-11^8$, pp. *i-iv* v-vi, 1 $2-158$ $159-170$, with prefixed and suffixed flyleaves. A half-title appears on p. i, with an Appleton advertisement for *The Red Badge of Courage*, boxed, on p. ii, the verso. The title occupies p. iii; on its verso, p. iv, are two copyright notices, one by Appleton in 1896 and one by

---

[1] Thomas Beer, *Stephen Crane: A Study in American Letters* (New York, 1923), pp. 90–91.

[2] Ripley Hitchcock, the Appleton editor, had been interested in *Maggie* as early as 1892 but did not feel at that time he could recommend its acceptance (Willis F. Johnson, "The Launching of Stephen Crane," *Literary Digest International Book Review*, IV [April, 1926], 289).

Crane in 1893. After the Publisher's Note on pp. v–vi, the text starts on p. 1 with the simple head title 'MAGGIE.' and ends on p. 158 with 'THE END.' Pages 159–170 contain integral Appleton book advertisements. According to a typed memorandum in the Appleton-Century MSS Collection in the Lilly Library of Indiana University, the contract was dated May 13, 1896, and Crane was to receive 15 per cent of the retail price as royalties. Copyright was applied for on May 28 and deposit was made in the Library of Congress on June 3, 1896. The book was advertised in the *Publishers' Weekly* of June 13. The price was seventy-five cents.

Machine collation reveals no worked-up or loosened types. All the evidence suggests, despite the lack of a stereotyper's notice, that the book was printed from plates.

Three impressions may be identified. The first (A2ᵃ) is on wove paper and its title-page is set in black-letter types: '𝕸𝖆𝖌𝖌𝖎𝖊 | 𝕬 𝕲𝖎𝖗𝖑 𝖔𝖋 𝖙𝖍𝖊 𝕾𝖙𝖗𝖊𝖊𝖙𝖘 | [leaf] | 𝕭𝖞 | 𝕾𝖙𝖊𝖕𝖍𝖊𝖓 𝕮𝖗𝖆𝖓𝖊 | 𝕬𝖚𝖙𝖍𝖔𝖗 𝖔𝖋 𝕿𝖍𝖊 𝕽𝖊𝖉 𝕭𝖆𝖉𝖌𝖊 𝖔𝖋 𝕮𝖔𝖚𝖗𝖆𝖌𝖊 | [Appleton device] | 𝕹𝖊𝖜 𝖄𝖔𝖗𝖐 | 𝕯. 𝕬𝖕𝖕𝖑𝖊𝖙𝖔𝖓 𝖆𝖓𝖉 𝕮𝖔𝖒𝖕𝖆𝖓𝖞 | 1896'. The last page of the advertisements (p. 170) contains the notice for The Story of the West Series. A few pieces of possible progressive type batter appear in the three A2ᵃ Barrett Collection copies and the McGregor copy at the University of Virginia, and also in the Ohio State University Libraries copy, when compared on the Hinman Collating Machine, but the evidence is insufficient to establish more than one printing.[3]

The second printing (A2ᵇ) is on laid paper, with vertical chainlines, watermarked with the Appleton device; its p. 170 also advertises The Story of the West Series, but its title-page is in a new setting, with different lining, all in roman type: 'MAGGIE | A GIRL OF THE STREETS | BY | STEPHEN CRANE | AUTHOR OF | THE RED | BADGE OF | COURAGE | [Appleton device] | NEW YORK | D. APPLETON AND COMPANY | 1896'. The hypothesis advanced by J. T. Winterich [4] would seem to be correct that the typographical change was instituted in order to emphasize that Crane was the author of the popular *Red Badge*

---

[3] Moreover, the evidence that A2ᵇ copies were ordered before the publication date (see below) suggests that only one printing was made on wove paper with the black-letter title-page.

[4] Quoted in Ames W. Williams and Vincent Starrett, *Stephen Crane: A Bibliography* (Glendale, Calif., 1948), p. 25.

of Courage.[5] The one clear-cut piece of batter evidence that serves to distinguish these two impressions occurs in the second *w* of *window* on p. 123, l. 17, which is perfect in all wove-paper copies examined but has its first half broken off or in some manner obscured in all examined copies of the laid-paper printings. Although the possibility exists that this defect may show up in some uncollated copy of the wove-paper form, the evidence favors the hypothesis that the damage was caused between printings and thus may be taken as a genuine typographical distinction. Another piece of evidence is less oracular. In the two known advance copies (see below) the hyphen that breaks *antici-|pating* in the first line of p. 136 is perfect. In the wove-paper copies this hyphen is so battered as to appear only as a dot; but in the laid-paper copies the hyphen is visible as a battered, bent-down mark about half its proper length. Since the total evidence for the priority of the wove-paper copies is incontestable, it is probable that some difference in the make-ready and its pressure caused the upper corner of a battered plate to print more fully in the later printing than in the earlier.

What would appear to be a third printing (A2^c) is owned by the Princeton University Library and by several private collectors, including Professor M. J. Bruccoli. This resembles the standard roman title-page laid-paper A2^b copies except that the final advertisement on p. 170 substitutes *The Three Musketeers* for The Story of the West series.

Each one of the four University of Virginia copies of A2^a and the two copies of A2^b has a pencil mark in connection with the announcement of the first of the series, *The Story of the Indian,* advertised as 'now ready.' This takes the form either of a diagonal line through the announcement or a large pencil cross against it, except for one copy of A2^a (Barrett 551429) which has only a short horizontal pencil line in the left margin against the preceding general announcement. Very few of the numerous copies observed (as, for instance, the Columbia University Libraries copy of A2^b) are not so marked in one of these three

---

[5] This black-letter typography for a title-page seems to have been conventional with Appleton at the time, as evidenced by its use for the titles of *The Red Badge* (1895), *The Little Regiment* (1896), and *The Third Violet* (1897). It is also found in *Yekl* by A. Cahan in 1896.

general ways. The purpose of this slash or cross is most obscure, especially since one observed copy of *The Three Musketeers* state also has it. *The Story of the Indian,* by George B. Grinnell, was registered in the Library of Congress Copyright Office on October 31, 1895, and two deposit copies were received on November 27. It was advertised in the *Publishers' Weekly,* December 7, 1895. In the same number a new popular edition of *The Three Musketeers* was also advertised but asterisked as an indication that a copy had not actually been received. This same number also mentions that Appleton was exhibiting an edition de luxe of the *Musketeers,* a special edition that had been published in 1894. The exact publication date of the cheap edition is not established, but since it had been listed as an autumn publication in the *Weekly* of September 28, 1895, and advertised in the undated 'Christmas Bookshelf' number, as well as on December 7, its issue must have been in November–December 1895 on the evidence that copyright was applied for on October 28 and two copies were deposited in the Library of Congress on November 2, 1895, well before the publication of *Maggie* in June, 1896. One may also notice that *Yekl: A Tale of the New York Ghetto,* published by Appleton in 1896 (advertised in the *Publishers' Weekly* of July 18, 1896, little more than a month after *Maggie*), concludes its advertisements with the same plate as *Maggie* for The Story of the West Series. Finally, what may be the second printing of *The Little Regiment,* which followed *Maggie* in late 1896, contains The Story of the West announcements on the final page of its advertisements as a substitute for S. R. Crockett's *Lilac Sunbonnet* advertised in the first printing. Here *The Story of the Mine,* announced in *Maggie* and in *Yekl* as in preparation, joins *The Story of the Indian* as 'now ready.'

One might conjecture that the pencil marks were intended in some manner as an indication of cancellation, but the presence of small pencil loop marks on the last advertisement page of *The Little Regiment* seems to destroy any cancellation hypothesis. The position of the pencil cross deep in the inner margin of one of Professor Bruccoli's copies demonstrates that, in this instance at least, the mark was made when the final gathering was still in sheet form unbound. Hence the best guess seems to be that these are collator's O.K.'s that the sheets are complete in the copy for binding.

Machine collation of Professor Bruccoli's copy of A2^c against A2^b reveals practically identical type batter, including the defects described above at 123.17 and 136.1. Thus it is just possible that A2^c represents not a complete reprinting but merely a reprinting for a cancellans final gathering containing the last of the text and the advertisements and then the binding up of the altered advertisement in the last copies to be sold. But the evidence of type batter in this book is not at all trustworthy except for the one definite piece of evidence on p. 123, l. 17; hence in view of the Appleton statement that there were four printings of *Maggie,* mentioned below, the odds would seem to favor the acceptance of this A2^c as a legitimate separate impression from A2^b, which it otherwise resembles.

Two examples of an advance-copy state on wove paper have been preserved, one as the deposit copy in the British Museum (shelf mark 012628.g.64) and the other in the Barrett Collection in the University of Virginia Library (acquisition 551431). Both share the same characteristics. The binding is not cloth but buff wrappers with blank spine and back wrapper. (The Barrett copy is perfect, but the British Museum copy has been rebound with only the front wrapper preserved.) On the front wrapper appears the black-letter title-page in the same setting as A2^a save that no imprint is present below the Appleton device and instead a purple rubber-stamped imprint reads: 'WM. HEINEMANN, | PUBLISHER, | 21, BEDFORD STREET, | LONDON, W.C.' The final gathering 11 wants the six pages of advertisements and is composed of a conjugate pair of leaves concluding the text (the BM leaves in this gathering have been strengthened and the evidence destroyed). The first gathering, though in 8's, has a different imposition whereby pp. i–ii are blank, p. iii is the half-title, p. iv blank, p. v tipped-in cancellans title, and p. vi blank. This imposition does not contain the Publisher's Note of the trade edition, and the advertisement for *The Red Badge* on the verso of the half-title is missing.

The Appleton title-leaf is canceled, and on slightly coated wove paper, different from the regular stock, the cancellans reads: 'MAGGIE | A GIRL OF THE STREETS | BY | STEPHEN CRANE | AUTHOR OF | THE RED | BADGE OF | COURAGE | LONDON | WILLIAM HEINEMANN | 1896'. In both the British

Museum and the Barrett copies the blank verso of the half-title reproduces in offset the black-letter Appleton title-page complete.

That these are true advance copies may be suggested not only by the unbattered hyphen on p. 136 but also by the preservation of physically similar wrappered copies of the Appleton *Little Regiment* (1896) and *Third Violet* (1897), as well as a previously unrecorded advance copy of *The Red Badge of Courage* in boards deposited in the British Museum, and one in wrappers in the Bodleian Library. The wrappers of *The Little Regiment* are blank, and all advertisements are present. But in the Columbia University *Third Violet* the front wrapper exactly reproduces the title-page in the same setting and, like *Maggie*, the verso of its half-title is blank, without the announcements of the trade edition. The British Museum's *Red Badge* in boards has its unique Appleton title-page reproduced on the front cover, and its trade-edition final gathering in 8's is imposed and sewn in 6's without the advertisements on the final two leaves of the book that appeared in the trade copies. A purple rubber stamp 'LONDON &' is placed above the imprint on the front cover and the title-page. A Bodleian Library deposit copy in wrappers exhibits the same characteristics.

Whether the lack of an imprint on the wrapper title of *Maggie* was designed for the convenience of a stamped imprint for another publisher (as actually used by Heinemann) or whether an imprint was thought to be inappropriate on the wrapper title cannot be determined. What seems evident, however, is that Heinemann was sent several copies of this advance state, and that he used one to secure copyright immediately by deposit in the British Museum on June 8, whereas his own London edition was not announced in the *Publishers' Circular* until September 19, 1896. (The British Museum, *contra* Williams and Starrett, does not have a deposit copy of the true 1896 Heinemann edition.) The 1896 Heinemann text was undoubtedly set up from one of the advance copies.

Three points of interest are raised by these advance copies of *Maggie*. First, the offset of the black-letter title on the verso of the half-title demonstrates that this black-letter setting was the original plate, as would indeed be suggested by the same types that printed the front wrapper save for the imprint. Second, the

use of an all-roman but wove-paper cancellans Heinemann title
that has the same unusual typography and the same font
(though not the identical types) as the Appleton roman laid-paper title indicates that the cancellans must have been printed in
imitation of the A2ᵇ Appleton title, which, therefore, must have
been in existence at an early date since the Appleton copyright
deposit was made in the Library of Congress on June 3, 1896,
with the black-letter title; but Heinemann was able to deposit his
copy, with the title imitating the roman setting, on June 8.
Whether this cancellans title was printed in the United States
and tipped in the copies sent to Heinemann, or whether Heinemann printed it for his own purposes cannot be demonstrated. If
Heinemann printed the title, the problem arises where he se-
cured the roman-setting model, for on the evidence of the offset
the black-letter setting had originally been bound in these wrappered copies. Since the essence of an advance copy is that it is,
indeed, an advance, made up before the regular trade printing
(or binding), the assumption is that these copies ought to have
been mailed to Heinemann before the second-impression laid-paper A2ᵇ copies would normally have been run off. Third, the
imposition of the final text gathering of the advance copies
without the plates for the advertisements (as in the advance *Red
Badge*), the absence of the plate for the advertisement on the
verso of the half-title (as in *The Third Violet*), and finally the
imposition of the preliminaries with an initial blank leaf and
without the Publisher's Note all blend to suggest that these are
not regularly machined examples of trade sheets in a special
binding but instead, probably, something close to final proofs for
special purposes, like the reviewers' and sales demonstration
copies of the present day, although the removal from these Appleton advance copies of Appleton advertisements (and of the
topical Publisher's Note in *Maggie* that would have no application in England) also suggests that their primary purpose was
perhaps what Heinemann used them for—deposit copies abroad
to preserve copyright. On certain pages of the Barrett copy what
appears to be the evidence of roller pressure can be seen, and the
impression of some furniture at the head of p. 42 also suggests
hand proofs, as does the special imposition of the first and last
gatherings.

The hypothesis to be drawn from this evidence indicates that after the manufacture of a few copies from hand proofs (whether pulled from type metal or the plates), Appleton ordered the printing started for the first trade impression, on wove paper and with the conventional black-letter title. However, before publication Appleton must have ordered a second impression, on laid paper and with the roman title. While this roman title was being approved in proof, either a proof of another setting was made up with the Heinemann imprint and the advance copies sent off to England, or else a proof of the Appleton roman title was enclosed with the advance copies mailed abroad and Heinemann made up an imitation of it with his own imprint for copyright purposes. What evidence there is seems to favor the latter possibility.[6] Thus if Heinemann deposited his copy at the earliest opportunity, on June 8, it is likely that Appleton mailed him the advance copies (perhaps including a proof of the roman title-leaf, or even a tipped-in roman title) very close in date to May 28, when the American copyright was applied for (though deposit was not made until June 3). Indeed, among the Appleton-Century MSS in the Lilly Library at Indiana University is a typescript copy of a letter dated May 11, 1896, and addressed to Heinemann from the Appleton offices at 33 Bedford Street, London, agreeing to let Heinemann have *Maggie*; Heinemann accepted on May 13. On May 11 William Appleton had written,

[6] It will be observed that the tipped-in title reads 'A Girl of the Streets' and not the later Heinemann version (E1), 'A Child of the Streets'. Whether the cancellans title was printed in the United States or in England is not certain, but the example of the Heinemann deposit copy of *The Little Regiment* in the New York sheets suggests that the title may have been English. The British Museum deposit copy of *The Little Regiment*, stamped October 30, 1896, has been rebound, and the Appleton advertisements on the last three leaves of gathering 13 are excised (instead of the gathering being reimposed to exclude them). Hence whether it was originally wrappered—like the copy preserved in the Bodleian Library and the one with an American title-page in the Barrett Collection—cannot be demonstrated: the British Museum binders were instructed to preserve such covers, as they did with the front cover of *Maggie*, but unfortunately they seem to have discarded blank wrappers, as with the back cover of *Maggie* and presumably as with the wrappers of *The Little Regiment*. At any rate, both this and the Bodleian copies contain a previously unrecorded cancellans title-page for *The Little Regiment*, with the Heinemann imprint as in *Maggie*; but in this case the watermark in the cancellans leaf 'Abbey Mills | Greenfield' shows that the paper was English. If in October, 1896, Heinemann printed his own cancellans title to secure copyright with American sheets before he printed his edition in 1897, it may be conjectured that he did so with *Maggie* in June, 1896.

" 'Maggie' we expect to publish in June, and I have no doubt that we should be able to send you proofs very shortly." Allowing time for a letter to reach New York from London after May 13, the advance copies must have been sent to Heinemann very close in date, as estimated, to the copyright entry. Thus since publication was announced by Appleton in the *Publishers' Weekly* of June 13, it would follow that the laid-paper printing must have been ordered before publication and might have been available very close to the first of the month, or even earlier, although the one remaining Library of Congress deposit copy is in the A2^a state.

Unfortunately, the Appleton records are sketchy and do not preserve any notice of the details of the advance copies or of the two early printings. All that we have is the copy, in the Appleton Collection in the Lilly Library of Indiana University, of the letter to Heinemann from Appleton's English office at 33 Bedford Street, dated May 11, 1896, and signed William W. Appleton. This begins: "We agree to let you have the publication in England etc. of Maggie and The Little Regiment and Other Stories on a royalty of 15 per cent of retail, you to pay an advance of £30 for each book. 'Maggie' we expect to publish in June, and I have no doubt that we should be able to send you proofs very shortly." According to another copy at Indiana, Heinemann on May 13 accepted the terms of this letter, and a copy of the contract is preserved dated May 13, 1896, agreeing on the 15 per cent of retail royalty rate.

What small evidence can be recovered from the batter in the plates does not suggest that the A2^a state consisted of more than a single printing. Indeed, if the hypothesis for the prepublication order for laid-paper copies is correct, the wove-paper copies would almost necessarily represent only one impression. On the other hand, if the advertisement for the fourth printing of *Maggie* that appears on the verso of the half-title of *The Little Regiment* in 1896 [7] is accurate and not an attempt to give a false appearance of popularity, at least three impressions may have been printed on laid paper. One of these would have been in the A2^b or A2^c state, but the batter in observed copies of the laid-pa-

---

[7] Copyright for *The Little Regiment* was applied for on October 7, 1896, with deposit on October 30. Publication was announced in the *Publishers' Weekly* of December 5.

per A2 does not serve to differentiate the missing printing.[8] Copies of A2ᵃ and A2ᵇ appear to be relatively common and without disproportion in their preserved numbers, except for the artificial preservation of larger numbers of A2ᵃ in libraries and in private collections, since it has long been recognized as the first printing and therefore has been more highly valued. Copies of A2ᶜ appear to be less common.

The first Heinemann English edition (E1) of 1896 collates π^4 A–I⁸ K⁴, pp. *i–iv* v–vii *viii, 1* 2–147 *148,* ²*1* 2–4. The half-title appears on p. i, advertisements for Crane books on p. ii, the title on p. iii, the copyright notice on p. iv, a specially written "Appreciation" by W. D. Howells on pp. v–vii, with p. viii blank. The text begins on p. 1 and ends on p. 148 with the colophon, '*Printed by* BALLANTYNE, HANDSON & CO. | *London and Edinburgh*'. Pages ²1–4 are inserted advertisements. Publication was announced in the *Publishers' Circular* of September 19, 1896. The British Museum does not possess a deposit copy, presumably because of the copyright and deposit of the advance copy of A2 on June 8. The copy for this edition (E1) was A2, almost certainly one of the advance copies that Appleton had sent instead of proofs. In William Appleton's letter to Heinemann of May 11, 1896, Heinemann was to pay a royalty of 15 per cent of retail, with an advance of £30. The publication price was two shillings.

The second English edition (E2) was published by Heinemann in 1900 and included, at a publication price of six shillings, *George's Mother* with *Maggie* under the general title of *Bowery Tales.* Two issues exist of this edition. In the first, or trade, issue of 1900 the binding cloth is tan buckram, with Heinemann's device and name on the spine, and the title-leaf is a cancel, reading 'Bowery Tales | George's Mother | Maggie | By | Stephen Crane | Author of | "The Red Badge of Courage," etc. | London | William Heinemann | 1900'. The collation is $A^2(\pm A2)$ B–P⁸ Q⁶, pp. *i–iv, 1–2* 3–109 *110–112* 113–236. Page i contains the general half-title with Crane book advertisements on p. ii, p. iii the cancel title, p. iv the Berne copyright formula with notice

---

[8] A copy in the Houghton Library at Harvard (AC.85.C8507.893mb) on wove paper (Story of the West final advertisement) has a cancellans laid-paper roman title-leaf tipped in. It would be mere speculation to suggest that Appleton could have treated some few remainder wove-paper copies in this manner and called them an 'edition'.

against import into the United States, together with the 1896 'first impression' record of the two titles. *George's Mother* begins on p. i with its half-title (verso blank), and *Maggie* with a half-title on p. 111, verso blank; pp. 113–114 hold Howells' "Appreciation" and pp. 115–236 the text. On p. 236 is the colophon, '[short rule] | *Richard Clay & Sons, Limited, London & Bungay.*' Sixteen quired leaves of publisher's advertisements signed A (the fifth leaf signed A2) are bound in these trade copies.

At some time after 1905, as Bruccoli and Katz have shown in *Studies in Bibliography*, XXII (1969), the remainder sheets without appended publisher's advertisements but with the original title-page were bound in blue cloth for the Times Book Club, the circular Times imprint substituting for Heinemann at the foot of the spine. In this issue the original and conjugate title-page reads as in the cancel except that 'George's Mother | Maggie' is wanting below 'Bowery Tales'. The cancel was printed, quite evidently, to advertise these two novels on the title-page.

These four represent the only editions of *Maggie* printed in Crane's lifetime; indeed, E2 was announced in the *Publishers' Circular* of June 30, 1900, and so appeared after Crane's death on June 5.

The privately printed 1893 edition (A1) is taken as the copy-text for the present edition since it is the only print set directly from the author's lost manuscript, perhaps a typescript of Crane's usual handwritten manuscript although typesetting direct from the holograph cannot be ruled out under the circumstances. In some though not in all respects it appears to be a fairly literal and sometimes even a naïve reproduction of its copy. For example, Crane's spelling *missle* for *missile* is reproduced at 39.23, at 49.6, and again at 49.14;[9] his characteristic misspelling *mode* for *mood* appears at 71.12, and also such aberrant spellings as *chrisanthemums* (21.15), *similiar* (26.1), *grimey* (26.25 and 70.12 versus *grimy*, 46.20), *begrimmed* (45.20), *sterness* (67.28). On the other hand, A1 does not usually reproduce Crane's characteristic *centre* or *theatre* spellings (although

[9] Unless otherwise specified, all page-line references are to the text in the present Virginia Edition.

theatre appears at 32.7), yet it more often than not agrees with his invariable spelling *grey*. Moreover, his somewhat characteristic single consonants appear in *unskilfull* (42.28), *quarreling* (57.13), *shriveling* (60.7, though *shrivelling* at 34.15), *marvelous* (48.30), but *appalling* at 35.39 and 75.17. *Gossiped* occurs at 11.10. His characteristic *bended* is usually preserved (18.36, 34.21, 45.31, 60.14, 63.24,37) and *strided* appears at 39.32 but *strode* at 44.18. Little house styling on the part of the compositor(s) is indicated by the variety of word-division forms like *upstairs* (18.17) and *up stairs* (42.22), or *side-walk* at 23.8 but *sidewalk* invariably elsewhere. The dialect wobbles between such variants as *tree* at 26.31 versus *t'ree* at 40.15, or *taut* at 26.13 versus *tau't* at 27.9, *tump* at 44.34 versus *t'ump* at 44.10, or *tink* at 42.10 versus *t'ink* at 44.37. Dialect-speaking characters say at random *somethin'*, *someting*, *somet'ing*, or *something*.

The punctuation system may not always be so close to the lost printer's copy (or to Crane's manuscript) as the forms of the other accidentals. An uncharacteristic comma ordinarily separates two adjectives before a noun, as in *small, convulsed faces* (7.13) or *tiny, insane demon* (7.20), and the distinction of parenthetical units by commas is rather more common than in Crane's manuscripts. On the other hand, more often than not A1 agrees with Crane's usual omission of the comma before the final element of a series, as in *buckets, brooms, rags and bottles* (11.6–7) or *excuses, explanations, apologies and prayers* (24.31–25.1). Moreover, with some frequency A1, like the manuscripts, dispenses with a comma separating the two clauses of a compound sentence, as in 'The orchestra . . . gave vent to a few bars of anticipatory music and a girl, in a pink dress with short skirts, galloped upon the stage (31.20–22) or 'some half tipsy men near the stage joined in the rollicking refrain and glasses were pounded rhythmically upon the tables' (31.27–29). The sparing use of exclamation marks in dialogue is also closer to manuscript habits than the free use found in the 1896 edition.

In general, it is accurate to remark that the accidentals of the 1893 print appear to resemble Crane's customary system (or lack of system) more than would be found in a professionally produced book.

A number of literals, easily set right, appear in A1. However, one series calls for special comment. Sheet 5, which consists of pp. 65–80, holds a most unusual concentration of such errors: p. 67, *amirable* for *admirable* (35.7) and *oblgied* for *obliged* (35.16); p. 68 *raking* for *racking* (35.24) and *trash* for *thrash* (35.31); just possibly the omission of a period after *monkeys* on p. 69 (35.34) although this particular error appears elsewhere several times; *ecstastic* for *ecstatic* on p. 70 (36.21); p. 74 *He* for *Her* (38.8); p. 77 *tin a dinner-pail* for *a tin dinner-pail* (39.26–27) and possibly *yer* for *yeh* (39.31); p. 78 *framed* for *frame* (39.34); and p. 80 *now, door* for *door, now* (40.32). This series within a single sheet suggests either that the sheet was never proofread or else that, after proofreading and before printing, the type partly pied and was reassembled without corrective proofreading. Whatever the explanation, it would seem that the typesetting in the 1893 *Maggie* pp. 65–80 (34.1–41.2 ['side.' ||]) is less authoritative on the whole than the rest of A1. It is useful that *raking* (35.24) appears in this area since the reading could be defended at need against the possible sophistication of A2 *racking*; but its occurrence on the same page with another and more readily identifiable corruption gives one confidence that A2 corrects a real error in A1. In this reset or unproofread sheet occur several doubtful readings, of which the most conspicuous is *Then they filed quietly in the way they had come* on p. 76 (39.6) altered in A2 to *filed off quietly in the way* . . . .

Elsewhere in the text there are no difficult cruxes indicative of more than casual corruption.[10] Thus the establishment of the 1893 (A1) text, as such, presents few serious problems. Comparison on the Hinman Collating Machine of the two copies at the University of Virginia (PS1449.C85M3 1893 [551432] and McG. A1893.C7M3 [244539] in the McGregor Collection) discloses no variation, nor does machine and sight collation of the Ohio State University Libraries Linson copy nor sight collation of

---

[10] The nearest approach to an unresolved crux is the word *observation* in 1893, unchanged in 1896, in the 1893 sentence, *He fell into the habit, when starting on a long journey, of fixing his eye on a high and distant object, commanding his horses to begin, and then going into a sort of a trance of observation* (22.12–14). Follett emends *observation* to *oblivion*, but see the Textual Note on this passage.

copies at Harvard and Yale universities against the University of Virginia McGregor copy. The indication is that the 1893 printed form of *Maggie* is invariant.

The 1896 Appleton edition (A2) represents a text altered at the publisher's insistence to remove most of the profanity and perhaps some of the sordid detail characteristic of the original version. Although Crane on February 2, 1896, wrote to Ripley Hitchcock of Appleton's, "I will set to work this month rewriting it",[11] the coincidence in hundreds of details in the accidentals shows that he did not mean he was making a fresh copy but instead that he annotated an example of the 1893 edition to serve as printer's copy for the 1896 and that this same copy was sent by the publishers to the printer. The general close relationship may be supported by such specific details of imperfect alteration as the attempt in 1896 to change the usual (though not invariable) 1893 dialect spelling *tink* to *t'ink* but the inadvertent retention of the A1 form in such places as 43.35 and 44.11. Similarly, at 44.34 both texts read *tump* but at 44.10 both *t'ump*. The variants *yehs* and *youse* generally coincide, as do other variable dialect forms of the kind that A2 was not intent on adjusting. What may be described as 'common errors' repeated in A2 from A1 appear in the unique dialect spelling *boat* at 47.26 (for *bote*, i.e. *both*); in the unique spelling *Jimmy* shared at 9.30; in the repetition of the error *smoked-filled atmosphere* at 52.12; in the omission of the apostrophe to note the elision in *an* (for *and*) at 55.8; and in *its* (for *it's*) at 76.8. The evidence points in only one direction: the printer's copy for A2 was a marked-up, edited example of A1.[12]

The incomplete series of letters to Hitchcock offers a few tantalizing details about the agreed-on revisions; what is preserved suggests that Appleton's major concern was to remove as much profanity as possible. In the first reference, on February 2, Crane writes, from Hartwood, "I am very glad to hear you speak as you do concerning *Maggie*. I will set to work this month rewriting it." Very shortly, in a letter conjecturally dated between

[11] References are to letters in the Stallman and Gilkes edition quoted by Professor Colvert in his Introduction.

[12] See also Crane's phrase 'edited chapters' in the letter of February 15, 1896, quoted in footnote 13 below.

February 4 and 6, he adds encouragingly: "I am working at *Maggie*. She will be down to you in a few days. I have dispensed with a goodly number of damns." A few days later, on February 10, another letter may possibly indicate that other words (or phrases) than profanity had offended the Appleton sensibilities: "I will send you *Maggie* by detail.[13] I have carefully plugged at the words which hurt."

The first sort of revision is perfectly obvious. Most of the *damn's* and *hell's* are omitted or else relatively innocuous substitutes are invented; and where they are retained they appear in the form *h—l* and *d—n*. References to the Deity as *God* are expunged whether or not in dialect. Even references that are not profane suffer mutilation, as *to meet God* in A1 becomes *go to heaven* in A2 (21.1), and a biblical quotation has its A1 introduction *As God says* excised (26.36–37). The second sort is more difficult to identify. Some of the 'words which hurt' may have included such a racially pejorative expression as *micks*, which becomes *mugs* in A2 (7.9) even though it is clear that Jimmie's chief antagonist from Devil's Row is an Irish boy (14.2). Others may perhaps have been graphic details that could be considered as unduly emphasizing the sordid, such as the A2 mention of the backless chair that the father *sat in*, not *crouched on* (13.1); the old woman who in A2 *had kicked the breath out of a huge policeman* instead of *almost kicked the stomach out of* (16.21);[14] or the description, omitted in A2, of the remnants of a meal that lay in a corner, ghastly, *like dead flesh* (29.37).

Yet if for the moment one excepts the question of the paragraph immediately preceding Maggie's death, the omissions of such sordid detail are so few as to raise the question whether they really stemmed from fixed principles of censorship; and it is true that all other deletions and substitutions in this category are likely also to involve the description of swearing even when the dialogue is not involved. Here we enter an area of some difficulty. The numerous deletions of described cursing are sufficient

---

[13] No one seems to have commented on the meaning of this phrase, but from parallels in "God Rest Ye, Merry Gentlemen" it can be translated as *in sections* or *bit by bit*. See "The army was going forward in detail as soon as the pieces landed" and especially "A low ridge before them was a bottling establishment blowing up in detail."

[14] A parallel may be A2 *kick d' face off* at 9.22 for A1 *guts out of.*

to establish the principle that too much of this would 'hurt'; nevertheless, various are retained in contrast to the consistent wiping out of the profane words themselves. Moreover, it is possible to argue that at least some of the deletions of this nature were for artistic effect, to relieve the monotony of repetition as much as to lighten the sordid atmosphere. For example, at 40.1 the A2 omission of *cursing blackly* appears to be motivated by censorship pure and simple; but the substitution of *madness* at 7.23 for *cursing fury* could be literary in its origin in view of the preserved statement of swearing in the very next sentence. Since at 10.13 the account of Jimmie following after his father is preserved in *He swore luridly*, it is not certain that at 9.6 *the little boys began to brag* for A1's *swear* was motivated by a desire to tone down excessive description of profanity. The dialogue that follows is at least as appropriate for *brag* as for *swear* and the A1 *hull damn Row* is preserved, even though as *d—n*. At 13.9 it is possible that the A2 deletion of *cursing and* from the phrase *where he limply lay cursing and weeping* was calculated to increase the reader's pity for the boy tossed in a corner. On the other hand, at 13.30–31 the A1 specification *in which they damned each other's souls with frequence* seems deleted in A2 as 'hurting' words more than as a superfluity; probably the *damned* and *souls* were enough to trigger the omission.

Crane's editing of the 1893 text did not confine itself to bowdlerizing or to the lightening of sordid detail, however. It is clear from many examples that he took the opportunity to make stylistic revisions as well as literary improvements. His attempts at a spare style continued. For example, *upreared its form* is reduced to *uprose* (7.25); *glittering eyes fastened on* becomes *eyes glittered on* (15.3); the redundant adjective *threateningly* is excised at 17.5 where the dialogue sufficiently exhibits the father's mood. Even interesting detail is sometimes sacrificed, such as the description of the father's throat as *hairy* (17.10); or that the little boy's tremendous howl was *hoarse* (8.26) and that Jimmie's eyes peered *from out his drawn face* (19.9); that Pete's patent-leather shoes looked like *murder-fitted* weapons (25.17); or that Mary drank from a *squdgy* bottle (54.23). *Kid-gloved* men become simply *men* (30.16) and *stereotyped enthusiasm* is cut to *enthusiasm* (32.4); *the most harrowing* is reduced to *harrowing*

(32.28). Many of these revisions sacrifice adjectives, but phrases like *leers, or smiles* reduced to *leers* (33.7) are not uncommon. Meaning is sharpened by the substitution of apter words, such as *tourists* for *gentlemen* (20.28), *punch* for *beat* (21.26), or *overcame* for *surmounted* (37.14). Inappropriate or redundant detail is excised. Perched on his truck and superior to the street-car drivers, Jimmie no longer becomes *immured like an African cow* (22.9–10); *He was afraid of nothing* substitutes for *He was afraid of neither the devil nor the leader of society* (21.17).

Crane's care with the style carried over even into the forms of the dialect. From other dialect pieces written about 1896 it is clear that the sporadic attempts in A2 to substitute *d'* for *deh* and *t'* for *teh* are his, not an editor's, and that he had changed his mind between 1893 and 1896 about the reporting of these sounds. These two comprise the major alterations of his 1893 dialect system, but various small changes in 1896 seem to represent his relatively careful efforts to improve uniformity, even though editorial or compositorial change cannot be ruled out entirely in such cases as the normalization of *or* to *er* at 24.12 or the alteration of *damn* to *tamn* at 35.5 (the one piece of profanity [except at 52.17] allowed in 1896, but only in dialect). Less certain are the few changes of *yehs* to *youse* as at 41.18, or of *someting* to *somethin'* at 27.27—although this latter may be partially confirmed by the presumably authorial substitution at 27.28 of *somethin'* for *all*.

No certain evidence exists that in 1896 Crane altered further details of the accidentals. It is true that in some respects A2 is closer to his usual punctuation system than A1. For example, manuscripts ordinarily show no comma separating two adjectives before a noun, whereas 1893 usually prints such commas and 1896 removes them. Examples are the already-noted *small, convulsed faces* in A1 versus *small convulsed* in A2 (7.13), or *tiny, insane demon* versus *tiny insane* (7.20); or else *squat, ignorant stables* versus A2 *squat ignorant* (7.26). Yet each instance of the concurrence of 1896 with general Crane punctuation habits (as at 7.17 in the omission of an A1 comma after *scuffle* between the two clauses of a compound sentence) can be matched by at least an equal number of the reverse. Typical of the sophistication is the 1896 insertion of a comma after *re-treated* at 13.16 in a compound sentence; typical also is the invariable 1896 addition of a comma before *and* marking the final element in a series, as at 14.25–26 in which A1 had characteristically read, *She delivered reproaches, swallowed potatoes and drank from a yellow-brown bottle,* but A2 inserts a noncharacteristic comma after *potatoes.* Perhaps the best example of unauthoritative change is the extremely characteristic punctuation of the sentence in A1 at 25.22–23 which must have followed the original copy—*He had certainly seen everything and with each curl of his lip, he declared that it amounted to nothing*—in which A2 conventionally removes the comma after *lip* and places it after *everything.*

Hence as in spelling, in which A2 uses the English *-our* ending for such words as *valour* (25.19) consistently, whereas—especially at this date—Crane employs the American *-or*; or in A2's change of Crane's habitual *grey* to *gray*; or in the numerous A2 differences in hyphenated compounds and word-division which often go contrary to Crane's established preferences, few 1896 alterations in the accidentals can be assigned to the author, and these are confined to such special cases as the insertion of quotes about *elegant* at 25.24 and the interesting addition of quotes about *bouncer* at 57.10. If Crane indeed concerned himself with the general texture of the accidentals (which is doubtful), his revisions are so obscured by the compositorial or editorial imposition of house style in 1896 as to be unidentifiable save for the dialect changes.

Crane was conscious that his revisions of objectionable features had to pass editorial scrutiny, as when he wrote on February 15 to Hitchcock from Hartwood, "I send you under two covers six edited chapters of Maggie to see if they suit." Later, he gave open permission for certain editorial changes in a letter of about April 2 from New York: "The proofs make me ill. Let somebody go over them—if you think best—and watch for bad grammatical form & bad spelling. I am too jaded with Maggie to be able to see it."

Under the circumstances of the revisions demanded by Appleton we may reasonably expect Hitchcock to have dealt as he chose with any remnants of profanity, and possibly with objectionable detail that Crane had left unaltered. This may be taken for granted. That he would also tinker with the style may also be taken for granted, since in some matters Crane was unconventional for his day and usually underwent such editing no matter where he published. The invariable A2 alteration of Crane's characteristic *bended* to *bent* is unquestionably editorial (or compositorial) for example, as are the italicizing of foreign words, complete with accents, as in *débris* (41.27), or *danseuse* 52.1–2); but this attention seems to have extended itself considerably further into questions of style and idiom. Crane commonly split infinitives and often used awkward syntactical order, and he continued to do so to the day of his death. As late as the Whilomville stories in 1898–99, for instance, we read in "The Lover and the Tell-Tale" manuscript *to at once recognize* and *to soon shy,* which were altered (certainly by an editor) in the *Harper's Magazine* text to *recognize at once* and *soon to shy.* Other examples of apparent editorial tinkering by the *Harper's* editor in these stories are, in "Lynx-Hunting," the manuscript *take out the gun* to *take the gun out,* and *as rabbit-cover* to *as a rabbit-cover;* or in "The Angel-Child" *of buffer* to *of a buffer;* or in "The Trial" *he now was* to *he was now;* in "The Fight" *would be probably* to *would probably be;* in "A Little Pilgrim" *ever you saw* to *you ever saw.*[15]

When to these are added the various stylistic constructions awkward by ordinary standards that the *Harper's* editor of the Whilomville material did not change, it is difficult to argue that in 1893 Crane wrote similar constructions in *Maggie,* recognized their awkwardness and revised them in 1896, only to continue to repeat them regularly in manuscripts of 1899. On the evidence of his relatively fixed stylistic habits, then, it is dangerous to assign as authoritative such changes in A2 as, for example, *grimly to bide his time* for A1 *to grimly bide* (14.4); *began frenziedly to seize* for *to frenziedly seize* (22.17); *she bawled persistently* for *she persistently bawled* (14.12); *one whose knuckles could ring defiantly against* for *could defiantly ring*

---

[15] That some of these alterations *may* have taken place in the lost typescript that intervened between the manuscripts and print does not alter the general proposition that editors, on occasion, took it upon themselves to 'improve' Crane's syntax. Indeed, the temptation would be irresistible.

against (28.5); *Pete walked aggressively up a side aisle* for *aggressively walked* (30.29); or *said Pete ominously* for *ominously said Pete* (48.4). These changes have been rejected as unauthoritative, therefore. That they make for smoother syntax is incontestable; that they are what Crane wrote is doubtful in the extreme.

More troublesome are minor changes in idiom. One may accept A2 *her eyes gleamed with fear* instead of A1 *gleamed from fear* (19.21) because of the possibility of A1 contamination from the antecedent clause, *Her features were haggard from weeping.* On the other hand, A2 *went to look out of the window* for A1 *out at the window* (13.25) appears to be wrong in view of the same phrase (similarly altered) at 43.22, A1 *began to stare out at the window* and A2 *out of the window*. Similarly, *infant's chair* (14.21) seems to be an A2 sophistication in view of A2's similar change of *panther den* to *panther's den* (18.17). Such examples cause one to be suspicious of A2 *in the ratio of ten to one* for A1 *at the ratio* (27.15), or of *he had a large acquaintance with pretty girls* for *acquaintance of pretty girls* (28.22).

Even more suspicious are the grammatical changes that Crane had specifically suggested could be made editorially. One cannot deny the possibility that in 1896 Crane tinkered with his 1893 ideas of grammar, particularly with concord between subject and verb, but the odds favor editorial supervision in such typical examples as A1 *The girl thought the arrogance and granite-heartedness of the magnate of the play was very accurately drawn* to A2 *were* (36.24); or A1 *and noted that wealth and prosperity was indicated by his clothes* to *were* (52.19).[16] Probably editorial are such changes in usage as A2 *amid* for A1's characteristic—in this work—*amidst* (29.23, 31.32); but definitely Crane's, on the evidence of the frequent alterations in his manuscripts, are the variations between *which* and *that* as at 21.35, 27.13, or 32.18.

More neutral, though still suspicious, are such changes as A2 *A wide dirty grin spread over each face* from A1 *Wide dirty grins* (38.20–22); or A2 *A woman of brilliance and audacity, accompanied by a mere boy, came into the place and took a seat near*

[16] Crane often used the collective singular in the manner of A1: see *There was valor and contempt* (25.19, unaltered in A2).

them from A1 *took seats* (58.6). So neutral, perhaps, as to require adjudication on a rather impressionistic basis are such small variants as A2 *A stone had smashed in Jimmie's mouth* from A1 *into* (8.1); or A2 *Eventually they entered a dark region* from *entered into* (11.1); or A2 *Jimmie crawled back into the shadows* from A1 *in* (19.7); or A2 *or of past drunks* from *past drunks* (34.22); or A2 *should love* from A1 *would love* (34.29). Sometimes, but not often, one can take comfort from identifying Crane's own very minor alterations as consequential or as in the area of a larger change: for instance, the insignificant substitution of A2 *this* for A1 *the* in the original phrase *the assemblage of the masses* (32.39) seems to be demonstrably authoritative by the fact that in A2 Crane changed the period after *masses* to a comma and added *most of them of foreign birth.*

Although there is something of a drumfire of small alterations in A2 requiring editorial selection, a series that cumulatively has a sufficient effect on the stylistics of *Maggie* to prevent its being ignored, critical attention has focused on the excisions at the end of Chapter XVII, the chapter that relates Maggie's journey to the river and her death. Actually, the major excision of the episode of the fat man (70.18 ff.), a powerful and terrifying piece of writing, is the crux.

That Crane was, in general, sincerely intent on improving the style of *Maggie* by revision of the 1893 text is incontestable on the evidence. The difficulty is, on some occasions, to distinguish his authoritative second thoughts from the editorial attention that the printer's copy received—unauthoritative alterations (whether or not 'accepted' by Crane by his passing them in proof) that must be rejected in a critical edition when identified. His letter of April 2, 1896, asking for editorial cleaning up in proof of his grammar and spelling is evidence that he was prepared for publisher's changes where he felt weakest. That censorship, chiefly of individual words, was a major requirement is quite clear from the specific references in the letters of February 4–6, 10, and 15; and it is reasonable to conjecture that Hitchcock or a substitute would check over Crane's omissions and substitutions and make others that he felt to be necessary.[17] It is

---

[17] Stallman conjectures that the excisions and substitutions of blasphemous epithets and swearing phrases were Crane's own work but says, "It was probably

clear from Crane's letter of February 4–6—"I have no more copies of the book or I would have sent you one"—that from the start Hitchcock was concerned to assist in the revision. However, unless he was able to find a copy independently, he was perhaps forced to wait upon Crane's presentation of the marked-up copy before beginning his own editorial work.

No evidence exists to suggest that Crane ever again saw this annotated copy he had prepared for the printer after the Appleton editors had surveyed it and given it their own series of alterations, certain of which can be identified with some confidence. That is, we have no indication that Crane had the opportunity to see the editorial changes and to discuss them with Hitchcock before they were set. According to every editorial custom of his day, as indeed of the present, he would be expected to accept normal stylistic revision, and—in this case—any further censorship of 'words that hurt' that Appleton chose to impose according to the original understanding about the nature of the changes he was supposed to supply.

That Crane was somewhat concerned about excessive deletion may be suggested by his letter of February 10 when he was engaged on the early chapters. After promising to send *Maggie* 'by detail,' he continues: "I have carefully plugged at the words which hurt. Seems to me the book wears quite a new aspect from very slight omissions. Did you know that the book is very short? Only about 20000 words?" Although these sentences have been taken as indicating Crane's feeling that the task imposed on him has resulted in an improvement in the book, the present editor believes quite the contrary. In the first place, the letter was written before Crane had progressed very far in his revision. In the letter of February 2 he promises, "I will set to work this month rewriting it." In the letter of about February 4–6 he states (though as the basis for a request for an advance), "I am working at *Maggie*. She will be down to you in a few days." Then comes the letter of February 10, and on February 15 a note about the dispatch of the first six chapters for Hitchcock's approval, these constituting slightly less than one-third of the whole.

---

the editor who turned what 'damns and 'hells' remained in the text into such ellipses as mark the 1896 edition: 'd—n' for 'damn,' and 'd'h—ll' for 'd'hell' " ("Stephen Crane's Revision of *Maggie*," *American Literature*, XXVI [1955], 531). This is plausible, but we have no evidence.

Under these circumstances it would seem that Crane is being defensive in his February 10 letter about the deletions he has been instructed to make and is intent on keeping them to a minimum. The tone is distinctly propitiatory. He has 'carefully' plugged at the words which hurt; the desirable 'new aspect,' he hopefully remarks, seems to have been achieved without draconian measures. The last two sentences are a palpable attempt to influence Hitchcock in the direction of Crane's point of view: the book is already very short—only 20,000 words—and you are endangering its acceptability as a novel if you insist on further omissions.

If this interpretation is the correct one, then Crane—very early in his marking up of printer's copy—was intent on making as few censorship deletions as possible other than the standard profanity omissions, and he was insinuating to Hitchcock how successfully the Appleton requirements might be met by minimal revision.[18] This is coupled with a tacit warning about any insistence on further cuts, presumably of another nature from the simple deletions of cursing that, on the evidence, comprise the majority of the excisions in the few chapters he could have completed at the date of the letter. With this interpretation it follows that Crane is not really expressing pleasure at the 'new aspect' he sees emerging; instead, he is hoping to influence Hitchcock into accepting as little nonliterary alteration as possible and he is afraid that more may be required.[19]

This survey of the general nature of the 1896 changes in the tender material of 1893 has emphasized the overwhelming and consistent revision of profanity and references to God, whether

[18] Since the nature of the material would have had a major effect on the nonprofanity cuts, it may be mere impressionism to record the sense that the removal or modification of sordid detail is more sweeping in the first chapter or two and thereupon seems to relax slightly.

[19] As a straw in the wind one may refer to his letter of February 4–6 in which he writes to Hitchcock that he has no more copies of the book or he would have sent one to him. This statement might be interpreted to indicate that Crane did not want Hitchcock to be editing the book independently before he saw the marked copy Crane was preparing. In his brother's house in Hartwood, it appears, there was a considerable stock of unsold copies, although the possibility exists that these had been forgotten. Stallman in *Stephen Crane: A Biography* (New York, 1968), p. 70, writes, "By 1896 he had only one copy left" and on p. 573 in footnote 8 cites the fact that "Unable to find another copy, Crane gave Charles J. Pike his own signed copy." Thus it is possible that Crane was candid and not endeavoring to keep Hitchcock from a copy until his revisions were complete.

or not profane, and the relatively few, if any, alterations of sordid detail not directly related to the profanity. That Crane accepted the first class as a necessity but feared for the second may be indicated by his February 10 letter. A remark in a later letter may bear on this point as well. In a letter from the Cosmos Club in Washington, D.C., conjecturally dated March 15, he writes to Hitchcock: 'You must send me the edited Maggie. I am going to settle down to New York work in lazy Washington.'

Stallman in a footnote interprets this reference as a request for copies of the 1896 book when published, but it would appear that in this instance he is mistaken. Between the last preserved letter of February 15 and this one, a month has elapsed in which Crane has submitted to Hitchcock the remaining thirteen chapters, the whole has been surveyed by the Appleton editors, and, one may suggest, copy has been sent to the printer and proof has started to arrive. For instance, from letter no. 156 we know that Crane had seen proofs as of April 2, although how many of them is uncertain. Yet the tone of the April 2 letter may well suggest that the body of the book has been typeset and proofed and that Crane does not wish to see any revises. On May 29, in no. 160, he inquires whether *Maggie* has been published.

These dates indicate that on March 15 Crane was either anticipating the receipt of proof or was already engaged with the early sheets (especially if he had completed reading proof by April 2 as seems likely). Under these circumstances it may be conjectured that his request for 'the edited Maggie' on March 15 perhaps was a plea that Hitchcock supply the only evidence Crane could have of the changes made from the 1893 text—that is, the marked printer's copy itself, which Crane had already referred to, using the word 'edited,' on February 15, 'I send you . . . six edited chapters of Maggie.' If this hypothesis is correct, Crane had not been sent the annotated 1893 copy (the only 'manuscript' that existed) with his proofs and he was concerned to see it, presumably in order to check the readings in his proof to identify which changes were editorial as against his own revisions, all of which he could scarcely be expected to recall.

Whether Hitchcock indeed sent the annotated 1893 book, or whatever sheets of it had been typeset, is unknown. Nonetheless, if Crane were actually concerned to identify the editorial work as it affected the 'new aspect' of *Maggie,* he would have had full opportunity to see the marked printer's copy by April 2 in New York when, presumably, Chapter XVII would have been in proof. Thus even if his memory had not been retentive enough to recall the fat-man episode (and this is a proposition one would not wish to defend), it is not at all likely that this cut was made without his ultimate knowledge.

We may now consider the evidence, such as it is, directly relating to the 1896 alterations in Chapter XVII. The crux of the matter is, of course, whether these changes were made (1) by Crane as a purely literary improvement without reference to censorship; (2) by Crane under the impression that they would be required by the general agreement with Appleton about the nature of the revisions; or (3) by the Appleton editors with or without Crane's approval. In the second and third contingencies the excised matter would need to be restored according to the editorial principles on which the present text is constructed. It would make no difference whether Crane agreed, perforce, to editorial censorship or whether he performed the censorship himself under what he regarded as general directions, and thus for nonliterary reasons: the cuts would be restored in order to provide the 'ideal' literary text of *Maggie.* Only in the first case could the 1896 version be accepted as truly authoritative, since it would represent the author's final and uninfluenced artistic intentions, which an editor must respect.

The third possibility—that Hitchcock or other Appleton editors made the cuts—does not agree with the total evidence for revision in this chapter. Crane made obligatory cuts of profanity at 70.2, 3, and 4. These have no significance for the question. On the other hand, he paid attention to stylistic revision. At 68.12–13 A1 *People having been comparatively silent* becomes in A2 *People who had been constrained to comparative silence,* and at 68.21–22 A1 *and of having just emerged from a place of forgetfulness* becomes *and of two hours in a place of forgetfulness.* At 68.28 the weak repetition *men* in A1 is revised by the substitution of *those*; at 69.36 *his hand buried in his overcoat* becomes *his hands buried in his overcoat pockets.* These show that Crane in this brief chapter was making rather more than usual literary revision on his own account, but they have nothing to do with Maggie's going to her death and the major cut about the fat man except to establish that Crane's revising hand was present earlier in the chapter. (Whether the small change of *from whence* in A1 to *whence* at 70.8 was Crane's or an editor's is undemonstrable.)

The first of the significant revisions comes at 70.10. In the two texts Maggie's encounters with the first seven men are reproduced verbatim except for the unimportant detail about the boy's hands noted at 69.36. On the last two pages of 1893, however, the text is altered to a degree that is unique in the history of the 1896 changes. This series of variants, all of which must be accounted significant, and of a piece, starts with the eighth man. In both editions the paragraph about the music, the dancing, and the laughter in the saloon ends, *there stood a man with blotched features.* In A2 the next two lines of A1 are omitted: *"Ah, there," said the girl.* | *"I've got a date," said the man.* It is difficult to argue for censorship (whether editorial or authorial) here. The act of solicitation conventionally implied by *"Ah, there"* (interestingly, the only words that Maggie speaks in the whole chapter) and by the man's answer is scarcely shocking or sordid; and this brief dialogue is indeed considerably less explicit than the words of the boy, *"Not this eve—some other eve!"* (69.40) or the lament of the drunken man: *"I ain' ga no money . . . . Ba' luck. Ain' ga no more money"* (70.2–4), relieved in 1896 only of three *damns.* Whatever the reason, therefore, censorship seems improbable and some other cause must be assigned.

The alteration of the ninth encounter is identical with that of the eighth in that once again the meeting is reproduced substantially verbatim in the two texts: *Further on in the darkness she met a ragged being with shifting, blood-shot eyes and grimy hands* (70.11–12). Her address to him is not recorded, but that there was one, or an action, is implied by his response in A1, deleted from A2: *"Ah, what deh hell? Tink I'm a millionaire?"* The profanity alone is not enough to account for the omission since the phrase in question had been readily subject to innocuous variation dozens of previous times in A2. Whatever literary reason obtained for the omission of the eighth man's response must hold as well for the ninth.

There follows a paragraph of description of the blackness of the final block that Maggie enters. Only one change, but that a significant substitution, appears when A1 *The structures seemed to have eyes that looked over her, beyond her, at other things* becomes in A2, *that looked over them, beyond them, at other things* (70.15–16).

The next paragraph in 1893, the encounter with the fat man, is completely excised in 1896:

When almost to the river the girl saw a great figure. On going forward she perceived it to be a huge fat man in torn and greasy garments. His grey hair straggled down over his forehead. His small, bleared eyes, sparkling from amidst great rolls of red fat, swept eagerly over the girl's upturned face. He laughed, his brown, disordered teeth gleaming under a grey, grizzled moustache from which beer-drops dripped. His whole body gently quivered and shook like that of a dead jelly fish. Chuckling and leering, he followed the girl of the crimson legions.

Finally, one consequential and one stylistic revision appear in the initial sentence of the following, final paragraph. A1 *At their feet the river,* which can refer only to the feet of the fat man and Maggie, becomes *At the feet of the tall buildings,* a phrase that links up with the emphasis placed on the buildings in the description of the final block (the immediately preceding paragraph in A2) and one that is perhaps accentuated by the revision of *her* to *them* at 70.15. The immediately following stylistic change by which A1 *the river appeared a deathly black hue* becomes in A2 *appeared the deathly black hue of the river* is of no pertinence except to suggest (as does the link with the buildings in the preceding words) that this literary revision was Crane's, like that at 70.15, and not editorial.

The presence of the revising author being established in this crucial area by two noneditorial changes, plus a consequential (and apparently authorial) alteration stemming from the omission of the fat man as Maggie's companion at the river, the third position becomes untenable that the deletions of the answers of the eighth and ninth men and the excision of the fat-man episode are editorial, even though the paragraph containing the fat man might be thought rather strong meat for Appleton's prospective readers.[20]

The second possibility exhibits something of the same incoherence. That is, we may suppose that Crane, either on specific instructions from Appleton or (less likely, perhaps) in the belief that he was following the intent of the original general instructions, removed the fat-man paragraph. This is possible, but such a theory of duress of one sort or another fails to explain the of-a-piece removal of the eighth and ninth responses, which seems to have a purely literary motivation, and thus it sets up a separate nonliterary category for the treatment of the fat man distinct from the unusually heavy literary revision that marks this chapter, especially in the crucial area but not confined to it alone. That Crane found himself forced by the external censorship of the fat-man paragraph to improvise a series of literary improvements in this whole area which had the effect of vitally altering the import of the entire chapter is not impossible to imagine but it may be thought difficult to credit. If necessary, the fat man could disappear with no further change than the substitution of *her* for *their* in the first sentence of the final paragraph.

However, if the first hypothesis is to prevail—and the editorial theory to be correspondingly adjusted—it must offer a more coherent and critically satisfying explanation than is possible for the alternatives.

We must start with the facts that Crane provides about Maggie in this chapter and see where they lead us. She is first introduced in the midst of a rainstorm *several months after the last chapter* (68.1–2) walking toward the theater district on a street where she attempts to pick up unsophisticated or rural men (68.26–30). The theater district had not been the starting

---

[20] In the first place, no editorial reason seems to exist for the omission of the responses of the eight and ninth men, whereas literary reasons may be adduced; in the second, since all editorial changes (owing to the nature of the printer's copy) must have been made after Crane had sent in the marked pages, or else (less likely) in proof, we should need to hypothesize original authorial revision, then the editorial excision of the paragraph, and finally the authorial patchwork of the start of the final paragraph. Finally, the view that the paragraph would have been thought offensive to the readers is based on an assumption that cannot be demonstrated. Although the details of the man's appearance may create a revulsion simply because they appear in a sexual context, the language itself is not offensive.

point, for she had come to it by *crossing glittering avenues* (68.31). It is important to observe, hence, that the pleasure-seeking crowds emerge from *the places of forgetfulness,* not of reality,[21] into the light and movement of the opening paragraphs of the chapter, the light that is to be referred to later as a symbol of joy against the blackness of despair (70.16–18 and perhaps 70.21–23). Maggie enters this area of light with its *atmosphere of pleasure and prosperity* (68.19–20), passes rapidly through it, and then leaves it behind.

Several significant details are presented. She is not driven to her death by any failure in her profession,[22] for she has a *handsome cloak* and *well-shod feet* (69.2–3). This is a matter of real importance: the motive for her death is vital, naturally, and the descent during her progress in the level of her possible clients from the monied though unsophisticated down to the dregs of the waterfront can scarcely account in any literal terms for a suicide in despair at her failure to attract custom that night. Indeed, Crane is at pains to give us clues that, despite her solicitation of various men, she has some other purpose in mind. *She hurried forward through the crowd as if intent upon reaching a distant home,* he remarks (68.32–69.1), and these are words pregnant with meaning, especially *home,*[23] just as the contrast is to be ironic between the water of the rainstorm and that of the river and between Maggie's *daintily lifting her skirts*

[21] We may profitably compare the contrast Crane has drawn between theatrical illusion and reality at 36.16–22, for example.

[22] Far too much significance has been given to her choice of men, and too little to Crane's description of her prosperity. That she chooses the unsophisticated or country visitors to accost and ignores the citified is only an indication of where the profitable custom lies. The typical reaction she would encounter elsewhere is illustrated by the description of the young man in evening dress who abruptly lost interest in accosting *her* when he recognized her profession (69.15–17; see also 69.31–32). In the light of these facts, such views as the following distort Crane's intentions: "It is a measure of the depth of her fall that she averts her face from all but boys, drunks, and the disreputable; this is the level to which she has descended" (Joseph Katz, "The *Maggie* Nobody Knows," *Modern Fiction Studies,* XII [1966], 210). Critics who take it that Maggie has failed as a prostitute or that she accosts each of the ten men mentioned have not followed Crane's account.

[23] In this connection, an inscription in Hamlin Garland's copy, preserved in in the Lilly Library (see Stallman and Gilkes, *Letters,* p. 14), is interesting: "For it tries to show that environment is a tremendous thing in the world and frequently shapes lives regardless. If one proves that theory one makes room in Heaven for all sorts of souls (notably an occasional street girl) who are not confidently expected to be there by many excellent people."

and picking for her well-shod feet the dryer spots upon the pavements and her final immersion.

Maggie has solicited men before she reached the district of light and pleasure (68.26–30), but she does not address herself to any within this district, not to the tall young man in evening dress, the stout gentleman, or the belated businessman. Indeed, she is in a hurry, not sauntering to invite custom, and the paradox is intensified when she moves directly from *the realm of restaurants and saloons,* passing more *glittering avenues* where she might have prospered, in order to plunge into *darker blocks than those where the crowd travelled* (69.25–27). Here she shoots a keen glance at a young man, speaks to a laborer, smiles at a boy, and possibly addresses a drunken man. Although she is rejected, her next destination is scarcely one calculated to produce customers, and there is no suggestion that she is, in fact, seriously seeking any, despite in the 1893 text her direct address to the man with the blotched face and presumably to the man with the bloodshot eyes.

Two matters are evident to any careful reader of this chapter: (1) Crane has kept the narrative absolutely objective; we have no inkling of Maggie's motives or reactions save those we may draw from the bare account of what she does. The only piece of interpretation he has inserted is the foreshadowing sentence, *She hurried forward through the crowd as if intent upon reaching a distant home.* (2) From start to finish she is moving swiftly forward on a predetermined journey, and the solicitation of men is not the primary purpose of her movement. It is scarcely necessary to point out that she neither patrols the glittering district where her customers have provided her with a handsome cloak and good shoes nor does she pause at any time in her flight to attempt to persuade a man to change his mind. The only inference suitable to draw from the details offered us is that from the beginning she has been in progress toward a planned suicide in the river. Since her motives are not financial, we are required in literal terms to assume that they must stem from what might be termed moral or spiritual despair. By blocking one possibility—hopeless failure and poverty—Crane leaves only one other reason open to inference at any ordinary level.

The problem then arises of the illogic of her actions during her course toward the river. If she is proposing suicide (as we must assume with all the advantages of hindsight), why does she solicit? To this difficulty there is no literal answer that is wholly satisfying. True, despite all talk of *painted cohorts* and (in 1893) of *crimson legions*, we are scarcely likely to accept Maggie as a professional prostitute without viewing her at her trade. But this difficulty could be solved in other ways, perhaps. That her actions might be thought of as simple reflex although her intentions were different is not at all satisfactory because the meaninglessness of such a portrait would be distracting in a chapter that by its position and its ending must in the nature of the case concentrate intense significance.

One part of an answer might be attempted by inquiring how else Crane could have handled the matter. He could, of course, merely have narrated her progress from the street on which she is first observed to the bank of the river, but if she has no connection with other people during this journey, the narrative would be in danger of proving mechanical and lifeless. If she is to have contacts, they must be with men, owing to her profession. If men address her in her progress but each time she were to ignore their advances, there is some improvement perhaps; but the journey would lack suspense since it would be more literal and obvious in its intent than Crane has contrived it. If the purpose of the journey is revealed from the start because of her unprofessional responses, if there is no tension set up by the mystery of human behavior, the progression from the glitter of the places of amusement to the black horror of the river would lack all but sentimental significance.

Each suggested alternative brings one back to two words—*literal* and *significant*—which oppose each other. The literal details by which Crane describes Maggie's journey are absurd on their face and in these terms have none of the significance promised the reader by the hint that Maggie is hurrying as if intent upon reaching a distant home.

Thus a critic is driven to the hypothesis that the journey is essentially symbolic. The use of water is interesting, but a more operative symbol has been stored at the end of the preceding chapter when Maggie, then in a redeemable state,[24] had sought

[24] "She did not feel like a bad woman. To her knowledge she had never seen any better" (52.24–26); "As they went out Maggie perceived two women seated at a table with some men. They were painted and their cheeks had lost their

grace by accosting a benevolent-appearing clergyman who, in horrified respectability, promptly rejected her. "He did not risk [his respectability] to save a soul. For how was he to know that there was a soul before him that needed saving?" (67.39–40).

We may take it that, for better or for worse, Crane's original intent in the series of confrontations between Maggie and the ten men of the 1893 version was to repeat this act of rejection, in various terms of the world. This is the major reason for the apparent paradox of a girl bent on suicide accosting men in the course of her passage, but without insistence and almost in a dreamlike state.[25] The externals may be realistic, but the rationale of the chapter, and its motivation, rests on another foundation that gives an air of unreality to the progress precisely because of the seeming clash between the superficial actions of this strangely impersonal girl and her secret intent.

In this symbolic passage the fat man plays his part. For a certain reason he is the climactic figure and he is introduced in a strangely portentous manner: *When almost to the river the girl saw a great figure.* She goes forward to look at him with *upturned face.* These days it is fashionable to see Christ-figures in most unlikely contexts, and one would not wish to be insistent here were it not for a strange parallel that seems to enforce the intention. One may mention the emphasis on size at this particular moment just before the river of death and the upturned face of the girl as bringing at least a momentary suggestion of the supernatural sacrificial figure; and it is perhaps Crane's private joke (for he enjoyed religious satire) that the figure turns out, in the end, to be satanic.

But this metamorphosis is no accident, for the fat man is the obverse of the stout clergyman whose rejection of Maggie at the end of the preceding chapter had led to her 'damnation' as a prostitute. The parallels are too exact to be anything but calculated. Highly significant is Maggie's progress from the saloon to

---

roundness. As she passed them the girl, with a shrinking movement, drew back her skirts" (53.7–10).

[25] The dreamlike state is perhaps more the effect on the reader of Crane's rapid series of scenes in which the girl hurries on her path, never making a second attempt to interest a man, her curious actions but never her words reported, the whole episode cut adrift from realism by its ambivalent motivation until the reader, along with Maggie, finds the answer in the dark.

her meeting with the clergyman. At first she walks with an aimlessness that attracts men *with calculating eyes,* whereupon "She quickened her step, frightened. As a protection she adopted a demeanor of intentness as if going somewhere" (67.22–24). In Chapter XVII Maggie *hurried forward through the crowd as if intent upon reaching a distant home.*[26] Just before meeting the clergyman she is affected by the appearance of the buildings she passes in a district apart from the avenues: "After a time she left rattling avenues and passed between rows of houses with sternness and stolidity [27] stamped upon their features. She hung her head for she felt their eyes grimly upon her." In Chapter XVII the avenues are *glittering* in the change from day to night and *She passed more glittering avenues and went into darker blocks. . . .* The buildings in the clergyman episode have sternness and stolidity stamped upon their features. She is in relation to them, and *She hung her head for she felt their eyes grimly upon her.* So in Chapter XVII (1893): "The shutters of the tall buildings were closed like grim lips. The structures seemed to have eyes that looked over her, beyond her, at other things."

In both episodes immediately after the buildings with their eyes Maggie meets a figure. In Chapter XVI, "Suddenly she came upon a stout gentleman . . . and she decided to approach this man." In Chapter XVII, "When almost to the river the girl saw a great figure. On going forward she perceived it to be a huge fat man. . . ." The clergyman's *silk hat and a chaste black coat, whose decorous row of buttons reached from his chin to his knees* contrast with the fat man's *torn and greasy garments.* The clergyman's *eyes shone good-will;* the fat man's *small, bleared eyes, sparkling from amidst great rolls of red fat, swept eagerly over the girl's upturned face.* The clergyman's *beaming, chubby face was a picture of benevolence and kind-heartedness.* The fat

[26] The use of the word *intentness* and *intent* here is interesting, as is, in another connection, the repetition of the word *home:* Maggie's progress toward her *distant home* recalls her flight from the advances of the *mere boy* and her insistence, *"I'm going home,"* she said (61.28).

[27] One need not insist on the *stolidity* of the buildings here and on the stout gentleman of Chapter XVII who *went stolidly* by her. However, a more plausible parallel is that between the man in Chapter XVI who *humorously took the questioning word as intended for him* but does not regard her as fair game (*"I didn't say anything,"* he laughingly said, and continued on his way [67.18–21]) and in Chapter XVII the belated businessman who bumps into her, jokes with her, and *then was running down the middle of the street.*

man's gray hair straggles over his forehead; he has small bleared eyes. Instead of beaming, he laughs, *his brown, disordered teeth gleaming under a grey, grizzled moustache from which beer-drops dripped.* The clergyman *gave a convulsive movement and saved his respectability by a vigorous side-step.* The fat man, *Chuckling and leering, he followed the girl of the crimson legions.*

Each encounter, then, has its parallel, for it was the meeting with the clergyman that decided her to turn prostitute, and the inevitable result is the similarly climactic meeting, before her death, with the fat man, who is no more culpable than the clergyman in his treatment of her, but is no hypocrite.[28]

The progress from the glittering avenues to the river has, however, another symbolic purport which bears even more directly on the paradox of the solicitations. For this I am indebted to a most perceptive insight of Professor Bruccoli, who remarks on the impossibility of the theory that Maggie commits suicide because of a failure on this one occasion and comments that no reason exists to peddle herself that night to increasingly revolting men. This point leads him to query whether we do not have two time schemes in Chapter XVII: the literal, depicting her progress to the river in one night; the other, a symbolic compression into this night of her whole future life in which after a prosperous start her rejection by each man represents her inevi-

[28] The closeness of detail, but especially the closeness of language, enforces Crane's conscious paralleling of the two incidents. Just so he had deliberately utilized much the same language and detail in the two scenes in which Jimmie rejects Hattie (62.17–63.3) and Pete rejects Maggie (66.26–67.27). It is no accident that each scene ends with the man telling the woman, "Oh, go t' hell," and that this is the climactic phrase in the mother's rejection of Maggie 41.17,29 also.

Whether Maggie actually accosts the fat man as she had *timidly accosted* the clergyman is moot. The episode is so ambiguously presented as to be subject to either interpretation. That her face is *upturned* does not necessarily mean that she speaks to him or invites him by a glance; she could merely be looking up at him to see who he was. For all we know, she looks up at him, passes him, and he follows her to the bank of the river, chuckling and leering. On the other hand, in an identical manner no speech or action on her part is recorded in the encounter with the ninth man, although from his response it is clear that she has accosted him: "Further on in the darkness she met a ragged being with shifting, blood-shot eyes and grimey hands. 'Ah, what deh hell? Tink I'm a millionaire?' " Whether she also accosted the drunken man who had no money is undemonstrable. On the whole, the parallel with the clergyman and also with every man whom she meets once she has left the pleasure district would seem to require us to believe that something passed between her and the fat man.

table downward slide over the course of time until she is acceptable only to the lowest and most revolting of mankind and the
river is the sole answer to the spiritual despair and physical
degeneration of one who has become the cheapest of whores.[29]

If this interpretation is valid—and it is the most comprehensive and persuasive yet advanced [30]—the question then arises
what reasons, except censorship, might have caused Crane in
1896 to alter his concept of the 1893 catastrophic chapter. That
the description of the fat man and the implications of his pursuit
of Maggie contain the most explicit sordid detail within a sexual
context found in the book may have been sufficient reason for
Crane to resurvey this chapter, although, as suggested above, it
is mere speculation to query the acceptability of this paragraph
to the public in the opinion of the Appleton editors. Moreover,
that if Crane found it on review to be what he still wanted, he
might have fought for its retention or have modified instead of
excising it (even assuming—what is dangerous—that it was
found objectionable), we may hope but we do not know. Given
the lack of all external evidence, the suggestion is possible that a
literary reason was the most powerful and indeed perhaps the
only operative force in the 1896 revision of this chapter.

If the original concept emphasized progressive rejection during a period of time symbolically encapsulated in the single night
described, and then a final acceptance on terms so degrading as
to be unbearable as a way of life, the episode of the fat man
introduced certain dissonances. Crane's reticence about the

[29] See "Maggie's Last Night," *Stephen Crane Newsletter*, II (1967), 10. One
may comment, also, it is possible that for his own purposes Crane has emphasized the nonbusinesslike nature of Maggie's solicitations by confining them
to the very districts where they were least likely to succeeed. It must be significant that though Maggie solicits on her way to the bright-light district
and then subsequently, she hurries through the best territory, and the reactions
of the three men she encounters there are not triggered by any word or sign
from her.

[30] Edwin Cady had an intimation of this compression, but did not altogether
carry it forward to its logical conclusion: "For this crucial Section XVII he
reverted to the earliest state of *Maggie*, when nobody had a name, and she
became simply 'a girl of the painted cohorts of the city,' soliciting. In swiftly
telescoped moments she steps down and down—compressing perhaps years as
she goes: James D. McCabe in *New York by Sunlight and Gaslight* (1882)
estimated that it took girls five to seven years to drop from the fashionable
'first-class houses' through the scale to utter waterfront degradation and to
death by disease, brutality, or the river" (*Stephen Crane*, New York, [1962], pp.
105–106).

meaning of the events in this whole chapter after his one clue
that Maggie was hurrying *as if intent on reaching a distant home*
leads to an ambiguity about the fat man in which the possibility
of rape-murder, or even rape-suicide, is as distinct as prostitution
and suicide.[31] This ambiguity so essential earlier to emphasize
the proper symbolic nature of the rapid series of events is distracting, and indeed even disintegrating, at the catastrophe. If in
1893 there had been present in Crane's mind the rounding off of
events by one that would show the degradation of her final
acceptance, which she then cannot face,[32] the fat man does not
entirely work. Prostitution to him, no matter how appropriate at
a symbolic level, clashes seriously on the literal plane with the
theme of her intent movement to the river and a suicide that
night. If one wishes to escape this dilemma by substituting the
more remote possibility of murder, or even of simple force, the
relation is no less jarring. If even a suggestion of violence is left
in the reader's mind, the pattern of rejection and acceptance is
broken and the irony gained is insufficient to restore the force of
the central theme that Maggie's mission that night has been a
voluntary and preconceived journey *to a distant home.*

For another consideration I am indebted to a private commu-
nication from Professor J. C. Levenson:

> The revision of Maggie's last walk shows that Crane's desire for
> simplicity of effect is consistently there, whether he cuts or adds.
> Cutting out that last customer makes the effect of somberness and
> pity much clearer by eliminating revulsion and fear; the indignity
> of that last physical mortification would have reduced her dignity of
> dying, the only dignity Crane attributes to her wretched little life.
> Crane's art, like his vocabulary, constantly surprises.

We may take it as at least a working hypothesis that by 1896
Crane had come to see the distracting effect, despite the irony, of
the fat man—what he does and what he stands for—and that he
had concluded the total effect of the chapter was worth more

---

[31] That is, even if Maggie accosts the fat man (as seems likely) and his following her to the river is in the nature of their assignation, the possibility of
murder is as present as that of suicide, given the degeneracy of the man in
Crane's vivid description.

[32] This of course combines with the intended satiric parallel with the clergyman, his rejection of Maggie, and its consequences.

than the sum of its parts. It is possible to speculate that by 1896, also, the parallel with the clergyman, which is the heart of the fat-man episode, came to seem too contrived and even juvenile. If, then, he decided to scrap this satiric parallel—which in turn would place more emphasis upon the now central symbol of the double time scheme for that night—the other changes made as Maggie nears her doom now demand consideration, for a critic arguing for the literary nature of the 1896 revisions of this chapter must show that they are all of a piece.

The impersonality of Crane's treatment of Maggie's progress has already been mentioned, the lack of any interpretation or guide to her actions save for the one planted clue at her first appearance. It is probable that in 1896 he saw that the most effective close to replace the clergyman parallel would emphasize this impersonality and that the fusion of the two time schemes called for an increasing generalization or personification of the girl. The more she became dissociated from her surroundings, the more effective she was as an impersonal, even fated object moving toward her willed doom.

This removal of any personal relation between Maggie and her surroundings is indicated by what is something of a key revision in 1896. In A1 when she goes *into the blackness of the final block,* the tall buildings—associated with the blackness and the *impossible distance* from the lights of the avenues—*seemed to have eyes that looked over her, beyond her, at other things.* Here she is in some relation to her surroundings, affected by her concept of the buildings, as she had been in the Chapter XVI passage that is being echoed with variation in Chapter XVII: "After a time she left the rattling avenues and passed between rows of houses with sternness and stolidity stamped upon their features. She hung her head for she felt their eyes grimly upon her." The deliberate change in A2 that removes her from any relation to the buildings cannot be overemphasized in its importance: "The structures seemed to have eyes that looked over them, beyond them, at other things." The wrench that took Maggie out of the picture may perhaps be observed in the uncertain referent of the new pronoun *them*: whether the noun should be the tall buildings that looked over other buildings or the shutters of the preceding sentence is uncertain (*The shutters of the tall buildings were closed like grim lips.*) although the first is the more probable.

This significant alteration, which can have only one purpose, is identical in its effect, and must be of a piece, with the removal of Maggie's personal relationship to the eighth and ninth men as performed by the A2 deletion of her address to the man with the blotched face and his reply, and also of the reply of the man with the bloodshot eyes to some undescribed word or glance. Once Maggie enters the gloomy factory district, the 1896 revisions cause nobody to pay attention to her and in turn she neither acts nor reacts. All interrelationship ceases, as in the pronoun substitutions and the cutting of the dialogue. A man stands outside a saloon; she passes a ragged being; she does this, she does that. Nowhere, now, in the chapter does she speak, and the closer she comes to the river the more she is hurried on by the swift, objective narrative. The symbolic solicitations would have been inappropriate here where the emphasis has changed in 1896 and she has reached that part of the city dominated by the river, her home—or at least its gateway—no longer distant.

If this is the intended effect of the three revisions, it is evident that the episode of the fat man had to go as well, for he put her into a human relationship (the most vivid of all) which conflicted with the preceding removal of any interaction, first with the blotched man, then with the bloodshot man, and finally—most significant of all—with the buildings. Strong as was the scene in its shock effect, in the words of Professor Levenson's acute analysis the 'revulsion and fear' that it created disrupted the superior calmness of pity and the dignity of death. Moreover, the lifting of the 'clever' satiric parallel to the clergyman together with the simplification of the means of Maggie's death removed all conflict with the clear intent of her symbolic or impressionistic (as well as literal) mission.[33] At the last district all interrup-

---

[33] The effect of the removal of the too obvious parallel of fat man and clergyman is to simplify the line of cause and effect. In the 1893 version the hypocrisy of the church was made the operative cause of her turning prostitute and, in turn, of her death. In 1896 this extraneous religious satire no longer interferes with the allocation of responsibility where it truly belongs as has been evident throughout the novel and is emphasized in the inscription in the Garland copy quoted in footnote 23 above about environment. Moreover, in 1893 the religious satire had joined so powerfully with the double-time-scheme requirement of rejection and acceptance as to make rather subsidiary the theme of a mission of

tions cease, and in Crane's splendid piece of spare narrative the girl shrouds herself in the anonymity and impersonality of death as she journeys from glittering lights to final darkness.

Neither English edition, of 1896 (E1) or 1900 (E2), shows signs of anything other than normal reprint corruption plus some minor publisher's alterations. It is obvious that Crane did not concern himself with them, as the record of their variants in the Historical Collation demonstrates. The first two American editions alone are substantive; thus in the divided authority of the 1893 and the revised 1896 edition of *Maggie* lies the key to the problem of the final critically edited text. The 1893 edition, obviously, has the superior claim to authoritative accidentals since it is the print that has the most immediate connection with the lost printer's copy and through it to the lost holograph. No evidence exists that enables an editor to isolate with any confidence more than a handful of 1896 accidentals (apart from the dialect) that stem from authorial revision. On the other hand, the 1896 (A2) substantives have undergone a considerable process of authorial alteration. Under ordinary circumstances, then, the A2 substantive variants would have generally superior authority to those of A1, and the editorial task would require an

---

suicide adumbrated by the hint given at Maggie's first appearance. Without the obscuring effect of the religious satire, the clash between the narrative line and the literal implications of this theme and the narrative line of the symbolic decline as condensed in the action of the one night showed its disruptive force. The excision of the fat-man paragraph and the accompanying revisions, therefore, allowed Crane to retain his symbolic night when in the new impersonality of the last four 1896 paragraphs describing Maggie's arrival in the river district he was able to merge skillfully the two themes. In the 1893 version the fat-man episode had elevated the theme of Maggie's symbolic degeneration above that of the planned suicide. In 1896 the stop put to the girl's solicitations once she reaches the last block permits the two motifs to join on equal terms in a superior unification that removes the clash of the literal and the symbolic both between the two themes and within each.

It may be that the serious revision given to this chapter in 1896, on recognition of its defects, stemmed from the 1893 form as having been closer to an earlier original which in other respects but not in this chapter had been revised to form the 1893 version. In Chapter XVII not only do we have the use of descriptive phrases, like *girl of the crimson legions* instead of names, which as Professor Cady has observed (see footnote 30) was characteristic of the reported early form of the novel, but we also have, especially in the fat-man episode, a much freer use of adjectives than was characteristic of Crane's later style, even in 1893 and certainly in 1896. The 1896 revision of the chapter, then, performed some of the work that ought to have been done in 1893 but was not.

eclectic union of these substantives with the accidentals texture of A1 (rejecing only those A2 verbals believed to arise from printer's errors or sophisticating editorial intervention). In this manner the final edited text would approach as closely as possible to an accurate reconstruction of the actual marked copy of the 1893 edition that was sent to the printer.

Usually this procedure would represent sound editorial theory; and, indeed, it would produce a logically constructed text of *Maggie* provided the principle were accepted that authorial change of any kind, and however motivated, must be incorporated in a critical text as constituting an authority so powerful that it should override all other considerations. According to this principle Crane's final verbal intentions conforming to the Appleton agreement that specified the nature of the required revision could be successfully united with the authoritative accidentals of 1893. In effect, this would produce an improved 'ideal' text of 1896, taken as the major substantive authority.

That A2 despite the Appleton editors' alterations does on the whole accurately represent Crane's verbal intentions in revising the novel according to the terms he had accepted is incontestable. Yet the query may usefully be made whether this A2 text represents what he would have produced in 1896 if he had been given the opportunity to revise the 1893 version according to his own lights, without the censorship instructions that must have been at the heart of the Appleton agreement to publish the book. That is, if an author yields to external forces of censorship and under pressure revises his text in a manner he would not have contemplated if only his literary intentions had shaped the nature of his alterations, the result can be only a distortion of his literary art. That Crane accepted the distortion in order to profit from a second edition of *Maggie* cannot be denied. The 1896 edition is a fact, and in any legal and practical sense he 'approved' its text.

Yet a narrow, legalistic imposition of the 1896 version as the definitive substantive text of *Maggie* would be mere pedantry in any rational terms of literary or textual criticism. The 1893 edition was written at a certain time and is a historical fact. The 1896 edition revised the earlier text according to certain principles, and this form is in turn a historical fact. Under normal circumstances the historical fact of 1896 would be given pre-eminence since the principles of revision would have been of the author's own contrivance and thus aimed solely at improving the literary quality of his work. But the Appleton edition from the start was based not on the theory of revision for literary excellence in Crane's own terms but on revision to make the novel more acceptable to the general reading public by the removal or lightening of what the publishers conceived to be offensive language. In short, from the Appleton point of view censorship was the only desideratum, and it was this point of view that Crane was forced to accept in order to see his book in print. The principle of censorship produced in large part the historical fact represented by the 1896 *Maggie*. If Appleton had contracted to publish a new edition without specification as to the nature of the revision, so that Crane could have devoted his attention exclusively to literary improvements, the historical fact of such an 1896 edition would have been very different from the fact as we have it.

Under these circumstances it is proper for a textual critic to inquire whether it is possible to construct a text from the available evidence that will represent in an ultimately satisfactory manner [34] the work as it would have been prepared for the press in revised form without censorship restrictions. Such a reconstruction will be more difficult than the relatively simple merging of the 1896 substantives with the 1893 accidentals according to the standard editorial theory of the present day. But difficulty is one of the hazards of editing; all that is pertinent is whether the evidence for *Maggie* permits such a reconstruction of the truly 'ideal' text on a rational and practicable basis.

In some literary works it is generally recognized that a revision may be so thoroughgoing—so motivated throughout by the author's altered political, social, or artistic concepts—as to require complete acceptance on its own terms as the final intention in every respect both of accidentals and of substantives. For instance, in concrete terms, the work may have been rewritten in

---

[34] By 'satisfactory' is meant 'critically satisfactory'; that is, not a subjective reconstruction of a work that could never have existed, but a rationally motivated attempt based on sufficient factual evidence to carry the conviction that the result does indeed represent—with sufficient closeness to be of superior value—what would have appeared under free conditions.

the form of a new manuscript which would replace the old in both kinds of authority. But even when an earlier edition has formed the physical basis for annotation to produce in whole or in part the revised text, the changes may be so extensive as to defy bibliographical or critical separation into their components. Under such conditions there is nothing for it but to treat the early and late texts as quite independent units and to establish each separately, perhaps in parallel form, with no attempt to merge the two in terms of the divided authority of accidentals and substantives. Divided authority does not exist and no synthetic text is possible for the early and revised editions of such works as Jonson's *Every Man in His Humour,* Wordsworth's *Prelude,* or Whitman's *Leaves of Grass.*

The 1896 text of *Maggie* does not bear comparison with these examples. The basis for the censorship being external and aimed chiefly at the profanity, Crane's enforced task to satisfy the Appleton demands was largely a mechanical operation and its precise details can usually be isolated. The only real difficulty in isolating the censorship changes concerns not the 'words which hurt' in the sense of the *damns* and *hells,* but the relatively small amount of excision or modification of sordid detail, including descriptions of cursing, some of which seem to have a literary motivation.[35] No evidence exists, then, to support the argument that Crane would have altered more than a handful of such details if he had not been forced into the rigorous bowdlerizing of his 1893 text.[36]

---

[35] That is, unnecessary repetition, as at 12.9 because of the similar detail at 12.11; or the possibility, at least, that at 13.9 the 1896 intention is to intensify the reader's pity without a distracting sordid element. That Crane may have felt the variety of his 1896 euphemisms for profanity was occasionally preferable to the monotonous and deadening repetitions of *what deh hell* and so on, is without evidence save for his comment about the *new aspect* given the book by relatively small adjustment, a comment that is at best neutral. Certainly one can believe that the 1893 deliberate repetition of an extremely limited range of profanity in circumstances, as Professor Katz points out, ranging from approval to disapproval, joy to pain, or merely as a normal mode of greeting, was intended to produce a particular literary effect, even without carrying the case so far as Katz does in arguing for an intentional portrait of hell itself on earth (*MFS,* XII [1966], 204–207).

[36] Nor can an argument be put up, of course, for critical acceptance of the editorial censorship of what Crane missed or of the house styling that altered syntax and idiom except for the correction of such positive error as a modern editor would himself wish to change on his own authority in a critical edition.

Indeed, powerful evidence to the contrary can be adduced. That Crane took the opportunity offered by his 1896 'editing' to make a number of purely stylistic improvements is quite clear. What is equally clear is—with the single exception of the end of Chapter XVII—he made no effort to rewrite the novel or to alter any aspect not covered by the Appleton instructions. His additions are confined to a sentence or two. His substitutions and small excisions are chiefly concerned with sharpening the style, not at all with changing in any way the presentation of the events narrated or what might be called their aspect. That he was operating from a strong literary conviction about the integrity of a text once written and published in this refusal to take advantage of the opportunity for a more sweeping revision is clearly evidenced by his sentiments against revising *The Third Violet* for book publication on the grounds that it would be dishonest to change a work already in print, even though in a newspaper and magazine version.[37]

On the evidence of Crane's recorded literary convictions, therefore, backed by the solid evidence of the limited nature of the actual literary and stylistic alterations that he chose to make in 1896 when he had the chance, a synthesis of the two editions is possible to create a form of the text that will represent his final artistic intentions divorced from the censorship alterations that were alien to him. This may properly be called the 'ideal' text of *Maggie* as a literary fact, not a limited 'ideal' text either of the 1893 or of the 1896 edition. It is the text presented in this edition.[38]

[37] This is different from the publication of *The Red Badge of Courage* in variant newspaper and book forms. In this case the text for the book had been written, and the newspaper version was an abridgment. *The Third Violet* would have involved the same kind of basic rewriting and recasting that he had declined to perform in *Maggie*.

[38] Since the present edition purports to be definitive, its apparatus permits the reconstruction in all significant detail (that is, in all substantive and in partial accidentals detail) of either edition. Indeed, by judicious use of the Historical Collation a critic without reference back to the originals can construct what might be called the ideal text of 1893 by incorporating the 1896 and some of the present editorial correction of 1893 errors and inadvertences, and very likely altering the dialect system to conform to the 1896 standards of reporting. Since all accidentals as well as substantive changes from the 1893 copy-text are recorded in the Editorial Emendations, the 1893 edition can be reconstituted in exact detail as well as in an edited version. The accidentals of the 1896 edition can be known from the apparatus only when they have been adopted as emendations, but the

Since the evidence indicates that for his own literary purposes Crane was intent chiefly on sharpening the stylistic presentation of his novel, the present edition accepts as authoritative all 1896 alterations not covered by the bowdlerizing operation or by the editorial 'correction' of Crane's grammar, syntax, or idiom. The estimate of the nature and extent of these unauthoritative editorial changes in *Maggie* has been based on a comparison with similar styling alterations performed by the editors of various American publishing houses on Crane's text as independently established from holograph or typescript form, and by comparison with the changes made unauthoritatively for book publication in Crane's stories where a magazine publication served as copy-text. That all such changes have been isolated is too much to expect: the conservatism of editorial treatment in which general authority within certain limited areas has been given to the 1896 edition,[39] though rejecting its authority completely in other limited areas, may have led to some acceptances as Crane's of

Historical Collation will record every substantive reading whether or not adopted. An ideal critical text of the 1896 text can be constructed quite readily by restoring the 1896 substantive readings from the data preserved in the Historical Collation but incorporating them in the 1893 accidentals of the present text, with whatever modification has otherwise been adopted.

[39] The problem of estimating whether a stylistic alteration in 1896 is Crane's or Hitchcock's has created the most serious textual difficulty faced by the editor. Modern editorial methods attempt to establish the superior general substantive authority of some one edition as the initial basis for judgment. However, any sophisticated application must thereupon eschew the quantitative theory which requires *all* substantives from this generally superior text to be accepted without further analysis, as well as its opposite—the travesty of the qualitative theory— by which an editor picks and chooses among variants in two or more authoritative editions without any principle other than personal taste. Once the general view was established that the noncensorship substantive variants in 1896 were on the whole the result of Crane's literary revision, they were taken as authoritative until proved guilty. Some few were inferred to be guilty when, despite a surface appearance to the contrary, censorship seemed to be the major reason for their variance from 1893. More were inferred to be nonauthoritative by direct comparison with the classes of changes editors made in other Crane substantive texts. In this manner evidence was sought as the basis for critical decision, and the rejection of any 1896 substantive reading was governed by fixed principles of selectivity that required coherent, interrelating reasons as a guide to critical judgment. An editor must be willing to back his judgment, of course, and to accept responsibility for the results while at the same time recognizing that whatever degree and scope of scholarly rigor he tries to apply will seldom end in uncontested perfection. All that can be done is to narrow the area of possible disagreement to the minimum by the application of recognized principles of editorial method.

what in fact may be Hitchcock's tinkerings.[40] However, the anticipated result is a text of *Maggie* that removes the effects on the
1893 copy-text of the 1896 censorship operation and of editorial
'improvements' but preserves those 1896 revisions that Crane
made for his own purposes and satisfaction.

Thus the end sought is a critical text that in every ascertaina-
ble detail reproduces Crane's own 1896 final artistic intentions,
that is, in physical terms the lost marked-up copy of the 1893
edition in the condition in which he mailed it to Hitchcock, but
minus the mutilations which Appleton forced on him in order to
make the work more palatable for a general audience.

There remain the housekeeping details of this edition. As
remarked earlier, the physical form of the 1893 copy-text was
established by machine collation of the two University of Virginia copies, the Barrett (PS1449.C85M3 1893 [551432]) and
the McGregor (A1893.C7M3 [244539]), the latter with the auto-
graph of William Crane on the front wrapper, a facsimile of the
McGregor then being machined against the Ohio State University Libraries Linson copy and also sight-collated against the
copies in the Harvard and the Yale University libraries. No variation was discovered in this process. Finally, a list of the literal
errors in 1893 was spot-checked, without sign of variation,
against the Columbia University copy (a mint, unopened example), and, further, by the courtesy of Professor Joseph Katz,
against several dozen copies throughout the country.

The physical form of the 1896 revised text was established by
machine collation of the three University of Virginia Barrett
copies (PS1449.C85.M3 1896a [426411, 551429, 551430]) and
the McGregor copy (A1896.C7M3 [281463]), these being A2ᵃ on
wove paper, and the two A2ᵇ copies, the Barrett [551428] and
the Taylor (1896.C73M3 [508267]). The Barrett advance copy

---

[40] This problem is not confined to the text of *Maggie*. Whenever holograph
manuscripts but not typescripts are preserved of Crane's works, the problem
arises to identify the differences between the manuscript and printed form as
authoritative or unauthoritative; and the same holds, although with a lesser
spread of lost textual transmission, between preserved typescripts and the print.
Even variation between preserved proof and print is not exempt from such
problems.

on wove paper with wrappers (PS1449.C85M3 1896c [551431]) was carefully sight-collated, and Professor Bruccoli's roman laid-paper copy with the variant final advertisement (A2^c) was machine-collated. No textual variation was discovered. Batter noticed in the machining was spot-checked against A2^a in the Yale and A2^b in the Columbia University Libraries.

The 1896 Heinemann edition (E1) was sight-collated in the Barrett copy (PS1449.C85.M3 1896b [551544]) against A2, its printer's copy, and the 1900 Heinemann edition in *Bowery Tales* (E2) was sight-collated in the Barrett copy of the trade edition (551497) against E1, its printer's copy.

The text of *Maggie* found in Volume 10 of Wilson Follett's edition of *The Work of Stephen Crane* (New York, 1926) was set up from a copy of E2 with editorial substantive variants added. In 1966 Joseph Katz edited for Scholars' Facsimiles and Reprints (Gainesville, Florida) a facsimile of the 1893 edition from the University of Virginia McGregor copy, which was followed in the same year by an edition of the 1893 text, with collations and illustrative critical and historical material in the form of a casebook, based on the Barrett copy, by Maurice Bassan (Wadsworth Publishing Co., Belmont, California). Another facsimile of the McGregor copy, edited by Donald Pizer, was published in 1968 by Chandler (San Francisco, California).

F. B.

MAGGIE: A GIRL OF THE STREETS

PUBLISHER'S NOTE

THE interest which has been shown in The Red Badge of Courage has been most gratifying, but it has also involved a few inaccuracies of statement in regard to the history of Mr. Crane's literary work. The Red Badge of Courage was offered to and accepted by the publishers in December, 1894, and it was published in October, 1895. As it happened, the actual publication in England came some two months later. By that time the American press had appreciated the quality of the book so cordially and unanimously as to dispose of the lingering tradition that only a well-known author, or an author with the hall mark of foreign approval, is recognised by our reviewers.

As to the book which succeeds The Red Badge of Courage, it should be said that Maggie has never been published before, even in serial form. The story was put into type and copyrighted by Mr. Crane three years ago, but this real and strenuous tale of New York life is now given to the public for the first time.

[*Prefixed to the 1896 Appleton edition*]

AN APPRECIATION

I THINK that what strikes me most in the story of "Maggie" is that quality of fatal necessity which dominates Greek tragedy. From the conditions it all had to be, and there were the conditions. I felt this in Mr. Hardy's "Jude," where the principle seems to become conscious in the writer; but there is apparently no consciousness of any such motive in the author of "Maggie." Another effect is that of an ideal of artistic beauty which is as present in the working out of this poor girl's squalid romance as in any classic fable. This will be foolishness, I know, to the many foolish people who cannot discriminate between the material and the treatment in art, and think that beauty is inseparable from daintiness and prettiness, but I do not speak to them. I appeal rather to such as feel themselves akin with every kind of human creature, and find neither high nor low when it is a question of inevitable suffering, or of a soul struggling vainly with an inexorable fate.

My rhetoric scarcely suggests the simple terms the author uses to produce the effect which I am trying to repeat again. They are simple, but always most graphic, especially when it comes to the personalities of the story; the girl herself, with her bewildered wish to be right and good, with her distorted perspective, her clinging and generous affections, her hopeless environments; the horrible old drunken mother, a cyclone of violence and volcano of vulgarity; the mean and selfish lover, dandy, rowdy, with his gross ideals and ambitions; her brother, an Ishmaelite from the cradle, who with his warlike instincts beaten back into cunning, is what the b'hoy of former times has become in our more strenuously policed days. He is, indeed, a wonderful figure in a group which betrays no faltering in the artist's hand. He, with his dull hates, his warped good-will, his cowed ferocity, is almost as fine artistically as Maggie, but he could not have been so hard to do, for all the pathos of her fate is rendered without one maudlin touch. So is that of the simple-minded and devoted and tedious old woman who is George's mother in the book of that name. This is scarcely a study at all, while Maggie is really and fully so. It is the study of a situation merely; a poor inadequate woman, of a commonplace religiosity, whose son goes to the bad. The wonder of it is the courage which deals with persons so absolutely average, and the art which graces them with the beauty of the author's compassion for everything that errs and suffers. Without this feeling the effects of his mastery would be impossible, and if it went further, or put itself into the pitying phrases, it would annul the effects. But it never does this; it is notable how in all respects the author keeps himself well in hand. He is quite honest with his reader. He never shows his characters or his situations in any sort of sentimental glamour; if you will be moved by the sadness of common fates you will feel his intention; but he does not flatter his portraits of people on conditions to take your fancy.

W. D. HOWELLS

[*Prefixed to the 1896 Heinemann edition*]

CHAPTER I

A VERY little boy stood upon a heap of gravel for the honor of Rum Alley. He was throwing stones at howling urchins from Devil's Row who were circling madly about the heap and pelting him.

His infantile countenance was livid with the fury of battle. His small body was writhing in the delivery of oaths.

"Run, Jimmie, run! Dey'll git yehs!" screamed a retreating Rum Alley child.

"Naw," responded Jimmie with a valiant roar, "dese micks can't make me run."

Howls of renewed wrath went up from Devil's Row throats. Tattered gamins on the right made a furious assault on the gravel heap. On their small, convulsed faces shone the grins of true assassins. As they charged, they threw stones and cursed in shrill chorus.

The little champion of Rum Alley stumbled precipitately down the other side. His coat had been torn to shreds in a scuffle, and his hat was gone. He had bruises on twenty parts of his body, and blood was dripping from a cut in his head. His wan features looked like those of a tiny, insane demon.

On the ground, children from Devil's Row closed in on their antagonist. He crooked his left arm defensively about his head and fought with madness. The little boys ran to and fro, dodging, hurling stones and swearing in barbaric trebles.

From a window of an apartment house that uprose from amid squat, ignorant stables, there leaned a curious woman. Some laborers, unloading a scow at a dock at the river, paused for a moment and regarded the fight. The engineer of a passive tug-boat hung lazily over a railing and watched. Over on the Island, a worm of yellow convicts came from the shadow of a grey ominous building and crawled slowly along the river's bank.

A stone had smashed in Jimmie's mouth. Blood was bubbling over his chin and down upon his ragged shirt. Tears made furrows on his dirt-stained cheeks. His thin legs had begun to tremble and turn weak, causing his small body to reel. His roaring curses of the first part of the fight had changed to a blasphemous chatter.

In the yells of the whirling mob of Devil's Row children there were notes of joy like songs of triumphant savagery. The little boys seemed to leer gloatingly at the blood upon the other child's face.

Down the avenue came boastfully sauntering a lad of sixteen years, although the chronic sneer of an ideal manhood already sat upon his lips. His hat was tipped over his eye with an air of challenge. Between his teeth, a cigar stump was tilted at the angle of defiance. He walked with a certain swing of the shoulders which appalled the timid. He glanced over into the vacant lot in which the little raving boys from Devil's Row seethed about the shrieking and tearful child from Rum Alley.

"Gee!" he murmured with interest. "A scrap. Gee!"

He strode over to the cursing circle, swinging his shoulders in a manner which denoted that he held victory in his fists. He approached at the back of one of the most deeply engaged of the Devil's Row children.

"Ah, what d' hell," he said, and smote the deeply-engaged one on the back of the head. The little boy fell to the ground and gave a tremendous howl. He scrambled to his feet, and perceiving, evidently, the size of his assailant, ran quickly off, shouting alarms. The entire Devil's Row party followed him. They came to a stand a short distance away and yelled taunting oaths at the boy with the chronic sneer. The latter, momentarily, paid no attention to them.

"What d' hell, Jimmie?" he asked of the small champion.

Jimmie wiped his blood-wet features with his sleeve.

"Well, it was dis way, Pete, see! I was goin' t' lick dat Riley kid and dey all pitched on me."

Some Rum Alley children now came forward. The party stood for a moment exchanging vainglorious remarks with Devil's Row. A few stones were thrown at long distances, and words of challenge passed between small warriors. Then the Rum Alley contingent turned slowly in the direction of their home street. They began to give, each to each, distorted versions of the fight. Causes of retreat in particular cases were magnified. Blows dealt in the fight were enlarged to catapultian power, and stones thrown were alleged to have hurtled with infinite accuracy. Valor grew strong again, and the little boys began to brag with great spirit.

"Ah, we blokies kin lick d' hull damn Row," said a child, swaggering.

Little Jimmie was striving to stanch the flow of blood from his cut lips. Scowling, he turned upon the speaker.

"Ah, where d' hell was yehs when I was doin' all d' fightin'?" he demanded. "Youse kids makes me tired."

"Ah, go ahn," replied the other argumentatively.

Jimmie replied with heavy contempt. "Ah, youse can't fight, Blue Billie! I kin lick yeh wid one han'."

"Ah, go ahn," replied Billie again.

"Ah," said Jimmie threateningly.

"Ah," said the other in the same tone.

They struck at each other, clinched, and rolled over on the cobble stones.

"Smash 'im, Jimmie, kick d' damn guts out of 'im," yelled Pete, the lad with the chronic sneer, in tones of delight.

The small combatants pounded and kicked, scratched and tore. They began to weep and their curses struggled in their throats with sobs. The other little boys clasped their hands and wriggled their legs in excitement. They formed a bobbing circle about the pair.

A tiny spectator was suddenly agitated.

"Cheese it, Jimmie, cheese it! Here comes yer fader," he yelled.

The circle of little boys instantly parted. They drew away and waited in ecstatic awe for that which was about to happen. The two little boys fighting in the modes of four thousand years ago, did not hear the warning.

Up the avenue there plodded slowly a man with sullen eyes. He was carrying a dinner-pail and smoking an apple-wood pipe.

As he neared the spot where the little boys strove, he regarded them listlessly. But suddenly he roared an oath and advanced upon the rolling fighters.

"Here, you Jim, git up, now, while I belt yer life out, yeh damned disorderly brat."

He began to kick into the chaotic mass on the ground. The boy Billie felt a heavy boot strike his head. He made a furious effort and disentangled himself from Jimmie. He tottered away, damning.

Jimmie arose painfully from the ground and confronting his father, began to curse him. His parent kicked him. "Come home, now," he cried, "an' stop yer jawin', er I'll lam the everlasting head off yehs."

They departed. The man paced placidly along with the apple-wood emblem of serenity between his teeth. The boy followed a dozen feet in the rear. He swore luridly, for he felt that it was degradation for one who aimed to be some vague kind of a soldier, or a man of blood with a sort of sublime license, to be taken home by a father.

CHAPTER II

EVENTUALLY they entered into a dark region where, from a careening building, a dozen gruesome doorways gave up loads of babies to the street and the gutter. A wind of early autumn raised yellow dust from cobbles and swirled it against an hundred windows. Long streamers of garments fluttered from fire-escapes. In all unhandy places there were buckets, brooms, rags and bottles. In the street infants played or fought with other infants or sat stupidly in the way of vehicles. Formidable women, with uncombed hair and disordered dress, gossiped while leaning on railings, or screamed in frantic quarrels. Withered persons, in curious postures of submission to something, sat smoking pipes in obscure corners. A thousand odors of cooking food came forth to the street. The building quivered and creaked from the weight of humanity stamping about in its bowels.

A small ragged girl dragged a red, bawling infant along the crowded ways. He was hanging back, baby-like, bracing his wrinkled, bare legs.

The little girl cried out: "Ah, Tommie, come ahn. Dere's Jimmie and fader. Don't be a-pullin' me back."

She jerked the baby's arm impatiently. He fell on his face, roaring. With a second jerk she pulled him to his feet, and they went on. With the obstinacy of his order, he protested against being dragged in a chosen direction. He made heroic endeavors to keep on his legs, denounced his sister and consumed a bit of orange peeling which he chewed between the times of his infantile orations.

As the sullen-eyed man, followed by the blood-covered boy, drew near, the little girl burst into reproachful cries. "Ah, Jimmie, youse bin fightin' agin."

The urchin swelled disdainfully.

"Ah, what d' hell, Mag. See?"

The little girl upbraided him. "Youse allus fightin', Jimmie, an' yeh knows it puts mudder out when yehs come home half dead, an' it's like we'll all get a poundin'.'"

She began to weep. The babe threw back his head and roared at his prospects.

"Ah, what d' hell!" cried Jimmie. "Shut up er I'll smack yer mout'. See?"

As his sister continued her lamentations, he suddenly struck her. The little girl reeled and, recovering herself, burst into tears and quaveringly cursed him. As she slowly retreated her brother advanced dealing her cuffs. The father heard and turned about.

"Stop that, Jim, d'yeh hear? Leave yer sister alone on the street. It's like I can never beat any sense into yer damned wooden head."

The urchin raised his voice in defiance to his parent and continued his attacks. The babe bawled tremendously, protesting with great violence. During his sister's hasty manœuvres, he was dragged by the arm.

Finally the procession plunged into one of the gruesome doorways. They crawled up dark stairways and along cold, gloomy halls. At last the father pushed open a door and they entered a lighted room in which a large woman was rampant.

She stopped in a career from a seething stove to a pan-covered table. As the father and children filed in she peered at them.

"Eh, what? Been fightin' agin, by Gawd!" She threw herself upon Jimmie. The urchin tried to dart behind the others and in the scuffle the babe, Tommie, was knocked down. He protested with his usual vehemence, because they had bruised his tender shins against a table leg.

The mother's massive shoulders heaved with anger. Grasping the urchin by the neck and shoulder she shook him until he rattled. She dragged him to an unholy sink, and, soaking a rag in water, began to scrub his lacerated face with it. Jimmie screamed in pain and tried to twist his shoulders out of the clasp of the huge arms.

The babe sat on the floor watching the scene, his face in contortions like that of a woman at a tragedy. The father, with a newly-ladened pipe in his mouth, sat in a backless chair near the stove. Jimmie's cries annoyed him. He turned about and bellowed at his wife:

"Let the damned kid alone for a minute, will yeh, Mary? Yer allus poundin' 'im. When I come nights I can't git no rest 'cause yer allus poundin' a kid. Let up, d'yeh hear? Don't be allus poundin' a kid."

The woman's operations on the urchin instantly increased in violence. At last she tossed him to a corner where he limply lay weeping.

The wife put her immense hands on her hips, and with a chieftain-like stride approached her husband.

"Ho," she said, with a great grunt of contempt. "An' what in the devil are you stickin' your nose for?"

The babe crawled under the table and, turning, peered out cautiously. The ragged girl retreated and the urchin in the corner drew his legs carefully beneath him.

The man puffed his pipe calmly and put his great muddied boots on the back part of the stove.

"Go t' hell," he said tranquilly.

The woman screamed and shook her fists before her husband's eyes. The rough yellow of her face and neck flared suddenly crimson. She began to howl.

He puffed imperturbably at his pipe for a time, but finally arose and went to look out at the window into the darkening chaos of back yards.

"You've been drinkin', Mary," he said. "You'd better let up on the bot', ol' woman, or you'll git done."

"You're a liar. I ain't had a drop," she roared in reply. They had a lurid altercation, in which they damned each other's souls with frequence.

The babe was staring out from under the table, his small face working in his excitement. The ragged girl went stealthily over to the corner where the urchin lay.

"Are yehs hurted much, Jimmie?" she whispered timidly.

"Not a damn bit! See?" growled the little boy.

"Will I wash d' blood?"

"Naw!"

"Will I——"

"When I catch dat Riley kid I'll break 'is face! Dat's right! See?"

He turned his face to the wall as if resolved to grimly bide his time.

In the quarrel between husband and wife, the woman was victor. The man seized his hat and rushed from the room, apparently determined upon a vengeful drunk. She followed to the door and thundered at him as he made his way down stairs.

She returned and stirred up the room until her children were bobbing about like bubbles.

"Git outa d' way," she persistently bawled, waving feet with their dishevelled shoes near the heads of her children. She shrouded herself, puffing and snorting, in a cloud of steam at the stove, and eventually extracted a frying-pan full of potatoes that hissed.

She flourished it. "Come t' yer suppers, now," she cried with sudden exasperation. "Hurry up, now, er I'll help yeh!"

The children scrambled hastily. With prodigious clatter they arranged themselves at table. The babe sat with his feet dangling high from a precarious infant chair and gorged his small stomach. Jimmie forced, with feverish rapidity, the grease-enveloped pieces between his wounded lips. Maggie, with side glances of fear of interruption, ate like a small pursued tigress.

The mother sat blinking at them. She delivered reproaches, swallowed potatoes and drank from a yellow-brown bottle. After a time her mood changed and she wept as she carried little Tommie into another room and laid him to sleep, with his fists doubled, in an old quilt of faded red and green grandeur. Then she came and moaned by the stove. She rocked to and fro upon a chair, shedding tears and crooning miserably to the two children about their "poor mother" and "yer fader, damn 'is soul."

The little girl plodded between the table and the chair with a dish-pan on it. She tottered on her small legs beneath burdens of dishes.

Jimmie sat nursing his various wounds. He cast furtive glances at his mother. His practised eye perceived her gradually emerge from a muddled mist of sentiment until her brain burned in drunken heat. He sat breathless.

Maggie broke a plate.

The mother started to her feet as if propelled.

"Good Gawd," she howled. Her glittering eyes fastened on her child with sudden hatred. The fervent red of her face turned almost to purple. The little boy ran to the halls, shrieking like a monk in an earthquake.

He floundered about in darkness until he found the stairs. He stumbled, panic-stricken, to the next floor. An old woman opened a door. A light behind her threw a flare on the urchin's face.

"Eh, Gawd, child, what is it dis time? Is yer fader beatin' yer mudder, or yer mudder beatin' yer fader?"

CHAPTER III

JIMMIE and the old woman listened long in the hall. Above the muffled roar of conversation, the dismal wailings of babies at night, the thumping of feet in unseen corridors and rooms, and the sound of varied hoarse shoutings in the street and the rattling of wheels over cobbles, they heard the screams of the child and the roars of the mother die away to a feeble moaning and a subdued bass muttering.

The old woman was a gnarled and leathery personage who could don, at will, an expression of great virtue. She possessed a small music box capable of one tune, and a collection of "God bless yehs" pitched in assorted keys of fervency. Each day she took a position upon the stones of Fifth Avenue, where she crooked her legs under her and crouched immovable and hideous, like an idol. She received daily a small sum in pennies. It was contributed, for the most part, by persons who did not make their homes in that vicinity.

Once, when a lady had dropped her purse on the sidewalk, the gnarled woman had grabbed it and smuggled it with great dexterity beneath her cloak. When she was arrested she had cursed the lady into a partial swoon, and with her aged limbs, twisted from rheumatism, had almost kicked the stomach out of a huge policeman whose conduct upon that occasion she referred to when she said, "The police, damn 'em!"

"Eh, Jimmie, it's cursed shame," she said. "Go, now, like a dear an' buy me a can, an' if yer mudder raises 'ell all night yehs can sleep here."

Jimmie took a tendered tin-pail and seven pennies and departed. He passed into the side door of a saloon and went to the bar. Straining up on his toes he raised the pail and pennies as high as his arms would let him. He saw two hands thrust down to take them. Directly the same hands let down the filled pail and he left.

In front of the gruesome doorway he met a lurching figure. It was his father, swaying about on uncertain legs.

"Give me d' can. See?" said the man.

"Ah, come off! I got dis can fer dat ol' woman an' it 'ud be dirt t' swipe it. See?" cried Jimmie.

The father wrenched the pail from the urchin. He grasped it in both hands and lifted it to his mouth. He glued his lips to the under edge and tilted his head. His throat swelled until it seemed to grow near his chin. There was a tremendous gulping movement and the beer was gone.

The man caught his breath and laughed. He hit his son on the head with the empty pail. As it rolled clanging into the street, Jimmie began to scream and kicked repeatedly at his father's shins.

"Look at d' dirt what yeh done me," he yelled. "D' ol' woman 'ill be raisin' hell."

He retreated to the middle of the street, but the man did not pursue. He staggered toward the door.

"I'll club hell outa yeh when I ketch yeh," he shouted, and disappeared.

During the evening he had been standing against a bar drinking whiskies and declaring to all comers, confidentially: "My home reg'lar livin' hell! Damndes' place! Reg'lar hell! Why do I come an' drin' whisk' here thish way? 'Cause home reg'lar livin' hell!"

Jimmie waited a long time in the street and then crept warily up through the building. He passed with great caution the door of the gnarled woman, and finally stopped outside his home and listened.

He could hear his mother moving heavily about among the furniture of the room. She was chanting in a mournful voice, occasionally interjecting bursts of volcanic wrath at the father, who, Jimmie judged, had sunk down on the floor or in a corner.

"Why d' blazes don' chere try t' keep Jim from fightin'? I'll break yer jaw," she suddenly bellowed.

The man mumbled with drunken indifference. "Ah, wha' d' hell. W'a's odds? Wha' makes kick?"

"Because he tears 'is clothes, yeh damn fool," cried the woman in supreme wrath.

The husband seemed to become aroused. "Go t' hell," he thundered fiercely in reply. There was a crash against the door and something broke into clattering fragments. Jimmie partially suppressed a yell and darted down the stairway. Below he paused and listened. He heard howls and curses, groans and shrieks—a confused chorus as if a battle were raging. With it all there was the crash of splintering furniture. The eyes of the urchin glared in his fear that one of them would discover him.

Curious faces appeared in doorways, and whispered comments passed to and fro. "Ol' Johnson's raisin' hell agin."

Jimmie stood until the noises ceased and the other inhabitants of the tenement had all yawned and shut their doors. Then he crawled up stairs with the caution of an invader of a panther den. Sounds of labored breathing came through the broken door-panels. He pushed the door open and entered, quaking.

A glow from the fire threw red hues over the bare floor, the cracked and soiled plastering, and the overturned and broken furniture.

In the middle of the floor lay his mother asleep. In one corner of the room his father's limp body hung across the seat of a chair.

The urchin stole forward. He began to shiver in dread of awakening his parents. His mother's great chest was heaving painfully. Jimmie paused and looked down at her. Her face was inflamed and swollen from drinking. Her yellow brows shaded eye-lids that had grown blue. Her tangled hair tossed in waves over her forehead. Her mouth was set in the same lines of vindictive hatred that it had, perhaps, borne during the fight. Her bare, red arms were thrown out above her head in an attitude of exhaustion, something, mayhap, like that of a sated villain.

The urchin bended over his mother. He was fearful lest she should open her eyes, and the dread within him was so strong, that he could not forbear to stare, but hung as if fascinated over the woman's grim face.

Suddenly her eyes opened. The urchin found himself looking straight into an expression, which, it would seem, had the power to change his blood to salt. He howled piercingly and fell backward.

The woman floundered for a moment, tossed her arms about her head as if in combat, and again began to snore.

Jimmie crawled back into the shadows and waited. A noise in the next room had followed his cry at the discovery that his mother was awake. He grovelled in the gloom, his eyes riveted upon the intervening door.

He heard it creak, and then the sound of a small voice came to him. "Jimmie! Jimmie! Are yehs dere?" it whispered. The urchin started. The thin, white face of his sister looked at him from the doorway of the other room. She crept to him across the floor.

The father had not moved, but lay in the same death-like sleep. The mother writhed in uneasy slumber, her chest wheezing as if she were in the agonies of strangulation. Out at the window a florid moon was peering over dark roofs, and in the distance the waters of a river glimmered pallidly.

The small frame of the ragged girl was quivering. Her features were haggard from weeping, and her eyes gleamed with fear. She grasped the urchin's arm in her little trembling hands and they huddled in a corner. The eyes of both were drawn, by some force, to stare at the woman's face, for they thought she need only to awake and all the fiends would come from below.

They crouched until the ghost-mists of dawn appeared at the window, drawing close to the panes, and looking in at the prostrate, heaving body of the mother.

CHAPTER IV

THE babe, Tommie, died. He went away in an insignificant coffin, his small waxen hand clutching a flower that the girl, Maggie, had stolen from an Italian.

She and Jimmie lived.

The inexperienced fibres of the boy's eyes were hardened at an early age. He became a young man of leather. He lived some red years without laboring. During that time his sneer became chronic. He studied human nature in the gutter, and found it no worse than he thought he had reason to believe it. He never conceived a respect for the world, because he had begun with no idols that it had smashed.

He clad his soul in armor by means of happening hilariously in at a mission church where a man composed his sermons of "you's." Once a philosopher asked this man why he did not say "we" instead of "you." The man replied, "What?"

While they got warm at the stove, he told his hearers just where he calculated they stood with the Lord. Many of the sinners were impatient over the pictured depths of their degradation. They were waiting for soup-tickets.

A reader of words of wind-demons might have been able to see the portions of a dialogue pass to and fro between the exhorter and his hearers.

"You are damned," said the preacher. And the reader of sounds might have seen the reply go forth from the ragged people: "Where's our soup?"

Jimmie and a companion sat in a rear seat and commented upon the things that didn't concern them, with all the freedom of English tourists. When they grew thirsty and went out their minds confused the speaker with Christ.

Momentarily, Jimmie was sullen with thoughts of a hopeless altitude where grew fruit. His companion said that if he should ever meet God he would ask for a million dollars and a bottle of beer.

Jimmie's occupation for a long time was to stand on street-corners and watch the world go by, dreaming blood-red dreams at the passing of pretty women. He menaced mankind at the inter-sections of streets.

On the corners he was in life and of life. The world was going on and he was there to perceive it.

He maintained a belligerent attitude toward all well-dressed men. To him fine raiment was allied to weakness, and all good coats covered faint hearts. He and his order were kings, to a certain extent, over the men of untarnished clothes, because these latter dreaded, perhaps, to be either killed or laughed at.

Above all things he despised obvious Christians and ciphers with the chrysanthemums of aristocracy in their button-holes. He considered himself above both of these classes. He was afraid of nothing.

When he had a dollar in his pocket his satisfaction with existence was the greatest thing in the world. So, eventually, he felt obliged to work. His father died and his mother's years were divided up into periods of thirty days.

He became a truck driver. There was given to him the charge of a pains-taking pair of horses and a large rattling truck. He invaded the turmoil and tumble of the down-town streets and learned to breathe maledictory defiance at the police who occa-sionally used to climb up, drag him from his perch and punch him.

In the lower part of the city he daily involved himself in hideous tangles. If he and his team chanced to be in the rear he preserved a demeanor of serenity, crossing his legs and bursting forth into yells when foot passengers took dangerous dives be-neath the noses of his champing horses. He smoked his pipe calmly for he knew that his pay was marching on.

If his charge was in the front and if it became the key-truck of chaos, he entered terrifically into the quarrel that was raging to and fro among the drivers on their high seats, and sometimes roared oaths and violently got himself arrested.

After a time his sneer grew so that it turned its glare upon all things. He became so sharp that he believed in nothing. To him the police were always actuated by malignant impulses and the rest of the world was composed, for the most part, of despicable creatures who were all trying to take advantage of him and with whom, in defense, he was obliged to quarrel on all possible occasions. He himself occupied a down-trodden position which had a private but distinct element of grandeur in its isolation.

The greatest cases of aggravated idiocy were, to his mind, rampant upon the front platforms of all of the street cars. At first his tongue strove with these beings, but he eventually became superior. In him grew a majestic contempt for those strings of street cars that followed him like intent bugs.

He fell into the habit, when starting on a long journey, of fixing his eye on a high and distant object, commanding his horses to start and then going into a trance of observation. Multitudes of drivers might howl in his rear, and passengers might load him with opprobrium, but he would not awaken until some blue policeman turned red and began to frenziedly seize bridles and beat the soft noses of the responsible horses.

When he paused to contemplate the attitude of the police toward himself and his fellows, he believed that they were the only men in the city who had no rights. When driving about, he felt that he was held liable by the police for anything that might occur in the streets, and that he was the common prey of all energetic officials. In revenge, he resolved never to move out of the way of anything, until formidable circumstances, or a much larger man than himself forced him to it.

Foot passengers were mere pestering flies with an insane disregard for their legs and his convenience. He could not comprehend their desire to cross the streets. Their madness smote him with eternal amazement. He was continually storming at them from his throne. He sat aloft and denounced their frantic leaps, plunges, dives and straddles.

When they would thrust at, or parry, the noses of his champing horses, making them swing their heads and move their feet, and thus disturbing a stolid dreamy repose, he swore at the men as fools, for he himself could perceive that Providence had caused it clearly to be written, that he and his team had the unalienable right to stand in the proper path of the sun chariot, and if they so minded, obstruct its mission or take a wheel off.

And if the god-driver had had a desire to step down, put up his flame-colored fists and manfully dispute the right of way, he would have probably been immediately opposed by a scowling mortal with two sets of hard knuckles.

It is possible, perhaps, that this young man would have derided, in an axle-wide alley, the approach of a flying ferry boat. Yet he achieved a respect for a fire engine. As one charged toward his truck, he would drive fearfully upon a sidewalk, threatening untold people with annihilation. When an engine struck a mass of blocked trucks, splitting it into fragments, as a blow annihilates a cake of ice, Jimmie's team could usually be observed high and safe, with whole wheels, on the sidewalk. The fearful coming of the engine could break up the most intricate muddle of heavy vehicles at which the police had been swearing for the half of an hour.

A fire engine was enshrined in his heart as an appalling thing that he loved with a distant dog-like devotion. It had been known to overturn a street car. Those leaping horses, striking sparks from the cobbles in their forward lunge, were creatures to be ineffably admired. The clang of the gong pierced his breast like a noise of remembered war.

When Jimmie was a little boy, he began to be arrested. Before he reached a great age, he had a fair record.

He developed too great a tendency to climb down from his truck and fight with other drivers. He had been in quite a number of miscellaneous fights, and in some general barroom rows that had become known to the police. Once he had been arrested for assaulting a Chinaman. Two women in different parts of the city, and entirely unknown to each other, caused him considerable annoyance by breaking forth, simultaneously, at fateful intervals, into wailings about marriage and support and infants.

Nevertheless, he had, on a certain star-lit evening, said wonderingly and quite reverently: "D' moon looks like hell, don't it?"

CHAPTER V

THE girl, Maggie, blossomed in a mud puddle. She grew to be a most rare and wonderful production of a tenement district, a pretty girl.

None of the dirt of Rum Alley seemed to be in her veins. The philosophers up stairs, down stairs and on the same floor, puzzled over it.

When a child, playing and fighting with gamins in the street, dirt disguised her. Attired in tatters and grime, she went unseen.

There came a time, however, when the young men of the vicinity, said: "Dat Johnson goil is a puty good looker." About this period her brother remarked to her: "Mag, I'll tell yeh dis! See? Yeh've edder got t' go t' hell er go t' work!" Whereupon she went to work, having the feminine aversion of going to hell.

By a chance, she got a position in an establishment where they made collars and cuffs. She received a stool and a machine in a room where sat twenty girls of various shades of yellow discontent. She perched on the stool and treadled at her machine all day, turning out collars with a name which might have been noted for its irrelevancy to anything connected with collars. At night she returned home to her mother.

Jimmie grew large enough to take the vague position of head of the family. As incumbent of that office, he stumbled up stairs late at night, as his father had done before him. He reeled about the room, swearing at his relations, or went to sleep on the floor.

The mother had gradually arisen to such a degree of fame that she could bandy words with her acquaintances among the police-justices. Court-officials called her by her first name. When she appeared they pursued a course which had been theirs for months. They invariably grinned and cried out: "Hello, Mary, you here again?" Her grey head wagged in many courts. She always besieged the bench with voluble excuses, explanations, apologies and prayers. Her flaming face and rolling eyes were a familiar sight on the Island. She measured time by means of sprees, and was eternally swollen and dishevelled.

One day the young man, Pete, who as a lad had smitten the Devil's Row urchin in the back of the head and put to flight the antagonists of his friend, Jimmie, strutted upon the scene. He met Jimmie one day on the street, promised to take him to a boxing match in Williamsburg, and called for him in the evening.

Maggie observed Pete.

He sat on a table in the Johnson home and dangled his checked legs with an enticing nonchalance. His hair was curled down over his forehead in an oiled bang. His pugged nose seemed to revolt from contact with a bristling moustache of short, wire-like hairs. His blue double-breasted coat, edged with black braid, was buttoned close to a red puff tie, and his patent-leather shoes looked like weapons.

His mannerisms stamped him as a man who had a correct sense of his personal superiority. There was valor and contempt for circumstances in the glance of his eye. He waved his hands like a man of the world, who dismisses religion and philosophy, and says "Rats!" He had certainly seen everything and with each curl of his lip, he declared that it amounted to nothing. Maggie thought he must be a very "elegant" bartender.

He was telling tales to Jimmie.

Maggie watched him furtively, with half-closed eyes, lit with a vague interest.

"Hully gee! Dey makes me tired," he said. "Mos' e'ry day some farmer comes in an' tries t' run d' shop. See? But dey gits t'rowed right out! I jolt dem right out in d' street before dey knows where dey is! See?"

"Sure," said Jimmie.

"Dere was a mug come in d' place d' odder day wid an idear he wus goin' t' own d' place! Hully gee, he wus goin' t' own d' place! I see he had a still on an' I didn' wanna giv 'im no stuff, so I says: 'Git d' hell outa here an' don' make no trouble,' I says like dat! See? 'Git d' hell outa here an' don' make no trouble'; like dat. 'Git d' hell outa here,' I says. See?"

Jimmie nodded understandingly. Over his features played an

eager desire to state the amount of his valor in a similar crisis, but the narrator proceeded.

"Well, d' blokie he says: 'T' hell wid it! I ain' lookin' for no scrap,' he says—see? 'But,' he says, 'I'm 'spectable cit'zen an' I wanna drink an' purtydamnsoon, too.' See? 'D' hell,' I says. Like dat! 'D' hell,' I says. See? 'Don' make no trouble,' I says. Like dat. 'Don' make no trouble.' See? Den d' mug he squared off an' said he was fine as silk wid his dukes—see? An' he wanned a drink damnquick. Dat's what he said. See?"

"Sure," repeated Jimmie.

Pete continued. "Say, I jes' jumped d' bar an' d' way I plunked dat blokie was outa sight. See? Dat's right! In d' jaw! See? Hully gee, he t'rowed a spittoon t'ru d' front windee. Say, I t'aut I'd drop dead. But d' boss, he comes in after an' he says, 'Pete, yehs done jes' right! Yeh've gota keep order an' it's all right.' See? 'It's all right,' he says. Dat's what he said."

The two held a technical discussion.

"Dat bloke was a dandy," said Pete, in conclusion, "but he hadn' oughta made no trouble. Dat's what I says t' dem: 'Don' come in here an' make no trouble,' I says, like dat. 'Don' make no trouble.' See?"

As Jimmie and his friend exchanged tales descriptive of their prowess, Maggie leaned back in the shadow. Her eyes dwelt wonderingly and rather wistfully upon Pete's face. The broken furniture, grimy walls, and general disorder and dirt of her home of a sudden appeared before her and began to take a potential aspect. Pete's aristocratic person looked as if it might soil. She looked keenly at him, occasionally, wondering if he was feeling contempt. But Pete seemed to be enveloped in reminiscence.

"Hully gee," said he, "dose mugs can't phase me. Dey knows I kin wipe up d' street wid any t'ree of dem."

When he said, "Ah, what d' hell!" his voice was burdened with disdain for the inevitable and contempt for anything that fate might compel him to endure.

Maggie perceived that here was the ideal man. Her dim thoughts were often searching for far away lands where, as God says, the little hills sing together in the morning. Under the trees of her dream-gardens there had always walked a lover.

CHAPTER VI

P ETE took note of Maggie.

"Say, Mag, I'm stuck on yer shape. It's outa sight," he said, parenthetically, with an affable grin.

As he became aware that she was listening closely, he grew still more eloquent in his descriptions of various happenings in his career. It appeared that he was invincible in fights.

"Why," he said, referring to a man with whom he had had a misunderstanding, "dat mug scrapped like a damned dago. Dat's right. He was dead easy. See? He t'aut he was a scrapper! But he foun' out diff'ent! Hully gee."

He walked to and fro in the small room, which seemed then to grow even smaller and unfit to hold his dignity, the attribute of a supreme warrior. That swing of the shoulders which had frozen the timid when he was but a lad had increased with his growth and education at the ratio of ten to one. It, combined with the sneer upon his mouth, told mankind that there was nothing in space which could appall him. Maggie marvelled at him and surrounded him with greatness. She vaguely tried to calculate the altitude of the pinnacle from which he must have looked down upon her.

"I met a chump d' odder day way up in d' city," he said. "I was goin' t' see a frien' of mine. When I was a-crossin' d' street d' chump runned plump inteh me, an' den he turns aroun' an' says, 'Yer insolen' ruffin,' he says, like dat. 'Oh, gee,' I says, 'oh, gee, go t' hell an' git off d' eart'!' I says, like dat. See? 'Go t' hell an' git off d' eart',' like dat. Den d' blokie he got wild. He says I was a con-tempt'ble scoun'el, er somethin' like dat, an' he says I was doom' t' everlastin' pe'dition, er somethin' like dat. 'Gee,' I says, 'gee! D' hell I am,' I says. 'D' hell I am,' like dat. An' den I slugged 'im. See?"

With Jimmie in his company, Pete departed in a sort of a blaze of glory from the Johnson home. Maggie, leaning from the window, watched him as he walked down the street.

Here was a formidable man who disdained the strength of a world full of fists. Here was one who had contempt for brass-clothed power; one whose knuckles could defiantly ring against the granite of law. He was a knight.

The two men went from under the glimmering street-lamp and passed into shadows.

Turning, Maggie contemplated the dark, dust-stained walls, and the scant and crude furniture of her home. A clock, in a splintered and battered oblong box of varnished wood, she suddenly regarded as an abomination. She noted that it ticked raspingly. The almost vanished flowers in the carpet-pattern, she conceived to be newly hideous. Some faint attempts which she had made with blue ribbon, to freshen the appearance of a dingy curtain, she now saw to be piteous.

She wondered what Pete dined on.

She reflected upon the collar and cuff factory. It began to appear to her mind as a dreary place of endless grinding. Pete's elegant occupation brought him, no doubt, into contact with people who had money and manners. It was probable that he had a large acquaintance of pretty girls. He must have great sums of money to spend.

To her the earth was composed of hardships and insults. She felt instant admiration for a man who openly defied it. She thought that if the grim angel of death should clutch his heart, Pete would shrug his shoulders and say, "Oh, ev'ryt'ing goes."

She anticipated that he would come again shortly. She spent some of her week's pay in the purchase of flowered cretonne for a lambrequin. She made it with infinite care and hung it to the slightly-careening mantel, over the stove, in the kitchen. She studied it with painful anxiety from different points in the room. She wanted it to look well on Sunday night when, perhaps, Jimmie's friend would come. On Sunday night, however, Pete did not appear.

Afterward the girl looked at it with a sense of humiliation. She was now convinced that Pete was superior to admiration for lambrequins.

A few evenings later Pete entered with fascinating innovations in his apparel. As she had seen him twice and he wore a different suit each time, Maggie had a dim impression that his wardrobe was prodigious.

"Say, Mag," he said, "put on yer bes' duds Friday night an' I'll take yehs t' d' show. See?"

He spent a few moments in flourishing his clothes and then vanished, without having glanced at the lambrequin.

Over the eternal collars and cuffs in the factory Maggie spent the most of three days in making imaginary sketches of Pete and his daily environment. She imagined some half dozen women in love with him and thought he must lean dangerously toward an indefinite one, whom she pictured as endowed with great charms of person, but with an altogether contemptible disposition.

She thought he must live in a blare of pleasure. He had friends, and people who were afraid of him.

She saw the golden glitter of the place where Pete was to take her. It would be an entertainment of many hues and many melodies where she was afraid she might appear small and mouse-colored.

Her mother drank whiskey all Friday morning. With lurid face and tossing hair she cursed and destroyed furniture all Friday afternoon. When Maggie came home at half-past six her mother lay asleep amidst the wreck of chairs and a table. Fragments of various household utensils were scattered about the floor. She had vented some phase of drunken fury upon the lambrequin. It lay in a bedraggled heap in the corner.

"Hah," she snorted, sitting up suddenly, "where d' hell yeh been? Why d' hell don' yeh come home earlier? Been loafin' 'round d' streets. Yer gettin' t' be a reg'lar devil."

When Pete arrived Maggie, in a worn black dress, was waiting for him in the midst of a floor strewn with wreckage. The curtain at the window had been pulled by a heavy hand and hung by one tack, dangling to and fro in the draft through the cracks at the sash. The knots of blue ribbons appeared like violated flowers. The fire in the stove had gone out. The displaced lids and open doors showed heaps of sullen grey ashes. The remnants of a meal, ghastly, lay in a corner. Maggie's mother, stretched on the floor, blasphemed and gave her daughter a bad name.

CHAPTER VII

A N ORCHESTRA of yellow silk women and bald-headed men on an elevated stage near the centre of a great green-hued hall, played a popular waltz. The place was crowded with people grouped about little tables. A battalion of waiters slid among the throng, carrying trays of beer glasses and making change from the inexhaustible vaults of their trousers pockets. Little boys, in the costumes of French chefs, paraded up and down the irregular aisles vending fancy cakes. There was a low rumble of conversation and a subdued clinking of glasses. Clouds of tobacco smoke rolled and wavered high in air about the dull gilt of the chandeliers.

The vast crowd had an air throughout of having just quitted labor. Men with calloused hands and attired in garments that showed the wear of an endless drudging for a living, smoked their pipes contentedly and spent five, ten, or perhaps fifteen cents for beer. There was a mere sprinkling of men who smoked cigars purchased elsewhere. The great body of the crowd was composed of people who showed that all day they strove with their hands. Quiet Germans, with maybe their wives and two or three children, sat listening to the music, with the expressions of happy cows. An occasional party of sailors from a war-ship, their faces pictures of sturdy health, spent the earlier hours of the evening at the small round tables. Very infrequent tipsy men, swollen with the value of their opinions, engaged their companions in earnest and confidential conversation. In the balcony, and here and there below, shone the impassive faces of women. The nationalities of the Bowery beamed upon the stage from all directions.

Pete aggressively walked up a side aisle and took seats with Maggie at a table beneath the balcony.

"Two beehs!"

Leaning back he regarded with eyes of superiority the scene before them. This attitude affected Maggie strongly. A man who could regard such a sight with indifference must be accustomed to very great things.

It was obvious that Pete had visited this place many times before, and was very familiar with it. A knowledge of this fact made Maggie feel little and new.

He was extremely gracious and attentive. He displayed the consideration of a cultured gentleman who knew what was due.

"Say, what d' hell? Bring d' lady a big glass! What d' hell use is dat pony?"

"Don't be fresh, now," said the waiter, with some warmth, as he departed.

"Ah, git off d' eart'," said Pete, after the other's retreating form.

Maggie perceived that Pete brought forth all his elegance and all his knowledge of high-class customs for her benefit. Her heart warmed as she reflected upon his condescension.

The orchestra of yellow silk women and bald-headed men gave vent to a few bars of anticipatory music and a girl, in a pink dress with short skirts, galloped upon the stage. She smiled upon the throng as if in acknowledgment of a warm welcome, and began to walk to and fro, making profuse gesticulations and singing, in brazen soprano tones, a song, the words of which were inaudible. When she broke into the swift rattling measures of a chorus some half-tipsy men near the stage joined in the rollicking refrain and glasses were pounded rhythmically upon the tables. People leaned forward to watch her and to try to catch the words of the song. When she vanished there were long rollings of applause.

Obedient to more anticipatory bars, she reappeared amidst the half-suppressed cheering of the tipsy men. The orchestra plunged into dance music and the laces of the dancer fluttered and flew in the glare of gas jets. She divulged the fact that she was attired in some half dozen skirts. It was patent that any one of them would have proved adequate for the purpose for which skirts are intended. An occasional man bent forward, intent upon the pink stockings. Maggie wondered at the splendor of the costume and lost herself in calculations of the cost of the silks and laces.

The dancer's smile of enthusiasm was turned for ten minutes upon the faces of her audience. In the finale she fell into some of those grotesque attitudes which were at the time popular among the dancers in the theatres up-town, giving to the Bowery public the diversions of the aristocratic theatre-going public, at reduced rates.

"Say, Pete," said Maggie, leaning forward, "dis is great."

"Sure," said Pete, with proper complacence.

A ventriloquist followed the dancer. He held two fantastic dolls on his knees. He made them sing mournful ditties and say funny things about geography and Ireland.

"Do dose little men talk?" asked Maggie.

"Naw," said Pete, "it's some damn fake. See?"

Two girls, set down on the bills as sisters, came forth and sang a duet which is heard occasionally at concerts given under church auspices. They supplemented it with a dance which of course can never be seen at concerts given under church auspices.

After they had retired, a woman of debatable age sang a negro melody. The chorus necessitated some grotesque waddlings supposed to be an imitation of a plantation darkey, under the influence, probably, of music and the moon. The audience was just enthusiastic enough over it to have her return and sing a sorrowful lay, whose lines told of a mother's love, and a sweetheart who waited and a young man who was lost at sea under harrowing circumstances. From the faces of a score or so in the crowd, the self-contained look faded. Many heads were bent forward with eagerness and sympathy. As the last distressing sentiment of the piece was brought forth, it was greeted by the kind of applause which rings as sincere.

As a final effort, the singer rendered some verses which described a vision of Britain annihilated by America, and Ireland bursting her bonds. A carefully prepared climax was reached in the last line of the last verse, when the singer threw out her arms and cried, "The star-spangled banner." Instantly a great cheer swelled from the throats of this assemblage of the masses, most of them of foreign birth. There was a heavy rumble of booted feet thumping the floor. Eyes gleamed with sudden fire, and calloused hands waved frantically in the air.

After a few moments' rest, the orchestra played noisily, and a small fat man burst out upon the stage. He began to roar a song and stamp back and forth before the foot-lights, wildly waving a silk hat and throwing leers broadcast. He made his face into fantastic grimaces until he looked like a devil on a Japanese kite. The crowd laughed gleefully. His short, fat legs were never still a moment. He shouted and roared and bobbed his shock of red wig until the audience broke out in excited applause.

Pete did not pay much attention to the progress of events upon the stage. He was drinking beer and watching Maggie.

Her cheeks were blushing with excitement and her eyes were glistening. She drew deep breaths of pleasure. No thoughts of the atmosphere of the collar and cuff factory came to her.

With the final crash of the orchestra they jostled their way to the sidewalk in the crowd. Pete took Maggie's arm and pushed a way for her, offering to fight with a man or two. They reached Maggie's home at a late hour and stood for a moment in front of the gruesome doorway.

"Say, Mag," said Pete, "give us a kiss for takin' yeh t' d' show, will yer?"

Maggie laughed, as if startled, and drew away from him.

"Naw, Pete," she said, "dat wasn't in it."

"Ah, what d' hell?" urged Pete.

The girl retreated nervously.

"Ah, what d' hell?" repeated he.

Maggie darted into the hall, and up the stairs. She turned and smiled at him, then disappeared.

Pete walked slowly down the street. He had something of an astonished expression upon his features. He paused under a lamp-post and breathed a low breath of surprise.

"Gawd," he said, "I wonner if I've been played fer a duffer."

CHAPTER VIII

AS THOUGHTS of Pete came to Maggie's mind, she began to have an intense dislike for all of her dresses.

"What d'hell ails yeh? What makes yeh be allus fixin' and fussin'? Good Gawd," her mother would frequently roar at her.

She began to note, with more interest, the well-dressed women she met on the avenues. She envied elegance and soft palms. She craved those adornments of person which she saw every day on the street, conceiving them to be allies of vast importance to women.

Studying faces, she thought many of the women and girls she chanced to meet, smiled with serenity as though forever cherished and watched over by those they loved.

The air in the collar and cuff establishment strangled her. She knew she was gradually and surely shriveling in the hot, stuffy room. The begrimed windows rattled incessantly from the passing of elevated trains. The place was filled with a whirl of noises and odors.

She became lost in thought as she looked at some of the grizzled women in the room, mere mechanical contrivances sewing seams and grinding out, with heads bended over their work, tales of imagined or real girl-hood happiness, or of past drunks, or the baby at home, and unpaid wages. She wondered how long her youth would endure. She began to see the bloom upon her cheeks as something of value.

She imagined herself, in an exasperating future, as a scrawny woman with an eternal grievance. She thought Pete to be a very fastidious person concerning the appearance of women.

She felt that she should love to see somebody entangle their fingers in the oily beard of the fat foreigner who owned the establishment. He was a detestable creature. He wore white socks with low shoes. He sat all day delivering orations, in the depths of a cushioned chair. His pocketbook deprived them of the power of retort.

"What een hell do you sink I pie fife dolla a week for? Play? No, py tamn!"

Maggie was anxious for a friend to whom she could talk about Pete. She would have liked to discuss his admirable mannerisms with a reliable mutual friend. At home, she found her mother often drunk and always raving. It seemed that the world had treated this woman very badly, and she took a deep revenge upon such portions of it as came within her reach. She broke furniture as if she were at last getting her rights. She swelled with virtuous indignation as she carried the lighter articles of household use, one by one, under the shadows of the three gilt balls, where Hebrews chained them with chains of interest.

Jimmie came when he was obliged to by circumstances over which he had no control. His well-trained legs brought him staggering home and put him to bed some nights when he would rather have gone elsewhere.

Swaggering Pete loomed like a golden sun to Maggie. He took her to a dime museum where rows of meek freaks astonished her. She contemplated their deformities with awe and thought them a sort of chosen tribe.

Pete, racking his brains for amusement, discovered the Central Park Menagerie and the Museum of Arts. Sunday afternoons would sometimes find them at these places. Pete did not appear to be particularly interested in what he saw. He stood around looking heavy, while Maggie giggled in glee.

Once at the Menagerie he went into a trance of admiration before the spectacle of a very small monkey threatening to thrash a cageful because one of them had pulled his tail and he had not wheeled about quickly enough to discover who did it. Ever after Pete knew that monkey by sight and winked at him, trying to induce him to fight with other and larger monkeys.

At the Museum, Maggie said, "Dis is outa sight."

"Oh hell," said Pete, "wait till next summer an' I'll take yehs to a picnic."

While the girl wandered in the vaulted rooms, Pete occupied himself in returning stony stare for stony stare, the appalling scrutiny of the watch-dogs of the treasures. Occasionally he would remark in loud tones: "Dat jay has got glass eyes," and sentences of the sort. When he tired of this amusement he would go to the mummies and moralize over them.

Usually he submitted with silent dignity to all that he had to go through, but, at times, he was goaded into comment.

"What d' hell," he demanded once. "Look at all dese little jugs! Hundred jugs in a row! Ten rows in a case an' 'bout a t'ousand cases! What d' blazes use is dem?"

In the evenings of week days he often took her to see plays in which the dazzling heroine was rescued from the palatial home of her treacherous guardian by the hero with the beautiful sentiments. The latter spent most of his time out at soak in pale-green snow storms, busy with a nickel-plated revolver, rescuing aged strangers from villains.

Maggie lost herself in sympathy with the wanderers swooning in snow storms beneath happy-hued church windows, while a choir within sang "Joy to the World." To Maggie and the rest of the audience this was transcendental realism. Joy always within, and they, like the actor, inevitably without. Viewing it, they hugged themselves in ecstatic pity of their imagined or real condition.

The girl thought the arrogance and granite-heartedness of the magnate of the play was very accurately drawn. She echoed the maledictions that the occupants of the gallery showered on this individual when his lines compelled him to expose his extreme selfishness.

Shady persons in the audience revolted from the pictured villainy of the drama. With untiring zeal they hissed vice and applauded virtue. Unmistakably bad men evinced an apparently sincere admiration for virtue. The loud gallery was overwhelmingly with the unfortunate and the oppressed. They encouraged the struggling hero with cries, and jeered the villain, hooting and calling attention to his whiskers. When anybody died in the pale-green snow storms, the gallery mourned. They sought out the painted misery and hugged it as akin.

In the hero's erratic march from poverty in the first act, to wealth and triumph in the final one, in which he forgives all the enemies that he has left, he was assisted by the gallery, which applauded his generous and noble sentiments and confounded the speeches of his opponents by making irrelevant but very sharp remarks. Those actors who were cursed with the parts of villains were confronted at every turn by the gallery. If one of them rendered lines containing the most subtile distinctions between right and wrong, the gallery was immediately aware that the actor meant wickedness, and denounced him accordingly.

The last act was a triumph for the hero, poor and of the masses, the representative of the audience, over the villain and the rich man, his pockets stuffed with bonds, his heart packed with tyrannical purposes, imperturbable amid suffering.

Maggie always departed with raised spirits from these melodramas. She rejoiced at the way in which the poor and virtuous eventually overcame the wealthy and wicked. The theatre made her think. She wondered if the culture and refinement she had seen imitated, perhaps grotesquely, by the heroine on the stage, could be acquired by a girl who lived in a tenement house and worked in a shirt factory.

CHAPTER IX

A GROUP of urchins were intent upon the side door of a saloon. Expectancy gleamed from their eyes. They were twisting their fingers in excitement.

"Here she comes," yelled one of them suddenly.

The group of urchins burst instantly asunder and its individual fragments were spread in a wide, respectable half-circle about the point of interest. The saloon door opened with a crash, and the figure of a woman appeared upon the threshold. Her grey hair fell in knotted masses about her shoulders. Her face was crimsoned and wet with perspiration. Her eyes had a rolling glare.

"Not a damn cent more of me money will yehs ever get—not a damn cent. I spent me money here fer t'ree years an' now yehs tells me yeh'll sell me no more stuff! T' hell wid yeh, Johnnie Murckre! 'Disturbance?' Disturbance be damned! T' hell wid yeh, Johnnie——"

The door received a kick of exasperation from within and the woman lurched heavily out on the sidewalk.

The gamins in the half-circle became violently agitated. They began to dance about and hoot and yell and jeer. Wide dirty grins spread over each face.

The woman made a furious dash at a particularly outrageous cluster of little boys. They laughed delightedly and scampered off a short distance, calling out over their shoulders to her. She stood tottering on the curb-stone and thundered at them.

"Yeh devil's kids," she howled, shaking her fists. The little boys whooped in glee. As she started up the street they fell in behind and marched uproariously. Occasionally she wheeled about and made charges on them. They ran nimbly out of reach and taunted her.

In the frame of a gruesome doorway she stood for a moment cursing them. Her hair straggled, giving her red features a look of insanity. Her great fists quivered as she shook them madly in the air.

The urchins made terrific noises until she turned and disappeared. Then they filed off quietly in the way they had come.

The woman floundered about in the lower hall of the tenement house and finally stumbled up the stairs. On an upper hall a door was opened and a collection of heads peered curiously out, watching her. With a wrathful snort the woman confronted the door, but it was slammed hastily in her face and the key was turned.

She stood for a few minutes, delivering a frenzied challenge at the panels.

"Come out in d' hall, Mary Murphy, damn yeh, if yehs want a scrap. Come ahn, yeh overgrown terrier, come ahn."

She began to kick the door. She shrilly defied the universe to appear and do battle. Her cursing trebles brought heads from all doors save the one she threatened. Her eyes glared in every direction. The air was full of her tossing fists.

"Come ahn, d' hull damn gang of yehs, come ahn," she roared at the spectators. An oath or two, cat-calls, jeers and bits of facetious advice were given in reply. Missiles clattered about her feet.

"What d' hell's d' matter wid yeh?" said a voice in the gathered gloom, and Jimmie came forward. He carried a tin dinner-pail in his hand and under his arm a truckman's brown apron done in a bundle. "What d' hell's wrong?" he demanded.

"Come out, all of yehs, come out," his mother was howling. "Come ahn an' I'll stamp yer damn brains under me feet."

"Shet yer face, an' come home, yeh damned old fool," roared Jimmie at her. She strided up to him and twirled her fingers in his face. Her eyes were darting flames of unreasoning rage and her frame trembled with eagerness for a fight.

"T' hell wid yehs! An' who d' hell are yehs? I ain't givin' a snap of me fingers fer yehs," she bawled at him. She turned her huge back in tremendous disdain and climbed the stairs to the next floor.

Jimmie followed, cursing blackly. At the top of the flight he seized his mother's arm and started to drag her toward the door of their room.

"Come home, damn yeh," he gritted between his teeth.

"Take yer hands off me! Take yer hands off me!" shrieked his mother.

She raised her arm and whirled her great fist at her son's face. Jimmie dodged his head and the blow struck him in the back of the neck. "Damn yeh," he gritted again. He threw out his left hand and writhed his fingers about her middle arm. The mother and the son began to sway and struggle like gladiators.

"Whoop!" said the Rum Alley tenement house. The hall filled with interested spectators.

"Hi, ol' lady, dat was a dandy!"

"T'ree t' one on d' red!"

"Ah, quit yer damn scrappin'!"

The door of the Johnson home opened and Maggie looked out. Jimmie made a supreme cursing effort and hurled his mother into the room. He quickly followed and closed the door. The Rum Alley tenement swore disappointedly and retired.

The mother slowly gathered herself up from the floor. Her eyes glittered menacingly upon her children.

"Here, now," said Jimmie, "we've had enough of dis. Sit down, an' don' make no trouble."

He grasped her arm, and twisting it, forced her into a creaking chair.

"Keep yer hands off me," roared his mother again.

"Damn yer ol' hide," yelled Jimmie, madly. Maggie shrieked and ran into the other room. To her there came the sound of a storm of crashes and curses. There was a great final thump and Jimmie's voice cried: "Dere, damn yeh, stay still." Maggie opened the door now, and went warily out. "Oh, Jimmie!"

He was leaning against the wall and swearing. Blood stood upon bruises on his knotty fore-arms where they had scraped against the floor or the walls in the scuffle. The mother lay screeching on the floor, the tears running down her furrowed face.

Maggie, standing in the middle of the room, gazed about her. The usual upheaval of the tables and chairs had taken place.

Crockery was strewn broadcast in fragments. The stove had been disturbed on its legs, and now leaned idiotically to one side. A pail had been upset and water spread in all directions.

The door opened and Pete appeared. He shrugged his shoulders. "Oh, Gawd," he observed.

He walked over to Maggie and whispered in her ear. "Ah, what d' hell, Mag? Come ahn and we'll have a hell of a time."

The mother in the corner upreared her head and shook her tangled locks.

"T' hell wid him and you," she said, glowering at her daughter in the gloom. Her eyes seemed to burn balefully. "Yeh've gone t' d' devil, Mag Johnson, yehs knows yehs have gone t' d' devil. Yer a disgrace t' yer people, damn yeh. An' now, git out an' go ahn wid dat doe-faced jude of yours. Go t' hell wid him, damn yeh, an' a good riddance. Go t' hell an' see how yeh likes it."

Maggie gazed long at her mother.

"Go t' hell now, an' see how yeh likes it. Git out. I won't have sech as yehs in me house! Git out, d'yeh hear! Damn yeh, git out!"

The girl began to tremble.

At this instant Pete came forward. "Oh, what d' hell, Mag, see," whispered he softly in her ear. "Dis all blows over. See? D' ol' woman 'ill be all right in d' mornin'. Come ahn out wid me! We'll have a hell of a time."

The woman on the floor cursed. Jimmie was intent upon his bruised fore-arms. The girl cast a glance about the room filled with a chaotic mass of debris, and at the writhing body of her mother.

"Go t' hell an' good riddance."

Maggie went.

CHAPTER X

JIMMIE had an idea it wasn't common courtesy for a friend to come to one's home and ruin one's sister. But he was not sure how much Pete knew about the rules of politeness.

The following night he returned home from work at rather a late hour in the evening. In passing through the halls he came upon the gnarled and leathery old woman who possessed the music box. She was grinning in the dim light that drifted through dust-stained panes. She beckoned to him with a smudged forefinger.

"Ah, Jimmie, what do yehs t'ink I tumbled to, las' night. It was d' funnies' t'ing I ever saw," she cried, coming close to him and leering. She was trembling with eagerness to tell her tale. "I was by me door las' night when yer sister and her jude feller came in late, oh, very late. An' she, the dear, she was a-cryin' as if her heart would break, she was. It was d' funnies' t'ing I ever saw. An' right out here by me door she asked him did he love her, did he. An' she was a-cryin' as if her heart would break, poor t'ing. An' him, I could see by d' way what he said it dat she had been askin' orften, he says: 'Oh, hell, yes,' he says, says he, 'Oh, hell, yes.'"

Storm-clouds swept over Jimmie's face, but he turned from the leathery old woman and plodded on up stairs.

"Oh, hell, yes," she called after him. She laughed a laugh that was like a prophetic croak. "'Oh, hell, yes,' he says, says he, 'Oh, hell, yes.'"

There was no one in at home. The rooms showed that attempts had been made at tidying them. Parts of the wreckage of the day before had been repaired by an unskilful hand. A chair or two and the table stood uncertainly upon legs. The floor had been newly swept. The blue ribbons had been restored to the curtains, and the lambrequin, with its immense sheaves of yellow wheat and red roses of equal size, had been returned, in a worn and sorry state, to its place at the mantel. Maggie's jacket and hat were gone from the nail behind the door.

Jimmie walked to the window and began to look through the blurred glass. It occurred to him to vaguely wonder, for an instant, if some of the women of his acquaintance had brothers.

Suddenly, however, he began to swear.

"But he was me frien'! I brought 'im here! Dat's d' hell of it!"

He fumed about the room, his anger gradually rising to the furious pitch.

"I'll kill d' jay! Dat's what I'll do! I'll kill d' jay!"

He clutched his hat and sprang toward the door. But it opened and his mother's great form blocked the passage.

"What d' hell's d' matter wid yeh?" exclaimed she, coming into the rooms.

Jimmie gave vent to a sardonic curse and then laughed heavily.

"Well, Maggie's gone t' d' devil! Dat's what! See?"

"Eh?" said his mother.

"Maggie's gone t' d' devil! Are yehs deaf?" roared Jimmie, impatiently.

"D' hell she has," murmured the mother, astounded.

Jimmie grunted, and then began to stare out at the window. His mother sat down in a chair, but a moment later sprang erect and delivered a maddened whirl of oaths. Her son turned to look at her as she reeled and swayed in the middle of the room, her fierce face convulsed with passion, her blotched arms raised high in imprecation.

"May Gawd curse her forever," she shrieked. "May she eat nothin' but stones and d' dirt in d' street. May she sleep in d' gutter an' never see d' sun shine again. D' damn——"

"Here, now," said her son. "Take a drop on yerself, an' quit dat."

The mother raised lamenting eyes to the ceiling.

"She's d' devil's own chil', Jimmie," she whispered. "Ah, who would t'ink such a bad girl could grow up in our fambly, Jimmie, me son. Many d' hour I've spent in talk wid dat girl an' tol' her if she ever went on d' streets I'd see her damned. An' after all her bringin' up an' what I tol' her and talked wid her, she goes t' d' bad, like a duck t' water."

The tears rolled down her furrowed face. Her hands trembled.

"An' den when dat Sadie MacMallister next door to us was sent t' d' devil by dat feller what worked in d' soap-factory, didn't I tell our Mag dat if she——"

"Ah, dat's anudder story," interrupted the brother. "Of course, dat Sadie was nice an' all dat—but—see—it ain't dessame as if —well, Maggie was diff'ent—see—she was diff'ent."

He was trying to formulate a theory that he had always unconsciously held, that all sisters, excepting his own, could advisedly be ruined.

He suddenly broke out again. "I'll go t'ump hell out a d' mug what done her d' harm. I'll kill 'im! He t'inks he kin scrap, but when he gits me a-chasin' 'im he'll fin' out where he's wrong, d' damned duffer. I'll wipe up d' street wid 'im."

In a fury he plunged out of the doorway. As he vanished the mother raised her head and lifted both hands, entreating.

"May Gawd curse her forever," she cried.

In the darkness of the hallway Jimmie discerned a knot of women talking volubly. When he strode by they paid no attention to him.

"She allus was a bold thing," he heard one of them cry in an eager voice. "Dere wasn't a feller come t' d' house but she'd try t' mash 'im. My Annie says d' shameless t'ing tried t' ketch her feller, her own feller, what we useter know his fader."

"I could a' tol' yehs dis two years ago," said a woman, in a key of triumph. "Yessir, it was over two years ago dat I says t' my ol' man, I says, 'Dat Johnson girl ain't straight,' I says. 'Oh, hell," he says. 'Oh, hell.' 'Dat's all right,' I says, 'but I know what I knows,' I says, 'an' it 'ill come out later. You wait an' see,' I says, 'you see.'"

"Anybody what had eyes could see dat dere was somethin' wrong wid dat girl. I didn't like her actions."

On the street Jimmie met a friend. "What d' hell?" asked the latter.

Jimmie explained. "An' I'll t'ump 'im till he can't stand."

"Oh, what d' hell," said the friend. "What's d' use! Yeh'll git pulled in! Everybody 'ill be onto it! An' ten plunks! Gee!"

Jimmie was determined. "He t'inks he kin scrap, but he'll fin' out diff'ent."

"Gee!" remonstrated the friend. "What d' hell?"

CHAPTER XI

O N A corner a glass-fronted building shed a yellow glare upon the pavements. The open mouth of a saloon called seductively to passengers to enter and annihilate sorrow or create rage.

The interior of the place was papered in olive and bronze tints of imitation leather. A shining bar of counterfeit massiveness extended down the side of the room. Behind it a great mahogany-imitation sideboard reached the ceiling. Upon its shelves rested pyramids of shimmering glasses that were never disturbed. Mirrors set in the face of the sideboard multiplied them. Lemons, oranges and paper napkins, arranged with mathematical precision, sat among the glasses. Many-hued decanters of liquor perched at regular intervals on the lower shelves. A nickel-plated cash register occupied a place in the exact centre of the general effect. The elementary senses of it all seemed to be opulence and geometrical accuracy.

Across from the bar a smaller counter held a collection of plates upon which swarmed frayed fragments of crackers, slices of boiled ham, dishevelled bits of cheese, and pickles swimming in vinegar. An odor of grasping, begrimed hands and munching mouths pervaded all.

Pete, in a white jacket, was behind the bar bending expectantly toward a quiet stranger. "A beeh," said the man. Pete drew a foam-topped glassful and set it dripping upon the bar.

At this moment the light bamboo doors at the entrance swung open and crashed against the wall. Jimmie and a companion entered. They swaggered unsteadily but belligerently toward the bar and looked at Pete with bleared and blinking eyes.

"Gin," said Jimmie.

"Gin," said the companion.

Pete slid a bottle and two glasses along the bar. He bended his head sideways as he assiduously polished away with a napkin at the gleaming wood. He wore a look of watchfulness.

Jimmie and his companion kept their eyes upon the bartender and conversed loudly in tones of contempt.

"He's a dindy masher, ain't he, by Gawd?" laughed Jimmie.

"Oh, hell, yes," said the companion, sneering. "He's great, he is. Git onto d' mug on d' blokie. Dat's enough to make a feller turn hand-springs in 'is sleep."

The quiet stranger moved himself and his glass a trifle further away and maintained an attitude of obliviousness.

"Gee! ain't he hot stuff!"

"Git onto his shape! Great Gawd!"

"Hey," cried Jimmie, in tones of command. Pete came along slowly, with a sullen dropping of the under lip.

"Well," he growled, "what's eatin' yehs?"

"Gin," said Jimmie.

"Gin," said the companion.

As Pete confronted them with the bottle and the glasses, they laughed in his face. Jimmie's companion, evidently overcome with merriment, pointed a grimy forefinger in Pete's direction.

"Say, Jimmie," demanded he, "what d' hell is dat behind d' bar?"

"Damned if I knows," replied Jimmie. They laughed loudly. Pete put down a bottle with a bang and turned a formidable face toward them. He disclosed his teeth and his shoulders heaved restlessly.

"You fellers can't guy me," he said. "Drink yer stuff an' git out an' don' make no trouble."

Instantly the laughter faded from the faces of the two men and expressions of offended dignity immediately came.

"Who d' hell has said anyt'ing t' you," cried they in the same breath.

The quiet stranger looked at the door calculatingly.

"Ah, come off," said Pete to the two men. "Don't pick me up for no jay. Drink yer rum an' git out an' don' make no trouble."

"Oh, d' hell," airily cried Jimmie.

"Oh, d' hell," airily repeated his companion.

"We goes when we git ready! See!" continued Jimmie.

"Well," said Pete in a threatening voice, "don' make no trouble."

Jimmie suddenly leaned forward with his head on one side. He snarled like a wild animal.

"Well, what if we does? See?" said he.

Hot blood flushed into Pete's face, and he shot a lurid glance at Jimmie.

"Well, den we'll see who's d' bes' man, you or me," he said.

The quiet stranger moved modestly toward the door.

Jimmie began to swell with valor.

"Don' pick me up fer no tenderfoot. When yeh tackles me yeh tackles one of d' bes' men in d' city. See? I'm a scrapper, I am. Ain't dat right, Billie?"

"Sure, Mike," responded his companion in tones of conviction.

"Oh, hell," said Pete, easily. "Go fall on yerself."

The two men again began to laugh.

"What d' hell is dat talkin'?" cried the companion.

"Damned if I knows," replied Jimmie with exaggerated contempt.

Pete made a furious gesture. "Git outa here now, an' don' make no trouble. See? Youse fellers er lookin' fer a scrap an' it's damn likely yeh'll fin' one if yeh keeps on shootin' off yer mout's. I know yehs! See? I kin lick better men dan yehs ever saw in yer lifes. Dat's right! See? Don' pick me up fer no stuff er yeh might be jolted out in d' street before yeh knows where yeh is. When I comes from behind dis bar, I t'rows yehs bote inteh d' street. See?"

"Oh, hell," cried the two men in chorus.

The glare of a panther came into Pete's eyes. "Dat's what I said! Unnerstan'?"

He came through a passage at the end of the bar and swelled down upon the two men. They stepped promptly forward and crowded close to him.

They bristled like three roosters. They moved their heads pugnaciously and kept their shoulders braced. The nervous muscles about each mouth twitched with a forced smile of mockery.

"Well, what d' hell yer goin' t' do?" gritted Jimmie.

Pete stepped warily back, waving his hands before him to keep the men from coming too near.

"Well, what d' hell yer goin' t' do?" repeated Jimmie's ally. They kept close to him, taunting and leering. They strove to make him attempt the initial blow.

"Keep back now! Don' crowd me," ominously said Pete.

Again they chorused in contempt. "Oh, hell!"

In a small, tossing group, the three men edged for positions like frigates contemplating battle.

"Well, why d' hell don' yeh try t' t'row us out?" cried Jimmie and his ally with copious sneers.

The bravery of bull-dogs sat upon the faces of the men. Their clenched fists moved like eager weapons.

The allied two jostled the bartender's elbows, glaring at him with feverish eyes and forcing him toward the wall.

Suddenly Pete swore furiously. The flash of action gleamed from his eyes. He threw back his arm and aimed a tremendous, lightning-like blow at Jimmie's face. His foot swung a step forward and the weight of his body was behind his fist. Jimmie ducked his head, Bowery-like, with the quickness of a cat. The fierce, answering blows of Jimmie and his ally crushed on Pete's bowed head.

The quiet stranger vanished.

The arms of the combatants whirled in the air like flails. The faces of the men, at first flushed to flame-colored anger, now began to fade to the pallor of warriors in the blood and heat of a battle. Their lips curled back and stretched tightly over the gums in ghoul-like grins. Through their white, gripped teeth struggled hoarse whisperings of oaths. Their eyes glittered with murderous fire.

Each head was huddled between its owner's shoulders, and arms were swinging with marvelous rapidity. Feet scraped to and fro with a loud scratching sound upon the sanded floor. Blows left crimson blotches upon pale skin. The curses of the first quarter minute of the fight died away. The breaths of the fighters came wheezingly from their lips and the three chests were straining and heaving. Pete at intervals gave vent to low, labored hisses, that sounded like a desire to kill. Jimmie's ally gibbered at times like a wounded maniac. Jimmie was silent, fighting with the face of a sacrificial priest. The rage of fear shone in all their eyes and their blood-colored fists whirled.

At a critical moment a blow from Pete's hand struck the ally and he crashed to the floor. He wriggled instantly to his feet and grasping the quiet stranger's beer glass from the bar, hurled it at Pete's head.

High on the wall it burst like a bomb, shivering fragments flying in all directions. Then missiles came to every man's hand. The place had heretofore appeared free of things to throw, but suddenly glasses and bottles went singing through the air. They were thrown point-blank at bobbing heads. The pyramid of shimmering glasses, that had never been disturbed, changed to cascades as heavy bottles were flung into them. Mirrors splintered to nothing.

The three frothing creatures on the floor buried themselves in a frenzy for blood. There followed in the wake of missiles and fists some unknown prayers, perhaps for death.

The quiet stranger had sprawled very pyrotechnically out on the sidewalk. A laugh ran up and down the avenue for the half of a block.

"Dey've t'rowed a bloke inteh d' street."

People heard the sound of breaking glass and shuffling feet within the saloon and came running. A small group, bending down to look under the bamboo doors, and watching the fall of glass and three pairs of violent legs, changed in a moment to a crowd.

A policeman came charging down the sidewalk and bounced through the doors into the saloon. The crowd bended and surged in absorbing anxiety to see.

Jimmie caught first sight of the on-coming interruption. On his feet he had the same regard for a policeman that, when on his truck, he had for a fire engine. He howled and ran for the side door.

The officer made a terrific advance, club in hand. One comprehensive sweep of the long night stick threw the ally to the floor and forced Pete to a corner. With his disengaged hand he made a furious effort at Jimmie's coat-tails. Then he regained his balance and paused.

"Well, well, you are a pair of pictures. What in hell have yeh been up to?"

Jimmie, with his face drenched in blood, escaped up a side

street, pursued a short distance by some of the more law-loving, or excited individuals of the crowd.

Later, from a safe dark corner, he saw the policeman, the ally and the bartender emerge from the saloon. Pete locked the doors and then followed up the avenue in the rear of the crowd-encompassed policeman and his charge.

At first Jimmie, with his heart throbbing at battle heat, started to go desperately to the rescue of his friend, but he halted.

"Ah, what d' hell?" he demanded of himself.

CHAPTER XII

IN A hall of irregular shape sat Pete and Maggie drinking beer. A submissive orchestra dictated to by a spectacled man with frowsy hair and in soiled evening dress, industriously followed the bobs of his head and the waves of his baton. A ballad singer, in a gown of flaming scarlet, sang in the inevitable voice of brass. When she vanished, men seated at the tables near the front applauded loudly, pounding the polished wood with their beer glasses. She returned attired in less gown, and sang again. She received another enthusiastic encore. She reappeared in still less gown and danced. The deafening rumble of glasses and clapping of hands that followed her exit indicated an overwhelming desire to have her come on for the fourth time, but the curiosity of the audience was not gratified.

Maggie was pale. From her eyes had been plucked all look of self-reliance. She leaned with a dependent air toward her companion. She was timid, as if fearing his anger or displeasure. She seemed to beseech tenderness of him.

Pete's air of distinguished valor had grown upon him until it threatened to reach stupendous dimensions. He was infinitely gracious to the girl. It was apparent to her that his condescension was a marvel.

He could appear to strut even while sitting still and he showed that he was a lion of lordly characteristics by the air with which he spat.

With Maggie gazing at him wonderingly, he took pride in commanding the waiters who were, however, indifferent or deaf.

"Hi, you, git a russle on yehs! What d' hell yehs lookin' at? Two more beehs, d'yeh hear?"

He leaned back and critically regarded the person of a girl with a straw-colored wig who upon the stage was flinging her heels about in somewhat awkward imitation of a well-known danseuse.

At times Maggie told Pete long confidential tales of her former home life, dwelling upon the escapades of the other members of the family and the difficulties she had had to combat in order to obtain a degree of comfort. He responded in the accents of philanthropy. He pressed her arm with an air of reassuring proprietorship.

"Dey was damn jays," he said, denouncing the mother and brother.

The sound of the music which, through the efforts of the frowsy-headed leader, drifted to her ears in the smoke-filled atmosphere, made the girl dream. She thought of her former Rum Alley environment and turned to regard Pete's strong protecting fists. She thought of a collar and cuff manufactory and the eternal moan of the proprietor: "What een hale do you sink I pie fife dolla a week for? Play? No, py tamn!" She contemplated Pete's man-subduing eyes and noted that wealth and prosperity was indicated by his clothes. She imagined a future, rose-tinted, because of its distance from all that she had experienced before.

As to the present she perceived only vague reasons to be miserable. Her life was Pete's and she considered him worthy of the charge. She would be disturbed by no particular apprehensions, so long as Pete adored her as he now said he did. She did not feel like a bad woman. To her knowledge she had never seen any better.

At times men at other tables regarded the girl furtively. Pete. aware of it, nodded at her and grinned. He felt proud.

"Mag, yer a bloomin' good-looker," he remarked, studying her face through the haze. The men made Maggie fear, but she blushed at Pete's words as it became apparent to her that she was the apple of his eye.

Grey-headed men, wonderfully pathetic in their dissipation, stared at her through clouds. Smooth-cheeked boys, some of them with faces of stone and mouths of sin, not nearly so pathetic as the grey heads, tried to find the girl's eyes in the smoke wreaths. Maggie considered she was not what they thought her. She confined her glances to Pete and the stage.

The orchestra played negro melodies and a versatile drummer pounded, whacked, clattered and scratched on a dozen machines to make noise.

Those glances of the men, shot at Maggie from under half-closed lids, made her tremble. She thought them all to be worse men than Pete.

"Come, let's go," she said.

As they went out Maggie perceived two women seated at a table with some men. They were painted and their cheeks had lost their roundness. As she passed them the girl, with a shrinking movement, drew back her skirts.

CHAPTER XIII

JIMMIE did not return home for a number of days after the fight with Pete in the saloon. When he did, he approached with extreme caution.

He found his mother raving. Maggie had not returned home. The parent continually wondered how her daughter could come to such a pass. She had never considered Maggie as a pearl dropped unstained into Rum Alley from Heaven, but she could not conceive how it was possible for her daughter to fall so low as to bring disgrace upon her family. She was terrific in denunciation of the girl's wickedness.

The fact that the neighbors talked of it, maddened her. When women came in, and in the course of their conversation casually asked, "Where's Maggie dese days?" the mother shook her fuzzy head at them and appalled them with curses. Cunning hints inviting confidence she rebuffed with violence.

"An' wid all d' bringin' up she had, how could she?" moaningly she asked of her son. "Wid all d' talkin' wid her I did an' d' t'ings I tol' her to remember? When a girl is bringed up d' way I bringed up Maggie, how kin she go t' d' devil?"

Jimmie was transfixed by these questions. He could not conceive how under the circumstances his mother's daughter and his sister could have been so wicked.

His mother took a drink from a bottle that sat on the table. She continued her lament.

"She had a bad heart, dat girl did, Jimmie. She was wicked t' d' heart an' we never knowed it."

Jimmie nodded, admitting the fact.

"We lived in d' same house wid her an' I brought her up an' we never knowed how bad she was."

Jimmie nodded again.

"Wid a home like dis an' a mudder like me, she went t' d' bad," cried the mother, raising her eyes.

One day Jimmie came home, sat down in a chair and began to wriggle about with a new and strange nervousness. At last he spoke shamefacedly.

"Well, look-a-here, dis t'ing queers us! See? We're queered! An' maybe it 'ud be better if I—well, I t'ink I kin look 'er up an'—maybe it 'ud be better if I fetched her home an'——"

The mother started from her chair and broke forth into a storm of passionate anger.

"What! Let 'er come an' sleep under d' same roof wid her mudder agin! Oh, yes, I will, won't I? Sure? Shame on yehs, Jimmie Johnson, fer sayin' such a t'ing t' yer own mudder—t' yer own mudder! Little did I t'ink when yehs was a babby playin' about me feet dat ye'd grow up t' say sech a t'ing t' yer mudder—yer own mudder. I never t'aut——"

Sobs choked her and interrupted her reproaches.

"Dere ain't nottin' t' raise sech hell about," said Jimmie. "I on'y says it 'ud be better if we keep dis t'ing dark, see? It queers us! See?"

His mother laughed a laugh that seemed to ring through the city and be echoed and re-echoed by countless other laughs. "Oh, yes, I will, won't I! Sure!"

"Well, yeh must take me for a damn fool," said Jimmie, indignant at his mother for mocking him. "I didn't say we'd make 'er inteh a little tin angel, ner nottin', but d' way it is now she can queer us! Don' che see?"

"Aye, she'll git tired of d' life atter a while an' den she'll wanna be a-comin' home, won' she, d' beast! I'll let 'er in den, won' I?"

"Well, I didn' mean none of dis prod'gal bus'ness anyway," explained Jimmie.

"It wa'n't no prod'gal dauter, yeh damn fool," said the mother. "It was prod'gal son, anyhow."

"I know dat," said Jimmie.

For a time they sat in silence. The mother's eyes gloated on the scene which her imagination called before her. Her lips were set in a vindictive smile.

"Aye, she'll cry, won' she, an' carry on, an' tell how Pete, or some odder feller, beats 'er an' she'll say she's sorry an' all dat an' she ain't happy, she ain't, and she wants to come home agin, she does."

With grim humor the mother imitated the possible wailing notes of the daughter's voice.

"Den I'll take 'er in, won't I? She kin cry 'er two eyes out on d' stones of d' street before I'll dirty d' place wid her. She abused an' ill-treated her own mudder—her own mudder what loved her an' she'll never git anodder chance dis side of hell."

Jimmie thought he had a great idea of women's frailty, but he could not understand why any of his kin should be victims.

"Damn her," he fervidly said.

Again he wondered vaguely if some of the women of his acquaintance had brothers. Nevertheless, his mind did not for an instant confuse himself with those brothers nor his sister with theirs. After the mother had, with great difficulty, suppressed the neighbors, she went among them and proclaimed her grief. "May Gawd forgive dat girl," was her continual cry. To attentive ears she recited the whole length and breadth of her woes.

"I bringed 'er up d' way a dauter oughta be bringed up, an' dis is how she served me! She went t' d' devil d' first chance she got! May Gawd forgive her."

When arrested for drunkenness she used the story of her daughter's downfall with telling effect upon the police-justices. Finally one of them said to her, peering down over his spectacles: "Mary, the records of this and other courts show that you are the mother of forty-two daughters who have been ruined. The case is unparalleled in the annals of this court, and this court thinks——"

The mother went through life shedding large tears of sorrow. Her red face was a picture of agony.

Of course Jimmie publicly damned his sister that he might appear on a higher social plane. But, arguing with himself, stumbling about in ways that he knew not, he, once, almost came to a conclusion that his sister would have been more firmly good had she better known why. However, he felt that he could not hold such a view. He threw it hastily aside.

CHAPTER XIV

IN A hilarious hall there were twenty-eight tables and twenty-eight women and a crowd of smoking men. Valiant noise was made on a stage at the end of the hall by an orchestra composed of men who looked as if they had just happened in. Soiled waiters ran to and fro, swooping down like hawks on the unwary in the throng; clattering along the aisles with trays covered with glasses; stumbling over women's skirts and charging two prices for everything but beer, all with a swiftness that blurred the view of the cocoanut palms and dusty monstrosities painted upon the walls of the room. A "bouncer" with an immense load of business upon his hands, plunged about in the crowd, dragging bashful strangers to prominent chairs, ordering waiters here and there and quarreling furiously with men who wanted to sing with the orchestra.

The usual smoke cloud was present, but so dense that heads and arms seemed entangled in it. The rumble of conversation was replaced by a roar. Plenteous oaths heaved through the air. The room rang with the shrill voices of women bubbling over with drink-laughter. The chief element in the music of the orchestra was speed. The musicians played in intent fury. A woman was singing and smiling upon the stage, but no one took notice of her. The rate at which the piano, cornet and violins were going, seemed to impart wildness to the half-drunken crowd. Beer glasses were emptied at a gulp and conversation became a rapid chatter. The smoke eddied and swirled like a shadowy river hurrying toward some unseen falls. Pete and Maggie entered the hall and took chairs at a table near the door. The woman who was seated there made an attempt to occupy Pete's attention and, failing, went away.

Three weeks had passed since the girl had left home. The air of spaniel-like dependence had been magnified and showed its direct effect in the peculiar off-handedness and ease of Pete's ways toward her.

She followed Pete's eyes with hers, anticipating with smiles gracious looks from him.

A woman of brilliance and audacity, accompanied by a mere boy, came into the place and took seats near them.

At once Pete sprang to his feet, his face beaming with glad surprise.

"By Gawd, dere's Nellie," he cried.

He went over to the table and held out an eager hand to the woman.

"Why, hello, Pete, me boy, how are you," said she, giving him her fingers.

Maggie took instant note of the woman. She perceived that her black dress fitted her to perfection. Her linen collar and cuffs were spotless. Tan gloves were stretched over her well-shaped hands. A hat of a prevailing fashion perched jauntily upon her dark hair. She wore no jewelry and was painted with no apparent paint. She looked clear-eyed through the stares of the men.

"Sit down, and call your lady-friend over," she said to Pete. At his beckoning Maggie came and sat between Pete and the mere boy.

"I thought yeh were gone away fer good," began Pete, at once. "When did yeh git back? How did dat Buff'lo bus'ness turn out?"

The woman shrugged her shoulders. "Well, he didn't have as many stamps as he tried to make out, so I shook him, that's all."

"Well, I'm glad t' see yehs back in d' city," said Pete, with gallantry.

He and the woman entered into a long conversation, exchanging reminiscences of days together. Maggie sat still, unable to formulate an intelligent sentence as her addition to the conversation and painfully aware of it.

She saw Pete's eyes sparkle as he gazed upon the handsome stranger. He listened smilingly to all she said. The woman was familiar with all his affairs, asked him about mutual friends, and knew the amount of his salary.

She paid no attention to Maggie, looking toward her once or twice and apparently seeing the wall beyond.

The mere boy was sulky. In the beginning he had welcomed the additions with acclamations.

"Let's all have a drink! What'll you take, Nell? And you, Miss What's-your-name. Have a drink, Mr. ——, you, I mean."

He had shown a sprightly desire to do the talking for the company and tell all about his family. In a loud voice he declaimed on various topics. He assumed a patronizing air toward Pete. As Maggie was silent, he paid no attention to her. He made a great show of lavishing wealth upon the woman of brilliance and audacity.

"Do keep still, Freddie! You talk like a clock," said the woman to him. She turned away and devoted her attention to Pete.

"We'll have many a good time together again, eh?"

"Sure, Mike," said Pete, enthusiastic at once.

"Say," whispered she, leaning forward, "let's go over to Billie's and have a heluva time."

"Well, it's dis way! See?" said Pete. "I got dis lady frien' here."

"Oh, t' hell with her," argued the woman.

Pete appeared disturbed.

"All right," said she, nodding her head at him. "All right for you! We'll see the next time you ask me to go anywheres with you."

Pete squirmed.

"Say," he said, beseechingly, "come wid me a minit an' I'll tell yer why."

The woman waved her hand.

"Oh, that's all right, you needn't explain, you know. You wouldn't come merely because you wouldn't come, that's all."

To Pete's visible distress she turned to the mere boy, bringing him speedily out of a terrific rage. He had been debating whether it would be the part of a man to pick a quarrel with Pete, or would he be justified in striking him savagely with his beer glass without warning. But he recovered himself when the woman turned to renew her smilings. He beamed upon her with an expression that was somewhat tipsy and inexpressibly tender.

"Say, shake that Bowery jay," requested he, in a loud whisper.

"Freddie, you are so funny," she replied.

Pete reached forward and touched the woman on the arm.

"Come out a minit while I tells yeh why I can't go wid yer. Yer doin' me dirt, Nell! I never t'aut ye'd do me dirt, Nell. Come on, will yer?" He spoke in tones of injury.

"Why, I don't see why I should be interested in your explanations," said the woman, with a coldness that seemed to reduce Pete to a pulp.

His eyes pleaded with her. "Come out a minit while I tells yeh. On d' level, now."

The woman nodded slightly at Maggie and the mere boy, saying, " 'Scuse me."

The mere boy interrupted his loving smile and turned a shriveling glare upon Pete. His boyish countenance flushed and he spoke, in a whine, to the woman:

"Oh, I say, Nellie, this ain't a square deal, you know. You aren't goin' to leave me and go off with that duffer, are you? I should think——"

"Why, you dear boy, of course I'm not," cried the woman, affectionately. She bended over and whispered in his ear. He smiled again and settled in his chair as if resolved to wait patiently.

As the woman walked down between the rows of tables, Pete was at her shoulder talking earnestly, apparently in explanation. The woman waved her hands with studied airs of indifference. The doors swung behind them, leaving Maggie and the mere boy seated at the table.

Maggie was dazed. She could dimly perceive that something stupendous had happened. She wondered why Pete saw fit to remonstrate with the woman, pleading for forgiveness with his eyes. She thought she noted an air of submission about her leonine Pete. She was astounded.

The mere boy occupied himself with cock-tails and a cigar. He was tranquilly silent for half an hour. Then he bestirred himself and spoke.

"Well," he said sighing, "I knew this was the way it would be. They got cold feet." There was another stillness. The mere boy seemed to be musing.

"She was pulling m' leg. That's the whole amount of it," he said, suddenly. "It's a bloomin' shame the way that girl does. Why, I've spent over two dollars in drinks to-night. And she goes off with that plug-ugly who looks as if he had been hit in the face with a coin-die. I call it rocky treatment for a fellah like me. Here, waiter, bring me a cock-tail and make it damned strong."

Maggie made no reply. She was watching the doors. "It's a

mean piece of business," complained the mere boy. He explained to her how amazing it was that anybody should treat him in such a manner. "But I'll get square with her, you bet. She won't get far ahead of yours truly, you know," he added, winking. "I'll tell her plainly that it was bloomin' mean business. And she won't come it over me with any of her 'now-Freddie-dears.' She thinks my name is Freddie, you know, but of course it ain't. I always tell these people some name like that, because if they got onto your right name they might use it sometime. Understand? Oh, they don't fool me much."

Maggie was paying no attention, being intent upon the doors. The mere boy relapsed into a period of gloom, during which he exterminated a number of cock-tails with a determined air, as if replying defiantly to fate. He occasionally broke forth into sentences composed of invectives joined together in a long chain.

The girl was still staring at the doors. After a time the mere boy began to see cobwebs just in front of his nose. He spurred himself into being agreeable and insisted upon her having a charlotte-russe and a glass of beer.

"They's gone," he remarked, "they's gone." He looked at her through the smoke wreaths. "Shay, lil' girl, we mightish well make bes' of it. You ain't such bad-lookin' girl, y'know. Not half bad. Can't come up to Nell, though. No, can't do it! Well, I should shay not! Nell fine-lookin' girl! F—i—n—ine. You look damn bad longsider her, but by y'self ain't so bad. Have to do anyhow. Nell gone. On'y you left. Not half bad, though."

Maggie stood up.

"I'm going home," she said.

The mere boy started.

"Eh? What? Home," he cried, struck with amazement. "I beg pardon, did hear say home?"

"I'm going home," she repeated.

"Great Gawd, what hav'a struck?" demanded the mere boy of himself, stupefied.

In a semi-comatose state he conducted her on board an uptown car, ostentatiously paid her fare, leered kindly at her through the rear window and fell off the steps.

CHAPTER XV

A FORLORN woman went along a lighted avenue. The street was filled with people desperately bound on missions. An endless crowd darted at the elevated station stairs and the horse cars were thronged with owners of bundles.

The pace of the forlorn woman was slow. She was apparently searching for some one. She loitered near the doors of saloons and watched men emerge from them. She furtively scanned the faces in the rushing stream of pedestrians. Hurrying men, bent on catching some boat or train, jostled her elbows, failing to notice her, their thoughts fixed on distant dinners.

The forlorn woman had a peculiar face. Her smile was no smile. But when in repose her features had a shadowy look that was like a sardonic grin, as if some one had sketched with cruel forefinger indelible lines about her mouth.

Jimmie came strolling up the avenue. The woman encountered him with an aggrieved air.

"Oh, Jimmie, I've been lookin' all over fer yehs——" she began.

Jimmie made an impatient gesture and quickened his pace.

"Ah, don't bodder me! Good Gawd!" he said, with the savageness of a man whose life is pestered.

The woman followed him along the sidewalk in somewhat the manner of a suppliant.

"But, Jimmie," she said, "yehs told me yeh'd——"

Jimmie turned upon her fiercely as if resolved to make a last stand for comfort and peace.

"Say, fer Gawd's sake, Hattie, don' foller me from one end of d' city t' d' odder. Let up, will yehs! Give me a minute's res', can't yehs? Yehs makes me tired, allus taggin' me. See? Ain' yehs got no sense? Do yehs want people t' get onto me? Go chase yerself, fer Gawd's sake."

The woman stepped closer and laid her fingers on his arm. "But, look-a-here——"

Jimmie snarled. "Oh, go t' hell."

He darted into the front door of a convenient saloon and a moment later came out into the shadows that surrounded the side door. On the brilliantly lighted avenue he perceived the forlorn woman dodging about like a scout. Jimmie laughed with an air of relief and went away.

When he arrived home he found his mother clamoring. Maggie had returned. She stood shivering beneath the torrent of her mother's wrath.

"Well, I'm damned," said Jimmie in greeting.

His mother, tottering about the room, pointed a quivering forefinger.

"Lookut her, Jimmie, lookut her. Dere's yer sister, boy. Dere's yer sister. Lookut her! Lookut her!"

She screamed at Maggie with scoffing laughter.

The girl stood in the middle of the room. She edged about as if unable to find a place on the floor to put her feet.

"Ha, ha, ha," bellowed the mother. "Dere she stands! Ain' she purty? Lookut her! Ain' she sweet, d' beast? Lookut her! Ha, ha! lookut her!"

She lurched forward and put her red and seamed hands upon her daughter's face. She bended down and peered keenly up into the eyes of the girl.

"Oh, she's jes' dessame as she ever was, ain' she? She's her mudder's putty darlin' yit, ain' she? Lookut her, Jimmie! Come here, fer Gawd's sake, and lookut her."

The loud, tremendous railing of the mother brought the denizens of the Rum Alley tenement to their doors. Women came in the hallways. Children scurried to and fro.

"What's up? Dat Johnson party on anudder tear?"

"Naw! Young Mag's come home!"

"D' hell yeh say?"

Through the open doors curious eyes stared in at Maggie. Children ventured into the room and ogled her, as if they formed the front row at a theatre. Women, without, bended toward each other and whispered, nodding their heads with airs of profound philosophy.

A baby, overcome with curiosity concerning this object at which all were looking, sidled forward and touched her dress, cautiously, as if investigating a red-hot stove. Its mother's voice rang out like a warning trumpet. She rushed forward and grabbed her child, casting a terrible look of indignation at the girl.

Maggie's mother paced to and fro, addressing the doorful of eyes, expounding like a glib showman. Her voice rang through the building.

"Dere she stands," she cried, wheeling suddenly and pointing with dramatic finger. "Dere she stands! Lookut her! Ain' she a dindy? An' she was so good as to come home t' her mudder, she was! Ain' she a beaut'? Ain' she a dindy? Fer Gawd's sake!"

The jeering cries ended in another burst of shrill laughter.

The girl seemed to awaken. "Jimmie——"

He drew hastily back from her.

"Well, now, yer a hell of a t'ing, ain' yeh?" he said, his lips curling in scorn. Radiant virtue sat upon his brow and his repelling hands expressed horror of contamination.

Maggie turned and went.

The crowd at the door fell back precipitately. A baby falling down in front of the door, wrenched a scream like that of a wounded animal from its mother. Another woman sprang forward and picked it up, with a chivalrous air, as if rescuing a human being from an on-coming express train.

As the girl passed down through the hall, she went before open doors framing more eyes strangely microscopic, and sending broad beams of inquisitive light into the darkness of her path. On the second floor she met the gnarled old woman who possessed the music box.

"So," she cried, " 'ere yehs are back again, are yehs? An' dey've kicked yehs out? Well, come in an' stay wid me t'-night. I ain' got no moral standin'."

From above came an unceasing babble of tongues, over all of which rang the mother's derisive laughter.

CHAPTER XVI

PETE did not consider that he had ruined Maggie. If he had thought that her soul could never smile again, he would have believed the mother and brother, who were pyrotechnic over the affair, to be responsible for it.

Besides, in his world, souls did not insist upon being able to smile. "What d' hell?"

He felt a trifle entangled. It distressed him. Revelations and scenes might bring upon him the wrath of the owner of the saloon, who insisted upon respectability of an advanced type.

"What d' hell do dey wanna raise such a smoke about it fer?" demanded he of himself, disgusted with the attitude of the family. He saw no necessity that people should lose their equilibrium merely because their sister or their daughter had stayed away from home.

Searching about in his mind for possible reasons for their conduct, he came upon the conclusion that Maggie's motives were correct, but that the two others wished to snare him. He felt pursued.

The woman whom he had met in the hilarious hall showed a disposition to ridicule him.

"A little pale thing with no spirit," she said. "Did you note the expression of her eyes? There was something in them about pumpkin pie and virtue. That is a peculiar way the left corner of her mouth has of twitching, isn't it? Dear, dear, Pete, what are you coming to?"

Pete asserted at once that he never was very much interested in the girl. The woman interrupted him, laughing.

"Oh, it's not of the slightest consequence to me, my dear young man. You needn't draw maps for my benefit. Why should I be concerned about it?"

But Pete continued with his explanations. If he was laughed at for his tastes in women, he felt obliged to say that they were only temporary or indifferent ones.

The morning after Maggie had departed from home, Pete stood behind the bar. He was immaculate in white jacket and apron and his hair was plastered over his brow with infinite correctness. No customers were in the place. Pete was twisting his napkined fist slowly in a beer glass, softly whistling to himself and occasionally holding the object of his attention between his eyes and a few weak beams of sunlight that found their way over the thick screens and into the shaded room.

With lingering thoughts of the woman of brilliance and audacity, the bartender raised his head and stared through the varying cracks between the swaying bamboo doors. Suddenly the whistling pucker faded from his lips. He saw Maggie walking slowly past. He gave a great start, fearing for the previously-mentioned eminent respectability of the place.

He threw a swift, nervous glance about him, all at once feeling guilty. No one was in the room.

He went hastily over to the side door. Opening it and looking out, he perceived Maggie standing, as if undecided, on the corner. She was searching the place with her eyes.

As she turned her face toward him Pete beckoned to her hurriedly, intent upon returning with speed to a position behind the bar and to the atmosphere of respectability upon which the proprietor insisted.

Maggie came to him, the anxious look disappearing from her face and a smile wreathing her lips.

"Oh, Pete——" she began brightly.

The bartender made a violent gesture of impatience.

"Oh, my Gawd," cried he, vehemently. "What d' hell do yeh wanna hang aroun' here fer? Do yeh wanna git me inteh trouble?" he demanded with an air of injury.

Astonishment swept over the girl's features. "Why, Pete! yehs tol' me——"

Pete's glance expressed profound irritation. His countenance reddened with the anger of a man whose respectability is being threatened.

"Say, yehs makes me tired. See? What d' hell do yeh wanna tag aroun' atter me fer? Yeh'll do me dirt wid d' ol' man an' dey'll be hell t' pay! If he sees a woman roun' here he'll go crazy an' I'll lose me job! See? Ain' yehs got no sense? Don' be allus bodderin' me. See? Yer brudder come in here an' raised hell an' d' ol' man hada put up fer it! An' now I'm done! See? I'm done."

The girl's eyes stared into his face. "Pete, don't yeh remem——"

"Oh, hell," interrupted Pete, anticipating.

The girl seemed to have a struggle with herself. She was apparently bewildered and could not find speech. Finally she asked in a low voice: "But where kin I go?"

The question exasperated Pete beyond the powers of endurance. It was a direct attempt to give him some responsibility in a matter that did not concern him. In his indignation he volunteered information.

"Oh, go t' hell," cried he. He slammed the door furiously and returned, with an air of relief, to his respectability.

Maggie went away.

She wandered aimlessly for several blocks. She stopped once and asked aloud a question of herself: "Who?"

A man who was passing near her shoulder, humorously took the questioning word as intended for him.

"Eh? What? Who? Nobody! I didn't say anything," he laughingly said, and continued his way.

Soon the girl discovered that if she walked with such apparent aimlessness, some men looked at her with calculating eyes. She quickened her step, frightened. As a protection, she adopted a demeanor of intentness as if going somewhere.

After a time she left rattling avenues and passed between rows of houses with sternness and stolidity stamped upon their features. She hung her head for she felt their eyes grimly upon her.

Suddenly she came upon a stout gentleman in a silk hat and a chaste black coat, whose decorous row of buttons reached from his chin to his knees. The girl had heard of the Grace of God and she decided to approach this man.

His beaming, chubby face was a picture of benevolence and kind-heartedness. His eyes shone good-will.

But as the girl timidly accosted him, he made a convulsive movement and saved his respectability by a vigorous side-step. He did not risk it to save a soul. For how was he to know that there was a soul before him that needed saving?

CHAPTER XVII

UPON a wet evening, several months after the last chapter, two interminable rows of cars, pulled by slipping horses, jangled along a prominent side street. A dozen cabs, with coat-enshrouded drivers, clattered to and fro. Electric lights, whirring softly, shed a blurred radiance. A flower dealer, his feet tapping impatiently, his nose and his wares glistening with rain-drops, stood behind an array of roses and chrysanthemums. Two or three theatres emptied a crowd upon the storm-swept pavements. Men pulled their hats over their eyebrows and raised their collars to their ears. Women shrugged impatient shoulders in their warm cloaks and stopped to arrange their skirts for a walk through the storm. People who had been constrained to comparative silence for two hours burst into a roar of conversation, their hearts still kindling from the glowings of the stage.

The pavements became tossing seas of umbrellas. Men stepped forth to hail cabs or cars, raising their fingers in varied forms of polite request or imperative demand. An endless procession wended toward elevated stations. An atmosphere of pleasure and prosperity seemed to hang over the throng, born, perhaps, of good clothes and of two hours in a place of forgetfulness.

In the mingled light and gloom of an adjacent park, a handful of wet wanderers, in attitudes of chronic dejection, was scattered among the benches.

A girl of the painted cohorts of the city went along the street. She threw changing glances at men who passed her, giving smiling invitations to those of rural or untaught pattern and usually seeming sedately unconscious of the men with a metropolitan seal upon their faces.

Crossing glittering avenues, she went into the throng emerging from the places of forgetfulness. She hurried forward through the crowd as if intent upon reaching a distant home, bending forward in her handsome cloak, daintily lifting her skirts and picking for her well-shod feet the dryer spots upon the pavements.

The restless doors of saloons, clashing to and fro, disclosed animated rows of men before bars and hurrying barkeepers.

A concert hall gave to the street faint sounds of swift, machine-like music, as if a group of phantom musicians were hastening.

A tall young man, smoking a cigarette with a sublime air, strolled near the girl. He had on evening dress, a moustache, a chrysanthemum, and a look of ennui, all of which he kept carefully under his eye. Seeing the girl walk on as if such a young man as he was not in existence, he looked back transfixed with interest. He stared glassily for a moment, but gave a slight convulsive start when he discerned that she was neither new, Parisian, nor theatrical. He wheeled about hastily and turned his stare into the air, like a sailor with a search-light.

A stout gentleman, with pompous and philanthropic whiskers, went stolidly by, the broad of his back sneering at the girl.

A belated man in business clothes, and in haste to catch a car, bounced against her shoulder. "Hi, there, Mary, I beg your pardon! Brace up, old girl." He grasped her arm to steady her, and then was away running down the middle of the street.

The girl walked on out of the realm of restaurants and saloons. She passed more glittering avenues and went into darker blocks than those where the crowd travelled.

A young man in light overcoat and derby hat received a glance shot keenly from the eyes of the girl. He stopped and looked at her, thrusting his hands in his pockets and making a mocking smile curl his lips. "Come, now, old lady," he said, "you don't mean to tell me that you sized me up for a farmer?"

A laboring man marched along with bundles under his arms. To her remarks, he replied, "It's a fine evenin', ain't it?"

She smiled squarely into the face of a boy who was hurrying by with his hands buried in his overcoat pockets, his blond locks bobbing on his youthful temples, and a cheery smile of unconcern upon his lips. He turned his head and smiled back at her, waving his hands.

"Not this eve—some other eve!"

A drunken man, reeling in her pathway, began to roar at her. "I ain' ga no money, dammit," he shouted, in a dismal voice. He lurched on up the street wailing to himself, "Dammit, I ain' ga no money. Damn ba' luck. Ain' ga no more money."

The girl went into gloomy districts near the river, where the tall black factories shut in the street and only occasional broad beams of light fell across the pavements from saloons. In front of one of these places, whence came the sound of a violin vigorously scraped, the patter of feet on boards and the ring of loud laughter, there stood a man with blotched features.

Further on in the darkness she met a ragged being with shifting, blood-shot eyes and grimy hands.

She went into the blackness of the final block. The shutters of the tall buildings were closed like grim lips. The structures seemed to have eyes that looked over them, beyond them, at other things. Afar off the lights of the avenues glittered as if from an impossible distance. Street-car bells jingled with a sound of merriment.

At the feet of the tall buildings appeared the deathly black hue of the river. Some hidden factory sent up a yellow glare, that lit for a moment the waters lapping oilily against timbers. The varied sounds of life, made joyous by distance and seeming unapproachableness, came faintly and died away to a silence.

CHAPTER XVIII

IN A partitioned-off section of a saloon sat a man with a half dozen women, gleefully laughing, hovering about him. The man had arrived at that stage of drunkenness where affection is felt for the universe.

"I'm good f'ler, girls," he said, convincingly. "I'm damn good f'ler. An'body treats me right, I allus trea's zem right! See?"

The women nodded their heads approvingly. "To be sure," they cried in hearty chorus. "You're the kind of a man we like, Pete. You're outa sight! What yeh goin' to buy this time, dear?"

"An't'ing yehs wants, damn it," said the man in an abandonment of good-will. His countenance shone with the true spirit of benevolence. He was in the proper mood of missionaries. He would have fraternized with obscure Hottentots. And above all, he was overwhelmed in tenderness for his friends, who were all illustrious.

"An't'ing yehs wants, damn it," repeated he, waving his hands with beneficent recklessness. "I'm good f'ler, girls, an' if an'body treats me right I——here," called he through an open door to a waiter, "bring girls drinks, damn it. What 'ill yehs have, girls? An't'ing yehs wants, damn it!"

The waiter glanced in with the disgusted look of the man who serves intoxicants for the man who takes too much of them. He nodded his head shortly at the order from each individual, and went.

"Damn it," said the man, "w're havin' heluva time. I like you girls! Damn'd if I don't! Yer right sort! See?"

He spoke at length and with feeling, concerning the excellencies of his assembled friends.

"Don' try pull man's leg, but have a heluva time! Das right! Das way t' do! Now, if I sawght yehs tryin' work me fer drinks, wouldn' buy damn t'ing! But yer right sort, damn it! Yehs know how ter treat a f'ler, an' I stays by yehs 'til spen' las' cent! Das right! I'm good f'ler an' I knows when an'body treats me right!"

Between the times of the arrival and departure of the waiter, the man discoursed to the women on the tender regard he felt for all living things. He laid stress upon the purity of his motives in all dealings with men in the world and spoke of the fervor of his friendship for those who were amiable. Tears welled slowly from his eyes. His voice quavered when he spoke to his companions.

Once when the waiter was about to depart with an empty tray, the man drew a coin from his pocket and held it forth.

"Here," said he, quite magnificently, "here's quar'."

The waiter kept his hands on his tray.

"I don' want yer money," he said.

The other put forth the coin with tearful insistence.

"Here, damn it," cried he, "tak't! Yer damn goo' f'ler an' I wan' yehs tak't!"

"Come, come, now," said the waiter, with the sullen air of a man who is forced into giving advice. "Put yer mon in yer pocket! Yer loaded an' yehs on'y makes a damn fool of yerself."

As the latter passed out of the door the man turned pathetically to the women.

"He don' know I'm damn goo' f'ler," cried he, dismally.

"Never you mind, Pete, dear," said the woman of brilliance and audacity, laying her hand with great affection upon his arm. "Never you mind, old boy! We'll stay by you, dear!"

"Das ri'!" cried the man, his face lighting up at the soothing tones of the woman's voice. "Das ri', I'm damn goo' f'ler an' w'en anyone trea's me ri', I trea's zem ri'! Shee?"

"Sure!" cried the women. "And we're not goin' back on you, old man."

The man turned appealing eyes to the woman. He felt that if he could be convicted of a contemptible action he would die.

"Shay, Nell, damn it, I allus trea's yehs shquare, didn' I? I allus been goo' f'ler wi' yehs, ain't I, Nell?"

"Sure you have, Pete," assented the woman. She delivered an oration to her companions. "Yessir, that's a fact. Pete's a square fellah, he is. He never goes back on a friend. He's the right kind an' we stay by him, don't we, girls?"

"Sure," they exclaimed. Looking lovingly at him they raised their glasses and drank his health.

"Girlsh," said the man, beseechingly, "I allus trea's yehs ri', didn' I? I'm goo' f'ler, ain' I, girlsh?"

"Sure," again they chorused.

"Well," said he finally, "le's have nozzer drink, zen."

"That's right," hailed a woman, "that's right. Yer no bloomin' jay! Yer spends yer money like a man. Dat's right."

The man pounded the table with his quivering fists.

"Yessir," he cried, with deep earnestness, as if someone disputed him. "I'm damn goo' f'ler, an' w'en anyone trea's me ri', I allus trea's—le's have nozzer drink."

He began to beat the wood with his glass.

"Shay!" howled he, growing suddenly impatient. As the waiter did not then come, the man swelled with wrath.

"Shay!" howled he again.

The waiter appeared at the door.

"Bringsh drinksh," said the man.

The waiter disappeared with the orders.

"Zat f'ler damn fool," cried the man. "He insul' me! I'm ge'man! Can' stan' be insul'! I'm goin' lickim when comes!"

"No, no!" cried the women, crowding about and trying to subdue him. "He's all right! He didn't mean anything! Let it go! He's a good fellah!"

"Din' he insul' me?" asked the man earnestly.

"No," said they. "Of course he didn't! He's all right!"

"Sure he didn' insul' me?" demanded the man, with deep anxiety in his voice.

"No, no! We know him! He's a good fellah. He didn't mean anything."

"Well, zen," said the man, resolutely, "I'm go 'pol'gize!"

When the waiter came, the man struggled to the middle of the floor.

"Girlsh shed you insul' me! I shay damn lie! I 'pol'gize!"

"All right," said the waiter.

The man sat down. He felt a sleepy but strong desire to straighten things out and have a perfect understanding with everybody.

"Nell, I allus trea's yeh shquare, din' I? Yeh likes me, don' yehs, Nell? I'm goo' f'ler?"

"Sure!" said the woman.

"Yeh knows I'm stuck on yehs, don' yehs, Nell?"

"Sure," she repeated, carelessly.

Overwhelmed by a spasm of drunken adoration, he drew two or three bills from his pocket, and with the trembling fingers of an offering priest, laid them on the table before the woman.

"Yehs knows, damn it, yehs kin have all I got, 'cause I'm stuck on yehs, Nell, damn 't, I—I'm stuck on yehs, Nell—buy drinksh —damn 't—we're havin' heluva time—w'en anyone trea's me ri' —I—damn 't, Nell—we're havin' heluva—time."

Presently he went to sleep with his swollen face fallen forward on his chest.

The women drank and laughed, not heeding the slumbering man in the corner. Finally he lurched forward and fell groaning to the floor.

The women screamed in disgust and drew back their skirts.

"Come ahn," cried one, starting up angrily, "let's get out of here."

The woman of brilliance and audacity stayed behind, taking up the bills and stuffing them into a deep, irregularly-shaped pocket. A guttural snore from the recumbent man caused her to turn and look down at him.

She laughed. "What a damn fool," she said, and went.

The smoke from the lamps settled heavily down in the little compartment, obscuring the way out. The smell of oil, stifling in its intensity, pervaded the air. The wine from an overturned glass dripped softly down upon the blotches on the man's neck.

CHAPTER XIX

IN A room a woman sat at a table eating like a fat monk in a
picture.

A soiled, unshaven man pushed open the door and
entered.

"Well," said he, "Mag's dead."

"What?" said the woman, her mouth filled with bread.

"Mag's dead," repeated the man.

"D' hell she is," said the woman. She continued her meal.
When she finished her coffee she began to weep.

"I kin remember when her two feet was no bigger dan' yer
t'umb, and she weared worsted boots," moaned she.

"Well, whata dat?" said the man.

"I kin remember when she weared worsted boots," she cried.

The neighbors began to gather in the hall, staring in at the
weeping woman as if watching the contortions of a dying dog. A
dozen women entered and lamented with her. Under their busy
hands the rooms took on that appalling appearance of neatness
and order with which death is greeted.

Suddenly the door opened and a woman in a black gown
rushed in with outstretched arms. "Ah, poor Mary," she cried,
and tenderly embraced the moaning one.

"Ah, what ter'ble affliction is dis," continued she. Her vocabu-
lary was derived from mission churches. "Me poor Mary, how I
feel fer yehs! Ah, what a ter'ble affliction is a disobed'ent chil'."

Her good, motherly face was wet with tears. She trembled in
eagerness to express her sympathy. The mourner sat with bowed
head, rocking her body heavily to and fro, and crying out in a
high, strained voice that sounded like a dirge on some forlorn
pipe.

"I kin remember when she weared worsted boots an' her two

feets was no bigger dan yer t'umb an' she weared worsted boots, Miss Smith," she cried raising her streaming eyes.

"Ah, me poor Mary," sobbed the woman in black. With low, coddling cries, she sank on her knees by the mourner's chair, and put her arms about her. The other women began to groan in different keys.

"Yer poor misguided chil' is gone now, Mary, an' let us hope it's fer d' bes'. Yeh'll fergive her now, Mary, won't yehs, dear, all her disobed'ence? All her t'ankless behavior to her mudder an' all her badness? She's gone where her ter'ble sins will be judged."

The woman in black raised her face and paused. The inevitable sunlight came streaming in at the window and shed a ghastly cheerfulness upon the faded hues of the room. Two or three of the spectators were sniffling, and one was weeping loudly. The mourner arose and staggered into the other room. In a moment she emerged with a pair of faded baby shoes held in the hollow of her hand.

"I kin remember when she used to wear dem," cried she. The women burst anew into cries as if they had all been stabbed. The mourner turned to the soiled and unshaven man.

"Jimmie, boy, go git yer sister! Go git yer sister an' we'll put d' boots on her feets!"

"Dey won't fit her now, yeh damn fool," said the man.

"Go git yer sister, Jimmie," shrieked the woman, confronting him fiercely.

The man swore sullenly. He went over to a corner and slowly began to put on his coat. He took his hat and went out, with a dragging, reluctant step.

The woman in black came forward and again besought the mourner.

"Yeh'll fergive her, Mary! Yeh'll fergive yer bad, bad chil'! Her life was a curse an' her days were black an' yeh'll fergive yer bad girl? She's gone where her sins will be judged."

"She's gone where her sins will be judged," cried the other women, like a choir at a funeral.

"D' Lord gives and d' Lord takes away," said the woman in black, raising her eyes to the sunbeams.

"D' Lord gives and d' Lord takes away," responded the others.

"Yeh'll fergive her, Mary!" pleaded the woman in black. The mourner essayed to speak but her voice gave way. She shook her great shoulders frantically, in an agony of grief. The tears seemed to scald her face. Finally her voice came and arose in a scream of pain.

"Oh, yes, I'll fergive her! I'll fergive her!"

APPENDIXES

TEXTUAL NOTES

11.25 denounced . . . consumed] At first sight the A2 change of the A1 infinitive series might appear to be a sophistication, probably by the Appleton editor; and indeed the possibility cannot be ruled out. But it is equally possible that Crane saw that the 'heroic endeavors' more properly applied only to the baby trying to keep his equilibrium. Certainly, the relative clause 'which he chewed between the times of his infantile orations' does not jibe with a 'heroic endeavor' to eat the orange peeling.

13.25 at] That A1 'look out at the window' was not inadvertent is indicated by the appearance of the same phrase later at 43.22, where A2 once again sophisticates, editorially no doubt, to 'look out of'. The same phrase with 'at' in 19.17–18 was repeated without change in A2.

14.21 infant] The addition in A2 of the possessive (infant's) would seem to be the same editorial interference found in the A2 alteration at 18.17 of 'panther' to 'panther's'.

19.7 into] Despite 26.23 'Maggie leaned back in the shadow', the phrase 'into shadows' at 28.8 suggests that the A2 change of A1 'in' to 'into' was here authoritative.

22.14 observation] Demonstrable common errors in A1 and A2 that are not simple misprints like 'smoked-filled' at 52.12 are hard to find, unless the present be an example. Follett emended 'observation' to 'oblivion', which is tempting. Nevertheless, the odds favor the authority of 'observation'. For example, Jimmie is described as 'fixing his eye on a high and distant object' and 'then going into a trance of observation', which makes sense if the 'observation' consists of the 'fixing' of the eye that induces a trancelike state resulting from this selection of an object to observe fixedly. It would be odd if Crane missed an error here since for the A2 revision he altered A1 'begin' to 'start' at 22.14, and at 22.14 deleted 'sort of' before 'trance'.

23.14 swearing for the half of an hour] That A2 'for half an hour' is an editorial alteration is indicated by A1 (and A2) 'ran up and down the avenue for the half of a block' at 49.17–18. If the editor's hand is to be seen here, then it is very likely that the A2 substitution of 'storming' for A1 'swearing' is part of the editorial censorship of Crane's language and is to be rejected.

35.24 racking] Although the common phrase 'racking his brains' found in A2 for A1's 'raking his brains' might arouse suspicion, the fact that this A1 reading occurs in a sheet that is so uniquely dotted with typographical errors as to cause one to believe it was not proofread should lead one to accept the A2 variant as a true correction of an A1 error like 'thrash' for 'trash' at 35.31. For this sheet, see the Textual Introduction, p. lxv.

36.24 was] The A2 change to 'were' of the A1 collective singular seems to be a sophistication, on the analogy of such other occurrences in A1 as 'wealth and prosperity was' (52.19) and 'a handful of wet wanderers . . . was scattered' (68.24), each of which was changed to 'were' in A2.

39.27 truckman's brown] This A2 transposition of A1 'brown truckman's' might seem to be a finicky editorial change were it not that it occurs in the supposedly unproofread sheet 5 of A1 which contains in the preceding line a transposed error 'tin a' for 'a tin' (39.26) and 'now, door' later (40.32) for 'door now,'.

40.9 he gritted] Crane was accustomed to inversions like 'whispered he softly' at 41.22, and thus it may be that the A2 'he gritted' for A1 'gritted he' is editorial. But this inversion is so awkward as perhaps to have called itself to Crane's attention when in A2 he censored the speech that was gritted.

58.6 seats] The assumption is that the A2 'took a seat' for A1 'took seats' is an editorial cleaning-up of Crane's false grammar. One may compare 30.29, 'Pete walked . . . and took seats with Maggie at a table' and also 57.27, 'Pete and Maggie . . . took chairs at a table'.

61.31 did hear] The agreement of all texts in this reading does not necessarily indicate that it is right. However, the omission of the pronoun in drunken speech is not unusual: see ' 'til spen' las' cent' (72.1) and 'I'm goin' lickim when comes' (73.21).

69.36 hands] The A1 reading 'hand' seems to be an error, even in the complete A1 phrase, 'his hand buried in his overcoat', in part on the analogy of 69.30, 'thrusting his hands in his pockets' and in part on the occurrence of the same use of a singular where a plural is required in "His New Mittens," for which see the Textual Introduction in Volume VII, *Tales of Whilomville*, p. 78.

76.12 window] Whether by good luck or good management, E1 corrects the A1–2 common error 'windows', which may have been Crane's own inadvertence. That there was only one window in the room is attested by 19.17–18, 26–27, but especially by 29.31–32. The reference here must be to the single window in the room, not to windows in other rooms.

EDITORIAL SUBSTANTIVE EMENDATIONS
IN THE COPY-TEXT

[NOTE: Every substantive editorial change made from the 1893 first edition of *Maggie* is listed here. For easier use of this editorial material, the alterations in the accidentals are presented in a separate list immediately following. Only the direct source of the emendation, with its antecedents, is noticed; the Historical Collation may be consulted for the complete history, within the editions collated, of any substantive readings that qualify for inclusion in that listing. An alteration assigned to the Virgina Edition (V) is made for the first time in the present text, if 'by the first time' is understood 'the first time in respect to the editions chosen for collation.' Asterisked readings are discussed in the Textual Notes. The following editions are referred to: A1 (1893), A2 (Appleton 1896), E1 (Heinemann 1896), E2 (Heinemann 1900).]

7.4   pelting] A2; pelting at A1
7.5   the fury of battle] A2; fury A1
7.6   oaths] A2; great, crimson oaths A1
7.13   shone] A2; there shone A1
7.20   looked like those] A2; wore a look A1
7.23   madness] A2; cursing fury A1
7.25   uprose] A2; upreared its form A1
7.29   over] A2; to A1
8.1   in] A2; into A1
8.13   tipped over his eye] A2; tipped A1
8.14   challenge] A2; challenge over his eye A1
8.26   tremendous] A2; hoarse, tremendous A1
9.6   brag] A2; swear A1
9.12   yehs] A2; yeh A1
10.14 kind of a] A2; *omit* A1
*11.25 denounced . . . consumed] A2; denounce . . . consume A1
12.9   struck] A2; swore and struck A1
13.1   sat in] A2; crouched on A1
13.9   lay] A2; lay cursing and A1
13.18 muddied] A2; mudded A1

13.20 said‸] A2; murmured, A1
13.25 went] A2; began A1
*13.25 at] *stet* A1
14.7   seized] A2; grabbed A1
*14.21 infant] *stet* A1
15.3   glittering eyes fastened] A2; eyes glittered A1
15.9   face] A2; quivering face A1
16.4   and] A2; mingled with A1
17.1   to] A2; and A1
17.5   man] A2; man, threateningly A1
17.10 throat] A2; hairy throat A1
18.8   yell] A2; howl A1
18.10 a confused] A2; confusingly in A1
18.10 it] A2; *omit* A1
18.10 there] A2; *omit* A1
18.12 his] A2; *omit* A1
18.33–34 an attitude . . . that] A2; positions . . . those A1
19.2   an] A2; that A1
*19.7 into] A2; that A1
19.9   his eyes] A2; the eyes from out his drawn face A1
19.21 with] A2; from A1
19.25 the] A2; *omit* A1
20.1   an insignificant] A2; a white, insignificant A1

83

20.14–15 Once. . . . What?] A2; omit A1
20.28 tourists] A2; gentlemen A1
21.17 nothing] A2; neither the devil nor the leader of society A1
21.22 There was given to him] A2; He was given A1
21.26 punch] A2; beat A1
21.34 If . . . became the] A2; If in the front and the A1
21.35 which] A2; that A1
22.5 which] A2; that A1
22.7 greatest] A2; most complete A1
22.9–10 became superior.] A2; was superior. He became immured like an African cow. A1
22.14 start₍] A2; begin, A1
22.14 trance] A2; sort of a trance A1
*22.14 observation] stet A1-E2
22.16 but] A2; omit A1
22.17 seize] A2; tear A1
22.22 that he] A2; omit A1
22.28–29 comprehend their desire] A2; conceive their maniacal desires A1
22.35 and thus] A2; omit A1
22.35 stolid] A2; solid A1
23.1 And] A2; And, perhaps, A1
23.1 had had a] A2; had an ungovernable A1
23.4 hard] A2; very hard A1
23.10 struck] A2; would strike A1
*23.14–15 swearing for the half of] stet A1
23.18 a street car] A2; street-cars A1
24.12 er] A2; or A1
24.18 with a name which might have been] A2; the name of whose brand could be A1
24.19 connected] A2; in connection A1
24.25 such a] A2; that A1
24.30 courts] A2; a court A1
25.1 a] A2; a sort of A1
25.13 pugged] A2; rather pugged A1
25.16 was] A2; omit A1
25.17 weapons] A2; murder-fitted weapons A1
25.22 Rats!] A2; Fudge. A1
25.24 "elegant"] A2; elegant and graceful A1
25.29 dey] V; deh A1; d' A2-E2
26.12 outa sight] A2; great A1
26.35 ideal] A2; beau ideal of a A1
27.13 which] A2; that A1
27.28 er somethin'] A2; an' all A1
28.3 of a] A2; omit a A1
28.14 which] A2; omit A1
29.1–2 wore a different suit] A2; had different suits on A1
29.3 prodigious] A2; prodigally extensive A1
29.12 as endowed] A2; omit A1
29.17 It would be] A2; omit A1
29.37 ghastly,] A2; ghastly, like dead flesh, A1
29.37 mother] A2; red mother A1
30.14 drudging] A2; trudge A1
30.16 men] A2; kid-gloved men A1
31.6 visited] A2; been to A1
32.4 enthusiasm] A2; stereotyped enthusiasm A1
32.8 diversions] A2; phantasies A1
32.10 is] A2; it A1
32.17 set down] A2; omit A1
32.18 which] A2; that A1
32.22 they] A2; the duettists A1
32.28 harrowing] A2; the most harrowing A1
32.32 the kind] A2; that kind A1
32.35 annihilated] A2; being annihilated A1
32.36 climax] A2; crisis A1
32.37 when] A2; where A1
32.39 this] A2; the A1
32.39–33.1 most of them of foreign birth] A2; omit A1
33.4 noisily] A2; crashingly A1
33.7 silk] A2; glossy silk A1
33.7 leers] A2; leers, or smiles, A1
33.8 devil] A2; pictured devil A1
33.17 With . . . orchestra₍] A2; When the orchestra crashed finally, A1

33.18 in] A2; with A1
34.19 became . . . looked at] A2; wondered as she regarded A1
34.22 or of] A2; *omit* A1
34.23 or] A2; *omit* A1
34.23 wondered] A2; speculated A1
34.25 something of value] A2; valuable A1
34.27 She] A2; Too, she A1
34.29 should] A2; would A1
35.5 tamn] A2; damn A1
35.9 seemed] A2; seems A1
*35.24 racking] A2; raking A1
35.31 thrash] A2; trash A1
36.5 that] A2; which A1
36.10 In . . . often took] A2; Evenings during the week he took A1
36.11 dazzling] 2; brain-clutching A1
36.12 her treacherous guardian] A2; her guardian, who is cruelly after her bonds, A1
36.17–18 windows, while . . . sang] A2; windows. And . . . singing A1
*36.24 was] *stet* A1
37.3–4 the parts of villains] A2; villainy parts A1
37.6 that] A2; if A1
37.12–13 these melodramas] A2; the showing places of the melodrama A1
37.14 overcame] A2; surmounted A1
38.26 her] A2; red A1
39.2 red] A2; crimson A1
39.6 off] A2; *omit* A1
39.16 scrap] A2; row A1
39.17 door] A2; door with her great feet A1
39.26 a tin] A2; tin a A1
*39.27 truckman's brown] A2; brown truckman's A1
39.31 yeh] A2; yer A1
39.34 frame] A2; framed A1
*40.9 he gritted] A2; gritted he A1

40.16 quit] A2; stop A1
40.32 door now,] A2; now, door A1
41.27 writhing] A2; red, writhing A1
41.30 Maggie] A2; She A1
42.10 tumbled to,] A2; got onto, A1
42.18 by] V; be A1-E2
42.23 she called] A2; called she A1
42.30 The blue] A2; Too, the blue A1
43.1 place] A2; position A1
43.31–32 an' quit dat] A2; *omit* A1
44.11 done] A2; did A1
45.8 -imitation] A2; -appearing A1
45.14 place] A2; position A1
45.21 all] A2; *omit* A1
45.26 wall] A2; siding A1
46.2 wore] A2; had A1
46.2 watchfulness] A2; watchfulness upon his features A1
46.6 sneering] A2; sneering widely A1
46.10 obliviousness] A2; oblivion A1
47.6 Hot] A2; Dark A1
48.14 furiously] A2; redly A1
48.19 Jimmie] A2; him A1
48.39 whirled] A2; swirled A1
49.1 critical] A2; tottering A1
49.8 glasses] A2; glass A1
49.22 and] A2; *omit* A1
50.3 safe dark corner] A2; corner safely dark A1
50.7 At first] A2; On first thoughts A1
51.3 in soiled evening dress] A2; a dress suit A1
51.5 gown] A2; dress A1
51.19 to reach] A2; *omit* A1
52.5 had had] A2; had A1
52.6 the accents] A2; tones A1
52.11 through] A2; by A1
52.12 in] A2; through A1
52.12 smoke-] E1; smoked- A1-2
52.16 hale] A2; hell A1
52.17 tamn!] A2; damn. A1
52.20 had experienced before] A2; previously had experienced A1
54.23 bottle] A2; squdgy bottle A1

55.35   the] A2; a A1
55.36   which] A2; omit A1
55.36   called] A2; could call A1
56.6   I?] A2; I, deh beast. A1
*58.6   seats] stet A1
58.20   said] A2; said cordially A1
58.28   gallantry] A2; awkward gallantry A1
58.31   as her addition to] A2; upon
A1
58.40   the additions with acclama-
tions] A2; with acclamations the
additions A1
59.9   talk like a clock] A2; gibber
like an ape, dear A1
59.26   all] A2; all there is of it A1
59.28   out of] A2; from A1
59.35   funny] A2; droll A1
60.4   On d' level, now.] A2; omit A1
60.6   saying,] A2; omit A1
60.31   They got cold feet.] A2; omit
A1
61.15   chain] A2; string A1
*61.31   did hear] stet A1-E2
62.7   furtively   scanned]   A2;
scanned furtively A1
62.24   yeh'd] V; ye'd A1–2; yehs
E1–2
63.17   at Maggie] A2; omit A1
63.24   bended] V; bent A1-E2
63.29   railing] A2; sneering A1
64.8   showman] A2; showman at a
museum A1
64.22   that of] A2; omit A1
65.12   that people should lose] A2;
for anyone's losing A1
65.19   woman] A2; woman of brilliance and audacity A1
65.24   Pete] A2; my cloud-compelling Pete A1
66.9   found] A2; had found A1
66.35   Pete's glance expressed] A2;
Pete glanced A1
66.38   do] V; deh A1 (omit A2-E2)
66.39   do me dirt] A2; get me inteh
trouble A1
67.36   made] A2; gave A1
68.12–13   who had . . . silence]
A2; having been comparatively
silent A1

68.21   two hours in] A2; having
just emerged from A1
68.24   was] stet A1
68.28   those] A2; men A1
*69.36   hands] A2; hand A1
69.36   pockets] A2; omit A1
70.8   whence] A2; from whence A1
70.10   features.] A2; features. ⌐
"Ah, there," said the girl. ⌐ "I've
got a date," said the man. A1
70.12   hands.] A2; hands. "Ah,
what deh hell? Tink I'm a millionaire?" A1
70.15   them . . . them] A2; her
. . . her A1
70.18   merriment.] A2; merriment.
⌐ When almost to the river the
girl saw a great figure. On going
forward she perceived it to be a
huge fat man in torn and greasy
garments. His grey hair straggled down over his forehead. His
small, bleared eyes, sparkling
from amidst great rolls of red
fat, swept eagerly over the girl's
upturned face. He laughed, his
brown, disordered teeth gleaming under a grey, grizzled moustache from which beer-drops
dripped. His whole body gently
quivered and shook like that of
a dead jelly fish. Chuckling and
leering, he followed the girl of
the crimson legions. A1
70.19   At the feet . . . river.] A2;
At their feet the river appeared
a deathly black hue. A1
71.12   mood] A2; mode A1
71.20   wants] V; want A1-E2
72.8   his companions] A2; them A1
72.23   the] A2; a A1
72.31; 74.3   woman] A2; woman of
brilliance and audacity A1
74.9   I] A2; omit A1
74.13   Presently] A2; Shortly A1
*76.12   window]   E1;   windows
A1–2
77.3   The] A2; Hot A1
77.4   face] A2; quivering face A1
77.4   in] A2; like A1

EDITORIAL ACCIDENTALS EMENDATIONS
IN THE COPY-TEXT

[NOTE: Except for such silent typographical alterations as are remarked in the prefatory "Text of the Virginia Edition," every editorial change made in the accidentals from the 1893 copy-text is listed here. The wavy dash ~ represents the same word that appears before the bracket and is used in recording punctuation variants. An inferior caret ∧ indicates the absence of a punctuation mark.]

7.7 git yehs!] A2; get yehs A1
8.19 interest.] V; ~ , A1-E2
8.24 d'] A2; deh A1
8.32 d'] V; deh A1 (*omit* A2-E2)
8.34 t'] V; teh A1-E2
8.36 forward] A2; foward A1
9.8 d'] A2; deh A1
9.12 d'] V; deh A1 (*omit* A2-E2)
9.12 d'] V; deh A1-E2
9.22 d'] A2; deh A1
9.30 Jimmie] E1; Jimmy A1–2
9.36 dinner-pail] E2; ~ ∧ ~ A1–2
11.31 disdainfully] A2; distain-fully A1
12.1 d'] A2; deh A1
12.2 him.] A2; ~ , A1
12.7 d'] V; deh A1 (*omit* A2-E2)
13.20 t'] A2; teh A1
13.33 The ragged (*no* ⚓)] A2; ⚓ A1
13.37 d'] A2; deh A1
14.1 I——"] A2; ~ "—— A1
14.12 d'] A2; deh A1
14.17 t'] A2; teh A1
14.28–29 sleep, . . . doubled,] A2; ~ ∧ . . . ~ ∧ A1
16.10 music∧ box] A2; ~ - ~ A1
17.5 d'] V; deh A1-E2
17.7 t'] V; teh A1-E2
17.17 d'] V; deh A1-E2
17.17 D'] V; Deh A1-E2
17.37 d' . . . t'] V; deh . . . teh A1-E2

18.1 d'] V; deh A1 (*omit* A2-E2)
18.5 t'] V; teh A1 (*omit* A2-E2)
18.9 shrieks—] A2; ~ , A1
18.13 doorways] A2; ~ - ~ A1
18.17 up stairs] V; upstairs A1-E1; up-stairs E2
19.14 doorway] A2; ~ - ~ A1
20.14 you's] V; yous A1-E2
20.16 ⚓ While] A2; no ⚓ A1
21.8 it.] A2; ~ ∧ A1
21.15 chrysanthemums] A2; chris-anthemums A1
21.25 breathe] A2; breath A1
21.31; 22.27 foot∧ passengers] A2; ~ - ~ A1
23.2 flame-colored] A2 (-coloured); ~ ∧ ~ A1
23.8 sidewalk] A2; ~ - ~ A1
23.16 fire∧ engine] A2; ~ - ~ A1
23.18 street∧ car] A2; ~ - ~ A1
23.33 D'] V; Deh A1-E2
24.5,22 up stairs] V; upstairs A2-E1; ~ - ~ A1, E2
24.5 down stairs] V; downstairs A2-E1; ~ - ~ A1, E2
24.12 t'] A2; teh A1
24.12 t' hell] V; teh hell A1 (*omit* A2-E2)
25.2 Island] V; island A1-E2
25.17 shoes∧] A2; ~ , A1
25.29 t' . . . d'] A2; teh . . . deh A1

25.30,33(*twice*),34   d'] A2; deh A1

25.34   t'] A2; teh A1

25.37   trouble';] V; ~ ;' A1-E2

26.1   similar] A2; similiar A1

26.3   d'] V; deh A1-E2

26.4   says—see?] A2; says (See?) A1

26.4   But] V; but A1-E2

26.4   'spectable] A2; spectable A1

26.7,11(*twice*),12,13,14   d']   A2; deh A1

26.8   dukes—see?] A2; dukes (See?) A1

26.8   An'] V; an' A1-E2

26.13   t'ru] V; true A1-E2

26.13   t'aut] V; taut A1-E2

26.19   hadn'] A2; had'n' A1

26.19   t'] A2; teh A1

26.21   See?] A2; ~ . A1

26.25   grimy] A2; grimey A1

26.31,32   d'] A2; deh A1

26.31   t'ree] V; tree A1-E2

27.2   sight,"] A2; ~ ,' A1

27.9   t'aut] V; tau't A1-E1; taut E2

27.21(*twice*),22(*twice*)   d'] V; deh A1-E2

27.22   t'] V; teh A1-E2

27.25(*twice*)   t'] V; teh A1 (*omit* A2-E2)

27.25,26   an'] V; and A1 (*omit* A2-E2)

27.26   Den d'] V; Den deh A1-E2

27.27   somethin'] A2; someting A1

27.28   t'] V; teh A1-E2

27.28   pe'dition,] A2; ~ ʌ A1

27.29(*twice*)   D'] V; Deh A1 (*omit* A2-E2)

29.5   t' d'] A2; teh deh A1

29.27–28   d' . . . d'] V; deh . . . deh A1 (*omit* A2-E2)

29.29   d'] A2; deh A1

29.29   t'] A2; teh A1

31.11(*twice*)   d' hell] V; deh hell A1 (*omit* A2-E2)

31.11   d'] A2; deh A1

31.27   half-tipsy] A2; ~ ʌ ~ A1

33.22   t' d'] A2; teh deh A1

33.26; 34.3   d'] V; deh A1 (*omit* A2-E2)

34.15   shriveling] V; shrivelling A1-E2

35.1   He sat (*no* ⸿)] A2; ⸿ A1

35.7   admirable] A2; amirable A1

35.9   It (*no* ⸿)] A2; ⸿ A1

35.14   one,] A2; ~ ʌ A1

35.16   obliged] A2; oblgied A1

35.34   monkeys.] A2; ~ ʌ A1

36.7   d'] V; deh A1 (*omit* A2-E2)

36.9   d'] A2; deh A1

36.21   ecstatic] A2; ecstastic A1

36.31   The loud (*no* ⸿)] A2; ⸿ A1

37.14   theatre] A2; theater A1

38.6   half-circle] V; ~ ʌ ~ A1-E2

38.8   Her] A2; He A1

38.9   grey] E1; gray A1–2

38.12   get—] A2; ~ , A1

39.15,21,25(*twice*)   d'] V; deh A1-E2

39.23   Missiles] A2; Missles A1

39.28,35   d'] V; deh A1 (*omit* A2-E2)

40.5   me—"] A2; ~ ," A1

40.15   t'] A2; to A1

40.15   d'] A2; deh A1

40.16   damn] V; dam A1 (*omit* A2-E2)

40.31   Dere,] A2; ~ ʌ A1

40.32   Jimmie!] A2; ~ . A1

41.7,12(*twice*),21,23   d'] A2; deh A1

41.10   T'] V; Teh A1 (*omit* A2-E2)

41.11,12,13   t'] A2; teh A1

41.14,15,17,29   t'] V; teh A1 (*omit* A2-E2)

41.18   Git] A2; Get A1

41.22   D'] A2; Deh A1

41.29   riddance."] V; ~ . ʌ A1 (*omit* A2-E2)

42.10   t'ink] A2; tink A1

42.11,15,18   d'] V; deh A1-E2

42.11,15   t'ing] A2; ting A1

42.19–20   'Oh . . . yes,' . . . 'Oh . . . yes.'] A2; " ~ . . . ~ ," . . . " ~ . . . ~ ." A1

42.29   table ʌ] A2; ~ , A1

43.7,17,19,34,36,37,38; 44.2(*twice*),
  10,11,12,13 d'] A2; deh A1
43.10(*twice*),29(*twice*),30 d'] V;
  deh A1-E2
43.13 d' hell's] V; deh hell's A1
  (*omit* A2-E2)
43.17,19,38,39; 44.2,21(*twice*),22,
  25 t'] V; teh A1-E2
43.21 D'] V; Deh A1 (*omit* A2-E2)
43.30 D'] A2; Deh A1
43.35 t'ink] V; tink A1-E2
44.11 t'inks] V; tinks A1-E2
44.13 'im."] A2; ~ . ∧ A1
44.21,22,35 d'] V; deh A1-E2
44.25 Yessir] V; Yesir A1; Yes sir
  A2-E2
44.32 friend.] V; ~ , A1-E2
44.34 t'ump] E2; tump A1-E1
44.35 use! ∧] A2; ~ !" A1
44.39 Gee!] A2; ~ , A1
45.14 centre] A2; center A1
45.20 begrimed] A2; begrimed A1
46.7(*twice*) d'] V; deh A1-E2
46.22,32,37,38; 47.17; 48.1,8 d']
  V; deh A1 (*omit* A2-E2)
46.22; 47.8,12(*twice*),25,26 d']
  A2; deh A1
46.32; 48.1,8 t'] A2; teh A1
47.8 who's] A2; whose A1
47.13 Billie?"] A2; ~ ? ∧ A1
47.17 talkin'] V; talkin A1; talking
  A2-E2
47.26 bote] V; boat A1-E2
47.29 eyes.] A2; ~ ∧ A1
49.6,14 missiles] A2; missles A1
49.9 point-blank] A2; ~ ∧ ~ A1
49.19 t'rowed] E2; trowed A1-E1
49.19 d'] V; deh A1-E2
50.9; 51.27 d'] V; deh A1 (*omit*
  A2-E2)
51.27 yehs] A2; yeh's A1
52.34 Smooth-cheeked] A2; ~ ∧ ~
  A1
54.4 home.] A2; ~ ∧ A1
54.16,17(*twice*),18,19,25,28; 55.1
  d'] A2; deh A1
54.19; 55.1,13,(*twice*),15(*twice*),
  18; 56.21 t'] V; teh A1-E2

54.25 t'] A2; teh A1
55.8 an'] E2; an A1-E1
55.11,26,28,29 d'] V; deh A1-E2
55.14 t'ink] E2; tink A1-E1
55.16 t'aut] V; taut A1-E2
55.18,26 nottin'] A2; nottin A1
55.23 won't] A2; wont A1
55.30 anyway,"] A2; ~ , ∧ A1
55.32 wa'n't] A2; wasn't A1
56.6,7,20,21(*twice*) d'] V; deh A1-
  E2
56.7 d'] A2; deh A1
56.24 police-justices] A2; ~ ∧ ~
  A1
57.10 "bouncer"] A2; ∧ ~ ∧ A1
57.11 an] A2; a A1
57.18 over] A2; o'er A1
58.9 dere's] A2; there's A1
58.27 t'] V; teh A1-E2
58.27 d'] V; deh A1-E2
59.2 What's-] A2; what's- A1
59.36 forward] A2; foward A1
59.38 t'aut] V; taut A1-E2
60.6 'Scuse] E1; Scuse A1–2
60.37 coin-die] A2 (~ ∧ ~); coin-
  dye A1
61.22 bad-lookin'] A2; ~ ∧ ~ A1
61.26 gone.] A2; ~ ∧ A1
61.26 On'y] V; O'ny A1-E2
61.33 hav'a] A2; hava A1
61.33 struck?] A2; ~ , A1
62.17 yehs——∧] A2; ~ —— , A1
62.27,28; 63.21 d'] V; deh A1-E2
62.27,30; 63.3; 64.12 t'] V; teh
  A1-E2
63.2 look-a-here] V; ~ - ~ ∧ ~
  A1-E2
63.14 forefinger] A2; ~ - ~ A1
63.31 hallways] A2; ~ - ~ A1
63.34 D'] V; Deh A1 (*omit* A2-E2)
64.1 ⊄ A baby] A2; *no* ⊄ A1
64.16 her.] A2; ~ ∧ A1
64.25 on-ccming] V; oncoming A1-
  E2
64.32 t'-night] A2; teh-night A1
65.6 d'] A2; deh A1
65.10 d'] V; deh A1 (*omit* A2-E2)
65.10 wanna] V; wanna' A1-E2
65.10 fer?"] A2; ~ ? ∧ A1

66.28 Pete——$_\wedge$"] E1; ~ —— ,"
A1–2

66.30,38,39; 67.2 d'] A2; deh A1

66.40; 67.13 t'] V; teh A1 (*omit* A2-E2)

67.20 didn't] A2; did'nt A1

67.27 sternness] A2; sterness A1

68.2 chapter,] A2; ~ $_\wedge$ A1

68.3 side street] A2; ~ - ~ A1

68.32 forgetfulness] A2; forget-|-ness A1

69.36 blond] V; blonde A1-E2

70.12 grimy] A2; grimey A1

70.15 eyes] A2; eyet A1

70.17 Street-car] A2; ~ $_\wedge$ ~ A1

71.10 An't'ing] A2; an'thin' A1

71.11 good-will] V; ~ $_\wedge$ ~ A1-E2

71.16,20 An't'ing] A2; An'thing A1

71.25 w're] A2; we're A1

71.30 t'] V; teh A1-E2

72.1 treat] A2; treata A1

72.11 magnificently,] A2; ~ $_\wedge$ A1

72.28 me$_\wedge$] A2; me' A1

72.28 trea's zem] A2; treats zem A1

72.28 Shee?] A2; ~ ! A1

73.14,16 Shay!] A2; ~ , A1

73.20 damn] V; dam A1 (*omit* A2-E2)

73.26 didn't!] A2; ~ ? A1

73.27 me?] A2; ~ , A1

74.1 din'] A2; ~ $_\wedge$ A1

74.11 heluva] V; heleva A1 (*omit* A2-E2)

74.29 glass] A2; glasss A1

75.8 D'] V; Deh A1-E2

75.11 t'umb] V; tumb A1–2; thumb E1–2

75.24 chil'] V; chile A1-E2

76.1 t'umb] V; tumb A1-E2

76.8 it's] E2; its A1-E1

76.8,21 d'] V; deh A1-E2

76.9 t'ankless] A2; tankless A1

76.36,38 D' . . . d'] V; Deh . . . deh A1-E2

WORD-DIVISION

1. *End-of-the-Line Hyphenation in the Virginia Edition*

[NOTE: No hyphenation of a possible compound at the end of a line in the Virginia text is present in the 1893 copy-text except for the following readings, which are hyphenated within the line in the 1893 edition. Hyphenated compounds in which both elements are capitalized are not included.]

10.11	apple-|wood	29.18	mouse-|colored
18.18	door-|panels	30.2	green-|hued
21.3	street-|corners	39.26	dinner-|pail
25.16	patent-|leather	53.3	half-|closed
28.4	brass-|clothed	61.35	up-|town

2. *End-of-the-Line Hyphenation in the 1893 Copy-Text*

[NOTE: The following compounds, or possible compounds, are hyphenated at the end of the line in the 1893 copy-text. The form in which they have been transcribed in the Virginia Edition, as listed below, represents the practice of the 1893 edition as ascertained by other appearances or by parallels within the edition. Crane manuscripts have been consulted when evidence was not available in the 1893 edition.]

23.26	barroom	49.35	coat-tails
31.32	reappeared	51.12	overwhelming
33.6	foot-lights	55.22	re-echoed
33.33	lamp-post	60.27	cock-tails
35.2	pocketbook	61.17	cobwebs
42.9	forefinger	68.10	eye-brows
49.25	sidewalk		

HISTORICAL COLLATION

[NOTE: Only substantive variants from the Virginia text are listed here, together with their appearances in the four editions collated for the establishment of this text: A1 (1893), A2 (Appleton 1896), E1 (Heinemann 1896), and E2 (Heinemann 1900). Purely typographical errors have been recorded in the Editorial Accidentals Emendations but are not listed here. Collated editions not noted for any reading agree with the Virginia Edition.]

7.4 pelting] pelting at A1
7.5 the fury of battle] fury A1
7.6 oaths] great, crimson oaths A1
7.9 micks] mugs A2-E2
7.13 shone] there shone A1
7.20 looked like those] wore a look A1
7.23 madness] cursing fury A1
7.25 uprose] upreared its form A1
7.29 over] to A1
8.1 in] into A1
8.13 tipped over his eye] tipped A1
8.14 challenge] challenge over his eye A1
8.24 hell] h—ll A2-E2
8.26 tremendous] hoarse, tremendous A1
8.32 What d' hell] What's wrong wi'che A2-E2
9.6 brag] swear A1
9.8 damn] d—n A2-E2
9.10 striving] trying E2
9.12 d' hell] omit A2-E2
9.12 yehs] yeh A1
9.22 damn guts out of] face off A2-E2
10.1 yeh] you A2-E2
10.2 damned] omit A2-E2
10.5–6 damning] omit A2-E2
10.14 kind of a] omit A1
11.1 entered into] entered A2-E2
11.5 an] a A2-E2

11.25 denounced] denounce A1
11.25 consumed] consume A1
12.1 hell] h—l A2-E2
12.7 what d' hell] omit A2-E2
12.9 struck] swore and struck A1
12.14 damned] omit A2-E2
12.26 agin, by Gawd!] agin! A2-E2
13.1 sat in] crouched A1
13.4 damned] omit A2-E2
13.5 git] get E1-2
13.9 lay] lay cursing and A1
13.18 muddied] mudded A1
13.20 hell] h—l A2-E2
13.20 said] murmured A1
13.25 went] began A1
13.25 at] of A2-E2
13.30–31 in which they damned each other's souls with frequence] omit A2-E2
13.36 damn] little A2-E2
14.4 to grimly] grimly to A2-E2
14.7 seized] grabbed A1
14.12 persistently bawled] bawled persistently A2-E2
14.21 infant] infant's A2-E2
14.32 damn] d—n A2-E2
14.38 muddled mist of] mist of muddled A2-E2
15.3 glittering eyes fastened] eyes glittered A1
15.9 face] quivering face A1
15.10 Gawd,] omit A2-E2

16.4   and] mingled with A1
16.21   almost kicked the stomach] kicked the breath A2-E2
16.23   damn] d—n A2-E2
16.24   cursed] a A2-E2
17.1   to] and A1
17.5   man] man, threateningly A1
17.10   throat] hairy throat
17.18   raisin' hell] trowin' fits A2-E2
17.19   man] old man E1-2
17.20   toward] towards E1-2
17.21   club hell outa] paste A2-E2
17.25,27   hell] h—l A2-E2
17.25   Damndes' place! Reg'lar hell!] omit A2-E2
18.1-2 wha' d' hell.] W'ats bitin' yeh? A2-E2
18.3   damn] omit A2-E2
18.5   t' hell,] chase yerself! A2-E2
18.8   yell] howl A1
18.10   a confused] confusingly in A1
18.10   it] omit A1
18.10   there] omit A1
18.12   his] omit A1
18.14   raisin' hell] playin' horse A2-E2
18.17   panther] panther's A2-E2
18.33-34   an attitude . . . that] positions . . . those A1
18.36   bended] bent A2-E2
19.2   an] that A1
19.7   into] in A1
19.9   his eyes] the eyes from out his drawn face A1
19.16   in uneasy] in an uneasy A2-E2
19.21   with] from A1
19.25   the] omit A1
20.1   an insignificant] a white, insignificant A1
20.10   for] from E1-2
20.14-15   Once. . . . What?"] omit A1
20.20   of words] of the words A2-E2
20.28   tourists] gentlemen A1
21.1   meet God] go to heaven A2-E2

21.3   on] at E1-2
21.9   toward] towards E1-2
21.11   order] orders E1-2
21.17   nothing] neither the devil nor the leader of society A1
21.22   There was given to him] He was given A1
21.26   punch] beat A1
21.34   If . . . became the] If in the front and the A1
22.5   which] that A1
22.7   greatest] most complete A1
22.9-10   became superior.] was superior. He became immured like an African cow. A1
22.14   start] begin A1
22.14   trance] sort of a trance A1
22.16   but] omit A1
22.17   policeman] policemen E1-2
22.17   to frenziedly] frenziedly to A2-E2
22.17   seize] tear A1
22.20   toward] towards E1-2
22.22   that he] omit A1
22.28-29   comprehend their desire] conceive their maniacal desires A1
22.35   and thus] omit A1
22.35   stolid] solid A1
22.39   obstruct] to obstruct A2-E2
23.1   And] And, perhaps, A1
23.1   had had a] had an ungovernable A1
23.4   hard] very hard A1
23.8   toward] towards E1-2
23.10   struck] would strike E1
23.14   swearing] storming A2-E2
23.15   the half of] half A2-E2
23.18   a street car] street-cars A2-E2
23.33   hell] h—l A2-E2
24.10   disguised] disgusted E1-2
24.12   t' hell] on d' toif A2-E2
24.12   er] or A1
24.13   of going to hell] to the alternative A2-E2
24.18   with . . . been] the name of whose brand could be A1
24.19   connected] in connection A1
24.25   such a] that A1

24.30 courts] a court A1
25.1 a] a sort of A1
25.3 eternally] *omit* E2
25.13 pugged] rather pugged A1
25.16 was] *omit* A1
25.17 weapons] murder-fitted weapons A1
25.19 was] were E1-2
25.22 Rats] Fudge A1
25.24 "elegant"] elegant and peaceful A1
25.29 dey] deh A1; d' A2-E2
25.36,37 d' hell] *omit* A2-E2
26.3 hell] blazes A2-E2
26.5 purtydamnsoon] quick A2-E2
26.5,6 D' hell] Aw, goahn A2-E2
26.9 damnquick] —quick A2-E2
26.12 outa sight] great A1
26.28 occasionally,] ~ ∧ A2-E2
26.29 reminiscence] eminiscence E1
26.32 hell] h—l A2-E2
26.35 ideal] beau ideal A1
26.36–37 , as God says,] *omit* A2-E2
27.8 damned] *omit* A2-E2
27.13 which] that A1
27.15 at] in A2-E2
27.24–25,25–26 go t' hell an'] *omit* A2-E2
27.28 er somethin'] an' all A1
27.29 D' hell I am] Yer joshin' me A2-E2
27.29 D' hell I am,' like dat] Yer joshin' me A2-E2
27.30 of a] of E2
28.3 of a] *omit* a A1
28.5 defiantly ring] ring defiantly A2-E2
28.14 which] *omit* A1
28.22 of] with A2-E2
28.36 Afterward] Afterwards E1-2
29.1–2 wore a different suit] had different suits on A1
29.3 prodigious] prodigiously extensive A1
29.11 toward] towards E1-2
29.12 as endowed] *omit* A1
29.17 It would be] *omit* A1
29.23 amidst] amid A2-E2

29.27,28 d' hell] *omit* A2-E2
29.37 ghastly,] ghastly, like dead flesh, A1
29.37 mother] red mother A1
30.3 hall] ball E1-2
30.10 about] above E2
30.14 drudging] trudge A1
30.16 men] kid-gloved men A1
30.29 aggressively walked] walked aggressively A2-E2
31.6 visited] been to A1
31.11 what d' hell] what's eatin' yeh? A2-E2
31.11 d'hell] *omit* A2-E2
31.32 amidst] amid A2; among E1-2
32.4 enthusiasm] stereotyped enthusiasm A1
32.8 diversions] phantasies A1
32.10 is] it A1
32.16 damn fake] big jolly A2-E2
32.17 set down] *omit* A1
32.18 which] that A1
32.22 they] the duettists A1
32.26 have] make E1-2
32.28 harrowing] the most harrowing A1
32.32 the] that A1
32.35 annihilated] being annihilated A1
32.36 climax] crisis A1
32.37 when] where A1
32.39 this] the A1
32.39–33.1 most of them of foreign birth] *omit* A1
33.4 noisily] crashingly A1
33.6 stamp] to stamp A2-E2
33.7 silk] glossy silk A1
33.7 leers] leers, or smiles A1
33.8 devil] pictured devil A1
33.17 With . . . orchestra] When the orchestra crashed finally, A1
33.18 in] with A1
33.26 what d' hell] why wasn't it A2-E2
33.28 what d'hell] go ahn! A2-E2
33.34 Gawd,] Gee! A2-E2
34.3 d' hell] *omit* A2-E2
34.3 yeh be] ye be A2-E2
34.4 Good Gawd,] *omit* A2-E2

34.19 became . . . looked at] wondered as she regarded A1

34.21 bended] bent A2-E2

34.22 or of] *omit* A1

34.23 or] *omit* A1

34.23 wondered] speculated A1

34.25 something of value] valuable A1

34.27 She] Too, she A1

34.29 should] would A1

35.4 een hell] *omit* A2-E2

35.5 tamn] damn A1, E1-2

35.9 seemed] seems A1

35.24 racking] raking A1

35.31 thrash] trash A1

35.36 Oh hell,] Aw, rats! A2-E2

36.5 that] which A1

36.7 What d' hell,] Aw! A2-E2

36.10 In . . . often] Evenings during the week he A1

36.11 dazzling] brain-clutching A1

36.12 her treacherous guardian] her guardian, who is cruelly after her bonds, A1

36.17–18 while . . . sang] And . . . singing A1

36.24 was] were A2-E2

37.3–4 the parts of villains] villainy parts A1

37.6 that] if A1

37.12–13 these melodramas] the showing places of the melodrama A1

37.14 overcame] surmounted A1

38.12 damn] *omit* A2-E2

38.13 damn cent.] red! A2-E2

38.14–15,15–16 T' hell wid yeh] Go fall on yerself A2-E2

38.15 damned] blowed A2-E2

38.20–21 Wide . . . grins] A wide dirty grin A2

38.24 over . . . to her.] to her over their shoulders. A2

38.26 her] red A1

39.2 red] crimson A1

39.6 off] *omit* A1

39.15 damn yeh,] *omit* A2-E2

39.16 scrap] row A1

39.17 door] door with her great feet A1

39.21 damn] *omit* A2-E2

39.25 what d' hells . . . yeh] What's wrong wi'che A2-E2

39.26 a tin] tin a A1

39.27 truckman's brown] brown truckman's A1

39.28 What d' hell's] What's A2-E2

39.30 damn . . . feet] faces tru d' floor A2-E2

39.31 yeh] yer A1

39.31 damned] *omit* A2-E3

39.32 strided] strode A2-E2

39.34 framed] frame A1

39.35 T' hell . . . yehs?] An' who are youse! A2-E2

39.36 yehs] youse A2-E2

40.1 cursing blackly. At] and at A2-E2

40.2 toward] towards E1-2

40.4 damn yeh] *omit* A2-E2

40.9 Damn yeh,] Come home! A2-E2

40.9 he gritted] gritted he A1

40.16 quit] stop A1

40.16 damn] *omit* A2-E2

40.28 Damn yer ol' hide,] Say, yeh ol' bat! Quit dat! A2-E2

40.31 damn yeh, stay] now! Stay A2-E2

40.32 door now,] now, door A1

41.5 Gawd,] gee! A2-E2

41.7 hell] h—l A2-E2

41.7 hell of a] out-a-sight A2-E2

41.10 T' hell . . . you] Aw, yer bote no good, needer of yehs A2-E2

41.13 damn yeh] *omit* A2-E2

41.14,15,17 t' hell] *omit* A2-E2

41.14 damn] curse A2-E2

41.18 yehs] youse A2-E2

41.18 Damn] D—n A2-E2

41.21 hell] h—l A2-E2

41.24 hell of a] out-a-sight A2-E2

41.27 debris] *débris* A2-E2

41.27 writhing] red, writhing A1

41.29 Go . . . riddance] Git th' devil outa here A2-E2

41.30 Maggie] She A1

42.4 rather a] a rather A2-E2

42.10 tumbled to] got onto A1

42.19,23 hell . . . hell] gee . . . gee A2-E2

42.23 she called] called she A1

42.24–25 " 'Oh, hell . . . yes.' "] *omit* A2-E2

42.28 unskilful] unskilled E1–2

42.30 The blue] Too, the blue A1

43.1 place] position A1

43.3 vaguely wonder] wonder vaguely A2-E2

43.7 hell] devil A2-E2

43.11 toward] towards E1–2

43.13 What d' hell's d'] What's d' A2-E2

43.21 D' hell she has,] Aw, git out! A2-E2

43.22 at] of A2-E2

43.28 Gawd curse her] she be cursed A2-E2

43.30 damn] bloomin' A2-E2

43.31 Take . . . yourself] Go fall on yerself A2-E2

43.31 yerself] yourself A1

43.31–32 an' quit dat] *omit* A1

43.37 damned] d—d A2-E2

44.10 hell outa] *omit* A2-E2

44.11 done] did A1

44.13 damned duffer.] big stiff! A2-E2

44.16 Gawd curse her] she be cursed A2-E2

44.26 hell,] rats! A2-E2

44.27 hell.] h—l! A2-E2

44.28 'ill] 'll E1-2

44.32 What d' hell] What's wrong A2-E2

44.35 what d' hell,] go ahn! A2-E2

44.39 What d' hell] what's d' use A2-E2

45.8 -imitation] -appearing A1

45.14 place] position A1

45.15 all] *omit* A1

45.26 wall] siding A1

45.31 bended] bent A2-E2

46.2 wore] had A1

46.2 watchfulness] watchfulness upon his features A1

46.5 dindy] dandy A2-E2

46.5 by Gawd] *omit* A2-E2

46.6 Oh, hell, yes,] Well, ain't he? A2-E2

46.6 sneering] sneering widely A1

46.9 further] farther A2-E2

46.10 obliviousness] oblivion A1

46.12 Great Gawd!] *omit* A2-E2

46.22 what d' hell is] what's A2-E2

46.24 Damned if I knows] Look's like some chump A2-E2

46.32 Who d' hell] Aw, who A2-E2

46.37,38 Oh, d' hell,] Aw, go ahn! A2-E2

47.6 Hot] Dark A1

47.15 Oh, hell,] Aw! A2-E2

47.17 d' hell] *omit* A2-E2

47.18 Damned if I knows] Don' ast me A2-E2

47.21–22 damn likely] like A2-E2

47.28 Oh, hell,] Aw, go ahn! A2-E2

47.37; 48.1,8 d' hell] *omit* A2-E2

48.4 ominously said Pete] said Pete ominously A2-E2

48.5 Oh, hell] Aw, go ahn A2-E2

48.11 clenched] clinched A2-E2

48.14 furiously] redly A1

48.19 Jimmie] him A1

48.32 pale] the pale A2-E2

48.34 wheezingly] wheezing E2

48.39 whirled] swirled A1

49.1 critical] tottering A1

49.8 glasses] glass A1

49.22 and] *omit* A1

49.26 bended] bent A2-E2

49.28 first] the first A2-E2

49.37 in hell] *omit* A2-E2

49.37 yeh] ye E2

50.3 safe dark corner] corner safely dark A1

50.7 At first] On first thoughts A1

50.9 what d' hell] what's d' use A2-E2

51.3 in soiled evening dress] a dress suit A1

51.5 gown] dress A1

51.9 to reach] *omit* A1

51.27 d' hell] *omit* A2

51.30–52.1 upon the stage . . . about] was flinging her heels about upon the stage A2

52.5 had had] had A1

52.6   the accents] tones A1
52.9   damn] cursed A2-E2
52.11   through] by A1
52.12   in] through A1
52.12   smoke-] smoked- A1–2
52.16   hale] hell A1
52.17   tamn!] damn. A1
52.19   was] were A2-E2
52.20   had experienced before] pre-
        viously had experienced A1
54.20   transfixed] tranfixed A2
54.23   bottle] squdgy bottle A1
55.13   t' yer own mudder—] omit
        E2
55.18   raise sech hell] make sech
        trouble A2-E2
55.24   damn] d—n A2-E2
55.30   didn'] didn't A2-E2
55.32   wa'n't] A2; wasn't A1
55.32   damn] omit A2-E2
55.35   the] a A1
55.36   which] omit A1
55.36   called] could call A1
56.6   I?] I, deh beast. A1
56.9   dis side of hell] omit A2-E2
56.12   Damn] Curse A2-E2
56.12   fervidly said] said fervidly
        A2-E2
56.18,22 Gawd] Heaven A2-E2
58.6   seats] a seat A2-E2
58.9   By Gawd] Hully gee A2-E2
58.20   said] said cordially A1
58.28   gallantry] awkward gal-
        lantry A1
58.31   as her addition to] upon A1
58.40   the additions with acclama-
        tions] with acclamations the ad-
        ditions A1
59.9   talk like a clock] gibber like
        an ape, dear A1
59.14   heluva] omit A2-E2
59.16   t' hell] g' way A2-E2
59.26   all] all there is of it A1
59.28   out of] from A1
59.35   funny] droll A1
60.4   On d' level, now] omit A1
60.6   saying] omit A1
60.14   bended] bent A2-E2
60.24   for] omit E1-2
60.31   They got cold feet.] omit A1

60.38   damned] omit A2-E2
61.15   chain] string A1
61.24   damn] omit A2-E2
61.33   Gawd,] heavens! A2-E2
62.7   furtively scanned] scanned
        furtively A1
62.20   Good Gawd!] omit A2-E2
62.24   yeh'd] ye'd A1–2; yehs E1–2
62.27,31 fer Gawd's sake,] omit
        A2-E2
63.3   hell] blazes A2-E2
63.12   damned] d—d A2-E2
63.17   at Maggie] omit A1
63.24   bended] bent A1-E2
63.28   , fer Gawd's sake,] omit
        A2-E2
63.29   railing] sneering A1
63.34   D' hell yeh say?] Git out!
        A2-E2
63.37   bended] bent A2-E2
64.8   showman] showman at a mu-
        seum A1
64.13   Fer Gawd's sake!] omit
        A2-E2
64.17   hell of a] omit A2-E2
64.22   that of] omit A1
65.6   hell] h—l A2-E2
65.10   d' hell] omit A2-E2
65.12   that people should lose] for
        anyone's losing A1
65.19   woman] woman of bril-
        liance and audacity A1
65.24   Pete] my cloud-compelling
        Pete A1
66.9   found] had found A1
66.10   room] rooms A2-E2
66.20   on] at E1-2
66.30   my Gawd,] say! A2-E2
66.30   hell do] omit A2-E2
66.31   yeh] yer A2-E2
66.35   Pete's glance expressed]
        Pete glanced A1
66.38   hell do] omit A2-E2
66.38   do] deh A1 (omit A2-E2)
66.39   do me dirt] git me inteh
        trouble A1
66.40   hell t' pay] trouble A2-E2
67.2   come] came E-2
67.2   raised hell] made trouble
        A2-E2

67.5　hell,] go ahn! A2-E2
67.13　hell] h—ll A2-E2
67.36　made] gave A1
68.12–13　who had . . . silence] having been comparatively silent A1
68.19　toward] towards E2
68.21　two hours in] having just emerged from A1
68.24　was] were A2-E2
68.28　those] men A1
69.12　ennui] *ennui* A2-E2
69.36　hands] hand A1
69.36　pockets] *omit* A1
70.2,3　dammit] *omit* A2-E2
70.4　Damn] *omit* A2-E2
70.8　whence] from whence A1
70.10　features.] features. ⸿ "Ah, there," said the girl. ⸿ "I've got a date," said the man A1
70.12　hands.] hands. "Ah, what deh hell? Tink I'm a millionaire?" A1
70.15　them . . . them] her . . . her A1
70.18　merriment.] merriment. ⸿ When almost to the river the girl saw a great figure. On going forward she perceived it to be a huge fat man in torn and greasy garments. His grey hair straggled down over his forehead. His small, bleared eyes, sparkling from amidst great rolls of red fat, swept eagerly over the girl's upturned face. He laughed, his brown, disordered teeth gleaming under a grey, grizzled moustache from which beer-drops dripped. His whole body gently quivered and shook like that of a dead jelly fish. Chuckling and leering, he followed the girl of the crimson legions. A1

70.19　At the feet . . . river.] At their feet the river appeared a deathly black hue. A1
71.5　damn] *omit* A2-E2
71.10,16,19,20　damn it] *omit* A2-E2
71.12　mood] mode A1
71.20　wants] want A1-E2
71.25　"Damn it," . . . time.] "We're havin' a great time," said the man. A2-E2
71.26　Damn'd if I don't!] *omit* A2-E2
71.29　heluva] good A2-E2
71.31　damn t'ing] not'ing A2-E2
71.31　damn it] *omit* A2-E2
72.8　his companions] them A1
72.15　Here, damn it,] Here's quar'! A2-E2
72.19,22,27　damn] *omit* A2-E2
72.23　the] a A1
72.31　woman] woman of brilliance and audacity A1
72.33　damn it,] *omit* A2-E2
73.11　damn] *omit* A2-E2
73.34　damn] —— A2-E2
74.3　woman] woman of brilliance and audacity A1
74.9,　damn it,] *omit* A2-E2
74.9　I] *omit* A1
74.10,12　damn 't] *omit* A2-E2
74.11　damn 't—] *omit* A2-E2
74.11　heluva] great A2-E2
74.13　Presently] Shortly A1
74.25　damn] *omit* A2-E2
75.8　hell] blazes A2-E2
75.11　t'umb] thumb E1–2
75.17　rooms] room E1–2
76.2　window] windows A1–2
76.23　damn] *omit* A2-E2
77.3　The] Hot A1
77.4　face] quivering face A1
77.4　in] like A1

George's Mother

INTRODUCTION

CRANE began *George's Mother,* his second novel of the slums, sometime early in 1893 shortly after the appearance of *Maggie: A Girl of the Streets.* It was once assumed the novel was first started in 1894, about the time he wrote Garland on May 9 that he was "writing another novel which is a bird." [1] But a recent discovery of two manuscript pages of *George's Mother* in the Barrett Collection at the University of Virginia shows that the initial composition must have been started a year earlier, [2] sometime in the spring of 1893,

[1] *Stephen Crane: Letters,* ed. R. W. Stallman and Lillian Gilkes (New York, 1960), p. 36.

[2] Maurice Bassan, "An Early Draft of *George's Mother,*" *American Literature,* XXXVI (January, 1965), 518–522. (Facsimile pages follow p. 110 below.)

This draft of the first five paragraphs of Chapter II of the published novel (noted as Chapter I in the draft) appears on the reverse sides of two pages of a complete manuscript of a Sullivan County sketch, "The Holler Tree." Seven of the ten Sullivan County stories were printed in the New York *Tribune* in 1892, and it is reasonably assumed that all of them were written this year or earlier, though "The Holler Tree" was not published until 1934. Since the draft of *George's Mother* is written on what would ordinarily be considered the "correct" sides of pages 5 and 6 of "The Holler Tree" manuscript, Bassan suggests that the novel was begun before Crane wrote "The Holler Tree," i.e., in 1892 or earlier. "Seeking fresh sheets for his Sullivan County story," Bassan writes, "Crane crossed out both pages of text [of the draft of *George's Mother*], which of course had been written on the 'correct' side of the page, and then turned these pages over and upside down."

But it is not necessary to assume that the draft of *George's Mother* was written first merely because it is on the "correct" side of the ruled legal paper. Crane wrote the title "The Holler Tree" on the "correct" side of one of the sheets, but for some reason, probably because he disfigured the page with a large ink blot just above the title, he apparently turned the pages over and upside down and wrote the sketch straight through on what would normally be considered the back sides of the sheets. Thus when he was seeking paper later for the draft of *George's Mother,* he found only the "correct" sides of the old Sullivan County story clean and usable.

This interpretation of the evidence is strongly supported by the fact that Crane did just this when he was seeking paper for another story which is known to have been written later than "The Holler Tree." Eight manuscript lines of the beginning of "The Reluctant Voyagers" (which Bassan does not mention) are also, like the fragment of *George's Mother,* written on the "correct" side of one of the pages of "The Holler Tree" manuscript (p. 3). Corwin K. Linson, the artist who

102 · George's Mother

though how much of the story was drafted before Crane laid it aside for *The Red Badge of Courage,* begun in April, 1893, and finished a year later, is not known. Another letter to Garland dated November 15, 1894, marks the approximate date *George's Mother* was finished: "I have just completed a New York book that leaves Maggie at the post. It is my best thing. Since you are not here, I am going to see if Mr. Howells will not read it." [3]

Except for these dates and a few other isolated facts, *George's Mother* has no concrete prepublication history. Crane almost never discussed his writing in his letters, except on rare occasions when he responded to requests of editors to supply brief biographical summaries for use in the preparation of newspaper notices and reviews. He was notoriously inaccurate with dates and other facts. He left no information whatsoever about his conversations with Howells, Garland, Henry James, Harold Frederic, H. G. Wells, Joseph Conrad, or any of the other literary men he knew well, in some cases intimately, during the nineties. He knew Garland well in the early years of the decade, and he was a welcome visitor in the home of Howells. He thought of these men as patrons and advisers, or as he put it in a characteristically scant and ambiguous phrase, "my literary fathers—Howells and Garland." [4] His article on Garland's lecture on Howells in the *Tribune* and his published interview with Howells in 1894 show a somewhat sophisticated grasp of literary theory. But he almost never discussed books or ideas in his letters or in any of his other writings.

He never reported, for example, whether or not Howells actually did read the manuscript of *George's Mother,* and the historian must be content to conjecture that a phrase in the critic's remark on the current situation in fiction, reported by Crane in

illustrated "The Reluctant Voyagers," positively dates this story in the spring of 1893 (*My Stephen Crane* [Syracuse, 1958], pp. 18 ff.). Linson's recollection of dates in his memoir of Crane is usually accurate, and he had particularly good reason to remember "The Reluctant Voyagers" since his elaborately prepared illustrations for the story were lost by a careless editor. His testimony establishes beyond reasonable doubt that Crane used the clean "correct" side of "The Holler Tree" as manuscript paper in the spring of 1893.

"The Reluctant Voyagers" does not, of course, precisely date the early draft of *George's Mother.* But it does establish almost certainly that the draft was begun *after* "The Holler Tree," not earlier than 1892, and most probably in the spring of 1893.

[3] New York, *Letters,* p. 41.

[4] Crane to Lily Brandon Munroe, New York, [March, 1894?], *Letters,* p. 31.

his article in the *Times*, is a reasonable indication that Howells at least knew of the existence of the novel in October, 1894, one month presumably before it was finished. "I like to see," Howells said, "the novelists treating some of the other important things of life—the relation of mother and son, of husband and wife, in fact all those things that we live in continually. The other can be but fragmentary." [5]

The remark not only alludes to the subject of *George's Mother*, the deterioration of the relationship between a pious, credulous, and doting woman and her self-indulgent and irresponsible son, but it seems to refer also, perhaps in a congratulatory way, to certain presumed improvements in Crane's conception of realistic fiction. Garland's review of *Maggie* complained that it failed of "rounded completeness." "It is typical only of the worst elements of the alley. The author should delineate the families living on the next street, who live lives of heroic purity and hopeless hardship." [6] As realists Howells and Garland held in common the idea that fiction should avoid a narrow focus on exceptional and bizarre subjects; realism, in their view, was properly concerned with the typical and ordinary, and one may suppose that Garland, who was articulate and vociferous in the expression of theoretical ideas, had taken pains to present these views to Crane when he took over the direction of the young man's literary affairs shortly after the first publication of *Maggie*. These ideas one may believe Crane also heard from Howells, who testified that he cautioned the author of *Maggie* about the unrestricted realism of its language, advising him that this "would shock the public from him." [7] A warning against a too narrow concern for the exceptional in life is implicit in the critic's reference to "grim if not grimy truth" in his 1895 review of *Maggie*.

The evidence is altogether circumstantial, but it seems to suggest that *George's Mother* was conceived as a response to Crane's "literary fathers." Crane's plan for the novel may be imagined. It would be a companion piece to *Maggie*, but it would show another, more "normal" life of the slums. The mother and

[5] "Fears Realists Must Wait," New York *Times* (Oct. 28, 1894), p. 20.

[6] "An Ambitious French Novel and a Modest American Story," *Arena*, VIII (June, 1893), xi.

[7] Howells to Cora Crane, Annisquam, Mass., July 29, 1900, *Letters*, p. 306.

son, the Kelceys, would live in the same tenement house as the Johnsons, but in contrast to the vicious Mrs. Johnson, the courageous and spirited Mrs. Kelcey, lately arrived from the country with her son George, would do battle against the arrayed forces of their hostile world. She would not like Maggie Johnson be defeated by the irresistible forces of her environment, but by the cruel rebuffs of her cowardly and weak-willed son. It would be a study in the psychology of moral deprivation, more subdued than *Maggie* and less conspicuously concentrated in execution. It would be, in short, the kind of realistic novel Howells or Garland might write. Howells could hardly have said as he did once in reference to *Maggie* that he "could not agree . . . in all points of theory." [8]

But he must have known that *George's Mother* was not in Crane's true idiom, though he was probably unconscious of the irony in the remarks he made about it two years later in his introduction to the English edition of *Maggie:* "This is scarcely a study at all," he wrote, "while Maggie is really and fully so. It is the study of a situation merely. . . . The wonder of it is the courage which deals with persons so absolutely average." [9] And though Howells intends to praise Crane for his art, guaranteed by his "compassion for everything that errs and suffers," Mencken reflects more general critical opinion in his observation that Crane's "method, in truth, was grossly ill-adapted to the novel, properly so-called. He had, so to speak, no literary small talk; he could not manage what the musicians call passage work. His superlative skill lay in the handling of isolated situations; he knew exactly how to depict them with a dazzling brilliance." [10] Mencken may have had in mind the graphic power of some of the street scenes in the novel, or the brilliance of the narrative account of old Bleecker's drunken party. But the characterization of the principals is all surface; they have little of the psychological depth which Howells' kind of realism requires. As he said, *George's Mother* is hardly a study at all.

[8] Howells to Crane, New York, April 8, 1893, *Letters*, p. 18.

[9] "An Appreciation," introduction to *Maggie: A Child of the Streets* (London, 1896), pp. vi–vii.

[10] H. L. Mencken, Introduction, in *The Work of Stephen Crane*, ed. Wilson Follett (New York, 1925), X, xi–xii.

II

The record, such as it is, can only lead to the conclusion that Crane was indifferent to the fate of *George's Mother*. Although he spoke of it enthusiastically in his letter to Garland as his "best thing," he did not mention it again in writing until 1899, when he remarked angrily that critics condemned just the passages in it that he "would like to write over again if that was honest." [11] He (or perhaps Howells or Garland) must have told someone at the *Bookman* about it, for a short article on Crane appearing in that journal in May, 1895, noted that "among other manuscripts which are now in the publisher's hands is one entitled 'A Woman Without Weapons,'" apparently the original title of the book.[12] But if it actually was at a publisher, nothing is known about it. Copeland and Day, having issued *The Black Riders* in May, approached Crane on the question of unpublished materials in June, and though the author admitted that he had "considerable work that is not in the hands of publishers," he did not offer, or indeed mention, the completed and idle *George's Mother*, offering instead his 1892 Sullivan County sketches. He may have thought the publisher's somewhat arty style of book design, exercised in the production of *The Black Riders* by printing the poems in large capitals and enclosing them in a cover decorated with a sprawling orchid, more appropriate for his eccentric poems and "grotesque little tales" than for *George's Mother*. *The Black Riders* at the time was attracting virulent ridicule from newspaper paragraphers, who were particularly scornful of the capitals and the orchid, and Crane observed that if the publishers chose to issue the sketches as one of their "swell little volumes of 10000, the tales would gain considerable lengthy abuse no doubt." [13]

But no explanation can be offered for the fact that Crane never mentioned *George's Mother*. As publisher of *The Red Badge* Appleton had as a matter of course first call on Crane's unpublished work. Appleton's editor, Ripley Hitchcock, accepted *The Third Violet* before it had advanced beyond the planning stage, as if it were understood at this time that Crane was an

[11] Crane to unknown recipient, [August, 1899], *Letters*, p. 226.
[12] "Stephen Crane," *Bookman*, I, 230.
[13] Crane to Copeland and Day, New York, [June? 1895], *Letters*, p. 59.

Appleton author. But Hitchcock knew nothing about the existence of *George's Mother* until it appeared in 1896 under the imprint of a competitor, Edward Arnold. And when Crane referred to it in a curiously oblique letter of apology, admitting that he had "perhaps in this case violated certain business courtesies" in handing work over to another publisher without consulting Appleton, he identified it by the wrong title:

As for Edward Arnold, his American manager is an old schoolmate and ten-year's friend of mine and he conducted such a campaign against me as is seldom seen. He appealed to my avarice and failing appealed to my humanity. Once I thought he was about to get "The Little Regiment," when you stepped in and saved it. Finally I thought of a satirical sketch of mine—an old thing, strong in satire but rather easy writing—called Dan Emmonds and I gave it to him.[14]

But "Dan Emmonds" is merely an unfinished sketch, not commercially publishable; what Crane's friend got for Arnold was *George's Mother*.

This curious concealment of the book suggests that Crane had no very high opinion of *George's Mother*. He may have thought it suffered too much from the drain on his creative energy by *The Red Badge*. He blamed the war novel for the inferiority of *The Third Violet*, describing this transparent little courtship comedy as "pretty rotten work" and explaining that he used himself up "in the accursed 'Red Badge.'"[15] But he did not withdraw it even when Hitchcock apparently hinted that he might. "I think it is as well to go ahead with The Third Violet. People may just as well discover now that the high dramatic key of The Red Badge cannot be sustained. . . . The Third Violet is a quiet little story but then it is serious work and I should say let it go."[16] He could have said much more for *George's Mother*, for despite its weaknesses it would have done *The Red Badge* more credit than the banal little love story.

III

It has been suggested that Crane drew on Zola's *L'Assommoir* for *George's Mother* as well as for *Maggie: A Girl of the Streets*,[17] but

[14] Crane to Hitchcock, Washington, D.C., March 26, [1896], *Letters*, p. 121.
[15] Crane to Curtis Brown, Hartwood, N.Y., Dec. 31, 1896 [1895], *Letters*, p. 87.
[16] Crane to Hitchcock, Hartwood, Jan. 27, [1896], *Letters*, pp. 106–107.
[17] Lars Åhnebrink, *The Beginnings of Naturalism in American Fiction, 1891–*

a more realistic view is that the novel is based on personal experience. The literature of the antisaloon movement, which dates back to the middle of the century, had impressed upon the popular mind of the time the idea of alcohol as an instrument of moral destruction. Crane's father, the Rev. Jonathan Townley Crane, was the author of a book on the evils of drink, *Arts of Intoxication* (1870), and the views he expressed on the evils of drink were reflected melodramatically and sentimentally in popular temperance literature, examples of which are the famous *Ten Nights in a Barroom* and its sequel *Three Years in a Man Trap* (1872). The elements of the common theme in these melodramatic exposés are the ruined victim of drink, the blighted career, the impoverishment of the victim's family, and the death of a loved one—child, wife, or mother—as a result of consequent shame or extreme poverty. Crane adopted this familiar motif for his account of George's decline, just as he adopted the popular conception about seduced and abandoned girls to account for the tragic demise of Maggie Johnson in his first novel of the slums.

But the germ for the mother and son relationship can be seen in Crane's experience with his own mother, Mary Helen Peck Crane, who is clearly the model for Mrs. Kelcey. Mrs. Crane was a devoted worker in the Methodist church who wrote newspaper articles on religion and was active in various reform projects. "After my father died," Crane wrote in 1899, "mother lived in and for religion. . . . My brother Will used to try to argue with her on religious subjects such as hell but he always gave it up. Don't understand that mother was bitter or mean but it hurt her that any of us should be slipping from Grace and giving up eternal damnation or salvation or those things." [18] The critical sense in Crane which enabled him to project his mother into the ironically contemplated Mrs. Kelcey was fully developed, according to a niece who knew him well, by the time he was twenty:

By this time [1891] he was in full rebellion against the traditions on which he had been nourished and reared. His mother's memory was dear to him, and although he never questioned her ways when he

---

1903 (University of Uppsala Essays and Studies on American Language and Literature, IX; Uppsala, Sweden, 1950), p. 271.
[18] Crane to Willis B. Clarke, [Brede Place, November, 1899], *Letters*, p. 242.

was outside the family portals, he did marvel always that such an intellectual woman, a university graduate, and capable of being a regular contributor to magazines and newspapers, could have wrapped herself so completely in the "vacuous, futile, psalm-singing that passed for worship" in those days.[19]

The regressive George is similarly a fictional adaptation of Crane himself as a young man:

I used to like church and prayer meetings when I was a kid but that cooled off and when I was thirteen or about that, my brother Will told me not to believe in Hell after my uncle had been boring me about the lake of fire and the rest of the sideshows. . . . Once when I was fourteen an organ grinder on the beach at Asbury gave me a nice long drink out of a nice red bottle for picking up his hat for him. I felt ecstatic walking home and then I was an Emperor and some Rajahs and Baron de Blowitz all at the same time. I had been sulky all morning and now I was perfectly willing to go to a prayer meeting and Mother was tickled to death. And, mind you, all because this nefarious Florentine gave me a red drink out of a bottle. I have frequently wondered how much mothers ever know about their sons, after all. She would not have found it much of a joke.[20]

The situation as he depicted it in his novel, the most personal of his books, must have had special significance for him. George's story is for one thing a fable of his own downward progress from the respectable Methodist parsonage to the disreputable Bowery saloon and bohemian studio. But if he felt in this condition a certain guilt, as he did consciously when he identified with the outcasts and renegades of the Bowery, he must have felt at the same time the justice of his disdain for the sentimental pieties of the middle-class orthodoxy he had repudiated. The significance of this contradiction is the undeveloped subject of the novel, given implicitly in the situation. But Crane was unable to exploit it. His lambent and witty impressionism, for all its peculiar strength, was unequal to this particular burden.

J. B. C.

[19] Helen R. Crane, "My Uncle, Stephen Crane," *American Mercury*, XXXI (January, 1934), 25.
[20] Crane to Clarke, *Letters*, pp. 242–243.

TEXTUAL INTRODUCTION

THE firm of Edward Arnold, which published *George's Mother* in 1896, applied for copyright on May 15, 1896, with deposit in the Library of Congress on May 29. The book was advertised in the *Publishers' Weekly* of June 6. The printer and binder was Trow Directory of New York. Only one edition was printed, probably from plates on the evidence of several out-of-line types constant in all eight copies collated. The title-page of this first edition (A1) reads: 'GEORGE'S MOTHER | BY | STEPHEN CRANE | AUTHOR OF "THE RED BADGE OF COURAGE," | "THE BLACK RIDERS," ETC. | EDWARD AR-NOLD | [to the left] NEW YORK | 70 FIFTH AVENUE | [vertical line] | [to the right] LONDON | 37 BEDFORD STREET | [centered] 1896'. Its collation is 1⁸ 2–11⁸ 12⁶, pp. 1–7 8–177 178–188. P. 1 holds the half-title 'GEORGE'S MOTHER'; p. 2 blank; p. 3 title; p. 4 copyright notice and printer's imprint; pp. 5–6 blank; p. 7 text ending on p. 177 with p. 178 blank; pp. 179–186 publisher's announcements; pp. 187–188 blank. The paper is white laid with horizontal chainlines and no watermark. The price was seventy-five cents.

Three copies of this edition (A1) at the University of Virginia have been collated on the Hinman Machine.[1] Three additional copies in the Ohio State University Libraries have been independently machined against each other. Finally, Barrett copy 1 has been sight-collated against the copies in the Berg Collection at the New York Public Library and the Houghton Library, Harvard, all without sign of textual variation. The batter lists of the three University of Virginia machined copies have been checked against those of the Ohio State University Libraries machined copies without evidence appearing for more than a single impression.

[1] These are Barrett PS1449.C85G4 1896, copy 1 (433775) and copy 2 (551387), and McGregor A1896.C7G4 (281461).

Arnold published the first London edition in 1896 (E1), the announcement in the *Publishers' Circular* being for June 13 and the British Museum deposit copy (shelf mark 012627.e.9) stamped June 30. The printer's copy was the New York edition A1. The title reads: 'GEORGE'S MOTHER | BY | STEPHEN CRANE | AUTHOR OF | 'THE RED BADGE OF COURAGE,' 'THE BLACK RIDERS,' ETC. | EDWARD ARNOLD | [to the left] LONDON | 37 BEDFORD STREET | [to the right] NEW YORK | 70 FIFTH AVENUE | [centered] 1896'. The book collates 1^8 $2-12^8$, the text beginning on p. 7 and ending on 185, with 186 blank and then on pp. 187–192 a series of publisher's advertisements. The price was two shillings. A constant error appears to be the dropping of the figure 3 from p. 34. The printers were Billing and Sons of Guildford. The University of Virginia Barrett copy PS1449.C85G4 1896a (551388) has been used for collation.

In 1900 the second English edition (E2) appeared under the Heinemann imprint joined with *Maggie* as *Bowery Tales*. This edition is described in the Textual Introduction to *Maggie*. The printer's copy was E1. Wilson Follett's edition in *The Work of Stephen Crane* appears to be printed from E2.

The text of *George's Mother* is simple in its history. Only the first New York edition (A1) has authority and it has automatically become the copy-text for the present edition. The changes in E1 appear to represent only normal editorial and compositorial tinkering, and E2 is a faithful reprint of E1. The copy-text A1 is remarkably uniform in its system of accidentals so that almost no editorial attention is required. As a result, however, the typical Crane features of the accidentals are fewer than in the more naïve print of *Maggie* despite the presence, for example, of his common misspelling *mode* for *mood*. Only two or three substantive cruxes occur in what appears to be an accurate and carefully printed text.

In the Barrett Collection at the University of Virginia is preserved an early draft of an opening for *George's Mother*, written on the versos of the fifth and sixth leaves of the Sullivan County Sketch "The Holler Tree." The following is a diplomatic reprint of this draft: [2]

[2] The draft was discovered by Professor Maurice Bassan and transcribed in "An Early Draft of *George's Mother*," *American Literature*, XXXVI (January, 1965), 518–522.

Chapter I.

A man with a red, mottled face put forth his head from a window and wrathfully cursed. He threw a bottle high across two back yards at a window of an opposite tenement. It broke against the bricks of the house and the fragments fell crackling upon the stones below. The man shook his fist.

A bare-armed woman, hanging out a small array of clothes in one of the yards, glanced casually up at the man and listened to his words. Her eyes followed his over to the other tenement. Two children, being in the proper places, picked up the bits of glass and began to fondle them as new toys.

From the window at which the man raged came the sound of an old voice, singing. It quavered and trembled ~~like a lamb~~ ~~and first~~ among the loud noises of the neighborhood.

"Should I be ~~w~~ car-reed tew th' skies,"
"O-on flow'ry be-eds of ee-ease,"
"While oth-hers fought tew w-win th' fight"
"~~And~~ sailed through blood-dee seas."

Draft of an early opening of *George's Mother*

The man across the block continued to swear.

A little old woman was the owner of the voice. In a third story room of the red and black tenement she was trudging ~~that~~ on a long journey, bearing pots and pans and sometimes a broom and d dust-pan. The weight of them seemed to have bended her back and crooked her limbs, until she walked with difficulty. ~~Sometimes~~ Often, she plunged her ~~arms~~ hands into hot water at the sink. She splashed about, the ~~muscles~~ dwindled muscles ~~of her arms~~ working to and fro under the loose skin of her arms. She came from it, be-draggled and steaming as if she had crossed some flooded river.

The room was changing under her hands. Her fingers went nervously ~~it~~ into disorder and wrought neatness.

Her broom was continually seeking dust-demons. It seemed a lance in the hands of a small determined warrior who was fighting her way to some place. There was the flurry of a

Second page of a draft of an early opening of *George's Mother*

[*first page*]

Chapter I

A man with a red,[a] mottled face put forth his head from a window and wrathfully cursed. He threw a bottle high across two back yards at a window of an opposite tenement. It broke against the bricks of the house and the fragments fell crackling upon the stones below. The man shook his fist.

A bare-armed woman, hanging out a small array of clothes in one of the yards, glanced casually up at the man and listened to his words. Her eyes followed his over to the other tenement. Two children, being in the proper place, picked up the bits of glass and began to fondle them as new toys.

From the window at which the man raged came the sound of an old voice, singing. It quavered and trembled [b] among the loud noises of the neighborhood.

"Should I be-[c] car-reed tew th' skies,"
"O-on flow'ry be-eds of ee-ease,"
"While oth-thers fought tew w-win th' fight
"An'[d] sailed through blood-dee seas."

[*second page*]

The man across the block continued to swear.

A little old woman was the owner of the voice. In a third story room of the red and black tenement she was trudging [e] on a long journey, bearing pots and pans and sometimes a broom and a dust-pan. The weight of them seemed to have bended her back and crooked her limbs,[f] until she walked with difficulty. Often,[g] she plunged her hands [h] into hot water at the sink. She splashed about, the dwindled [i] muscles [j] working to and fro under the loose skin of her [k] arms. She came from it, be-draggled and steaming as if she had crossed some flooded river.

The room was changing under her hands. Her fingers went nervously [l] into disorder and wrought neatness.

her broom was continually seeking dust-demons.[m] It seemed a lance in the [n] hands of a small determined warrior who was fighting her way to some place. There was the flurry of a

[a] red,] *followed by deleted* 'sin-stained' *with* 'mottled' *interlined*
[b] trembled] *followed by deleted* 'like a lame sound spirit'
[c] be-] *originally* 'be-e' *but final* 'e' *deleted*
[d] An'] *final* 'd' *deleted and apostrophe added*
[e] trudging] *followed by deleted* 'about'
[f] limbs,] *comma added after a deleted period*
[g] Often] *preceded by deleted* 'Sometimes,'
[h] hands] *interlined above deleted* 'arms'

[i] dwindled] *preceded by deleted* 'muscles'
[j] muscles] *followed by deleted* 'of her arms'
[k] her] *interlined with a caret*
[l] nervously] *followed by deleted* 'it'
[m] -demons] *hyphen follows a deleted period*
[n] the] *interlined with a caret*

So far as is known, no other part of a manuscript of *George's Mother* is preserved.

F. B.

GEORGE'S MOTHER

I

IN THE swirling rain that came at dusk the broad avenue glistened with that deep bluish tint which is so widely condemned when it is put into pictures. There were long rows of shops, whose fronts shone with full, golden light. Here and there, from druggists' windows, or from the red street-lamps that indicated the positions of fire-alarm boxes, a flare of uncertain, wavering crimson was thrown upon the wet pavements.

The lights made shadows, in which the buildings loomed with a new and tremendous massiveness, like castles and fortresses. There were endless processions of people, mighty hosts, with umbrellas waving, banner-like, over them. Horse-cars, aglitter with new paint, rumbled in steady array between the pillars that supported the elevated railroad. The whole street resounded with the tinkle of bells, the roar of iron-shod wheels on the cobbles, the ceaseless trample of the hundreds of feet. Above all, too, could be heard the loud screams of the tiny newsboys, who scurried in all directions. Upon the corners, standing in from the dripping eaves, were many loungers, descended from the world that used to prostrate itself before pageantry.

A brown young man went along the avenue. He held a tin lunch-pail under his arm in a manner that was evidently uncomfortable. He was puffing at a corn-cob pipe. His shoulders had a self-reliant poise, and the hang of his arms and the raised veins of his hands showed him to be a man who worked with his muscles.

As he passed a street-corner a man in old clothes gave a shout of surprise, and rushing impetuously forward, grasped his hand.

"Hello, Kelcey, ol' boy," cried the man in old clothes. "How's th' boy, anyhow? Where in thunder yeh been fer th' last seventeen years? I'll be hanged if you ain't th' last man I ever expected t' see."

The brown youth put his pail to the ground and grinned.

"Well, if it ain't ol' Charley Jones," he said, ecstatically shaking hands. "How are yeh, anyhow? Where yeh been keepin' yerself? I ain't seen yeh fer a year!"

"Well, I should say so! Why, th' last time I saw you was up in Handyville!"

"Sure! On Sunday, we——"

"Sure! Out at Bill Sickles's place. Let's go get a drink!"

They made toward a little glass-fronted saloon that sat blinking jovially at the crowds. It engulfed them with a gleeful motion of its two widely smiling lips.

"What'll yeh take, Kelcey?"

"Oh, I guess I'll take a beer."

"Gimme little whiskey, John."

The two friends leaned against the bar and looked with enthusiasm upon each other.

"Well, well, I'm thunderin' glad t' see yeh," said Jones.

"Well, I guess," replied Kelcey. "Here's to yeh, ol' man."

"Let 'er go."

They lifted their glasses, glanced fervidly at each other, and drank.

"Yeh ain't changed much, on'y yeh've growed like th' devil," said Jones, reflectively, as he put down his glass. "I'd know yeh anywheres!"

"Certainly yeh would," said Kelcey. "An' I knew you, too, th' minute I saw yeh. Yer changed, though!"

"Yes," admitted Jones, with some complacency, "I s'pose I am." He regarded himself in the mirror that multiplied the bottles on the shelf back of the bar. He should have seen a grinning face with a rather pink nose. His derby was perched carelessly on the back part of his head. Two wisps of hair straggled down over his hollow temples. There was something very worldly and wise about him. Life did not seem to confuse him. Evidently he understood its complications. His hand thrust into his trousers' pocket, where he jingled keys, and his hat perched back on his head expressed a young man of vast knowledge. His extensive acquaintance with bartenders aided him materially in this habitual expression of wisdom.

Having finished he turned to the barkeeper. "John, has any of th' gang been in t'-night yet?"

"No—not yet," said the barkeeper. "Ol' Bleecker was aroun' this afternoon about four. He said if I seen any of th' boys t' tell 'em he'd be up t'-night if he could get away. I saw Connor an' that other fellah goin' down th' avenyeh about an hour ago. I guess they'll be back after awhile."

"This is th' hang-out fer a great gang," said Jones, turning to Kelcey. "They're a great crowd, I tell yeh. We own th' place when we get started. Come aroun' some night. Any night, almost. T'-night, b' jiminy. They'll almost all be here, an' I'd like t' inter-duce yeh. They're a great gang! Gre-e-at!"

"I'd like teh," said Kelcey.

"Well, come ahead, then," cried the other, cordially. "Yeh'd like t' know 'em. It's an outa sight crowd. Come aroun' t'-night!"

"I will if I can."

"Well, yeh ain't got anything t' do, have yeh?" demanded Jones. "Well, come along, then. Yeh might just as well spend yer time with a good crowd 'a fellahs. An' it's a great gang. Great! Gre-e-at!"

"Well, I must make fer home now, anyhow," said Kelcey. "It's late as blazes. What'll yeh take this time, ol' man?"

"Gimme little more whiskey, John!"

"Guess I'll take another beer!"

Jones emptied the whiskey into his large mouth and then put the glass upon the bar. "Been in th' city long?" he asked. "Um—well, three years is a good deal fer a slick man. Doin' well? Oh, well, nobody's doin' well these days." He looked down mournfully at his shabby clothes. "Father's dead, ain't 'ee? Yeh don't say so? Fell off a scaffoldin', didn't 'ee? I heard it somewheres. Mother's livin', of course? I thought she was. Fine ol' lady—fi-i-ne. Well, you're th' last of her boys. Was five of yeh onct, wasn't there? I knew four m'self. Yes, five! I thought so. An' all gone but you, hey? Well you'll have t' brace up an' be a comfort t' th' ol' mother. Well, well, well, who would 'a thought that on'y you'd be left out 'a all that mob 'a tow-headed kids. Well, well, well, it's a queer world, ain't it?"

A contemplation of this thought made him sad. He sighed and moodily watched the other sip beer.

"Well, well, it's a queer world—a damn queer world."

"Yes," said Kelcey, "I'm th' on'y one left!" There was an accent of discomfort in his voice. He did not like this dwelling upon a sentiment that was connected with himself.

"How is th' ol' lady, anyhow?" continued Jones. "Th' last time I remember she was as spry as a little ol' cricket, an' was helpeltin' aroun' the' country lecturin' before W.C.T.U.'s an' one thing an' another."

"Oh, she's pretty well," said Kelcey.

"An' outa five boys you're th' on'y one she's got left? Well, well —have another drink before yeh go."

"Oh, I guess I've had enough."

A wounded expression came into Jones's eyes. "Oh, come on," he said.

"Well, I'll take another beer!"

"Gimme little more whiskey, John!"

When they had concluded this ceremony, Jones went with his friend to the door of the saloon. "Good-by, ol' man," he said, genially. His homely features shone with friendliness. "Come aroun', now, sure. T'-night! See? They're a great crowd. Gre-e-at!"

MAN with a red, mottled face put forth his head from a window and cursed violently. He flung a bottle high across two backyards at a window of the opposite tenement. It broke against the bricks of the house and the fragments fell crackling upon the stones below. The man shook his fist.

A bare-armed woman, making an array of clothes on a line in one of the yards, glanced casually up at the man and listened to his words. Her eyes followed his to the other tenement. From a distant window, a youth with a pipe, yelled some comments upon the poor aim. Two children, being in the proper yard, picked up the bits of broken glass and began to fondle them as new toys.

From the window at which the man raged came the sound of an old voice, singing. It quavered and trembled out into the air as if a sound-spirit had a broken wing.

"Should I be car-reed tew th' skies
O-on flow'ry be-eds of ee-ease,
While others fought tew win th' prize
An' sailed through blood-ee seas."

The man in the opposite window was greatly enraged. He continued to swear.

A little old woman was the owner of the voice. In a fourth-story room of the red and black tenement she was trudging on a journey. In her arms she bore pots and pans, and sometimes a broom and dust-pan. She wielded them like weapons. Their weight seemed to have bended her back and crooked her arms until she walked with difficulty. Often she plunged her hands into water at a sink. She splashed about, the dwindled muscles working to and fro under the loose skin of her arms. She came from the sink, steaming and bedraggled as if she had crossed a flooded river.

There was the flurry of a battle in this room. Through the clouded dust or steam one could see the thin figure dealing mighty blows. Always her way seemed beset. Her broom was continually poised, lance-wise, at dust demons. There came clashings and clangings as she strove with her tireless foes.

It was a picture of indomitable courage. And as she went on her way her voice was often raised in a long cry, a strange war-chant, a shout of battle and defiance, that rose and fell in harsh screams, and exasperated the ears of the man with the red, mottled face.

> "Should I be car-reed tew th' skies
> O-on flow'ry be-eds of ee-ease——"

Finally she halted for a moment. Going to the window she sat down and mopped her face with her apron. It was a lull, a moment of respite. Still it could be seen that she even then was planning skirmishes, charges, campaigns. She gazed thoughtfully about the room and noted the strength and position of her enemies. She was very alert.

At last, she turned to the mantel. "Five o'clock," she murmured, scrutinizing a little, swaggering, nickel-plated clock.

She looked out at chimneys growing thickly on the roofs. A man at work on one seemed like a bee. In the intricate yards below, vine-line lines had strange leaves of cloth. To her ears there came the howl of the man with the red, mottled face. He was engaged in a furious altercation with the youth who had called attention to his poor aim. They were like animals in a jungle.

In the distance an enormous brewery towered over the other buildings. Great gilt letters advertised a brand of beer. Thick smoke came from funnels and spread near it like vast and powerful wings. The structure seemed a great bird, flying. The letters of the sign made a chain of gold hanging from its neck. The little old woman looked at the brewery. It vaguely interested her, for a moment, as a stupendous affair, a machine of mighty strength.

Presently she sprang from her rest and began to buffet with her shrivelled arms. In a moment the battle was again in full swing. Terrific blows were given and received. There arose the clattering uproar of a new fight. The little intent warrior never hesitated nor faltered. She fought with a strong and relentless will. Beads and lines of perspiration stood upon her forehead.

Three blue plates were leaning in a row on the shelf back of the stove. The little old woman had seen it done somewhere. In front of them swaggered the round nickel-plated clock. Her son had stuck many cigarette pictures in the rim of a looking-glass that hung near. Occasional chromos were tacked upon the yellowed walls of the room. There was one in a gilt frame. It was quite an affair, in reds and greens. They all seemed like trophies.

It began to grow dark. A mist came winding. Rain plashed softly upon the window-sill. A lamp had been lighted in the opposite tenement; the strong orange glare revealed the man with a red, mottled face. He was seated by a table, smoking and reflecting.

The little old woman looked at the clock again. "Quarter 'a six."

She had paused for a moment, but she now hurled herself fiercely at the stove that lurked in the gloom, red-eyed, like a dragon. It hissed, and there was renewed clangor of blows. The little old woman dashed to and fro.

III

AS IT grew toward seven o'clock the little old woman became nervous. She often would drop into a chair and sit staring at the little clock.

"I wonder why he don't come," she continually repeated. There was a small, curious note of despair in her voice. As she sat thinking and staring at the clock the expressions of her face changed swiftly. All manner of emotions flickered in her eyes and about her lips. She was evidently perceiving in her imagination the journey of a loved person. She dreamed for him mishaps and obstacles. Something tremendous and irritating was hindering him from coming to her.

She had lighted an oil-lamp. It flooded the room with vivid yellow glare. The table, in its oil-cloth covering, had previously appeared like a bit of bare, brown desert. It now was a white garden, growing the fruits of her labor.

"Seven o'clock," she murmured, finally. She was aghast.

Then suddenly she heard a step upon the stair. She sprang up and began to bustle about the room. The little fearful emotions passed at once from her face. She seemed now to be ready to scold.

Young Kelcey entered the room. He gave a sigh of relief, and dropped his pail in a corner. He was evidently greatly wearied by a hard day of toil.

The little old woman hobbled over to him and raised her wrinkled lips. She seemed on the verge of tears and an outburst of reproaches.

"Hello!" he cried, in a voice of cheer. "Been gettin' anxious?"

"Yes," she said, hovering about him. "Where yeh been, George? What made yeh so late? I've been waitin' th' longest while. Don't throw your coat down there. Hang it up behind th' door."

The son put his coat on the proper hook, and then went to splatter water in a tin wash-basin at the sink.

"Well, yeh see, I met Jones—you remember Jones? Ol' Handyville fellah. An' we had t' stop an' talk over ol' times. Jones is quite a boy."

The little old woman's mouth set in a sudden straight line. "Oh, that Jones," she said. "I don't like him."

The youth interrupted a flurry of white towel to give a glance of irritation. "Well, now, what's th' use of talkin' that way?" he said to her. "What do yeh know 'bout 'im? Ever spoke to 'im in yer life?"

"Well, I don't know as I ever did since he grew up," replied the little old woman. "But I know he ain't th' kind 'a man I'd like t' have you go around with. He ain't a good man. I'm sure he ain't. He drinks."

Her son began to laugh. "Th' dickens he does?" He seemed amazed, but not shocked at this information.

She nodded her head with the air of one who discloses a dreadful thing. "I'm sure of it! Once I saw 'im comin' outa Simpson's Hotel, up in Handyville, an' he could hardly walk. He drinks! I'm sure he drinks!"

"Holy smoke!" said Kelcey.

They sat down at the table and began to wreck the little white garden. The youth leaned back in his chair, in the manner of a man who is paying for things. His mother bended alertly forward, apparently watching each mouthful. She perched on the edge of her chair, ready to spring to her feet and run to the closet or the stove for anything that he might need. She was as anxious as a young mother with a babe. In the careless and comfortable attitude of the son there was denoted a great deal of dignity.

"Yeh ain't eatin' much t'-night, George?"

"Well, I ain't very hungry, t' tell th' truth."

"Don't yeh like yer supper, dear? Yeh must eat somethin', chile. Yeh mustn't go without."

"Well, I'm eatin' somethin', ain't I?"

He wandered aimlessly through the meal. She sat over behind the little blackened coffee-pot and gazed affectionately upon him.

After a time she began to grow agitated. Her worn fingers were gripped. It could be seen that a great thought was within her. She was about to venture something. She had arrived at a supreme moment. "George," she said, suddenly, "come t' prayer-meetin' with me t'-night."

The young man dropped his fork. "Say, you must be crazy," he said, in amazement.

"Yes, dear," she continued, rapidly, in a small pleading voice, "I'd like t' have yeh go with me onct in a while. Yeh never go with me any more, dear, an' I'd like t' have yeh go. Yeh ain't been anywhere at all with me in th' longest while."

"Well," he said, "well, but what th' blazes——"

"Ah, come on," said the little old woman. She went to him and put her arms about his neck. She began to coax him with caresses.

The young man grinned. "Thunderation!" he said, "what would I do at a prayer-meetin'?"

The mother considered him to be consenting. She did a little antique caper.

"Well, yeh can come an' take care 'a yer mother," she cried, gleefully. "It's such a long walk every Thursday night alone, an' don't yeh s'pose that when I have such a big, fine, strappin' boy, I want 'im t' beau me aroun' some? Ah, I knew ye'd come."

He smiled for a moment, indulgent of her humor. But presently his face turned a shade of discomfort. "But—" he began, protesting.

"Ah, come on," she continually repeated.

He began to be vexed. He frowned into the air. A vision came to him of dreary blackness arranged in solemn rows. A mere dream of it was depressing.

"But—" he said again. He was obliged to make great search for an argument. Finally he concluded, "But what th' blazes would I do at prayer-meetin'?"

In his ears was the sound of a hymn, made by people who tilted their heads at a prescribed angle of devotion. It would be too apparent that they were all better than he. When he entered they would turn their heads and regard him with suspicion. This would be an enormous aggravation, since he was certain that he was as good as they.

"Well, now, y' see," he said, quite gently, "I don't wanta go, an' it wouldn't do me no good t' go if I didn't wanta go."

His mother's face swiftly changed. She breathed a huge sigh, the counterpart of ones he had heard upon like occasions. She put a tiny black bonnet on her head, and wrapped her figure in an old shawl. She cast a martyr-like glance upon her son and went mournfully away. She resembled a limited funeral procession.

The young man writhed under it to an extent. He kicked moodily at a table-leg. When the sound of her footfalls died away he felt distinctly relieved.

IV

THAT night, when Kelcey arrived at the little smiling saloon, he found his friend Jones standing before the bar engaged in a violent argument with a stout man.

"Oh, well," this latter person was saying, "you can make a lot of noise, Charlie, for a man that never says anything—let's have a drink!"

Jones was waving his arms and delivering splintering blows upon some distant theories. The stout man chuckled fatly and winked at the bartender.

The orator ceased for a moment to say, "Gimme little whiskey, John." At the same time he perceived young Kelcey. He sprang forward with a welcoming cry. "Hello, ol' man, didn't much think ye'd come." He led him to the stout man.

"Mr. Bleecker—my friend Mr. Kelcey!"

"How d'yeh do!"

"Mr. Kelcey, I'm happy to meet you, sir; have a drink."

They drew up in line and waited. The busy hands of the bartender made glasses clink. Mr. Bleecker, in a very polite way, broke the waiting silence.

"Never been here before, I believe, have you, Mr. Kelcey?"

The young man felt around for a high-bred reply. "Er—no—I've never had that—er—pleasure," he said.

After a time the strained and wary courtesy of their manners wore away. It became evident to Bleecker that his importance slightly dazzled the young man. He grew warmer. Obviously, the youth was one whose powers of perception were developed. Directly, then, he launched forth into a tale of by-gone days, when the world was better. He had known all the great men of that age. He reproduced his conversations with them. There were traces of pride and of mournfulness in his voice. He rejoiced at the glory of the world of dead spirits. He grieved at the youth and flippancy of the present one. He lived with his head in the clouds of the past, and he seemed obliged to talk of what he saw there.

Jones nudged Kelcey ecstatically in the ribs. "You've got th' ol' man started in great shape," he whispered.

Kelcey was proud that the prominent character of the place talked at him, glancing into his eyes for appreciation of fine points.

Presently they left the bar, and going into a little rear room, took seats about a table. A gas-jet with a colored globe shed a crimson radiance. The polished wood of walls and furniture gleamed with faint rose-colored reflections. Upon the floor saw-dust was thickly sprinkled.

Two other men presently came. By the time Bleecker had told three tales of the grand past, Kelcey was slightly acquainted with everybody.

He admired Bleecker immensely. He developed a brotherly feeling for the others, who were all gentle-spoken. He began to feel that he was passing the happiest evening of his life. His companions were so jovial and good-natured; and everything they did was marked by such courtesy.

For a time the two men who had come in late did not presume to address him directly. They would say: "Jones, won't your friend have so and so, or so and so?" And Bleecker would begin his orations: "Now, Mr. Kelcey, don't you think——"

Presently he began to believe that he was a most remarkably fine fellow, who had at last found his place in a crowd of most remarkably fine fellows.

Jones occasionally breathed comments into his ear.

"I tell yeh, Bleecker's an ol'-timer. He was a husky guy in his day, yeh can bet. He was one 'a th' best known men in N' York onct. Yeh ought to hear him tell about——"

Kelcey listened intently. He was profoundly interested in these intimate tales of men who had gleamed in the rays of old suns.

"That O'Connor's a damn fine fellah," interjected Jones once, referring to one of the others. "He's one 'a th' best fellahs I ever knowed. He's always on th' dead level. An' he's always jest th' same as yeh see 'im now—good-natured an' grinnin'."

Kelcey nodded. He could well believe it.

When he offered to buy drinks there came a loud volley of

protests. "No, no, Mr. Kelcey," cried Bleecker, "no, no. To-night you are our guest. Some other time——"

"Here," said O'Connor, "it's my turn now."

He called and pounded for the bartender. He then sat with a coin in his hand warily eying the others. He was ready to frustrate them if they offered to pay.

After a time Jones began to develop qualities of great eloquence and wit. His companions laughed. "It's the whiskey talking now," said Bleecker.

He grew earnest and impassioned. He delivered speeches on various subjects. His lectures were to him very imposing. The force of his words thrilled him. Sometimes he was overcome.

The others agreed with him in all things. Bleecker grew almost tender, and considerately placed words here and there for his use. As Jones became fiercely energetic the others became more docile in agreeing. They soothed him with friendly interjections.

His mood changed directly. He began to sing popular airs with enthusiasm. He congratulated his companions upon being in his society. They were excited by his frenzy. They began to fraternize in jovial fashion. It was understood that they were true and tender spirits. They had come away from a grinding world filled with men who were harsh.

When one of them chose to divulge some place where the world had pierced him, there was a chorus of violent sympathy. They rejoiced at their temporary isolation and safety.

Once a man, completely drunk, stumbled along the floor of the saloon. He opened the door of the little room and made a show of entering. The men sprang instantly to their feet. They were ready to throttle any invader of their island. They elbowed each other in rivalry as to who should take upon himself the brunt of an encounter.

"Oh!" said the drunken individual, swaying on his legs and blinking at the party, "oh! thish private room?"

"That's what it is, Willie," said Jones. "An' you git outa here er we'll throw yeh out."

"That's what we will," said the others.

"Oh," said the drunken man. He blinked at them aggrievedly for an instant and then went away.

They sat down again. Kelcey felt, in a way, that he would have liked to display his fidelity to the others by whipping the intruder.

The bartender came often. "Gee, you fellahs er tanks," he said, in a jocular manner, as he gathered empty glasses and polished the table with his little towel.

Through the exertions of Jones the little room began to grow clamorous. The tobacco-smoke eddied about the forms of the men in ropes and wreaths. Near the ceiling there was a thick gray cloud.

Each man explained, in his way, that he was totally out of place in the before-mentioned world. They were possessed of various virtues which were unappreciated by those with whom they were commonly obliged to mingle; they were fitted for a tree-shaded land, where everything was peace. Now that five of them had congregated it gave them happiness to speak their inmost thoughts without fear of being misunderstood.

As he drank more beer Kelcey felt his breast expand with manly feeling. He knew that he was capable of sublime things. He wished that some day one of his present companions would come to him for relief. His mind pictured a little scene. In it he was magnificent in his friendship.

He looked upon the beaming faces and knew that if at that instant there should come a time for a great sacrifice he would blissfully make it. He would pass tranquilly into the unknown, or into bankruptcy, amid the ejaculations of his companions upon his many virtues.

They had no bickerings during the evening. If one chose to momentarily assert himself, the others instantly submitted.

They exchanged compliments. Once old Bleecker stared at Jones for a few moments. Suddenly he broke out: "Jones, you're one of the finest fellows I ever knew!" A flush of pleasure went over the other's face, and then he made a modest gesture, the protest of an humble man. "Don't flim-flam me, ol' boy," he said, with earnestness. But Bleecker roared that he was serious about it. The two men arose and shook hands emotionally. Jones bunted against the table and knocked off a glass.

Afterward a general hand-shaking was inaugurated. Brotherly sentiments flew about the room. There was an uproar of fraternal feeling.

Jones began to sing. He beat time with precision and dignity. He gazed into the eyes of his companions, trying to call music from their souls. O'Connor joined in heartily, but with another tune. Off in a corner old Bleecker was making a speech.

The bartender came to the door. "Gee, you fellahs er making a row. It's time fer me t' shut up th' front th' place, an' you mugs better sit on yerselves. It's one o'clock."

They began to argue with him. Kelcey, however, sprang to his feet. "One o'clock," he said. "Holy smoke, I mus' be flyin'!"

There came protesting howls from Jones. Bleecker ceased his oration. "My dear boy—" he began. Kelcey searched for his hat. "I've gota go t' work at seven," he said.

The others watched him with discomfort in their eyes. "Well," said O'Connor, "if one goes we might as well all go." They sadly took their hats and filed out.

The cold air of the street filled Kelcey with vague surprise. It made his head feel hot. As for his legs, they were like willow-twigs.

A few yellow lights blinked. In front of an all-night restaurant a huge red electric lamp hung and sputtered. Horse-car bells jingled far down the street. Overhead a train thundered on the elevated road.

On the sidewalk the men took fervid leave. They clutched hands with extraordinary force and proclaimed, for the last time, ardent and admiring friendships.

When he arrived at his home Kelcey proceeded with caution. His mother had left a light burning low. He stumbled once in his voyage across the floor. As he paused to listen he heard the sound of little snores coming from her room.

He lay awake for a few moments and thought of the evening. He had a pleasurable consciousness that he had made a good impression upon those fine fellows. He felt that he had spent the most delightful evening of his life.

ELCEY was cross in the morning. His mother had been obliged to shake him a great deal, and it had seemed to him a most unjust thing. Also, when he, blinking his eyes, had entered the kitchen, she had said: "Yeh left th' lamp burnin' all night last night, George. How many times must I tell yeh never t' leave th' lamp burnin'?"

He ate the greater part of his breakfast in silence, moodily stirring his coffee and glaring at a remote corner of the room with eyes that felt as if they had been baked. When he moved his eyelids there was a sensation that they were cracking. In his mouth there was a singular taste. It seemed to him that he had been sucking the end of a wooden spoon. Moreover, his temper was rampant within him. It sought something to devour.

Finally he said, savagely: "Damn these early hours!"

His mother jumped as if he had flung a missile at her. "Why, George—" she began.

Kelcey broke in again. "Oh, I know all that—but this gettin' up in th' mornin' so early makes me sick. Jest when a man is gettin' his mornin' nap he's gota get up. I——"

"George, dear," said his mother, "yeh know how I hate yeh t' swear, dear. Now please don't." She looked beseechingly at him.

He made a swift gesture. "Well, I ain't swearin', am I?" he demanded. "I was on'y sayin' that this gettin'-up business gives me a pain, wasn't I?"

"Well, yeh know how swearin' hurts me," protested the little old woman. She seemed about to sob. She gazed off retrospectively. She apparently was recalling persons who had never been profane.

"I don't see where yeh ever caught this way a' swearin' out at everything," she continued, presently. "Fred, ner John, ner Willie never swore a bit. Ner Tom neither, except when he was real mad."

The son made another gesture. It was directed into the air, as if he saw there a phantom injustice. "Oh, good thunder," he said, with an accent of despair. Thereupon, he relapsed into a mood of silence. He sombrely regarded his plate.

This demeanor speedily reduced his mother to meekness. When she spoke again it was in a conciliatory voice. "George, dear, won't yeh bring some sugar home t'-night?" It could be seen that she was asking for a crown of gold.

Kelcey aroused from his semi-slumber. "Yes, if I kin remember it," he said.

The little old woman arose to stow her son's lunch into the pail. When he had finished his breakfast he stalked for a time about the room in a dignified way. He put on his coat and hat, and taking his lunch-pail went to the door. There he halted, and without turning his head, stiffly said: "Well, good-by!"

The little old woman saw that she had offended her son. She did not seek an explanation. She was accustomed to these phenomena. She made haste to surrender.

"Ain't yeh goin' t' kiss me good-by," she asked in a little woful voice.

The youth made a pretence of going on, deaf-heartedly. He wore the dignity of an injured monarch.

Then the little old woman called again in forsaken accents: "George—George—ain't yeh goin' t' kiss me good-by?" When he moved he found that she was hanging to his coat-tails.

He turned eventually with a murmur of a sort of tenderness. "Why, 'a course I am," he said. He kissed her. Withal there was an undertone of superiority in his voice, as if he were granting an astonishing suit. She looked at him with reproach and gratitude and affection.

She stood at the head of the stairs and watched his hand sliding along the rail as he went down. Occasionally she could see his arm and part of his shoulder. When he reached the first floor she called to him: "Good-by!"

The little old woman went back to her work in the kitchen with a frown of perplexity upon her brow. "I wonder what was th' matter with George this mornin'," she mused. "He didn't seem a bit like himself!"

As she trudged to and fro at her labor she began to speculate.

She was much worried. She surmised in a vague way that he was a sufferer from a great internal disease. It was something no doubt that devoured the kidneys or quietly fed upon the lungs. Later, she imagined a woman, wicked and fair, who had fascinated him and was turning his life into a bitter thing. Her mind created many wondrous influences that were swooping like green dragons at him. They were changing him to a morose man, who suffered silently. She longed to discover them, that she might go bravely to the rescue of her heroic son. She knew that he, generous in his pain, would keep it from her. She racked her mind for knowledge.

However, when he came home at night he was extraordinarily blithe. He seemed to be a lad of ten. He capered all about the room. When she was bringing the coffee-pot from the stove to the table, he made show of waltzing with her so that she spilled some of the coffee. She was obliged to scold him.

All through the meal he made jokes. She occasionally was compelled to laugh, despite the fact that she believed that she should not laugh at her own son's jokes. She uttered reproofs at times, but he did not regard them.

"Golly," he said once, "I feel fine as silk. I didn't think I'd get over feelin' bad so quick. It——" He stopped abruptly.

During the evening he sat content. He smoked his pipe and read from an evening paper. She bustled about at her work. She seemed utterly happy with him there, lazily puffing out little clouds of smoke and giving frequent brilliant dissertations upon the news of the day. It seemed to her that she must be a model mother to have such a son, one who came home to her at night and sat contented, in a languor of the muscles after a good day's toil. She pondered upon the science of her management.

The week thereafter, too, she was joyous, for he stayed at home each night of it, and was sunny-tempered. She became convinced that she was a perfect mother, rearing a perfect son. There came often a love-light into her eyes. The wrinkled, yellow face frequently warmed into a smile of the kind that a maiden bestows upon him who to her is first and perhaps last.

THE little old woman habitually discouraged all outbursts of youthful vanity upon the part of her son. She feared that he would get to think too much of himself, and she knew that nothing could do more harm. Great self-esteem was always passive, she thought, and if he grew to regard his qualities of mind as forming a dazzling constellation, he would tranquilly sit still and not do those wonders she expected of him. So she was constantly on the alert to suppress even a shadow of such a thing. As for him he ruminated with the savage, vengeful bitterness of a young man, and decided that she did not comprehend him.

But despite her precautions he often saw that she believed him to be the most marvellous young man on the earth. He had only to look at those two eyes that became lighted with a glow from her heart whenever he did some excessively brilliant thing. On these occasions he could see her glance triumphantly at a neighbor, or whoever happened to be present. He grew to plan for these glances. And then he took a vast satisfaction in detecting and appropriating them.

Nevertheless, he could not understand why, directly after a scene of this kind, his mother was liable to call to him to hang his coat on the hook under the mantel, her voice in a key of despair as if he were negligent and stupid in what was, after all, the only important thing in life.

"If yeh'll only get in the habit of doin' it, it'll be jest as easy as throwin' it down anywheres," she would say to him. "When yeh pitch it down anywheres, somebody's got t' pick it up, an' that'll most likely be your poor ol' mother. Yeh can hang it up yerself, if yeh'll on'y think." This was intolerable. He usually went then and hurled his coat savagely at the hook. The correctness of her position was maddening.

It seemed to him that anyone who had a son of his glowing attributes should overlook the fact that he seldom hung up his coat. It was impossible to explain this situation to his mother. She was unutterably narrow. He grew sullen.

There came a time, too, that, even in all his mother's tremendous admiration for him, he did not entirely agree with her. He was delighted that she liked his great wit. He spurred himself to new and flashing effort because of this appreciation. But for the greater part he could see that his mother took pride in him in quite a different way from that in which he took pride in himself. She rejoiced at qualities in him that indicated that he was going to become a white and looming king among men. From these she made pictures in which he appeared as a benign personage, blessed by the filled hands of the poor, one whose brain could hold massive thoughts and awe certain men about whom she had read. She was fêted as the mother of this enormous man. These dreams were her solace. She spoke of them to no one because she knew that, worded, they would be ridiculous. But she dwelt with them, and they shed a radiance of gold upon her long days, her sorry labor. Upon the dead altars of her life she had builded the little fires of hope for another.

He had a complete sympathy for as much as he understood of these thoughts of his mother. They were so wise that he admired her foresight. As for himself, however, most of his dreams were of a nearer time. He had many of the distant future when he would be a man with a cloak of coldness concealing his gentleness and his faults, and of whom the men and, more particularly, the women, would think with reverence. He agreed with his mother that at that time he would go through the obstacles to other men like a flung stone. And then he would have power and he would enjoy having his bounty and his wrath alike fall swiftly upon those below. They would be awed. And above all he would mystify them.

But then his nearer dreams were a multitude. He had begun to look at the great world revolving near to his nose. He had a vast curiosity concerning this city in whose complexities he was buried. It was an impenetrable mystery, this city. It was a blend of many enticing colors. He longed to comprehend it completely, that he might walk understandingly in its greatest marvels, its mightiest march of life, its sin. He dreamed of a comprehension whose pay was the admirable attitude of a man of knowledge. He remembered Jones. He could not help but admire a man who knew so many bartenders.

VII

N INDEFINITE woman was in all of Kelcey's dreams. As a matter of fact it was not he whom he pictured as wedding her. It was a vision of himself greater, finer, more terrible. It was himself as he expected to be. In scenes which he took mainly from pictures, this vision conducted a courtship, strutting, posing, and lying through a drama which was magnificent from glow of purple. In it he was icy, self-possessed; but she, the dream-girl, was consumed by wild, torrential passion. He went to the length of having her display it before the people. He saw them wonder at his tranquillity. It amazed them infinitely to see him remain cold before the glory of this peerless woman's love. She was to him as beseeching for affection as a pet animal, but still he controlled appearances and none knew of his deep abiding love. Some day, at the critical romantic time, he was going to divulge it. In these long dreams there were accessories of castle-like houses, wide lands, servants, horses, clothes.

They began somewhere in his childhood. When he ceased to see himself as a stern general pointing a sword at the nervous and abashed horizon, he became this sublime king of a vague woman's heart. Later when he had read some books, it all achieved clearer expression. He was told in them that there was a goddess in the world whose business it was to wait until he should exchange a glance with her. It became a creed, subtly powerful. It saved discomfort for him and for several women who flitted by him. He used her as a standard.

Often he saw the pathos of her long wait, but his faith did not falter. The world was obliged to turn gold in time. His life was to be fine and heroic, else he would not have been born. He believed that the common-place lot was the sentence, the doom of certain people who did not know how to feel. His blood was a tender current of life. He thought that the usual should fall to others whose nerves were of lead. Occasionally he wondered how fate was going to begin in making an enormous figure of him; but he had no doubt of the result. A chariot of pink clouds was coming for him. His faith was his reason for existence. Meanwhile he could dream of the indefinite woman and the fragrance of roses that came from her hair.

One day he met Maggie Johnson on the stairs. She had a pail of beer in one hand and a brown-paper parcel under her arm. She glanced at him. He discovered that it would wither his heart to see another man signally successful in the smiles of her. And the glance that she gave him was so indifferent and so unresponsive to the sudden vivid admiration in his own eyes that he immediately concluded that she was magnificent in two ways.

As she came to the landing, the light from a window passed in a silver gleam over the girlish roundness of her cheek. It was a thing that he remembered.

He was silent for the most part at supper that night. He was particularly unkind when he did speak. His mother, observing him apprehensively, tried in vain to picture the new terrible catastrophe. She eventually concluded that he did not like the beef-stew. She put more salt in it.

He saw Maggie quite frequently after the meeting upon the stairs. He reconstructed his dreams and placed her in the full glory of that sun. The dream-woman, the goddess, pitched from her pedestal, lay prostrate, unheeded, save when he brought her forth to call her insipid and childish in the presence of his new religion.

He was relatively happy sometimes when Maggie's mother would get drunk and make terrific uproars. He used then to sit in the dark and make scenes in which he rescued the girl from her hideous environment.

He laid clever plans by which he encountered her in the halls, at the door, on the street. When he succeeded in meeting her he was always overcome by the thought that the whole thing was obvious to her. He could feel the shame of it burn his face and neck. To prove to her that she was mistaken he would turn away his head or regard her with a granite stare.

After a time he became impatient of the distance between them. He saw looming princes who would aim to seize her.

Hours of his leisure and certain hours of his labor he spent in contriving. The shade of this girl was with him continually. With her he builded his grand dramas so that he trod in clouds, the matters of his daily life obscured and softened by a mist.

He saw that he need only break down the slight conventional barriers and she would soon discover his noble character. Sometimes he could see it all in his mind. It was very skilful. But then his courage flew away at the supreme moment. Perhaps the whole affair was humorous to her. Perhaps she was watching his mental contortions. She might laugh. He felt that he would then die or kill her. He could not approach the dread moment. He sank often from the threshold of knowledge. Directly after these occasions, it was his habit to avoid her to prove that she was a cipher to him.

He reflected that if he could only get a chance to rescue her from something, the whole tragedy would speedily unwind.

He met a young man in the halls one evening who said to him: "Say, me frien', where d' d' Johnson birds live in heh? I can't fin' me feet in dis bloomin' joint. I been battin' round heh fer a half-hour."

"Two flights up," said Kelcey stonily. He had felt a sudden quiver of his heart. The grandeur of the clothes, the fine worldly air, the experience, the self-reliance, the courage that shone in the countenance of this other young man made him suddenly sink to the depths of woe. He stood listening in the hall, flushing and ashamed of it, until he heard them coming down-stairs together. He slunk away then. It would have been a horror to him if she had discovered him there. She might have felt sorry for him.

They were going out to a show, perhaps. That pig of the world in his embroidered cloak was going to dazzle her with splendor. He mused upon how unrighteous it was for other men to dazzle women with splendor.

As he appreciated his handicap he swore with savage, vengeful bitterness. In his home his mother raised her voice in a high key of monotonous irritability. "Hang up yer coat, can't yeh, George?" she cried at him. "I can't go round after yeh all th' time. It's jest as easy t' hang it up as it is t' throw it down that way. Don't yeh ever git tired 'a hearin' me yell at yeh!"

"Yes," he exploded. In this word he put a profundity of sudden anger. He turned toward his mother a face, red, seamed, hard with hate and rage. They stared a moment in silence. Then she turned and staggered toward her room. Her hip struck violently against the corner of the table during this blind passage. A moment later the door closed.

Kelcey sank down in a chair with his legs thrust out straight and his hands deep in his trousers' pockets. His chin was forward upon his breast and his eyes stared before him. There swept over him all the self-pity that comes when the soul is turned back from a road.

VIII

URING the next few days Kelcey suffered from his first gloomy conviction that the earth was not grateful to him for his presence upon it. When sharp words were said to him, he interpreted them with what seemed to be a lately acquired insight. He could now perceive that the universe hated him. He sank to the most sublime depths of despair.

One evening of this period he met Jones. The latter rushed upon him with enthusiasm. "Why, yer jest th' man I wanted t' see! I was comin' round t' your place t'-night. Lucky I met yeh! Ol' Bleecker's goin' t' give a blow-out t'-morrah night. Anything yeh want t' drink! All th' boys'll be there an' everything. He tol' me expressly that he wanted yeh t' be there. Great time! Great! Can yeh come?"

Kelcey grasped the other's hand with fervor. He felt now that there was some solacing friendship in space. "You bet I will, ol' man," he said, huskily. "I'd like nothin' better in th' world!"

As he walked home he thought that he was a very grim figure. He was about to taste the delicious revenge of a partial self-destruction. The universe would regret its position when it saw him drunk.

He was a little late in getting to Bleecker's lodging. He was delayed while his mother read aloud a letter from an old uncle, who wrote in one place: "God bless the boy! Bring him up to be the man his father was." Bleecker lived in an old three-storied house on a side-street. A Jewish tailor lived and worked in the front parlor, and old Bleecker lived in the back parlor. A German, whose family took care of the house, occupied the basement. Another German, with a wife and eight children, rented the dining-room. The two upper floors were inhabited by tailors, dressmakers, a pedler, and mysterious people who were seldom seen. The door of the little hall-bedroom, at the foot of the

second flight, was always open, and in there could be seen two
bended men who worked at mending opera-glasses. The German
woman in the dining-room was not friends with the little dress-
maker in the rear room of the third floor, and frequently they
yelled the vilest names up and down between the balusters. Each
part of the woodwork was scratched and rubbed by the contact of
innumerable persons. In one wall there was a long slit with
chipped edges, celebrating the time when a man had thrown a
hatchet at his wife. In the lower hall there was an eternal
woman, with a rag and a pail of suds, who knelt over the worn
oil-cloth. Old Bleecker felt that he had quite respectable and
high-class apartments. He was glad to invite his friends.

Bleecker met Kelcey in the hall. He wore a collar that was
cleaner and higher than his usual one. It changed his appearance greatly. He was now formidably aristocratic. "How are yeh,
ol' man?" he shouted. He grasped Kelcey's arm, and, babbling
jovially, conducted him down the hall and into the ex-parlor.

A group of standing men made vast shadows in the yellow
glare of the lamp. They turned their heads as the two entered.
"Why, hello, Kelcey, ol' man," Jones exclaimed, coming rapidly
forward. "Good fer you! Glad yeh come! Yeh know O'Connor, 'a
course! An' Schmidt! an' Woods! Then there's Zeusentell! Mr.
Zeusentell—my friend Mr. Kelcey! Shake hands—both good fellows, damnitall! Then here is—oh, gentlemen, my friend Mr.
Kelcey! A good fellow, he is, too! I've known 'im since I was a kid!
Come, have a drink!" Everybody was excessively amiable. Kelcey
felt that he had social standing. The strangers were cautious and
respectful.

"By all means," said old Bleecker. "Mr. Kelcey, have a drink!
An' by th' way, gentlemen, while we're about it, let's all have a
drink!" There was much laughter. Bleecker was so droll at times.

With mild and polite gesturing they marched up to the table.
There were upon it a keg of beer, a long row of whiskey bottles, a
little heap of corn-cob pipes, some bags of tobacco, a box of
cigars, and a mighty collection of glasses, cups, and mugs. Old
Bleecker had arranged them so deftly that they resembled a
primitive bar. There was considerable scuffling for possession of
the cracked cups. Jones politely but vehemently insisted upon
drinking from the worst of the assortment. He was quietly op-

posed by others. Everybody showed that they were awed by Bleecker's lavish hospitality. Their demeanors expressed their admiration at the cost of this entertainment.

Kelcey took his second mug of beer away to a corner and sat down with it. He wished to socially reconnoitre. Over in a corner a man was telling a story, in which at intervals he grunted like a pig. A half dozen men were listening. Two or three others sat alone in isolated places. They looked expectantly bright, ready to burst out cordially if anyone should address them. The row of bottles made quaint shadows upon the table, and upon a sidewall the keg of beer created a portentous black figure that reared toward the ceiling, hovering over the room and its inmates with spectral stature. Tobacco-smoke lay in lazy cloud-banks overhead.

Jones and O'Connor stayed near the table, occasionally being affable in all directions. Kelcey saw old Bleecker go to them and heard him whisper: "Come, we must git th' thing started. Git th' thing started." Kelcey saw that the host was fearing that all were not having a good time. Jones conferred with O'Connor and then O'Connor went to the man named Zeusentell. O'Connor evidently proposed something. Zeusentell refused at once. O'Connor beseeched. Zeusentell remained implacable. At last O'Connor broke off his argument, and going to the centre of the room, held up his hand. "Gentlemen," he shouted loudly, "we will now have a recitation by Mr. Zeusentell, entitled 'Patrick Clancy's Pig'!" He then glanced triumphantly at Zeusentell and said: "Come on!" Zeusentell had been twisting and making pantomimic appeals. He said, in a reproachful whisper: "You son of a gun."

The men turned their heads to glance at Zeusentell for a moment and then burst into a sustained clamor. "Hurray! Let 'er go! Come—give it t' us! Spring it! Spring it! Let it come!" As Zeusentell made no advances, they appealed personally. "Come, ol' man, let 'er go! Whatter yeh 'fraid of? Let 'er go! Go ahn! Hurry up!"

Zeusentell was protesting with almost frantic modesty. O'Connor took him by the lapel and tried to drag him; but he leaned back, pulling at his coat and shaking his head. "No, no, I don't know it, I tell yeh! I can't! I don't know it! I tell yeh I don't know it! I've forgotten it, I tell yeh! No—no—no—no. Ah, say, lookahere, le' go me, can't yeh? What's th' matter with yeh? I tell yeh I don't know it!" The men applauded violently. O'Connor did not relent. A little battle was waged until all of a sudden Zeusentell was seen to grow wondrously solemn. A hush fell upon the men. He was about to begin. He paused in the middle of the floor and nervously adjusted his collar and cravat. The audience became grave. " 'Patrick Clancy's Pig,' " announced Zeusentell in a shrill, dry, unnatural tone. And then he began in rapid singsong:

> "Patrick Clancy had a pig
>   Th' pride uv all th' nation,
> The half uv him was half as big
>   As half uv all creation——"

When he concluded the others looked at each other to convey their appreciation. They then wildly clapped their hands or tinkled their glasses. As Zeusentell went toward his seat a man leaned over and asked: "Can yeh tell me where I kin git that." He had made a great success. After an enormous pressure he was induced to recite two more tales. Old Bleecker finally led him forward and pledged him in a large drink. He declared that they were the best things he had ever heard.

The efforts of Zeusentell imparted a gayety to the company. The men having laughed together were better acquainted, and there was now a universal topic. Some of the party, too, began to be quite drunk.

The invaluable O'Connor brought forth a man who could play the mouth-organ. The latter, after wiping his instrument upon his coat-sleeve, played all the popular airs. The men's heads swayed to and fro in the clouded smoke. They grinned and beat time with their feet. A valor, barbaric and wild, began to show in their poses and in their faces, red and glistening from perspiration. The conversation resounded in a hoarse roar. The beer would not run rapidly enough for Jones, so he remained behind to tilt the keg. This caused the black shadow on the wall to retreat and advance, sinking mystically to loom forward again with sudden menace, a huge dark figure controlled, as by some unknown emotion. The glasses, mugs, and cups travelled swift and regular, catching orange reflections from the lamp-light. Two or three men were grown so careless that they were continually spilling their drinks. Old Bleecker, cackling with pleasure, seized time to glance triumphantly at Jones. His party was going to be a success.

OF A sudden Kelcey felt the buoyant thought that he was having a good time. He was all at once an enthusiast, as if he were at a festival of a religion. He felt that there was something fine and thrilling in this affair isolated from a stern world, and from which the laughter arose like incense. He knew that old sentiment of brotherly regard for those about him. He began to converse tenderly with them. He was not sure of his drift of thought, but he knew that he was immensely sympathetic. He rejoiced at their faces, shining red and wrinkled with smiles. He was capable of heroisms.

His pipe irritated him by going out frequently. He was too busy in amiable conversations to attend to it. When he arose to go for a match he discovered that his legs were a trifle uncertain under him. They bended and did not precisely obey his intent. At the table he lit a match and then, in laughing at a joke made near him, forgot to apply it to the bowl of his pipe. He succeeded with the next match after annoying trouble. He swayed so that the match would appear first on one side of the bowl and then on the other. At last he happily got it directly over the tobacco. He had burned his fingers. He inspected them, laughing vaguely.

Jones came and slapped him on the shoulder. "Well, ol' man, let's take a drink fer ol' Handyville's sake!"

Kelcey was deeply affected. He looked at Jones with moist eyes. "I'll go yeh," he said. With an air of profound melancholy, Jones poured out some whiskey. They drank reverently. They exchanged a glistening look of tender recollections and then went over to where Bleecker was telling a humorous story to a circle of giggling listeners. The old man sat like a fat, jolly god. "—and just at that moment th' old woman put her head out of th' window an' said: 'Mike, yez lezy divil, fer phwat do yez be slapin' in me new geranium bid?' An' Mike woke up an' said: 'Domn a washwoman thot do niver wash her own bidclues. Here do I be slapin' in nothin' but dhirt an' wades.'" The men slapped their knees, roaring loudly. They begged him to tell another. A clamor of comment arose concerning the anecdote, so that when old Bleecker began a fresh one nobody was heeding.

It occurred to Jones to sing. Suddenly he burst forth with a ballad that had a rippling waltz movement, and seizing Kelcey, made a furious attempt to dance. They sprawled over a pair of outstretched legs and pitched headlong. Kelcey fell with a yellow crash. Blinding lights flashed before his vision. But he arose immediately, laughing. He did not feel at all hurt. The pain in his head was rather pleasant.

Old Bleecker, O'Connor, and Jones, who now limped and drew breath through his teeth, were about to lead him with much care and tenderness to the table for another drink, but he laughingly pushed them away and went unassisted. Bleecker told him: "Great Gawd, your head struck hard enough t' break a trunk."

He laughed again, and with a show of steadiness and courage he poured out an extravagant portion of whiskey. With cold muscles he put it to his lips and drank it. It chanced that this addition dazed him like a powerful blow. A moment later it affected him with blinding and numbing power. Suddenly unbalanced, he felt the room sway. His blurred sight could only distinguish a tumbled mass of shadow through which the beams from the light ran like swords of flame. The sound of the many voices was to him like the roar of a distant river. Still, he felt that if he could only annul the force of these million winding fingers that gripped his senses, he was capable of most brilliant and entertaining things.

He was at first of the conviction that his feelings were only temporary. He waited for them to pass away, but the mental and physical pause only caused a new reeling and swinging of the room. Chasms with inclined approaches were before him; peaks leaned toward him. And withal he was blind and numb with surprise. He understood vaguely in his stupefaction that it would disgrace him to fall down a chasm.

At last he perceived a shadow, a form, which he knew to be Jones. The adorable Jones, the supremely wise Jones, was walking in this strange land without fear or care, erect and tranquil.

Kelcey murmured in admiration and affection, and fell toward his friend. Jones's voice sounded as from the shores of the unknown. "Come, come, ol' man, this will never do. Brace up." It appeared after all that Jones was not wholly wise. "Oh, I'm—all ri' Jones! I'm all ri'! I wan' shing song! Tha's all! I wan' shing song!"

Jones was stupid. "Come now, sit down an' shut up."

It made Kelcey burn with fury. "Jones, le' me alone, I tell yeh! Le' me alone! I wan' shing song er te' story! G'l'm'n, I lovsh girl live down my shtreet. Thash reason 'm drunk, 'tis! She——"

Jones seized him and dragged him toward a chair. He heard him laugh. He could not endure these insults from his friend. He felt a blazing desire to strangle his companion. He threw out his hand violently, but Jones grappled him close and he was no more than a dried leaf. He was amazed to find that Jones possessed the strength of twenty horses. He was forced skilfully to the floor.

As he lay, he reflected in great astonishment upon Jones's muscle. It was singular that he had never before discovered it. The whole incident had impressed him immensely. An idea struck him that he might denounce Jones for it. It would be a sage thing. There would be a thrilling and dramatic moment in which he would dazzle all the others. But at this moment he was assailed by a mighty desire to sleep. Sombre and soothing clouds of slumber were heavily upon him. He closed his eyes with a sigh that was yet like that of a babe.

When he awoke, there was still the battleful clamor of the revel. He half arose with a plan of participating, when O'Connor came and pushed him down again, throwing out his chin in affectionate remonstrance and saying, "Now, now," as to a child.

The change that had come over these men mystified Kelcey in a great degree. He had never seen anything so vastly stupid as their idea of his state. He resolved to prove to them that they were dealing with one whose mind was very clear. He kicked and squirmed in O'Connor's arms, until, with a final wrench, he scrambled to his feet and stood tottering in the middle of the room. He would let them see that he had a strangely lucid grasp of events. "G'l'm'n, I lovsh girl! I ain' drunker'n yeh all are! She——"

He felt them hurl him to a corner of the room and pile chairs and tables upon him until he was buried beneath a stupendous mountain. Far above, as up a mine's shaft, there were voices, lights, and vague figures. He was not hurt physically, but his feelings were unutterably injured. He, the brilliant, the good, the sympathetic had been thrust fiendishly from the party. They had had the comprehension of red lobsters. It was an unspeakable barbarism. Tears welled piteously from his eyes. He planned long diabolical explanations!

T FIRST the gray lights of dawn came timidly into the room, remaining near the windows, afraid to approach certain sinister corners. Finally, mellow streams of sunshine poured in, undraping the shadows to disclose the putrefaction, making pitiless revelation. Kelcey awoke with a groan of undirected misery. He tossed his stiffened arms about his head for a moment and then leaning heavily upon his elbow stared blinking at his environment. The grim truthfulness of the day showed disaster and death. After the tumults of the previous night the interior of this room resembled a decaying battle-field. The air hung heavy and stifling with the odors of tobacco, men's breaths, and beer half filling forgotten glasses. There was ruck of broken tumblers, pipes, bottles, spilled tobacco, cigar stumps. The chairs and tables were pitched this way and that way, as after some terrible struggle. In the midst of it all lay old Bleecker stretched upon a couch in deepest sleep, as abandoned in attitude, as motionless, as ghastly as if it were a corpse that had been flung there.

A knowledge of the thing came gradually into Kelcey's eyes. He looked about him with an expression of utter woe, regret, and loathing. He was compelled to lie down again. A pain above his eyebrows was like that from an iron-clamp.

As he lay pondering, his bodily condition created for him a bitter philosophy, and he perceived all the futility of a red existence. He saw his life problems confronting him like granite giants and he was no longer erect to meet them. He had made a calamitous retrogression in his war. Spectres were to him now as large as clouds.

Inspired by the pitiless ache in his head, he was prepared to reform and live a white life. His stomach informed him that a good man was the only being who was wise. But his perception of his future was hopeless. He was aghast at the prospect of the old routine. It was impossible. He trembled before its exactions.

Turning toward the other way, he saw that the gold portals of vice no longer enticed him. He could not hear the strains of alluring music. The beckoning sirens of drink had been killed by this pain in his head. The desires of his life suddenly lay dead like mullein stalks. Upon reflection, he saw, therefore, that he was perfectly willing to be virtuous if somebody would come and make it easy for him.

When he stared over at old Bleecker, he felt a sudden contempt and dislike for him. He considered him to be a tottering old beast. It was disgusting to perceive aged men so weak in sin. He dreaded to see him awaken lest he should be required to be somewhat civil to him.

Kelcey wished for a drink of water. For some time he had dreamed of the liquid, deliciously cool. It was an abstract, uncontained thing that poured upon him and tumbled him, taking away his pain like a kind of surgery. He arose and staggered slowly toward a little sink in a corner of the room. He understood that any rapid movement might cause his head to split.

The little sink was filled with a chaos of broken glass and spilled liquids. A sight of it filled him with horror, but he rinsed a glass with scrupulous care, and filling it, took an enormous drink. The water was an intolerable disappointment. It was insipid and weak to his scorched throat and not at all cool. He put down the glass with a gesture of despair. His face became fixed in the stony and sullen expression of a man who waits for the recuperative power of morrows.

Old Bleecker awakened. He rolled over and groaned loudly. For awhile he thrashed about in a fury of displeasure at his bodily stiffness and pain. Kelcey watched him as he would have watched a death agony. "Good Gawd," said the old man, "beer an' whiskey make th' devil of a mix. Did yeh see th' fight?"

"No," said Kelcey, stolidly.

"Why, Zeusentell an' O'Connor had a great old mill. They were scrappin' all over th' place. I thought we were all goin' t' get pulled. Thompson, that fellah over in th' corner, though, he sat down on th' whole business. He was a dandy! He had t' poke Zeusentell! He was a bird! Lord, I wish I had a Manhattan!"

Kelcey remained in bitter silence while old Bleecker dressed. "Come an' get a cocktail," said the latter briskly. This was part of his aristocracy. He was the only man of them who knew much about cocktails. He perpetually referred to them. "It'll brace yeh right up! Come along! Say, you get full too soon. You oughter wait until later, me boy! You're too speedy!" Kelcey wondered vaguely where his companion had lost his zeal for polished sentences, his iridescent mannerisms.

"Come along," said Bleecker.

Kelcey made a movement of disdain for cocktails, but he followed the other to the street. At the corner they separated. Kelcey attempted a friendly parting smile and then went on up the street. He had to reflect to know that he was erect and using his own muscles in walking. He felt like a man of paper, blown by the winds. Withal, the dust of the avenue was galling to his throat, eyes, and nostrils, and the roar of traffic cracked his head. He was glad, however, to be alone, to be rid of old Bleecker. The sight of him had been as the contemplation of a disease.

His mother was not at home. In his little room he mechanically undressed and bathed his head, arms, and shoulders. When he crawled between the two white sheets he felt a first lifting of his misery. His pillow was soothingly soft. There was an effect that was like the music of tender voices.

When he awoke again his mother was bending over him giving vent to alternate cries of grief and joy. Her hands trembled so that they were useless to her. "Oh, George, George, where have yeh been? What has happened t' yeh? Oh, George, I've been so worried! I didn't sleep a wink all night."

Kelcey was instantly wide awake. With a moan of suffering he turned his face to the wall before he spoke. "Never mind, mother, I'm all right. Don't fret now! I was knocked down by a truck last night in th' street, an' they took me t' th' hospital; but it's all right now. I got out jest a little while ago. They told me I'd better go home an' rest up."

His mother screamed in pity, horror, joy, and self-reproach for something unknown. She frenziedly demanded the details. He sighed with unutterable weariness. "Oh—wait—wait—wait," he said shutting his eyes as from the merciless monotony of a pain. "Wait—wait—please wait. I can't talk now. I want t' rest."

His mother condemned herself with a little cry. She adjusted his pillow, her hands shaking with love and tenderness. "There, there, don't mind, dearie! But yeh can't think how worried I was —an' crazy. I was near frantic. I went down t' th' shop, an' they said they hadn't seen anything 'a yeh there. The foreman was awful good t' me. He said he'd come up this afternoon t' see if yeh had come home yet. He tol' me not t' worry. Are yeh sure yer all right? Ain't there anythin' I kin git fer yeh? What did th' docter say?"

Kelcey's patience was worn. He gestured, and then spoke querulously. "Now—now—mother, it's all right, I tell yeh! All I need is a little rest an' I'll be as well as ever. But it makes it all th' worse if yeh stand there an' ask me questions an' make me think. Jest leave me alone fer a little while, an' I'll be as well as ever. Can't yeh do that?"

The little old woman puckered her lips funnily. "My, what an old bear th' boy is!" She kissed him blithely. Presently she went out, upon her face a bright and glad smile that must have been a reminiscence of some charming girlhood.

AT ONE time Kelcey had a friend who was struck in the head by the pole of a truck and knocked sense- less. He was taken to the hospital, from which he emerged in the morning an astonished man, with rather a dim recollection of the accident. He used to hold an old brier-wood pipe in his teeth in a manner peculiar to himself, and, with a brown derby hat tilted back on his head, recount his strange sensations. Kelcey had always remembered it as a bit of curious history. When his mother cross-examined him in regard to the accident, he told this story with barely a variation. Its truthful- ness was incontestable.

At the shop he was welcomed on the following day with con- siderable enthusiasm. The foreman had told the story and there were already jokes created concerning it. Mike O'Donnell, whose wit was famous, had planned a humorous campaign, in which he made charges against Kelcey, which were, as a matter of fact, almost the exact truth. Upon hearing it, Kelcey looked at him suddenly from the corners of his eyes, but otherwise remained imperturbable. O'Donnell eventually despaired. "Yez can't goiy that kid! He tekes ut all loike mate an' dhrink." Kelcey often told the story, his pipe held in his teeth peculiarly, and his derby tilted back on his head.

He remained at home for several evenings, content to read the papers and talk with his mother. She began to look around for the tremendous reason for it. She suspected that his nearness to death in the recent accident had sobered his senses and made him think of high things. She mused upon it continually. When he sat moodily pondering she watched him. She said to herself that she saw the light breaking in upon his spirit. She felt that it was a very critical period of his existence. She resolved to use all her power and skill to turn his eyes toward the lights in the sky.

Accordingly she addressed him one evening. "Come, go t' prayer-meetin' t'-night with me, will yeh, George?" It sounded more blunt than she intended.

He glanced at her in sudden surprise. "Huh?"

As she repeated her request, her voice quavered. She felt that it was a supreme moment. "Come, go t' prayer-meetin' t'-night, won't yeh?"

He seemed amazed. "Oh, I don't know," he began. He was fumbling in his mind for a reason for refusing. "I don't wanta go. I'm tired as th' dickens!" His obedient shoulders sank down languidly. His head mildly drooped.

The little old woman, with a quick perception of her helplessness, felt a motherly rage at her son. It was intolerable that she could not impart motion to him in a chosen direction. The waves of her desires were puny against the rocks of his indolence. She had a great wish to beat him. "I don't know what I'm ever goin' t' do with yeh," she told him, in a choking voice. "Yeh won't do anything I ask yeh to. Yeh never pay th' least bit 'a attention t' what I say. Yeh don't mind me any more than yeh would a fly. Whatever am I goin' t' do with yeh?" She faced him in a battleful way, her eyes blazing with a sombre light of despairing rage.

He looked up at her ironically. "I don't know," he said, with calmness. "What are yeh?" He had traced her emotions and seen her fear of his rebellion. He thrust out his legs in the easy scorn of a rapier-bravo. "What are yeh?"

The little old woman began to weep. They were tears without a shame of grief. She allowed them to run unheeded down her cheeks. As she stared into space her son saw her regarding there the powers and influences that she had held in her younger life. She was in some way acknowledging to fate that she was now but withered grass, with no power but the power to feel the winds. He was smitten with a sudden shame. Besides, in the last few days he had gained quite a character for amiability. He saw something grand in relenting at this point. "Well," he said, trying to remove a sulky quality from his voice, "well, if yer bound t' have me go, I s'pose I'll have t' go."

His mother, with strange, immobile face, went to him and kissed him on the brow. "All right, George!" There was in her wet eyes an emotion which he could not fathom.

She put on her bonnet and shawl, and they went out together. She was unusually silent, and made him wonder why she did not appear gleeful at his coming. He was resentful because she did not display more appreciation of his sacrifice. Several times he thought of halting and refusing to go farther, to see if that would not wring from her some acknowledgment.

In a dark street the little chapel sat humbly between two towering apartment-houses. A red street-lamp stood in front. It threw a marvellous reflection upon the wet pavements. It was like the death-stain of a spirit. Farther up the brilliant lights of an avenue made a span of gold across the black street. A roar of wheels and a clangor of bells came from this point, interwoven into a sound emblematic of the life of the city. It seemed somehow to affront this solemn and austere little edifice. It suggested an approaching barbaric invasion. The little church, pierced, would die with a fine, illimitable scorn for its slayers.

When Kelcey entered with his mother he felt a sudden quaking. His knees shook. It was an awesome place to him. There was a menace in the red padded carpet and the leather doors, studded with little brass tacks that penetrated his soul with their pitiless glances. As for his mother, she had acquired such a new air that he would have been afraid to address her. He felt completely alone and isolated at this formidable time.

There was a man in the vestibule who looked at them blandly. From within came the sound of singing. To Kelcey there was a million voices. He dreaded the terrible moment when the doors should swing back. He wished to recoil, but at that instant the bland man pushed the doors aside and he followed his mother up the centre aisle of the little chapel. To him there was a riot of lights that made him transparent. The multitudinous pairs of eyes that turned toward him were implacable in their cool valuations.

They had just ceased singing. He who conducted the meeting motioned that the services should wait until the new-comers found seats. The little old woman went slowly on toward the first rows. Occasionally she paused to scrutinize vacant places, but they did not seem to meet her requirements. Kelcey was in agony. He thought the moment of her decision would never come. In his unspeakable haste he walked a little faster than his mother. Once she paused to glance in her calculating way at some seats and he forged ahead. He halted abruptly and returned, but by that time she had resumed her thoughtful march up the aisle. He could have assassinated her. He felt that everybody must have seen his torture, during which his hands were to him like monstrous swollen hides. He was wild with a rage in which his lips turned slightly livid. He was capable of doing some furious, unholy thing.

When the little old woman at last took a seat, her son sat down beside her slowly and stiffly. He was opposing his strong desire to drop.

When from the mists of his shame and humiliation the scene came before his vision, he was surprised to find that all eyes were not fastened upon his face. The leader of the meeting seemed to be the only one who saw him. He stared gravely, solemnly, regretfully. He was a pale-faced, but plump young man in a black coat that buttoned to his chin. It was evident to Kelcey that his mother had spoken of him to the young clergyman, and that the latter was now impressing upon him the sorrow caused by the contemplation of his sin. Kelcey hated the man.

A man seated alone over in a corner began to sing. He closed his eyes and threw back his head. Others, scattered sparsely throughout the innumerable light-wood chairs, joined him as they caught the air. Kelcey heard his mother's frail, squeaking soprano. The chandelier in the centre was the only one lighted, and far at the end of the room one could discern the pulpit swathed in gloom, solemn and mystic as a bier. It was surrounded by vague shapes of darkness on which at times was the glint of brass, or of glass that shone like steel, until one could feel there the presence of the army of the unknown, possessors of the great eternal truths, and silent listeners at this ceremony. High up, the stained-glass windows loomed in leaden array like dull-hued banners, merely catching occasional splashes of dark wine-color from the lights. Kelcey fell to brooding concerning this indefinable presence which he felt in a church.

One by one people arose and told little tales of their religious faith. Some were tearful and others calm, emotionless, and convincing. Kelcey listened closely for a time. These people filled him with a great curiosity. He was not familiar with their types.

At last the young clergyman spoke at some length. Kelcey was amazed, because, from the yound man's appearance, he would not have suspected him of being so glib; but the speech had no effect on Kelcey, excepting to prove to him again that he was damned.

XII

KELCEY sometimes wondered whether he liked beer. He had been obliged to cultivate a talent for imbibing it. He was born with an abhorrence which he had steadily battled until it had come to pass that he could drink from ten to twenty glasses of beer without the act of swallowing causing him to shiver. He understood that drink was an essential to joy, to the coveted position of a man of the world and of the streets. The saloons contained the mystery of a street for him. When he knew its saloons he comprehended the street. Drink and its surroundings were the eyes of a superb green dragon to him. He followed a fascinating glitter, and the glitter required no explanation.

Directly after old Bleecker's party he almost reformed. He was tired and worn from the tumult of it, and he saw it as one might see a skeleton emerged from a crimson cloak. He wished then to turn his face away. Gradually, however, he recovered his mental balance. Then he admitted again by his point of view that the thing was not so terrible. His headache had caused him to exaggerate. A drunk was not the blight which he had once remorsefully named it. On the contrary, it was a mere unpleasant incident. He resolved, however, to be more cautious.

When prayer-meeting night came again his mother approached him hopefully. She smiled like one whose request is already granted. "Well, will yeh go t' prayer-meetin' with me t'-night again?"

He turned toward her with eloquent suddenness, and then riveted his eyes upon a corner of the floor. "Well, I guess not," he said.

His mother tearfully tried to comprehend his state of mind. "What has come over yeh?" she said, tremblingly. "Yeh never used t' be this way, George. Yeh never used t' be so cross an' mean t' me——"

"Oh, I ain't cross an' mean t' yeh," he interpolated, exasperated and violent.

"Yes, yeh are, too! I ain't hardly had a decent word from yeh in ever so long. Yer as cross an' as mean as yeh can be. I don't know what t' make of it. It can't be—" There came a look in her eyes that told that she was going to shock and alarm him with her heaviest sentence—"it can't be that yeh've got t' drinkin'."

Kelcey grunted with disgust at the ridiculous thing. "Why, what an old goose yer gettin' t' be."

She was compelled to laugh a little, as a child laughs between tears at a hurt. She had not been serious. She was only trying to display to him how she regarded his horrifying mental state. "Oh, of course, I didn't mean that, but I think yeh act jest as bad as if yeh did drink. I wish yeh would do better, George!"

She had grown so much less frigid and stern in her censure that Kelcey seized the opportunity to try to make a joke of it. He laughed at her, but she shook her head and continued: "I do wish yeh would do better. I don't know what's t' become 'a yeh, George. Yeh don't mind what I say no more'n if I was th' wind in th' chimbly. Yeh don't care about nothin' 'cept goin' out nights. I can't ever get yeh t' prayer-meetin' ner church; yeh never go out with me anywheres unless yeh can't get out of it; yeh swear an' take on sometimes like everything, yeh never——"

He gestured wrathfully in interruption. "Say, lookahere, can't yeh think 'a something I do?"

She ended her oration then in the old way. "An' I don't know what's goin' t' become 'a yeh."

She put on her bonnet and shawl and then came and stood near him, expectantly. She imparted to her attitude a subtle threat of unchangeableness. He pretended to be engrossed in his newspaper. The little swaggering clock on the mantel became suddenly evident, ticking with loud monotony. Presently she said, firmly: "Well, are yeh comin'?"

He was reading.

"Well, are yeh comin'?"

He threw his paper down, angrily. "Oh, why don't yeh go on an' leave me alone?" he demanded in supreme impatience.

"What do yeh wanta pester me fer? Yeh'd think there was rob-bers. Why can't yeh go alone er else stay home? You wanta go an' I don't wanta go, an' yeh keep all time tryin' t' drag me. Yeh know I don't wanta go." He concluded in a last defiant wounding of her. "What do I care 'bout those ol' bags-'a-wind anyhow? They gimme a pain!"

His mother turned her face and went from him. He sat staring with a mechanical frown. Presently he went and picked up his newspaper.

Jones told him that night that everybody had had such a good time at old Bleecker's party that they were going to form a club. They waited at the little smiling saloon, and then amid much enthusiasm all signed a membership-roll. Old Bleecker, late that night, was violently elected president. He made speeches of thanks and gratification during the remainder of the meeting. Kelcey went home rejoicing. He felt that at any rate he would have true friends. The dues were a dollar for each week.

He was deeply interested. For a number of evenings he fairly gobbled his supper in order that he might be off to the little smiling saloon to discuss the new organization. All the men were wildly enthusiastic. One night the saloon-keeper announced that he would donate half the rent of quite a large room over his saloon. It was an occasion for great cheering. Kelcey's legs were like whalebone when he tried to go up-stairs upon his return home, and the edge of each step was moved curiously forward.

His mother's questions made him snarl. "Oh, nowheres!" At other times he would tell her: "Oh, t' see some friends 'a mine! Where d' yeh s'pose?"

Finally, some of the women of the tenement concluded that the little old mother had a wild son. They came to condole with her. They sat in the kitchen for hours. She told them of his wit, his cleverness, his kind heart.

XIII

AT A certain time Kelcey discovered that some young men who stood in the cinders between a brick wall and the pavement, and near the side-door of a corner saloon, knew more about life than other people. They used to lean there smoking and chewing, and comment upon events and persons. They knew the neighborhood extremely well. They debated upon small typical things that transpired before them until they had extracted all the information that existence contained. They sometimes inaugurated little fights with foreigners or well-dressed men. It was here that Sapristi Glielmi, the pedler, stabbed Pete Brady to death, for which he got a life-sentence. Each patron of the saloon was closely scrutinized as he entered the place. Sometimes they used to throng upon the heels of a man and in at the bar assert that he had asked them in to drink. When he objected, they would claim with one voice that it was too deep an insult and gather about to thrash him. When they had caught chance customers and absolute strangers, the barkeeper had remained in stolid neutrality, ready to serve one or seven, but two or three times they had encountered the wrong men. Finally, the proprietor had come out one morning and told them, in the fearless way of his class, that their pastime must cease. "It quits right here! See? Right here! Th' nex' time yeh try t' work it, I come with th' bung-starter, an' th' mugs I miss with it git pulled. See? It quits!" Infrequently, however, men did ask them in to drink.

The policeman of that beat grew dignified and shrewd whenever he approached this corner. Sometimes he stood with his hands behind his back and cautiously conversed with them. It was understood on both sides that it was a good thing to be civil.

In winter this band, a trifle diminished in numbers, huddled in their old coats and stamped little flat places in the snow, their faces turned always toward the changing life in the streets. In the summer they became more lively. Sometimes, then, they walked out to the curb to look up and down the street. Over in a trampled vacant lot, surrounded by high tenement-houses, there was a sort of a den among some bowlders. An old truck was made to form a shelter. The small hoodlums of that vicinity all avoided the spot. So many of them had been thrashed upon being caught near it. It was the summer-time lounging-place of the band from the corner.

They were all too clever to work. Some of them had worked, but these used their experiences as stores from which to draw tales. They were like veterans with their wars. One lad in particular used to recount how he whipped his employer, the proprietor of a large grain and feed establishment. He described his victim's features and form and clothes with minute exactness. He bragged of his wealth and social position. It had been a proud moment of the lad's life. He was like a savage who had killed a great chief.

Their feeling for contemporaneous life was one of contempt. Their philosophy taught that in a large part the whole thing was idle and a great bore. With fine scorn they sneered at the futility of it. Work was done by men who had not the courage to stand still and let the skies clap together if they willed.

The vast machinery of the popular law indicated to them that there were people in the world who wished to remain quiet. They awaited the moment when they could prove to them that a riotous upheaval, a cloud-burst of destruction would be a delicious thing. They thought of their fingers buried in the lives of these people. They longed dimly for a time when they could run through decorous streets with crash and roar of war, an army of revenge for pleasures long possessed by others, a wild sweeping compensation for their years without crystal and gilt, women and wine. This thought slumbered in them, as the image of Rome might have lain small in the hearts of the barbarians.

Kelcey respected these youths so much that he ordinarily used the other side of the street. He could not go near to them, because if a passer-by minded his own business he was a disdainful prig and had insulted them; if he showed that he was aware of them they were likely to resent his not minding his own business and prod him into a fight if the opportunity were good. Kelcey longed for their acquaintance and friendship, for with it came social safety and ease; they were respected so universally.

Once in another street Fidsey Corcoran was whipped by a short, heavy man. Fidsey picked himself up, and in the fury of defeat hurled pieces of brick at his opponent. The short man dodged with skill and then pursued Fidsey for over a block. Sometimes he got near enough to punch him. Fidsey raved in maniacal fury. The moment the short man would attempt to resume his own affairs, Fidsey would turn upon him again, tears and blood upon his face, with the lashed rage of a vanquished animal. The short man used to turn about, swear madly, and make little dashes. Fidsey always ran and then returned as pursuit ceased. The short man apparently wondered if this maniac was ever going to allow him to finish whipping him. He looked helplessly up and down the street. People were there who knew Fidsey, and they remonstrated with him; but he continued to confront the short man, gibbering like a wounded ape, using all the eloquence of the street in his wild oaths.

Finally the short man was exasperated to black fury. He decided to end the fight. With low snarls, ominous as death, he plunged at Fidsey.

Kelcey happened there then. He grasped the short man's shoulder. He cried out in the peculiar whine of the man who interferes. "Oh, hol' on! Yeh don't wanta hit 'im any more! Yeh've done enough to 'im now! Leave 'im be!"

The short man wrenched and tugged. He turned his face until his teeth were almost at Kelcey's cheek: "Le' go me! Le' go me, you——" The rest of his sentence was screamed curses.

Kelcey's face grew livid from fear, but he somehow managed to keep his grip. Fidsey, with but an instant's pause, plunged into the new fray.

They beat the short man. They forced him against a high board-fence where for a few seconds their blows sounded upon his head in swift thuds. A moment later Fidsey descried a running policeman. He made off, fleet as a shadow. Kelcey noted his going. He ran after him.

Three or four blocks away they halted. Fidsey said: "I'd 'a licked dat big stuff in 'bout a minute more," and wiped the blood from his eyes.

At the gang's corner, they asked: "Who soaked yeh, Fidsey?" His description was burning. Everybody laughed. "Where is 'e now?" Later they began to question Kelcey. He recited a tale in which he allowed himself to appear prominent and redoubtable. They looked at him then as if they thought he might be quite a man.

Once when the little old woman was going out to buy something for her son's supper, she discovered him standing at the side-door of the saloon engaged intimately with Fidsey and the others. She slunk away, for she understood that it would be a terrible thing to confront him and his pride there with youths who were superior to mothers.

When he arrived home he threw down his hat with a weary sigh, as if he had worked long hours, but she attacked him before he had time to complete the falsehood. He listened to her harangue with a curled lip. In defence he merely made a gesture of supreme exasperation. She never understood the advanced things in life. He felt the hopelessness of ever making her comprehend. His mother was not modern.

XIV

THE little old woman arose early and bustled in the preparation of breakfast. At times she looked anxiously at the clock. An hour before her son should leave for work she went to his room and called him in the usual tone of sharpness, "George! George!"

A sleepy growl came to her.

"Come, come it's time t' git up," she continued. "Come now, git right up!"

Later she went again to the door. "George, are yeh gittin' up?"

"Huh?"

"Are yeh gittin' up?"

"Yes, I'll git right up!" He had introduced a valor into his voice which she detected to be false. She went to his bedside and took him by the shoulder. "George—George—git up!"

From the mist-lands of sleep he began to protest incoherently. "Oh, le' me be, won' yeh? 'M sleepy!"

She continued to shake him. "Well, it's time t' git up. Come—come—come on, now."

Her voice, shrill with annoyance, pierced his ears in a slender, piping thread of sound. He turned over on the pillow to bury his head in his arms. When he expostulated, his tones came half-smothered. "Oh le' me be, can't yeh? There's plenty 'a time! Jest fer ten minutes! 'M sleepy!"

She was implacable. "No, yeh must git up now! Yeh ain't got more'n time enough t' eat yer breakfast an' git t' work."

Eventually he arose, sullen and grumbling. Later he came to his breakfast, blinking his dry eyelids, his stiffened features set in a mechanical scowl.

Each morning his mother went to his room, and fought a battle to arouse him. She was like a soldier. Despite his pleadings, his threats, she remained at her post, imperturbable and unyielding. These affairs assumed large proportions in his life. Sometimes he grew beside himself with a bland, unformulated wrath. The whole thing was a consummate imposition. He felt that he was being cheated of his sleep. It was an injustice to compel him to arise morning after morning with bitter regularity, before the sleep-gods had at all loosened their grasp. He hated that unknown force which directed his life.

One morning he swore a tangled mass of oaths, aimed into the air, as if the injustice poised there. His mother flinched at first; then her mouth set in the little straight line. She saw that the momentous occasion had come. It was the time of the critical battle. She turned upon him valorously. "Stop your swearin', George Kelcey. I won't have yeh talk so before me! I won't have it! Stop this minute! Not another word! Do yeh think I'll allow yeh t' swear b'fore me like that? Not another word! I won't have it! I declare I won't have it another minute!"

At first her projected words had slid from his mind as if striking against ice, but at last he heeded her. His face grew sour with passion and misery. He spoke in tones dark with dislike. "Th' 'ell yeh won't? Whatter yeh goin' t' do 'bout it?" Then, as if he considered that he had not been sufficiently impressive, he arose and slowly walked over to her. Having arrived at point-blank range he spoke again. "Whatter yeh goin' t' do 'bout it?" He regarded her then with an unaltering scowl, albeit his mien was as dark and cowering as that of a condemned criminal.

She threw out her hands in the gesture of an impotent one. He was acknowledged victor. He took his hat and slowly left her.

For three days they lived in silence. He brooded upon his mother's agony and felt a singular joy in it. As opportunity offered, he did little despicable things. He was going to make her abject. He was now uncontrolled, ungoverned; he wished to be an emperor. Her suffering was all a sort of compensation for his own dire pains.

She went about with a gray, impassive face. It was as if she had survived a massacre in which all that she loved had been torn from her by the brutality of savages.

One evening at six he entered and stood looking at his mother as she peeled potatoes. She had hearkened to his coming listlessly, without emotion, and at his entrance she did not raise her eyes.

"Well, I'm fired," he said, suddenly.

It seemed to be the final blow. Her body gave a convulsive movement in the chair. When she finally lifted her eyes, horror possessed her face. Her under jaw had fallen. "Fired? Outa work? Why—George?" He went over to the window and stood with his back to her. He could feel her gray stare upon him.

"Yep! Fired!"

At last she said, "Well—whatter yeh goin' t' do?"

He tapped the pane with his finger-nail. He answered in a tone made hoarse and unnatural by an assumption of gay careless-ness, "Oh, nothin'!"

She began, then, her first weeping. "Oh—George—George— George——"

He looked at her scowling. "Ah, whatter yeh givin' us? Is this all I git when I come home f'm being fired? Anybody 'ud think it was my fault. I couldn't help it."

She continued to sob in a dull, shaking way. In the pose of her head there was an expression of her conviction that comprehen-sion of her pain was impossible to the universe. He paused for a moment, and then, with his usual tactics, went out, slamming the door. A pale flood of sunlight, imperturbable at its vocation, streamed upon the little old woman, bowed with pain, forlorn in her chair.

XV

KELCEY was standing on the corner next day when three little boys came running. Two halted some distance away, and the other came forward. He halted before Kelcey, and spoke importantly.

"Hey, your ol' woman's sick."

"What?"

"Your ol' woman's sick."

"Git out!"

"She is, too!"

"Who tol' yeh?"

"Mis' Callahan. She said fer me t' run an' tell yeh. Dey want yeh."

A swift dread struck Kelcey. Like flashes of light little scenes from the past shot through his brain. He had thoughts of a vengeance from the clouds. As he glanced about him the familiar view assumed a meaning that was ominous and dark. There was prophecy of disaster in the street, the buildings, the sky, the people. Something tragic and terrible in the air was known to his nervous, quivering nostrils. He spoke to the little boy in a tone that quavered. "All right!"

Behind him he felt the sudden contemplative pause of his companions of the gang. They were watching him. As he went rapidly up the street he knew that they had come out to the middle of the walk and were staring after him. He was glad that they could not see his face, his trembling lips, his eyes wavering in fear. He stopped at the door of his home and stared at the panel as if he saw written thereon a word. A moment later he entered. His eye comprehended the room in a frightened glance.

His mother sat gazing out at the opposite walls and windows. She was leaning her head upon the back of the chair. Her face was overspread with a singular pallor, but the glance of her eyes was strong and the set of her lips was tranquil.

He felt an unspeakable thrill of thanksgiving at seeing her seated there calmly. "Why, mother, they said yeh was sick," he cried, going toward her impetuously. "What's th' matter?"

She smiled at him. "Oh, it ain't nothin'! I on'y got kinda dizzy, that's all." Her voice was sober and had the ring of vitality in it.

He noted her common-place air. There was no alarm or pain in her tones, but the misgivings of the street, the prophetic twinges of his nerves made him still hesitate. "Well—are you sure it ain't? They scared me 'bout t' death."

"No, it ain't anything, o'ny some sorta dizzy feelin'. I fell down b'hind th' stove. Missis Callahan, she came an' picked me up. I must 'a laid there fer quite a while. Th' docter said he guessed I'd be all right in a couple 'a hours. I don't feel nothin'!"

Kelcey heaved a great sigh of relief. "Lord, I was scared." He began to beam joyously, since he was escaped from his fright. "Why, I couldn't think what had happened," he told her.

"Well, it ain't nothin'," she said.

He stood about awkwardly, keeping his eyes fastened upon her in a sort of surprise, as if he had expected to discover that she had vanished. The reaction from his panic was a thrill of delicious contentment. He took a chair and sat down near her, but presently he jumped up to ask: "There ain't nothin' I can git fer yeh, is ther?" He looked at her eagerly. In his eyes shone love and joy. If it were not for the shame of it he would have called her endearing names.

"No, ther ain't nothin'," she answered. Presently she continued, in a conversational way, "Yeh ain't found no work yit, have yeh?"

The shadow of his past fell upon him then and he became suddenly morose. At last he spoke in a sentence that was a vow, a declaration of change. "No, I ain't, but I'm goin' t' hunt fer it hard, you bet."

She understood from his tone that he was making peace with her. She smiled at him gladly. "Yer a good boy, George!" A radiance from the stars lit her face.

Presently she asked, "D' yeh think yer old boss would take yeh on ag'in if I went t' see him?"

"No," said Kelcey, at once. "It wouldn't do no good! They got all th' men they want. There ain't no room there. It wouldn't do no good." He ceased to beam for a moment as he thought of certain disclosures. "I'm goin' t' try to git work everywheres. I'm goin' t' make a wild break t' git a job, an' if there's one anywheres I'll git it."

She smiled at him again. "That's right, George!"

When it came supper-time he dragged her in her chair over to the table and then scurried to and fro to prepare a meal for her. She laughed gleefully at him. He was awkward and densely ignorant. He exaggerated his helplessness sometimes until she was obliged to lean back in her chair to laugh. Afterward they sat by the window. Her hand rested upon his hair.

XVI

WHEN Kelcey went to borrow money from old Bleecker, Jones and the others, he discovered that he was below them in social position. Old Bleecker said gloomily that he did not see how he could loan money at that time. When Jones asked him to have a drink, his tone was careless. O'Connor recited at length some bewildering financial troubles of his own. In them all he saw that something had been reversed. They remained silent upon many occasions, when they might have grunted in sympathy for him.

As he passed along the street near his home he perceived Fidsey Corcoran and another of the gang. They made eloquent signs. "Are yeh wid us?"

He stopped and looked at them. "What's wrong with yeh?"

"Are yeh wid us er not," demanded Fidsey. "New barkeep'! Big can! We got it over in d' lot. Big can, I tell yeh." He drew a picture in the air, so to speak, with his enthusiastic fingers.

Kelcey turned dejectedly homeward. "Oh, I guess not, this roun'."

"What's d' matter wi'che?" said Fidsey. "Yer gittin' t' be a reg'lar willie! Come ahn, I tell yeh! Youse gits one smoke at d' can b'cause yeh b'longs t' d' gang, an' yeh don't wanta give it up widout er scrap! See? Some udder john'll git yer smoke. Come ahn!"

When they arrived at the place among the bowlders in the vacant lot, one of the band had a huge and battered tin-pail tilted afar up. His throat worked convulsively. He was watched keenly and anxiously by five or six others. Their eyes followed carefully each fraction of distance that the pail was lifted. They were very silent.

Fidsey burst out violently as he perceived what was in progress. "Heh, Tim, yeh big sojer, le' go d' can! What 'a yeh tink! Wese er in dis! Le' go dat!"

He who was drinking made several angry protesting contortions of his throat. Then he put down the pail and swore. "Who's a big sojer? I ain't gittin' more'n me own smoke! Yer too bloomin' swift! Yeh'd tink yeh was d' on'y mug what owned dis can! Close yer face while I gits me smoke!"

He took breath for a moment and then returned the pail to its tilted position. Fidsey went to him and worried and clamored. He interfered so seriously with the action of drinking that the other was obliged to release the pail again for fear of choking.

Fidsey grabbed it and glanced swiftly at the contents. "Dere! Dat's what I was hollerin' at! Lookut d' beer! Not 'nough t' wet yer t'roat! Yehs can't have not'in' on d' level wid youse damn' tanks! Youse was a reg'lar resevoiy, Tim Connigan! Look what yeh lef' us! Ah, say, youse was a dandy! What 'a yeh tink we ah? Willies? Don' we want no smoke? Say, lookut dat can! It's drier'n hell! What 'a yeh tink?"

Tim glanced in at the beer. Then he said: "Well, d' mug what come b'fore me, he on'y lef' me dat much. Blue Billee, he done d' swallerin'! I on'y had a tas'e!"

Blue Billie, from his seat near, called out in wrathful protest: "Yeh lie, Tim. I never had more'n a mouf-ful!" An inspiration evidently came to him then, for his countenance suddenly brightened, and, arising, he went toward the pail. "I ain't had me reg'lar smoke yit! Guess I come in aheader Fidsey, don' I?"

Fidsey, with a sardonic smile, swung the pail behind him. "I guess nit! Not dis minnet! Youse hadger smoke. If yeh ain't, yeh don't git none. See?"

Blue Billie confronted Fidsey determinedly. "D' 'ell I don't!"

"Nit," said Fidsey.

Billie sat down again.

Fidsey drank his portion. Then he manœuvred skilfully before the crowd until Kelcey and the other youth took their shares. "Youse er a mob 'a tanks," he told the gang. "Nobody 'ud git not'in' if dey wasn't on t' yehs!"

Blue Billie's soul had been smouldering in hate against Fidsey. "Ah, shut up! Youse ain't gota take care 'a dose two mugs, dough. Youse hadger smoke, ain't yeh? Den yer tr'u. G' home!"

"Well, I hate t' see er bloke use 'imself fer a tank," said Fidsey. "But youse don't wanta go jollyin' 'round 'bout d' can, Blue, er youse'll git done."

"Who'll do me?" demanded Blue Billie, casting his eye about him.

"Kel' will," said Fidsey, bravely.

"D' 'ell he will?"

"Dat's what he will!"

Blue Billie made the gesture of a warrior. "He never saw d' day 'a his life dat he could do me little finger. If 'e says much t' me, I'll push 'is face all over d' lot."

Fidsey called to Kelcey. "Say, Kel, hear what dis mug is chewin'?"

Kelcey was apparently deep in other matters. His back was half-turned.

Blue Billie spoke to Fidsey in a battleful voice. "Did 'e ever say 'e could do me?"

Fidsey said: "Soitenly 'e did. Youse is dead easy, 'e says. He says he kin punch holes in you, Blue!"

"When did 'e say it?"

"Oh—any time. Youse is a cinch, Kel' says."

Blue Billie walked over to Kelcey. The others of the band followed him exchanging joyful glances.

"Did youse say yeh could do me?"

Kelcey slowly turned, but he kept his eyes upon the ground. He heard Fidsey darting among the others telling of his prowess, preparing them for the downfall of Blue Billie. He stood heavily on one foot and moved his hands nervously. Finally he said, in a low growl, "Well, what if I did?"

The sentence sent a happy thrill through the band. It was the formidable question. Blue Billie braced himself. Upon him came the responsibility of the next step. The gang fell back a little upon all sides. They looked expectantly at Blue Billie.

He walked forward with a deliberate step until his face was close to Kelcey.

"Well, if you did," he said, with a snarl between his teeth, "I'm goin' t' t'ump d' life outa yeh right heh!"

A little boy, wild of eye and puffing, came down the slope as from an explosion. He burst out in a rapid treble, "Is dat Kelcey feller here? Say, yeh ol' woman's sick again. Dey want yeh! Yehs better run! She's awful sick!"

The gang turned with loud growls. "Ah, git outa here!" Fidsey threw a stone at the little boy and chased him a short distance, but he continued to clamor, "Youse better come, Kelcey feller! She's awful sick! She was hollerin'! Dey been lookin' fer yeh over'n hour!" In his eagerness he returned part way, regardless of Fidsey!

Kelsey had moved away from Blue Billie. He said: "I guess I'd better go!" They howled at him. "Well," he continued, "I can't—I don't wanta—I don't wanta leave me mother be—she—"

His words were drowned in the chorus of their derision. "Well, lookahere"—he would begin and at each time their cries and screams ascended. They dragged at Blue Billie. "Go fer 'im, Blue! Slug 'im! Go ahn!"

Kelcey went slowly away while they were urging Blue Billie to do a decisive thing. Billie stood fuming and blustering and explaining himself. When Kelcey had achieved a considerable distance from him, he stepped forward a few paces and hurled a terrible oath. Kelcey looked back darkly.

XVII

WHEN he entered the chamber of death, he was
brooding over the recent encounter and devising
extravagant revenges upon Blue Billie and the
others.

The little old woman was stretched upon her bed. Her face
and hands were of the hue of the blankets. Her hair, seemingly
of a new and wondrous grayness, hung over her temples in
whips and tangles. She was sickeningly motionless, save for her
eyes, which rolled and swayed in maniacal glances.

A young doctor had just been administering medicine.
"There," he said, with a great satisfaction, "I guess that'll do her
good!" As he went briskly toward the door he met Kelcey. "Oh,"
he said. "Son?"

Kelcey had that in his throat which was like fur. When he
forced his voice, the words came first low and then high as if
they had broken through something. "Will she—will she——"

The doctor glanced back at the bed. She was watching them as
she would have watched ghouls, and muttering. "Can't tell," he
said. "She's wonderful woman! Got more vitality than you and I
together! Can't tell! May—may not! Good-day! Back in two
hours."

In the kitchen Mrs. Callahan was feverishly dusting the furniture, polishing this and that. She arranged everything in decorous rows. She was preparing for the coming of death. She
looked at the floor as if she longed to scrub it.

The doctor paused to speak in an undertone to her, glancing at
the bed. When he departed she labored with a renewed speed.

Kelcey approached his mother. From a little distance he called
to her. "Mother—mother——" He proceeded with caution lest
this mystic being upon the bed should clutch at him.

"Mother—mother—don't yeh know me?" He put forth apprehensive, shaking fingers and touched her hand.

There were two brilliant steel-colored points upon her eyeballs. She was staring off at something sinister.

Suddenly she turned to her son in a wild babbling appeal. "Help me! Help me! Oh, help me! I see them coming."

Kelcey called to her as to a distant place. "Mother! Mother!" She looked at him, and then there began within her a struggle to reach him with her mind. She fought with some implacable power whose fingers were in her brain. She called to Kelcey in stammering, incoherent cries for help.

Then she again looked away. "Ah, there they come! There they come! Ah, look—look—loo—" She arose to a sitting posture without the use of her arms.

Kelcey felt himself being choked. When her voice pealed forth in a scream he saw crimson curtains moving before his eyes. "Mother—oh, mother—there's nothin'—there's nothin'——"

She was at a kitchen-door with a dish-cloth in her hand. Within there had just been a clatter of crockery. Down through the trees of the orchard she could see a man in a field ploughing. "Bill—o-o-oh, Bill—have yeh seen Georgie? Is he out there with you? Georgie! Georgie! Come right here this minnet! Right—this —minnet!"

She began to talk to some people in the room. "I want t' know what yeh want here! I want yeh t' git out! I don't want yeh here! I don't feel good t'-day, an' I don't want yeh here! I don't feel good t'-day! I want yeh t' git out!" Her voice became peevish. "Go away! Go away! Go away!"

Kelcey lay in a chair. His nerveless arms allowed his fingers to sweep the floor. He became so that he could not hear the chatter from the bed, but he was always conscious of the ticking of the little clock out on the kitchen shelf.

When he aroused, the pale-faced but plump young clergyman was before him.

"My poor lad——" began this latter.

The little old woman lay still with her eyes closed. On the table at the head of the bed was a glass containing a water-like medicine. The reflected lights made a silver star on its side. The two men sat side by side, waiting. Out in the kitchen Mrs. Callahan had taken a chair by the stove and was waiting.

Kelcey began to stare at the wall-paper. The pattern was clusters of brown roses. He felt them like hideous crabs crawling upon his brain.

Through the door-way he saw the oil-cloth covering of the table catching a glimmer from the warm afternoon sun. The window disclosed a fair, soft sky, like blue enamel, and a fringe of chimneys and roofs, resplendent here and there. An endless roar, the eternal trample of the marching city, came mingled with vague cries. At intervals the woman out by the stove moved restlessly and coughed.

Over the transom from the hall-way came two voices.

"Johnnie!"

"Wot!"

"You come right here t' me! I want yehs t' go t' d' store fer me!"

"Ah, ma, send Sally!"

"No, I will not! You come right here!"

"All right, in a minnet!"

"Johnnie!"

"In a minnet, I tell yeh!"

"Johnnie——" There was the sound of a heavy tread, and later a boy squealed. Suddenly the clergyman started to his feet. He rushed forward and peered. The little old woman was dead.

Appendixes

TEXTUAL NOTES

116.4 you] This appearance of 'you' in a context where the consistent 'yeh' seems called for may be inadvertent, but the possibility remains that it may be used for emphasis, as it may be also at 161.2.

136.1 its sin] A1 reads, "might walk understandingly in its greatest marvels, its mightiest march of life, sin." The E1–2 reading 'life, of sin' can be only an editorial or compositorial guess. That a word is missing is certain, since 'sin' can scarcely be in apposition to 'march of life,' and the fact that 'life,' ends a line may help to explain the dropping of the word. On the whole, it seems simplest to take it that Crane is constructing a standard series of three independent elements, each prefaced by 'its'; thus the emendation has been made accordingly.

147.27 fingers] No need exists to accept the E1–2 reading 'figures' for A1 'fingers' in view of such expressions as "They thought of their fingers buried in the lives of these people" (163.29) and especially "She fought with some implacable power whose fingers were in her brain" (177.9–10), which offers an exact parallel to 147.27, "these million winding fingers that gripped his senses".

153.8 docter] Crane very frequently misspelled 'doctor' as 'docter'. Thus both here and at 170.15 it is difficult to know whether 'docter' is intended as a dialect spelling or whether Crane's possible misspellings were faithfully retained by the compositor since they appeared in a dialect context.

176.19 She's wonderful woman] Every reason exists to retain this example of the doctor's brisk speech instead of sophisticating with E1–2 as "She's a wonderful woman", implying the omission of a word by a printer's error. For a similar E1–2 addition, see 'in a rapid sing-song' for A1 'in rapid sing-sing' (144.8–9).

EDITORIAL EMENDATIONS IN THE COPY-TEXT

[NOTE: Every editorial change, whether in the substantives or accidentals, made from the 1896 first edition of *George's Mother* is listed here. Only the direct source of the emendation, with its antecedents, is noticed; the Historical Collation may be consulted for the complete history, within the editions collated, of any substantive readings that qualify for inclusion in that listing. An alteration assigned to the Virginia Edition (V) is made for the first time in the present text if 'by the first time' is understood 'the first time in respect to the editions chosen for collation.' Asterisked readings are discussed in the Textual Notes. The wavy dash ~ represents the same word that appears before the bracket and is used in recording punctuation variants. An inferior caret ∧ indicates the absence of a punctuation mark. The following editions are referred to: A1 (Arnold, New York, 1896), E1 (Arnold, London, 1896), E2 (Heinemann 1900).]

116.3   year!] ; ~ ? A1
*116.4   you] *stet* A1-E2
117.12   Yeh'd] V; Ye'd A1-E2
120.19   o'clock,] E1; ~ ∧ A1
120.20; 121.5   nickel-] E1; nickle- A1
124.23   But—] E1; ~ , A1
128.17   mood] E2; mode A1-E1
130.11   boy—"] E1 (~ '); ~ "——A1
134.26   yeh] V; ye A1-E2
*136.1   its sin] V; sin A1; of sin E1-2
141.11   drink!] E1; ~ ? A1
141.23   the] V; th' A1-E2
142.11   oil-cloth] V; oilcloth A1-E2
143.25   Pig'!"] ; ~ ! ' " A1
147.2   an'] E1; an A1

*147.27   fingers] *stet* A1
151.37   though] E1; 'though A1
*153.8   docter] *stet* A1
161.1   Yeh'd] V; Ye'd A1-E2
161.5   -'a-] E1; -a- A1
166.17   Oh,] E2; ~ ' A1; ~ ∧ E1
170.25; 171.6   git] V; get A1-E2
172.31   le'] V; let A1-E2
173.4   Yeh'd] V; Ye'd A1-E2
173.12   not'in'] V; notin' A1; nottin' E1-2
173.30   Billie] E1; Billee A1
174.30; 175.6   Billie.] E1; ~ ! A1
174.37   Yehs] V; Yeh's A1-E2
*176.19   She's wonderful] *stet* A1
177.17   nothin'] E1; nothin A1
177.35   lad——"] V; ~ "——A1; ~ !" E1-2

182

WORD-DIVISION

1. *End-of-the-Line Hyphenation in the Virginia Edition*

[NOTE: No hyphenation of a possible compound at the end of a line in the Virginia text is present in the copy-text except for the following readings, which are hyphenated within the line in A1. Hyphenated compounds in which both elements are capitalized are not included.]

119.22	fourth-|story	144.8	sing-|song
124.2,31	prayer-|meetin'	155.1	prayer-|meetin'
130.17	willow-|twigs	166.22	half-|smothered
141.18	self-|destruction	167.33	point-|blank
143.10	side-|wall		

2. *End-of-the-Line Hyphenation in the Copy-Text*

[NOTE: The following compounds, or possible compounds, are hyphenated at the end of the line in the copy-text. The form in which they have been transcribed in the Virginia text, listed below, represents the practice of A1 as ascertained by other appearances or by parallels.]

115.13	railroad	143.13	tobacco-smoke
116.38	barkeeper	144.27	mouth-organ
118.16	Good-by	150.11	battle-field
121.18	red-eyed	155.6	prayer-meetin'
127.11	sawdust	157.33	stained-glass
128.4	bartender	161.13	membership-roll
129.11	before-mentioned	168.11	finger-nail
132.18,19	good-by	175.25	tin-pail
138.24	dream-woman	178.3	wall-paper
142.34	corn-cob	178.6	oil-cloth

HISTORICAL COLLATION

[NOTE: Only substantive variants from the Virginia text are listed here, together with their appearances in the three editions collated for the establishment of this text: A1 (Arnold, New York, 1896), E1 (Arnold, London, 1896), and E2 (Heinemann 1900). Purely typographical errors have been recorded in the Editorial Emendations but are not listed here. Collated editions not noted for any reading agree with the Virginia Edition.]

116.1   said,   ecstatically∧] ~ ∧ ~ , E1–2
116.7   Sickles's] Sickles' E1–2
116.10   two] too E1–2
116.33   trousers' pocket] trousers-pocket E1–2
117.12   Yeh'd] Ye'd A1-E2
120.19   turned] returned E1–2
127.37   'im] him E1–2
128.5   in his hand] in hand E1–2
128.17   mood] mode A1-E1
129.33   an] a E1–2
129.36   bunted] butted E1–2
134.2   upon] on E1–2
134.26   yeh] ye A1-E2
135.16   fêted] *fêted* E2
135.22   He] Kelcey E1–2
135.29   the] what were E1–2
136.1   its sin] sin A1; of sin E1–2
136.3   help but admire] help admiring E1–2
137.2   he whom] himself E1–2
137.3   himself] a man E1–2
138.7   pail] can E1–2
139.39   hearin'] hearing E1–2
140.8   trousers' pockets] trousers-pockets E1–2

141.23   the] th' A1-E2
143.3   cost] cast E1–2
144.8   in rapid] in a rapid E1–2
147.27   fingers] figures E1–2
155.10   th'] the E1–2
156.5,10   farther] further E1–2
156.12   clangor] clang E1–2
156.25   was] were E1–2
156.34   services] service E1–2
159.19   drunk] 'drunk' E1–2
161.1   Yeh'd] Ye'd A1-E2
161.2   er] or E1–2
163.38   passer-by] passer E1–2
168.9   Yep] Yes E1–2
169.25   wavering] quavering E1–2
170.25   git] get A1-E2
170.25   fer] for E1–2
170.34; 171.5   goin'] going E1–2
171.5; 172.22   git] get E1–2
171.6   git] get A1-E2
172.25,28; 173.2,6,9,23,25 pail] can E1–2
172.31   le'] let A1-E2
173.4   Yeh'd] Ye'd A1-E2
173.38; 175.3,11   fer] for E1–2
176.12   toward] towards E1–2
176.19   She's] She's a E1–2

The University of Virginia Edition of
The Works of Stephen Crane

was composed, printed, and bound by
Kingsport Press, Inc., Kingsport, Tennessee.
The paper is Mohawk Superfine,
and the types are Primer and Chisel.
Design is by Edward G. Foss.